Also by Lynn Franklin

Jeweler's Gemstone Mystery Series

The Blue Diamond: Jeweler's Gemstone Mystery #1
The Pirate's Ruby: Jeweler's Gemstone Mystery #2
The Carolina Emerald: Jeweler's Gemstone Mystery #3

Readers' Specials

The Diamond Digest
Hidden Gems

www.LynnFranklin.com
Lynn@LynnFranklin.com

The Pirate's Ruby

Lynn Franklin

Lynn Franklin (signature)

Franklin & Franklin

The Pirate's Ruby
© 2014 by Lynn Franklin

eBook: ISBN 978-0-9855457-2-7
Print: ISBN 978-0-9855457-4-1

To Jon,
Thank you for your love, your friendship, your eternal
support.
You are the love of my life

Prologue

22 years ago
Osprey Beach, Maryland

"You take that back right now!" Kimberley West planted her feet and glared up at Brittany Bonnet.

Behind them, most of the other fifth graders whooped and hollered and dashed around the school playground, enjoying the mid-day recess. A few girls glanced their way, but carefully kept their distance. Seagulls circled overhead, waiting for snacks to fall from pockets.

A gust of wind carrying the distinctive salt/not-salt fragrance of the Chesapeake Bay loosened a hank of brown hair from Kim's messy ponytail. Tucking the strand behind an ear, she pushed her glasses more firmly onto her nose.

"Take what back?" Brittany lifted her hands in a palms-up shrug and turned to the girl standing beside her. "Did I say something wrong?"

Brittany's friend, Leslie, tossed her blond hair and giggled.

"You called Grandpa a liar!" Too late, Grandpa's advice flashed through her mind: *Ignore the bully's words.*

"Yeah?" A seagull landed near them, dodged the foot Brittany swung at it and launched back into the air. Brittany stepped forward until the toes of her sneakers touched Kim's. "What if I did? What are you going to do about it?"

Brittany's breath smelled of garlic from the pizza served an hour ago. Kim wrinkled her nose but resisted the urge to step back. Grandpa had also said bullies thrive on fear.

"Kim?" Brooke Swann, her voice high-pitched with fear, touched Kim's shoulder. "Maybe we should go back to class."

Kim stiffened. Class? Class was where everything had started.

Today's history class should have been Kim's moment of triumph, the day she proved to everyone that her family was just as good as Brittany's. Just because Brittany's dad was rich and her mom wore designer clothes and her Aunt Dorothy bossed everyone on the school board, that didn't make Brittany a princess.

Besides, princesses didn't bite and scratch when they got mad.

Most of Kim's teachers, however, must have believed the princess thing. Why else would they allow Brittany to lord her family's wealth and status over the other kids?

So when Mrs. Thomas first told everyone to research their ancestors and create an oral presentation, Kim assumed this was just another way to impress Brittany's parents. Surely the Bonnet's ancestors did something interesting to make all of that money.

Kim's own family was boring, boring, boring. Mom and Dad worked as teachers. Mom's sisters -- Emerald, Ruby and Sapphire -- stayed home with their children. Dad's sister, Aunt Ginny, worked for Maryland's Department of Motor Vehicles.

Grandpa was the only interesting family member. He owned his jewelry store. Brittany's family bought stuff there all the time.

Maybe Grandpa would allow her to bring some diamonds, rubies and sapphires to class. Those always impressed people. People liked emeralds, too, but they scratched easily and Kim didn't want to worry about that.

When she told Grandpa about the assignment, however, he'd insisted she do her report without trying to dazzle with gemstones. People, he'd said, were always more interesting than things.

To prove it, he'd shown her photos of snow-capped mountains and lush valleys and told her stories about his ancestors who'd lived in Switzerland.

They were good stories, too, which is why this morning she'd focused most of her oral presentation on Grandpa's family.

"My great-great-great-great... er..." She'd turned to Mrs. Thomas. "I don't remember how many greats."

Mrs. Thomas had smiled. "That's okay, Kim. Why don't you tell us the year you're discussing?"

Kim turned to the flip-chart she'd prepared and pointed at the year 1541.

"Grandpa's family -- the Hershey family -- owned a jewelry store in Switzerland. Grandpa said Swiss jewelers were world-famous for bending and twisting and molding gold into necklaces, bracelets and earrings.

"But in 1541, some guy named John Calvert convinced the government in Geneva to forbid people from wearing jewelry. So the jewelers lost their jobs and..."

Mrs. Thomas interrupted. "Are you talking about John Calvert, one of the Protestant Reformers?"

"Yes, ma'am."

"Do you know why Mr. Calvert suggested they ban the wearing of jewelry?" Mrs. Thomas said.

Kim nodded, grateful now that she'd paid attention to Grandpa's story. "Grandpa said Mr. Calvert thought people shouldn't show off their wealth." She couldn't resist glancing at Brittany. Brittany folded her arms and scowled.

"That's correct." Mrs. Thomas turned to the class. "We'll be studying John Calvert when we talk about The Reformation period of history. Please continue, Kim."

Kim cleared her throat. Telling stories in front of class was harder than telling them to her friends. "Because no one was allowed to wear jewelry, jewelers needed to find something else to do. My great-great-er... My ancestor learned to make beautiful gold watches. He could do that 'cause watches were considered practical and people were allowed to wear them. Lots of other jewelers did the same thing and that was the start of the Swiss watch-making industry."

Wanting to finish her report and return to her seat, Kim quickly skimmed through her ancestors' roles in the Swiss peasant revolts in the 1600s and 1700s. She mentioned the ancestor who'd joined a chocolate-making factory in the 1800s and how Swiss chocolate tastes different from other chocolate.

And she told how, in the late 1800s, her great-great-great grandmother insisted the family start selling jewelry again.

"They still made watches," Kim said, "but they also opened a jewelry store. And when Great-great-great Grandmother had a baby girl, she named her Diamond. Grandpa said she did this to defy that earlier ban on wearing jewelry."

He'd also said Kim shared her ancestor's rebellious nature, but Kim didn't mention that.

"Ever since then, my family has named girls after jewelry stuff." She risked a glance at Brooke, the only person in the room who knew the origins of Kim's own name. "That's why I have aunts named Ruby, Sapphire and Emerald and cousins named Tiffany, Opal, Amber and Pearl. Mom's name is Diamondtina, but everyone calls her Tina."

As she rattled off names, her face heated. Why did everyone else get pretty names while Kim was named after a big hole in the ground?

Brooke met her eyes and offered an encouraging nod. Kim hurried through the rest of her report. She described Grandpa's birth in Switzerland, his family's immigration to Maryland, how he met Grandma and created Osprey Beach's only jewelry store.

"Grandpa still repairs watches and clocks and he sells beautiful jewelry. And that's the story of my family. The End."

"Excellent report, Kim," Mrs. Thomas said. "Does anyone have a question?"

Brittany's hand shot into the air.

Kim bit her lip. Brittany never asked questions unless she was trying to embarrass someone.

"You said all the girls in your family were named for jewelry." Brittany's eyes glittered. "What gem were you named after?"

Kim's stomach clenched and her ears felt funny.

"That's a good question, Brittany," Mrs. Thomas said. Her voice sounded like she was standing at the other end of a long tunnel. "Kim, were you named after some exotic gemstone?"

"No, Mrs. Thomas." Kim glanced at Brooke; her friend's eyes glistened in sympathy. Kim swallowed, then stuck out her chest. "I was named after the very first diamond mine in Africa."

Brittany and Leslie giggled. Kim felt her face flush.

"Grandpa said the Kimberley Mine contained the most spectacular formation of diamonds in the world."

"Yeah." Brittany flashed a smug smile. "But it's still nothing but a big hole in the ground."

No way did Brittany make that up just now. But how did she know Kim hated her name?

As the class started laughing, Kim glanced at Brooke. Her best friend wouldn't meet her eyes. Mrs. Thomas silenced everyone with a look. Kim scurried to her seat.

"Who would like to go next?" Mrs. Thomas said.

Brittany's hand shot into the air. As she swaggered to the front of the room, Kim leaned close to Brooke.

"How did she know?" she whispered.

"Remember when you told me about your name?" Brooke said. "And you said the Kimberley mine is just a big hole in the ground? Brittany was standing behind you."

"Why didn't you *tell* me?"

"Didn't see her until it was too late."

"Girls." Mrs. Thomas gave them her behave-or-else look.

Kim slumped into her seat and watched Brittany arrange her flip chart on the provided stand.

Brittany turned, beamed at the group and announced, "My father is descended from a world-famous pirate."

Several people gasped, masking Kim's groan. Pirates. Why did it have to be pirates?

Ever since last week's field trip to Osprey Beach's dusty old pirate museum, her classmates had elevated pirates to celebrity status. They'd staged mock sword fights in the playground and strutted around saying stupid things like "ahoy, mate" and "shiver me timbers."

Brittany couldn't have invented a more appealing ancestor.

"His name was Stede Bonnet, like my dad, but people called him the Gentleman Pirate." Brittany puffed out her chest. "He was even friends with Blackbeard."

Mrs. Thomas leaned forward, eyes bright, as Brittany described her ancestor as some swashbuckling hero who hunted treasure and saved damsels in distress. No one seemed to remember the museum director telling them that pirates had been killers and thieves.

Kim glanced around the room. Everyone, including Brooke, stared at Brittany with wide eyes.

Well, almost everyone. Mary Schultz, the new girl who dressed in too-large clothes, looked bored.

Sensing Kim's attention, Mary's brown eyes suddenly bored into Kim's.

Kim glanced away, then back. Mary continued to stare. Guilt washed over Kim.

Mary had arrived in school a week ago. She'd been chatty and bubbly, anxious to make everyone a friend. But her poodle curls, horned-rimmed glasses and dorky clothes had drawn Brittany's ire. Brittany had taunted Mary and anyone who tried to befriend her. After only two days, most everyone had been afraid to approach the new girl.

Truth was, Kim liked Mary. Before Brittany launched her campaign against her, Mary had listened avidly to Kim re-telling Grandpa's jewelry stories. Mary agreed that the Hardy Boys books were better than Nancy Drew and supported Kim's assertion that every girl should have a dog. Mary wanted a golden retriever while Kim had her heart set on a standard poodle, but, hey, all dogs were wonderful and dog lovers were the best.

But once Brittany started ridiculing Mary and anyone near her, Kim had backed away from the growing friendship. Ever since kindergarten, Brittany had used her larger size and willingness to scratch and bite to subdue anyone who challenged her. She'd once slammed Kim's face into the snow, holding her there until lack of oxygen made Kim stop struggling.

Fearing reprisal, Kim joined the others in ignoring Mary. The new girl retreated into herself.

Brittany's voice cut through Kim's thoughts.

"And this," Brittany said, "is the ruby amulet Stede Bonnet wore into battle."

Brittany removed a pendant from her neck and held it high. Maybe an inch long, the pendant had been shaped in gold filigree. In its center, a red stone, faceted in an old-fashioned style that Grandpa called "rose cut," caught the overhead light and glimmered.

Brittany pointed at the stone. "This ruby is the best. It's almost flawless, just like the stone in England's crown jewels, the one called the Black Prince's Ruby."

Kim straightened. What Brittany just said wasn't right.

She raised her hand. "Excuse me, Mrs. Thomas, but the Black Prince's Ruby isn't a real ruby. It's a red spinel."

Brittany's face flushed. "Of course it's a ruby! It's called the Black Prince's *ruby*, not the Black Prince's *spinel*."

"Grandpa says that's a mistake, that throughout most of history all red stones were called rubies. But later they discovered that red stones aren't all made of the same minerals. So they called some garnets and some spinels and the one in the crown jewels is a natural spinel." Kim pointed at the pendant Brittany clutched. "That might even be spinel. Have you had it checked?"

"This --" Brittany displayed the amulet. "This is a ruby just like the Black Prince's is a ruby and if your grandfather says different then he's lying."

"Grandpa's not a liar!"

"Is so!"

"Girls, that's enough," Mrs. Thomas said.

"But, Mrs. Thomas, Grandpa's not..."

"I said that's enough, Kimberley. You had your chance to talk, now give Brittany her time."

"But she's lying..."

Mrs. Thomas rose, pointed toward the front corner of the room and ordered Kim to stand in it.

"But...".

Mrs. Thomas folded her arms. "The next move is to the principal's office."

Leslie snickered, Brittany sneered. Kim trudged to the front of the room and listened while Brittany told more lies about her stupid ancestors.

When the bell rang for recess, Kim ran outside without even bothering to collect her backpack.

Brooke followed. But so did Brittany and her friend Leslie.

And then, right there in the playground, Brittany shouted so everyone could hear "Your grandfather is a liar and so are you."

Now Kim lifted her chin.

"Grandpa is not a liar," she said. "The Black Prince's stone *is* a spinel and you could look it up yourself if you weren't so stupid."

Brittany's eyes narrowed. She turned and searched the playground, probably looking for teachers.

Kim's mouth suddenly felt dry and she couldn't swallow. She really didn't want to tangle with Brittany again; she still had scabs on her elbows from the last time. But if she backed down, she'd invite more torment from Brittany.

Clenching her fists, Kim bent her knees and balanced her weight the way Grandpa showed her.

But before Brittany could throw the first punch, a small voice behind her said, "I don't know why you're fighting over that stupid pirate; he was a total loser."

Brittany wheeled around, revealing Mary Schultz.

What was she doing?

"Do you see this?" Brittany brandished the ancient gold pendant that had started the entire mess. "Blackbeard himself gave this amulet to my ancestor."

Kim leaned forward, trying to get a closer look at the red stone. Seeing her interest, Brittany immediately tucked the pendant inside her blouse.

"Read the history books," Mary said. "Stede Bonnet was so incompetent that Blackbeard took his ship away and made someone else captain. Bonnet sailed with Blackbeard, but the other pirates laughed at him behind his back."

"That's a lie!"

"Is not." Mary crossed her arms, her eyes flicking from Brittany to Kim and back to Brittany. "Besides, if the Gentleman Pirate was such a success, why did he survive only a year before he was caught and hanged? He was a loser."

With a screech that startled a nearby flock of seagulls, Brittany tackled Mary. Mary hit the ground with a sickening thunk, then flung up her arms, trying to block Brittany's long nails from her face.

Leslie stepped back but made no move to help Brittany. Brooke tugged on Kim's arm.

"C'mon," Brooke hissed. "Let's get out of here."

Kim let Brooke pull her a step, then stopped and glanced over her shoulder. Mary had curled into a ball, but Brittany continued to hammer her.

"That's not fair," Kim said. "Brittany's bigger."

"You wanna tell her that? Let's go."

Kim took another step. Mary screamed. Wheeling around, Kim launched herself at Brittany.

The impact carried Brittany off of Mary and onto the sandy ground.

"Mary, run!" Kim yelled.

Brittany roared and grabbed Kim's pony tail, tugging hard. Pain shot through Kim's scalp, bringing tears to her eyes. She slammed an elbow into Brittany's arm, breaking the hold. Jabbing with her right fist, she managed to connect with Brittany's stomach.

But the larger girl used her weight to flip Kim onto her back.

A clawed hand aimed for her eyes. Kim blocked the strike with her forearm, felt the sharp nails piercing her skin. Suddenly, Brittany was all nails and elbows and teeth.

Years of pent-up animosity surged through Kim, the anger giving her the strength to push Brittany to the side. She pounced and began swinging. Her fists connected with Brittany's shoulder, arm, stomach. Brittany tore at Kim's clothes and blood trickled down Kim's arm.

Strong arms wrapped around Kim, trapping her arms and swinging her into the air.

"What is going on here?" Mr. Jefferson roared.

Recognizing the dark hands that held her, Kim stopped struggling. Which is why she was unprepared when Brittany landed a punch onto her diaphragm.

Air rushed through her mouth and she couldn't breathe, omygosh, she couldn't breathe!

Through watery eyes, she watched Brittany pull back for another strike, saw Mary and Brooke tackle her and the three girls tumble to the ground, heard Mrs. Thomas screech "Girls, stop that!" and still she couldn't breathe. She felt Mr. Jefferson gently lower her to the ground and her legs crumpled and she curled into a ball and gasped for air.

And finally -- finally! -- she inhaled a huge breath and her nose identified the normally comforting odor of Chesapeake Bay, sand and early autumn leaves.

She blinked tears away and adjusted her glasses. Mrs. Thomas gripped Brooke and Mary. Brittany lay on the ground, making a big production out of injuries nowhere near as serious as what she'd inflicted on Mary and Kim. Leslie was nowhere in sight, having fled when the teachers appeared.

As she gulped air and the roaring in her ears subsided, Kim tuned in to Mrs. Thomas. "...principal's office. Ganging up on poor Brittany!"

"That's not what I saw," Mr. Jefferson said. "They were all fighting."

"But who started it?"

Hearing her cue, Brittany started whimpering. Brooke protested, but Mrs. Thomas shushed her. Mary met Kim's eyes.

Help. She needed to get help.

Pushing to her feet, Kim tore through the school yard.

She heard shouts and the thudding of large feet. A spurt of speed carried her over the short fence and into the street. Horns honked, but she'd already reached the far sidewalk.

Glancing over her shoulder, she spotted Mr. Jefferson by the road waiting for a break in traffic. Kim veered right and dashed into the nearest yard, hoping she wouldn't encounter a dog. She cleared another hedge and her feet connected with the gravel alley that ran behind Grandpa's house.

She skidded left and, keeping the houses that bordered the Chesapeake Bay on her right, charged down the alley. The crunch of gravel beneath her feet hid any sounds of pursuit. Finally, Grandpa's driveway came into view.

Her sneakers slapped asphalt. Slamming to a halt, she opened the gate to the yard. Even though there was no sign of Mr. Jefferson, she pounded up the outside steps to the first floor and swung open the door to Grandpa's office.

The chair in front of his jewelry bench was empty, but bare spots in his normally meticulously arranged tweezers, pliers and files indicated an interruption of his work. Voices drifted in from the storefront, Aunt Ruby, another woman and...

"Grandpa!"

Kim burst into the store, skirted the first display case and threw her arms around Grandpa's waist. The tears she'd held at bay flowed, streaking her glasses. Grandpa knelt and wrapped his arms around her. She transferred her arms to his neck and sobbed into his shoulder. He cooed nonsense, the sound of his tender voice giving her courage.

Leaning back, she stared into Grandpa's kind eyes. He dabbed her tears with a large, fluffy handkerchief and handed it to her to blow her nose.

"Why the tears..." He broke off as he spotted the blood on her arms. He caught her hands in his and studied the scratches. "Who did this?"

"Brittany."

"Stede and Jessica's daughter?" Aunt Ruby snorted. "I'm not surprised. They've always spoiled that child."

Sensing an ally, Kim turned to include her aunt in the conversation. But the words froze in her mouth when she spotted the woman standing next to Aunt Ruby: Dorothy Tyson.

The wealthy busybody's eyes narrowed as she scanned Kim's messy ponytail, scratches and dirt-covered jeans.

"*I* find it hard to believe my niece would stoop to roughhousing."

The woman's superior tone freed Kim from her deer-in-the-headlights reaction. Dorothy Tyson might be Brittany's aunt, but she wouldn't be the only one proclaiming Brittany's innocence. Kim needed Grandpa's help.

She squeezed his hand. "You've got to come to the principal's office and explain that Brooke and Mary were only trying to help, that Brittany started it all and she was going to kill Mary and..."

"Whoa, whoa, whoa, slow down sweetie..."

"I can't slow down! They need our help now!" She bit her lip, fighting a new set of tears.

"We're going to help. But first I need to know what we're dealing with. Start from the beginning."

Kim nodded and launched into her story, how Mrs. Thomas had praised Kim's report, how Brittany ridiculed Kim's name, how Brittany said her family's ruby was just like the Black Prince's, how she'd explained about ruby and spinel, how Brittany called Grandpa a liar. She described Brittany's playground challenge, Mary's attempt to distract her and Brittany's attack on Mary.

"I really, really thought she was going to kill Mary," Kim said.

"Nonsense," Dorothy Tyson said. "Brittany has an explosive temper, but she'd never resort to physical violence."

Grandpa frowned. "I'm afraid you don't know your niece very well. Ruby, would you please lock up for me? Dorothy, I'm afraid we'll have to finish our discussion at another time."

Without waiting for a response, he took Kim's hand and led her out to his car.

Five minutes later, he parked the car next to a black Mercedes with the license plate "Bonnet." Brittany's parents had arrived. The Subaru that belonged to Brooke's family was parked farther away.

Kim's stomach clenched. While she'd been explaining to Grandpa what happened, someone in the principal's office must have called the other parents. That they'd arrived already was not a good sign.

Grandpa turned off the car. But instead of opening the door, he said, "Kim, why did you interrupt Brittany's talk?"

"Because what Brittany was saying isn't true!" How could Grandpa even ask such a question? "The Black Prince's Ruby is a spinel, not a ruby."

"If Brooke made a mistake in her talk, would you have interrupted?"

Though Grandpa's voice was gentle, Kim detected a touch of sadness. She bit her lip and looked away. "No."

"You'd have waited until after the class, told her in private and let her correct the mistake, right?"

Kim picked at a hangnail. "I guess."

A warm hand closed over hers. She looked back at Grandpa.

"Sometimes," he said, "telling the truth can hurt people."

"How? Isn't the truth always right?"

"Not if you're using truth as a weapon."

"A weapon?"

Grandpa nodded. "What you said was true. But you used the truth to embarrass Brittany. Words can hurt every bit as much as fists or..." He nodded at her arms. "Fingernails."

"But don't people need to know the truth?"

"Usually. But not always. Not if your motive is to hurt someone. Brittany is a bully and you told the truth to make her seem less powerful. Right?"

"I... I guess."

Grandpa hugged her. "It's okay, Monkey. We all make mistakes. What's important is that we learn from them. Next time think twice before using truth as a weapon."

"But... But what about Mary? She said Brittany's pirate was a loser because he was caught and hanged. Was Mary wrong, too?"

Grandpa's eyebrows drew together and he gazed into the distance. Recognizing his thoughtful look, Kim folded her hands and waited in silence. Years ago she'd made him promise to treat her like an adult, to tell her when he didn't know the answer to a question rather than making something up. She trusted him to give her a real answer when he was done thinking.

Besides, she had no desire to rush into the principal's office.

"The answer is yes and no," Grandpa finally said. "Mary said those things because she was trying to prevent Brittany from hitting you. So in a way, Mary did right.

"But don't kid yourself: Mary knew what she said about Brittany's ancestor would hurt her."

"But why would Brittany care? That pirate guy has been dead for ages."

"You've studied the kings and queens of England in school, right? And you know that in order to be queen, you have to be related to royalty?"

"Brittany's not a princess."

"True. But she *thinks* like a princess. Her whole image of herself is based on her ancestors. And didn't you say everyone was impressed when Brittany revealed she has a pirate ancestor?"

"Yeah. They acted like it was a big deal, like that made her special or something."

Grandpa patted her hand. "There you go. Brittany thinks she needs the Gentleman Pirate to be important."

He brushed a lock of hair from her face, tucking it behind her ear. "Brittany isn't unusual. There are a lot of people who worry more about the past than the present. They define themselves by whether or not their ancestors sailed on the Mayflower or fought in the Civil War."

"That's silly."

"They don't think so. But if they live too much in the past and not enough in the present, well, then it's sad. Don't get me wrong: History is important." He peered at her over the top of his glasses. "I don't want to see your history grades go down."

Kim resisted the impulse to roll her eyes. Grandpa didn't like that.

"But," he continued, "if Brittany is really looking to the past for her identity, you should feel sorry for her."

She felt her mouth drop open. Brittany? Snotty Brittany with her snide comments, Ralph Lauren shirts and mansion on the hill? Mean Brittany who'd made school a living nightmare?

Grandpa hugged her. "Just think about it, okay?" He reached for the car door. "Let's go straighten out this mess."

The walk to the principal's office was all too short. The school secretary sat just inside the reception area, a phone pressed to her ear. She looked up as they entered and frowned.

"Never mind, Mrs. West," she said into the phone. "She just walked in with her grandfather. Yes, I'll tell him to call." Hanging up the phone, she peered over her glasses at Kim. "You are in big trouble, young lady." To Grandpa, she added "Thank you for coming, Mr. Hershey. Go right in. The other parents are already here."

Kim's stomach knotted and her mouth was so dry she thought she'd gag. What story had the secretary told Mom? Could Grandpa make it all better? She clung to his hand as they entered the crowded office.

Mr. Lloyd, the principal, loomed behind his huge walnut desk. The sun filtering through the window behind him made his bald head gleam. To his right, Brittany -- flanked by both parents -- shed pretend tears into a dry handkerchief. Across the room, Brooke huddled against her mom. Mrs. Swann's face was as white as Brooke's.

Mary Schultz stood alone, one arm bent across her stomach as if it hurt. Blood oozed from the scratches Brittany had inflicted.

Kim reached out, took Mary's hand and pulled her close.

Mr. Lloyd cleared his throat. "I understand Ms. Schultz's parents won't be able to join us, so let's get started, shall we?" He frowned and swept solemn eyes around the room. "I must confess, I'm not used to girls fighting in the schoolyard."

"She started it!" Brittany pointed at Kim.

Kim gasped. "Did not! You called Grandpa a liar and..." A squeeze on her shoulder -- Grandpa's warning -- stopped her.

"It doesn't matter who started it," Mr. Lloyd said. "I didn't call everyone in here to discuss who did what. School policy is very clear. There is to be no fighting on school grounds. Anyone who engages in physical violence will be placed in after-school detention for five days."

"That is totally unacceptable." Stede Bonnet lifted his chin. "My wife and I have busy schedules. We can't be expected to drop everything to play chauffer just because you made Brittany miss the school bus."

"Mr. Bonnet, school policy was designed for the safety of our children, not your convenience," the principal said.

"Fine," Mr. Bonnet said. "Punish the three who started this mess and leave my daughter out of it."

"We have no way of knowing how the fight started," Grandpa said. "Every story can be told from different perspectives and you've only heard one side."

"But look." Mr. Bonnet pointed to a bruise forming on Brittany's chin. "Look at what that hellion did to my daughter." Now the finger pointed at Kim.

Grandpa stepped in front of her.

"Name calling and affixing blame isn't going to help the situation." Though Grandpa's voice was level, Kim heard the anger. "All four girls have been injured."

"Which is why we have a no tolerance policy," the principal said. "Normally, punishment begins immediately, but I'll give you time to make transportation arrangements." Mr. Lloyd paused to stare briefly at Brittany's father. "Detention will begin tomorrow." He stood. "Again, I'd like to thank you all for coming so quickly."

Kim followed Grandpa out into the hall. As they walked toward the front door, Grandpa offered to drive Mary home; she readily agreed.

Once outside, however, Grandpa handed the keys to Kim and told the girls to go ahead of him. Kim started toward the car, but when she heard the school door open, she stopped and turned.

Brittany, still flanked by her parents, stepped into the sunshine.

"Stede, can you spare a moment?" Grandpa said.

Mr. Bonnet nodded. "Jessica, you and Brittany wait in the car."

As Brittany and her mother moved away, Kim slid closer to the two men. Grandpa lowered his voice.

"Don't you ever call my granddaughter names again," he said.

Mr. Bonnet's eyebrows shot up. "Who do you think..."

"I don't think, I know. I know that if you don't start setting a better example for your daughter, she'll never have any friends. I know that all of the jewelry you've purchased from me didn't go to your wife. And I know that if you ever again describe Kim in anything other than glowing terms, an accounting of those purchases will appear in your wife's mailbox."

Not waiting for a response, Grandpa turned away. He should have seen Kim eavesdropping, but for the moment his eyes focused inward. Kim snagged Mary's hand and trotted toward Grandpa's car. As they passed the Bonnet's Mercedes, she glanced inside.

Brittany slouched in the back seat, shoulders hunched, eyes staring out at nothing. She looked so unlike the cocky girl in class that for a minute Kim wondered if Brittany had a sister. But, no, that was the pink top Brittany had worn in class.

So why did she look different? She'd almost looked... Lonely?

No, that couldn't be right. Brittany had lots of friends. Maybe she was pouting because her father couldn't stop the principal from putting her in detention, too.

Yeah, that had to be it. Brittany had caused today's disaster and now she was sad because she was getting punished, too.

There was no reason to feel sorry for her, despite Grandpa's earlier words.

No, Kim would never, ever feel sorry for Brittany. Not even if Brittany was run over by a truck or eaten by a shark or... or nibbled to death by ducks.

Not even if Brittany's stupid pirate ancestor came back to haunt her.

Chapter 1

Present Day
Osprey Beach, Maryland

The three-month-old osprey glided over Pirate's Cove, spotted the activity on the beach below and emitted an annoyed screech. He was hungry and his favorite hunting tree jutted from the eroding cliff that surrounded the cove. The tree's gnarled branches leaned toward the Chesapeake Bay and provided the perfect launch pad for the newly independent young bird.

Normally on a hot August morning, only a handful of fossil hunters and dog walkers populated this particular strip of land. There were wider stretches of sand farther north, as well as boardwalks in Osprey, Chesapeake and North beaches, plenty of places for sun bathers and swimmers.

Several hours earlier, however, the cove's tranquil atmosphere began to change. The beach was still shrouded in twilight when the elderly man and young woman arrived.

The osprey recognized the pair. They were usually accompanied by a standard poodle that chased seagulls but, at the insistence of his companions, honored the osprey's privacy. Today the dog was absent, but the osprey wasn't concerned; he knew these two humans wouldn't bother him.

So he'd perched on his tree and watched the woman draw a rope across the entrance to Pirate's Cove and help the man erect a canopy on the beach. The woman then scattered armloads of tiny treasure chests across a mound of imported white sand. While the man noted locations on a hand-drawn map, the woman buried each chest.

An hour later, the first wave of would-be treasure hunters arrived and the noise and cacophony had begun.

How could the osprey possibly hunt with all that going on? He screed his annoyance.

Kimberley West stepped from beneath the canopy, shaded her eyes with her hand and called "I'm sorry! Tomorrow everything will be back to normal."

She watched the bird veer away and sighed, wishing she could fly away with him. Like the osprey, she hated to see her sleepy hometown inundated with strangers.

And it was all Brittany's fault.

The childish thought made her wince. She was 32 years old, a professor of psychology and Brittany could still make her angry.

She hadn't seen her childhood nemesis since she graduated from high school. The no-Brittany years had been pure bliss. No more vicious rumors, no more stolen boyfriends, no more ridicule.

No more wondering when Brittany's sly insults would explode into an actual physical attack.

The years hadn't been completely Brittany-free, of course. Brittany might have snagged a wealthy husband and moved to New York, but the psychological damage she'd inflicted had lingered. To this day, Kim grew tongue-tied whenever confronted with insult masked as compliment -- a ploy Brittany learned from her aunt, Dorothy Tyson.

Such backhanded compliments had been rife in the small Oregon college where Kim had labored for six years in her quest for tenure. Not surprisingly, the psychology professors were particularly adept at slicing colleagues' confidence with a well-turned phrase.

Kim had persevered and not only earned that tenure, but she'd also landed an associate professorship at the University of Maryland.

Her triumphant return home, however, had turned into a nightmare when she'd interrupted a burglary that landed Grandpa in the hospital. With Kim's help, the police eventually arrested the assailant.

Three weeks ago, the hospital released Grandpa with admonitions to rest. Kim had enforced the doctor's orders by taking control of Grandpa's jewelry store, thus eliminating his "but I need to" excuses. Under Kim's care, his strength began to return.

Even so, his skin was still too pale and he tired easily. Kim feared his participation in this week's pirate festival would push him back into bed.

The festival celebrating the opening of the new Osprey Beach Pirate Museum was originally planned as a one-day affair. Local business owners would have sponsored day-time children's activities while vendors sold pirate memorabilia. In the evening, donors, local hotshots and museum board members would attend a black-tie banquet held in the museum's roof-top restaurant.

Brittany, however, had insisted the festival expand to encompass an entire week. Her demand divided the museum board. Grandpa and two others urged restraint. Brittany's father and aunt supported Brittany's demands.

Given that Brittany personally financed the new museum -- Kim suspected the money came from the settlement from Brittany's recent divorce -- she ultimately prevailed.

In true Brittany fashion, she'd scheduled a press conference and managed to convince *The Washington Post* to run an article about the museum's opening. As a result, local hotels filled quickly. Attendance at last night's special fireworks rivaled the Three Beaches' annual July 4 celebration. Today people from all over Maryland,

Washington and Virginia crowded the shops along the boardwalk and the vendor booths erected for the occasion. The beaches teemed with sunbathers and squealing children. By any measure, the festival was a surprising success.

And therein lay the problem.

The children's treasure hunt Grandpa had planned should have ended long ago. Kim wanted to take Grandpa home to rest before the heat and humidity grew too intense. But so many children wanted to participate that they'd had to divide them into smaller, manageable groups. Each group had to be escorted from the Pirate's Cove parking lot, provided instructions and then supervised during the digging. Unlike most of the children Kim encountered in Calvert County, some of the out-of-town visitors either didn't understand the rule of one treasure per person or chose to ignore it. Kim had to closely watch the digging to ensure everyone played fairly.

So here it was, almost noon, she was dripping with sweat and the last group of treasure hunters hadn't yet arrived. Too bad Hurricane Dan was still far out in the Atlantic. Maybe it'd come close enough to break the heat wave that gripped the East Coast.

She wiped her sweaty brow. Now that she thought about it, she decided she was justified in blaming her misery on Brittany.

The *Raider's March* from *Indiana Jones* sounded in her pocket. She pulled out her cell phone and checked caller I.D.

Mary.

"You are not going to believe what Brittany did now!"

A wave of guilt washed over Kim. She might be hot, miserable and worried about Grandpa, but at least she hadn't tangled directly with Brittany.

Her childhood friend, however, had waged a one-woman war against Brittany. Years ago, Mary had been hired as director of Osprey Beach's Pirate Museum. She'd taken that dusty, forgotten piece of Calvert County history and turned it into a serious, educational institution.

Then along came pirate-obsessed Brittany and her offer to build a bigger, better museum. In typical Brittany fashion, she'd assumed the donation entitled her to dictate the contents and layout of the exhibits. Mary claimed Brittany was trying to turn the museum into Coney Island. Battle lines were drawn and Brittany made no secret of her desire to replace Mary with a hand-picked museum director.

"I'm almost afraid to ask," Kim said into the phone.

"You know how she's been nagging Kevin about the case for her pirate amulet?" Mary said. "Like she thinks it's the Hope Diamond or something?"

Mary's husband Kevin constructed all of the museum's specialty display cases, including the case for Brittany's ruby amulet. Her nitpicking had pushed the poor man far behind schedule.

"What did she change now?" Kim said. "Does she require gold inlay on the case?"

Mary snorted. "That would actually be preferable to what she did. You know how she insisted on taking the plaque for the case to her own inscriber? She finally gave Kevin the finished plaque to hang.

"Guess what it says? No, here, I'll read it to you. Ah, something about Bonnet wearing the ruby into battle, blah, blah, blah... Here it is."

Mary cleared her voice and, with a faint British accent, read "'The quality of Stede Bonnet's ruby rivals the Black Prince's Ruby found in Britain's Crown Jewels.'

"Brittany knows darn well the Black Prince's Ruby is really a spinel. Didn't she listen in school when you told everyone? I'm trying to run an educational museum and she's not only turning it into an amusement park, she's disseminating incorrect information!"

Mary continued her rant, but Kim only half-way listened.

Why had Brittany given Kevin incorrect information for her exhibit? Did she really believe the red stone in the Crown Jewels was ruby, not spinel? Or was there a more sinister reason for waiting until the last minute to install a plaque with verifiably incorrect information?

Kim had yet to meet Brittany face-to-face. She'd probably see her at tonight's banquet. Unlike Mary, however, she'd assumed she had nothing to fear from the childhood bully. After all, normal people didn't hold grudges for decades.

Or did they?

"Kim? Are you still there?"

"Oh. I'm sorry, Mary. I'm just trying to figure out Brittany's motive."

"Don't bother trying to psychoanalyze her," Mary said. "You don't need a psychology degree to know Brittany did this as a warning... Oh, crap, here comes Dorothy Tyson. I'd better run. See you later."

Kim hung up and jammed the phone into her pocket. She suddenly felt cold.

"Everything okay, Monkey?"

Pasting a smile on her face, Kim turned toward Grandpa and searched for signs of exhaustion.

Though his cheeks were slightly pale, his eyes sparkled. Despite hours of heat and humidity, Grandpa's white shirt and black pants looked newly pressed. He still wore his pirate hat at a jaunty angle and the eye patch and boots added the final authentic touch.

In contrast, Kim's white shirt dripped in sweat. She'd long ago tossed off her pirate hat and boots, preferring to brave the hot sand in bare feet to sweltering in leather that chafed her calves. She wished she'd taken Tiffany's advice and worn shorts instead of long pants.

"Everything's fine," she said. "How do you stay so cool looking?"

"Don't change the subject." Grandpa crossed his arms. "You look worried. Was that Mary on the phone again?"

"Yeah. Brittany messed up the plaque for her pirate ruby exhibit."

"Messed up how?"

"She says her ruby rivals the Black Prince's Ruby."

Grandpa sighed. "That girl has a fragile ego."

"*Brittany?* How can you say that? She thinks the world revolves around her."

"That may be. But her whole identity is tied up in her family name. She doesn't know how to be an individual." He peered over his glasses at her. "Unlike some people."

Kim grinned and playfully swatted Grandpa's arm. "I resemble that."

The sound of children's laughter drew their eyes to the roped off trail. Aunt Ginny had arrived with the last group of pint-sized treasure hunters.

While some children stared at the mound of sand where they'd be digging, most gawked up at Ginny.

Instead of the traditional pirate costume, Ginny wore a brightly colored flounced skirt and ruffled blouse. The serving-wench costume may not have suited her plump figure, but it matched her bubbly personality.

Besides, the gypsy-like clothes allowed Ginny to drape herself in bangles and beads and crazy earrings.

Several children's eyes suddenly widened as they stared at Ginny's ears. Kim grinned. They'd probably spotted the dangling fish earrings. The upside-down trout sported a plastic eye whose pupil rolled every time Ginny moved.

No one knew why Ginny began pasting the cartoon-like eyes on everything, but Kim would be forever grateful for her favorite aunt's quirky humor. Her first encounter with googly eyes came on her 28th birthday. She was living in Oregon and feeling homesick when a birthday card arrived.

The card featured a photo of the Mona Lisa with some kind of saying about a niece being one-of-a-kind. The saccharine message, however, was lightened by Ginny's addition: Plastic googly eyes covered Lisa's famous ones.

Suddenly the gray day seemed to brighten and she could face the stack of Psychology 101 papers she needed to grade. First, however, she'd called her aunt and thanked her profusely for making her laugh.

Turns out, however, that loving aunts had much in common with standard poodles: If you laughed at something they did, the behavior never went away.

After that day googly eyes appeared on holiday cards (Santa and Rudolph), collectible stuffed toys and, most recently, jewelry. Kim had to admit that the dangling fish were the most inventive.

"Show time," Grandpa whispered before swaggering over to the children. Kim attempted her own swagger walk to the sand pile, but each step was accompanied by a painful "ouch" as her bare feet touched hot sand.

She reached the dig site, turned, planted her legs and crossed her arms in what she hoped was true cocky pirate fashion.

"Well, shiver me timbers, this is a hearty crew," Grandpa proclaimed. "Are ye ready to dig for treasure?"

"Yes!" the children cried as one.

"Well, now, let's first discuss the pirate rules of conduct."

Kim tried hard not to smile as Grandpa explained that there was to be no shoving, no stealing, no rough-housing. There was plenty of treasure for all. Only one treasure chest per crew member. Once you find your treasure, step away from the dig site. Otherwise, the first mate -- here Grandpa gestured toward Kim -- would make you walk the plank.

Muscles tensed as Aunt Ginny started the countdown. On the word "Go," several dozen boys and girls rushed at Kim. She resisted the urge to jump out of the way. A real pirate commanded respect by holding her position. If this group of children was as avaricious as the previous two, she needed to maintain the illusion of authority to enforce the one-treasure-only rule.

The wave of skinny arms and legs swept around her, landed on the "dig site" and began flinging stinging sand onto her exposed calves.

As the heat beat down on her bare head, she tried to imagine sitting in Grandpa's air conditioned living room, iced tea beside her, Rorschach laying at her feet... Nah, that image didn't work. During the heat wave, Rory had commandeered the a/c vent in whatever room she occupied. He was probably sprawled over a vent right now. No dogs were allowed on the beach during the pirate celebration, not even well-behaved standard poodles.

Lucky dog.

"Told ya you should have worn shorts."

Kim turned and stared at Tiffany. Her gorgeous cousin looked cool and sexy in a sleeveless blouse, black short-shorts and flat sandals laced up her curvy calves. A bandana wrapped around her head provided a pirate look while preventing wavy blond locks from whipping into her face.

"I wish I'd listened to you," Kim said. "Unfortunately, I don't have your legs."

"Nonsense. All Hershey women have gorgeous legs."

Kim grinned and shook her head. What she wouldn't give for half of Tiff's confidence.

"Thought you were manning the refreshment booth," she said.

"Amber took over. One of the treasure hunters brought me a message from Grandpa saying you were walking around barefoot." Tiffany held up a pair of rubber flipflops. "Good thing someone was selling tourist junk."

"Lifesaver!" Kim hugged Tiffany, accepted the shoes and slipped them on. The relief to her sandy, bare feet was immediate.

"Now go get out of the sun. I'll deal with the kids."

Kim felt her mouth drop open. When had her younger cousin turned so bossy? Or, for that matter, motherly? Throughout their lives, Kim had always done the mothering, protecting Tiffany, Amber and Crystal from their older cousins' verbal bullying. Though Kim had never mastered the art of the biting comment -- she preferred direct confrontation -- she'd never hesitated to defend the younger girls. Odd to hear Tiff ordering her around.

Tiffany gave her a mild shove. "Go sit in the shade. You don't want to look like a lobster for Professor Hotstuff tonight." Turning her back on Kim, she reached out to snag the t-shirt of a boy trying to sneak off with three treasure chests. "You seriously want to walk the plank, bud?"

Kim turned away so the boy couldn't see her grin. Tiffany may not know pirate-speak, but she had the attitude down pat. Obviously, Kim could leave this duty in good hands.

Besides, she didn't want to get into a discussion about her date for tonight, Scott Wilson.

She wasn't sure why Tiffany referred to Scott as "Professor Hotstuff." The Pulitzer-prize winning journalist turned history professor wasn't classically handsome. He was tall -- maybe six feet -- but his dark hair was receding and most people would describe his hazel eyes as nondescript. But he had an Indiana Jones smile and a charming manner and he treated people with respect.

A month ago they'd been total strangers. Then Grandpa was attacked, Scott's uncle was murdered and Kim and Scott were thrown together, dodging bullets and thugs while trying to unmask the murderous thieves intent on stealing a rare blue diamond.

Tonight they'd attend the museum banquet, their first official date since Grandpa returned home from the hospital. With Tiffany's help, she'd bought a special dress for the occasion. She looked forward to seeing Scott wearing a tuxedo.

Crossing to the shaded area, she plopped into a chair beside Grandpa and Aunt Ginny.

"I'd say your treasure hunt was a success," she said.

Grandpa grinned. "Not still mad that I insisted on following through with this?"

"Not as long as you don't make yourself sick." She kissed his cheek.

"Hi, remember me?"

Kim looked up, using her hand to shade her eyes from the glare. A boy and girl, maybe nine or ten years old, fidgeted in front of her.

Like the other children, they were dressed in flip flops, shorts and dirt-smudged t-shirts. The little boy was nondescript: Brown hair, brown eyes, slight build.

The little girl, however...

Kim grinned as she recognized the dishwater blond. "Liz! Wonderful to see you." Remembering Liz's fierce independence, Kim resisted the urge to hug the child, opting instead for a hand squeeze.

Liz's smile lit her face. "You do remember!"

"How can I forget a fellow traveler?" Escorting Liz around the Smithsonian's gem collection had provided a much-needed break from investigating the attack on Grandpa.

"Uh, is your grandmother with you?" *Oh, please don't be nearby.* The last time she'd seen Liz's grandmother, the woman hadn't been happy with Kim's investigation.

"Grandma couldn't come, so I rode over with Bobby's folks."

Bobby? Kim looked closer at the shy boy. "Oh, my gosh, you're Mary's son! You've gotten so tall since I last saw you!"

Bobby blushed, so Kim quickly changed the subject.

"I didn't see you two out here digging." She indicated the sand pile with the squealing children.

"Oh, no," Liz said. "We don't do baby stuff. We dig for real." She nudged Bobby. "Show her."

Bobby pulled a blue bandana from his shorts pocket, gently unwrapped it, and removed something. "Hold out your hand," he said.

Assuming they'd found one of the fossilized shark's teeth that dotted the nearby cliffs, she extended her hand. With great reverence, Bobby positioned a faceted gemstone on her palm.

Kim's first thought was that some poor woman had lost a stone from a ring. That happened more often than people realized. Over time, the prongs that held gemstones in place could loosen. That was why Grandpa always told his customers to bring their jewelry in once a year for a free cleaning; it gave him the opportunity to check the prongs and, if necessary, tighten them.

Most women knew to leave their diamonds, emeralds and sapphires at home when going to the beach. Rings could slip off, necklace clasps could come undone, earrings could catch in hair and pull loose. Hard enough to find lost jewelry in the sand; impossible if the item landed in the water.

However, people seemed more cavalier with the less expensive gemstones. Kim frequently found amethyst, citrine and blue topaz buried in the sand.

In the shade, Bobby's find appeared dark red. Garnet, maybe? Flat and wide on the bottom, its facets curved in a rounded shape to end at a point on top, an old-fashioned style called "rose."

Developed in the 1500s, the cutting style had been one of the early attempts to enhance color and brilliance in gemstones. Much later, new tools enabled more precise placement of facets which, in turn, produced more sparkle. Styles like the rose cut went out of fashion.

Which meant this stone might be very old.

"Is it real?" Liz said.

Kim couldn't help smiling at the excitement on Liz's face. "Let's take a closer look."

She turned to show the stone to Grandpa only to find him deep in conversation with Aunt Ginny, something about the seating arrangements for tonight.

Not wanting to interrupt, she snaked her hand into his shirt pocket. He never went anywhere without one of his loupes and, sure enough, he had one today.

Holding the loupe to her eye, she brought the stone into focus and searched for the telltale bubbles that would indicate the stone was glass. No bubbles. Instead, she saw the small feather-like inclusions that formed in many natural stones.

She frowned. Did someone lose a gem from an antique ring?

Setting the loupe aside, she stepped away from the protective umbrella and held the stone to the light. A sunbeam sent flashes of red in all directions.

But not just any old red.

Kim's mouth dropped open. The children and beach and heat faded away as her mind flashed back to the first time she'd seen this color.

She'd just turned ten and, in celebration, Grandpa took her on one of his New York buying trips. The rumbling train ride followed by a speeding taxi set the stage for an entire day of wonders. They'd stepped from the taxi onto West 47th Street, the very heart of New York's diamond district.

Store windows glittered with diamonds in every size and shape. Wide-eyed tourists shuffled from one display to the next. A man with a briefcase handcuffed to his wrist exchanged a jewelry envelope with a bearded fellow wearing a long black coat.

Clutching his own battered briefcase, Grandpa guided her to a nondescript door tucked into a brick wall. The creaky stairs led up one flight to another plain door. Grandpa pushed a button on the wall and announced his name. A buzzer sounded and they stepped into a scene right out of *The Arabian Nights.*

The walls were wallpapered, floor to ceiling, with jewels. Small jewelry boxes with clear lids had been mounted to display their contents from a distance. Diamond tennis bracelets, sapphire earrings and emerald pendants competed for attention with less expensive gems: amethyst, citrine, turquoise, carnelian, topaz, malachite, peridot, garnet. Kim stepped close to a wall of purple and yellow and imagined herself in an Egyptian tomb, the first archeologist to discover the Pharaoh's treasure.

All too soon, Grandpa led her back to the street, through other doors, into other sparkling rooms.

By the time they reached their last stop -- a nondescript shop with the distinctive barred door -- Kim thought she couldn't absorb any more. Just as well because, after being admitted inside, there wasn't much to see. The small room held a single wall of shelves holding what looked like black shoe boxes. Nothing glittered except for the eyes of the wizened woman standing behind a wooden counter.

Like the other store owners, the woman beamed at Grandpa and began pulling jewelry envelopes from beneath the counter. Kim tuned out their chatter. Her stomach grumbled, reminding her that Grandpa had promised to treat her to dinner at a fancy restaurant with real tablecloths. Maybe she'd even order her favorite meal: baked beans mixed with sliced hotdogs.

She jumped when a hand landed on her shoulder.

"Wanna see something amazing?" Grandpa pointed to a small stone laying on a piece of black velvet. "What color is that?"

Kim opened her mouth to say "red," but then stopped. Grandpa had taught her to be more precise when describing a color. Subtle, almost imperceptible differences – a hint of yellow, orange or blue - could raise or lower a colored gemstone's value. She peered closer.

The stone was red, but it was the oddest shade she'd ever seen. Not blue-red like the rubies in Grandpa's showcase or purple-red like the garnets. This was a real red, a rich, true color with maybe a hint of purple. The gemstone was almost the same shade as the dorky new fruit Grandpa had insisted she try, the one that was nothing but juice-covered seeds.

"Er, pomegranate red?"

The smile on Grandpa's face lit the entire dingy room. "That's my girl! The color is actually called 'pigeon's blood.'"

Kim wrinkled her nose. "Pigeon's blood? Ewwww..."

Giving a quick tweak of her ponytail, he added "This is the most valuable color for a ruby. And also the rarest. Look at it closely because you won't often see rubies this color."

Talk about understatement! The "pigeon's blood" red was so rare that, outside of that odd little shop, she'd *never* seen a ruby that color.

Until now.

There was no other way to describe the stone that glistened in her hand: pigeon's blood red.

She turned back to the children. "Where did you find this?"

Bobby's eyes slid left before he pointed vaguely toward the recently imported sand. Liz gawked at him, opened her mouth, then closed it.

Kim's eyes narrowed. Now that she looked closely, the dirt on the children's shirts wasn't the white-beige color of the imported sand. It was the ruddy brown shade of the surrounding cliffs.

Bobby was lying. But why?

"There you are!" a woman's voice called. "We've been looking all over."

Kim turned and smiled as Mary and her husband approached. In the years since high school, her childhood friend had blossomed.

Mary was still tiny, maybe 5'3" compared to Kim's 5'6. But she'd traded her glasses for contact lenses and wore her highlighted brown hair in a chic bob. Today's turquoise tank and shorts displayed a slender, toned body.

She gripped the hand of her younger child, five-year-old Kimberley spelled l-E-y. The adult Kim had been horrified as well as flattered when Mary said she'd named her daughter after Kim. She hoped the little girl never learned about the Kimberley Diamond Mine.

Mary's husband held Kimmy's other hand. Kim couldn't help admiring the man's fashion-magazine looks. Dark, wavy hair -- the source of the children's curls -- swept away from intense blue eyes. Though tall and slender, firm muscles peeked from beneath his Redskins t-shirt. He'd shortened his stride to match his daughter's steps yet somehow still managed to swagger.

"Thought you'd still be working at the museum," Kim said to him.

Kevin shrugged. "I need to get back, but I promised Kimmy I'd take her for ice cream." His smile turned mischievous. "So, you gonna beat up Brittany again for claiming the Black Prince's Ruby is ruby and not spinel?"

Kim turned to Mary. "You *told* him?"

Mary giggled. "Hey, our rumble was the high spot of grade school."

Before Kim could respond, Bobby snatched the gemstone from her hand. "Dad, look what I found!"

Kevin accepted his son's offering with the respect it deserved. After turning it this way and that, he handed it back saying "Looks like you found a nice piece of glass."

"Not glass!" Bobby turned to Kim. "Tell him!"

"Er, I think Bobby's right, that it is a real gemstone. Grandpa will need to look at it, but I think it might be ruby." She glanced over her shoulder. Grandpa and Aunt Ginny were still absorbed in their discussion.

She turned back to Bobby. "If you'll trust me to keep the gemstone safe, I'll have Grandpa study it when we get back to the store. And I might be able to find a spare treasure chest for you to store this in."

Bobby's eyes widened at the mention of the treasure chest. After a moment's hesitation, he handed the stone to Kim.

Then he grinned. "I found real pirate treasure, didn't I?"

Kevin smiled down at his son. "Now, Bobby, you know there isn't pirate treasure around here."

Though his voice was gentle, the effect on Bobby was like a slap. The boy's face fell and his shoulders drooped.

Liz glared at Kevin while Kim tried to think of something encouraging to cheer Bobby. Then Liz's eyes slid to the side and her mouth tilted at one corner.

Kim stiffened. She knew that expression. As a child, she'd probably worn it herself whenever she'd devised a new way to terrorize the adults.

"Mrs. Klein, look, I added something!" Liz reached into her backpack and started to pull something out.

The thing suddenly wiggled and now Kim recognized the black turtle-shaped head, round eyes and white chin: black rat snake.

She's testing the adults. Even as the thought formed, Kim fought the urge to step back. Heaven knows, she'd collected enough garden snakes herself. Still, her mouth was suddenly dry.

Mary's husband, however, failed the test miserably. He stumbled backward, almost tripping over his daughter. His face drained of color.

"Liz." Mary's voice was stern. "You know Mr. Klein doesn't like snakes."

"But it's not real!" She pulled the snake completely free, gripping it just behind the head.

Now Kim could see that the head was, in fact, rubber or plastic. It'd been glued to what looked like a series of long, narrow box cars. Instead of the bright colors of a toy train, however, these cars were functional steel with odd, mechanical parts sticking up. The wheels appeared to be made of the ball caster sort of things found on office chairs. The cars were connected by flat hinges, which rotated side to side creating the slithering motion.

As Kim studied it, she realized that the lead car was slightly longer with an extra rectangular box located just behind the attached head.

She pointed. "Is that some kind of motor?"

Liz beamed. "Yeah. And these are solenoids." She pointed at the smaller boxes on top of each car. "You know, the part that generates electricity. My teacher said Homer might win this year's science fair!"

"You *made* this?"

Hearing the awe in Kim's voice, Liz puffed out her chest.

"Yeah, but it can't crawl on sand," Bobby said. "My robot jeep can climb rocks."

"You didn't make your stupid jeep," Liz said. "Besides, my teacher said snake motion is the hardest to make with a robot." She turned to Kim. "Did you know that snakes use four different ways to move? There's lateral undulation -- that's what Homer does -- and sidewinding and concertina progression and... and rectilinear locomotion!"

Not quite sure how to respond to that, Kim simply smiled. "Rory would love Homer."

"Who's Rory?"

"My dog."

Liz sighed. "I want a dog, but Mom says Tommy and Tina are too little."

Kim had met Liz's younger siblings at the Smithsonian's Natural History Museum. Tina was maybe kindergarten age while Tommy was a couple of years younger. Presumably, both had been on their best behavior for the grandmother who'd taken them to the museum. Even so, Kim had been glad she hadn't been the one trying to control them.

"You're welcome to visit Rory whenever you want," she said.

"I want a dog, too," Bobby said, "but Dad won't let me get one."

"That's because your father is allergic to dogs," Mary said.

Throughout the conversation, Kevin had been drifting backward, away from the robotic serpent. He stood as far from the fake snake as he could without getting his feet wet.

"If you really want a dog, there are breeds that don't shed and seem to work for people with allergies," Kim said. "Rory is one. He's a standard poodle. That's the big one." She held her hand above the ground at about the height of Rory's head.

"A poodle?" Kevin grimaced. "No way am I going to live with a poodle."

Kim stiffened. "Poodles are not frou-frou dogs. They were bred for fishing and hunting and..."

"No dogs." Kevin's face still hadn't regained its color, but he managed to impart a superior tone that made her want to throw Homer at him.

Instead, she said to Liz "You know, Rory has an old toy that he no longer plays with. It used to be a stuffed snake. I bet we could remove the stuffing and use the skin on your snake; make it more realistic."

"Oh, wow, that'd be great," Liz said.

"Daddy, you promised me ice cream."

Mary smiled down at her daughter. "And I think it's time to collect. Liz, why don't you put the snake away and you and Bobby can get ice cream, too."

Liz pulled a remote controller from her pack and pushed a button. Homer stopped moving.

"C'mon, Mr. Klein, I promise not to pull out Homer again." Liz's words, however, didn't quite soften the glint in her eyes.

To his credit, Kevin didn't press for reassurance. Instead, he kneeled down so Kimmy could crawl onto his back, then led the older children toward the concession stands.

"Snake phobia?" Kim said.

"Big time. When he was six, his older brother threw a black snake at him." Mary shivered. "The thing dug its fangs into his arm. Thank goodness his mother was nearby to pull it off. He..."

Mary's eyes suddenly widened as she focused on something over Kim's shoulder. Kim glanced back. Aunt Ruby and Dorothy Tyson trudged toward them.

Aunt Ruby exuded cool efficiency. Despite the heat, humidity and sand, her shorts and shirt looked freshly pressed, her sunhat crisp.

Next to her, Brittany's aunt drooped. Though a few years younger than Aunt Ruby, the harsh sun illuminated Dorothy's every frown line. Kim wondered why Grandpa's best customer never had plastic surgery. She could certainly afford it. Was it possible Dorothy was more sensible than she acted?

As they passed the digging children, Aunt Ruby paused long enough to plunk a spare sunhat onto Tiffany's head.

Then she marched over to Kim and demanded "Where's your hat? I know I saw you in a hat this morning."

"Too hot."

Aunt Ruby shook her head. "When you're my age, you girls are going to regret not caring for your skin now."

Ruby continued on to talk with Grandpa. Dorothy Tyson, however, planted herself in front of Mary.

"Mary, I have a job for you." Dorothy whipped out a key. "The locksmith finished changing the museum locks this morning. This is the only key. You need to have copies made."

Mary's mouth dropped open. "You've already changed the locks?"

"Of course. We can't allow minimum wage workers free access now that the exhibits are complete."

"But Kevin has a few more things to do inside."

"Then you'll have to let him in before you have the copies made. He can use the back door when he leaves; that door will automatically lock behind him."

"But I promised the kids we'd get pizza and I have to check on the caterers and the florists and then change for dinner..."

"No one wants to hear about your problems." Dorothy glared. "If you can't handle your duties, then step aside so we can hire someone more competent."

Before Kim or Mary could respond, Dorothy tramped away.

"She's trying to get me fired," Mary said. "Brittany has a friend she wants to hire to direct the new museum and Dorothy is looking for ways to get rid of me."

"Dorothy is only one member of the museum board," Kim said. "Grandpa supports you and so does Aunt Ginny's friend Wilma. And I've heard Aunt Ruby say good things about what you've done."

Unfortunately, her friend didn't look reassured.

"Mary, is there anything I can do to help? Want me to take the key to be copied?"

"Nah, that'd just give Dorothy something else to criticize." Mary shook her head. "Some day someone's going to strangle that woman."

Chapter 2

Seven hours later, Kim swallowed a lump of anxiety as Scott pulled into the museum parking lot and joined the line of cars waiting for valet parking. The evening festivities would begin with cocktails served in the ground-floor exhibit area. Afterwards, dinner would be served in the roof-top restaurant.

Grandpa had left early for the reception, saying board members were required to greet the elite guests. Kim and Scott had opted for arriving fashionably late. In hindsight, that may have been a mistake; the extra time allowed her to worry about what she'd say when she encountered Brittany.

Somehow "Guess you were too stupid to look up the Black Prince's Ruby" didn't seem appropriate.

Up ahead, attendants hired for the evening helped women attired in long gowns exit passenger seats. Kim studied the women's movements, trying to figure out how they stepped out of their cars without catching a high heel in their black gowns.

And the gowns were black, each and every one of them.

She gazed down at her own cobalt blue gown, the one Tiffany insisted she buy because "the color enhances your skin tone."

When Tiff pulled the gown from the Nordstrom sales rack, Kim had instantly fallen in love. The straps were wide enough to accommodate a regular bra, the bodice accentuated her waist and created the illusion of boobs and the skirt fell away in a graceful swish of beaded chiffon. Best of all, the price had been reduced several times, bringing the gown into range of her starving-professor salary.

Now, however, looking at a sea of black ascending the museum stairs, she questioned her decision. True, numerous satires had been written about the Washington-area women's propensity for wearing black, black and nothing but black. But what if tonight the abundance of black stemmed from some unwritten social rule, like wearing only black or white to the opening of an art exhibit?

She crossed her arms, hugging the thin shawl close.

"Cold?" Scott reached over to adjust the air conditioning.

Kim gazed at her handsome date. With that crooked smile and the tuxedo he wore, he looked like a cross between

Indiana Jones and James Bond. Tonight Kim would be the envy of most of those black-clad females.

She marveled that in less than a month, being with Scott felt so *right.*

"Not really," she answered his question. "Just a little nervous."

"Don't be." Warm eyes appraised her. "You look lovely."

Muttering "thank you," Kim looked away so he couldn't see the blush she felt climbing up her cheeks. Oh, she was so in over her head.

As if sensing her discomfort, Scott changed the subject. "Looks like they pulled out all the stops tonight."

"Yeah, leave it to Brittany to orchestrate an Academy Awards production in Osprey Beach."

"I sense a story there."

Mercifully, before she answered, their turn arrived. The attendant opened the passenger door. Kim waved away his assistance; she needed both hands to keep her full skirt from tripping her. Trying to mimic the other women, she swung her feet out first, then made sure her shoes were steady before rising.

She took one step forward and stood wobbling on the high heels while she surveyed the area. At seven p.m. on a late-summer evening, dusk was still two hours away.

Up close, the three-story building, with its hexagonal shape and shiny walls, resembled a spaceship. Mary was right; the design did not suit the beach atmosphere.

The builders, however, had minimized the damage to the ecology. They'd cleared just enough of the straggly forest to make room for the museum and parking lot. A low stone wall separated the asphalt lot from the narrow strip of land edging the cliff. Beyond the wall, a single tree remained. It leaned over the cliff, its gnarly branches stretching toward the Bay, a perfect tree for climbing.

"Gorgeous view, isn't it?" she said.

"Yeah, gorgeous."

It took a moment before she realized Scott was looking at her, not the bay. Feeling another blush starting, she lifted her skirt and headed up the stairs. After a few steps, Scott's warm hand pressed against her back.

He leaned in and whispered "You can run, but you're still gorgeous."

His breath tickled her ear and she couldn't help giggling.

Scott grinned. "That's better." At the top, he offered his arm. "Shall we?"

Smiling, she accepted his arm, strolled inside... and slammed to a halt. Directly in front of her, an unmanned ticket booth announced admission prices: Ten dollars for adults, five for children ten and under.

"They're *charging* admission?"

"Don't worry," Scott said. "They won't charge us tonight."

"That's not the point." Kim crossed her arms. "None of the local museums charge admission. Museums and libraries and nature parks should be free. How else will children learn about worlds beyond their every-day life?" She pointed at the offending sign. "Those prices are going to prevent many children from ever visiting."

"Sounds like a problem the museum board should consider." Scott inclined his head toward the first exhibit. As Kim fell into step beside him, he added "Isn't Max a board member?"

"Of course! I bet Grandpa won't be happy when he sees they're planning to charge admission... Oh, doesn't that look like fun?"

She pointed at the half-scale replica of a pirate ship that'd been erected in the middle of the room. The single-mast sloop might be bare of sails, but its sleek lines created the illusion of speed. A wooden ramp outfitted with rope hand rails invited guests to board and explore the interior. None of the women had boarded, but a cluster of tuxedo-clad men clomped around the deck and stern.

"Makes you wish you were ten again, huh?" Kim gazed longingly at the ramp. If she removed her shoes, she could probably ascend without slipping. Unfortunately, at the top she'd have to swing a leg over the gunwale to board. Not easy to do in a long dress, darn it.

"Says this is a replica of a pirate ship owned by someone called Stede Bonnet." Scott pointed to an exhibit sign. "Isn't Bonnet the name of the donor who built this museum?"

With one last look at the ramp, she dropped her gaze to the detailed description of the Gentleman Pirate's short stint on the high seas. "I'm afraid so."

"Thought I knew all of the pirates," Scott said, "but I've never heard of this one."

"Probably because he wasn't very successful. He was a wealthy plantation owner who knew nothing about sailing. Then one day he had a ship built -- I guess it looked like *this* ship -- hired some thugs and set sail. The other pirates considered him a laughing stock and he didn't last a year before he was captured and hanged."

"So why'd he turn pirate?" Scott said.

"No one knows." Kim quickly scanned the sign, but it didn't address Bonnet's early life. "I did a paper on him for one of my psychology classes. Some historians blame a nagging wife. Others say the death of a child made him depressed. And there was some speculation about mental illness.

"Thing is, while he was incompetent as a pirate, I couldn't find any evidence of crazy behavior like hearing voices. Although, I suppose abandoning his wife and children was pretty crazy. It's not like his wife could get a job or anything."

"You can't fault him for that," said a voice behind them. "It was a different time and place."

Recognizing Brittany's superior tone, Kim's fingers curled. The scent of a musk-heavy perfume wafted over her shoulder. Silk rustled and high heels clicked, headed toward Scott.

Oh no you don't...

Kim turned, placing her body physically in front of Scott and effectively halting Brittany's advance. Face-to-face with her childhood adversary, she took a moment to study her.

Not a wrinkle or blemish marred Brittany's porcelain skin. She'd styled her strawberry blond mane into Veronica Lake waves that fell to bare shoulders. Somewhere along the way, she'd had breast implants. The strapless gown -- black, of course -- hugged her curves until just below the hip where it flared out in a fishtail hem. She'd completed the 1940s look with bright red lipstick that accented her Cruella de Vil sneer.

Kim lifted her chin and forced her hands to unclench. "Good evening, Brittany." There, that sounded mature, right?

Something in her tone or body language must have reminded Brittany of their playground tussle. Brittany took a step back.

With a flirtatious toss of her peekaboo hair, Brittany extended a hand toward Scott. "And who is this handsome gentleman?"

Reluctantly, Kim introduced them. To her delight, Scott appeared unaffected by Brittany's Hollywood glamour. He briefly shook her hand before snaking an arm around Kim's shoulders.

"I understand this is all your doing." He used his free hand to gesture around the room.

"I was the catalyst, but of course we couldn't have accomplished all of this without the help of our wonderful donors..."

Blah, blah, blah... Brittany had obviously launched into canned public relations stuff. She must have spent the afternoon rehearsing it. All the town's movers and shakers were supposed to be here tonight.

Kim peered into the sea of black, searching for familiar faces. She easily picked out Mayor Gaynor's laughing red face, probably telling silly jokes to the mayors of Chesapeake and North Beaches. She spotted several county commissioners (current and past), the dude who managed the 24-hour gym, other Osprey Beach shop owners.

In the far corner, Brittany's elegant parents huddled with a ferret faced man who studied the nearby display with possessive interest. Beyond them, Dorothy Tyson shook a finger at her henpecked husband before turning on her heel and sailing through an open doorway. Mr. Tyson's scowl reminded Kim of Mary's earlier statement: *Some day someone's going to strangle that woman.*

A flash of purple and red drew Kim's eyes to the other side of the room. Standing on tiptoes, she identified Aunt Ginny.

Her favorite aunt's idea of formal wear was a long black skirt topped with a satin blouse swirled with purple and red. It was the red and purple feathers pinned in her hair, however, that had captured Kim's attention. The dyed ostrich plumes added half a foot to Ginny's height. Every time she moved, one of the long feathers brushed the face of the man beside her... Oh, yuk, the art teacher from elementary school. Mr. Personality. Not.

Rescue Ginny?

But Kim couldn't convince her feet to move. She'd never been comfortable in crowds, let alone phony glad-handing. She longed to run outside, kick off her heels and climb the tree that stretched toward the bay.

No, she'd promised Grandpa she'd be here to support him. She needed to stay till the bitter end.

"So what brings the prodigal child back to Osprey Beach?"

Kim turned her attention back to Brittany. "Job promotion. But I've always loved Osprey Beach. I'm kinda surprised you came back."

In high school, Brittany couldn't find enough things to criticize about Osprey Beach. The people were too parochial, the beaches too small, the winters too cold.

Brittany shrugged. "Haven't decided if I'm going to stay yet." Her eyes narrowed. "I see you haven't had time to find a decent beautician. Let me give you Ryan Hardy's phone number. He's absolutely the best."

Oh, yes, Kim had forgotten. Brittany always used "the best."

"Ryan's cuts are amazing," Brittany continued. "And he's the only one I know who can do something with mousy brown.

"Now, excuse me but I must see to my other guests."

She turned and headed into the crowd. Kim glared at Brittany's bare back, simultaneously hating the woman for her snide remark and herself for once again letting the class bully rattle her self-confidence. Mousy brown?

"I'm not sure what just happened," Scott whispered in her ear, "But I think your hair is beautiful."

"Really?" She turned an eager face toward him and melted at the warmth in his eyes.

"Really."

Impulsively, she leaned over and pecked him on the cheek, then grabbed his hand. "C'mon. I think I know where Grandpa's hiding."

Scott grinned and allowed her to tug him through the crowd.

"All week Grandpa's been talking about the old-fashioned gemstones that are now on display," she said as she led him around the ship.

"Old fashioned?"

"I'm sorry. I meant that the stones are cut in old-fashioned styles... Excuse me, coming through... Lapidarists had to develop special tools before they could execute the precise faceting you see today... Ah, there's the exit."

Expecting another open room lined with exhibits, she was surprised to enter a dimly lit, narrow hallway that veered to the right. The walls on each side held illustrations, photos and maps that traced the history of pirating from ancient times to the present.

She paused to read one of the exhibits. Apparently, Brittany's ancestor had taken to the high seas during the "Golden Age of Piracy."

Scott stopped in front of an illustration of a swashbuckling pirate aboard his ship. "Kinda looks like people romanticized piracy even before Errol Flynn's movies."

"Yeah, that was another reason people think Stede Bonnet turned pirate. The romance of it all. I still don't understand how people could idolize thieves."

A photo of modern-day pirates caught her eye. Greasy-haired men stared back at her with cold eyes. They posed with spread legs and smirks, clutching scary looking guns.

She shivered. Nothing like a slap of reality to remind her that the Gentleman Pirate and his pals were cold-blooded killers. She hurried on.

The hallway emptied into another open room, this one featuring interactive exhibits and video. At the far side, a sign above an open doorway indicated the entrance to "pirate treasure." She wove her way through the door.

The small room was lined with glass cases containing treasure chests, pieces of eight, gold doubloons, jeweled daggers, swords and cutlasses. On the far right, a crowd clustered around what must surely be the gemstones. And in the center space, on its own glass-enclosed pedestal, stood Brittany's ruby amulet. Curious, Kim tugged Scott to the back of the line waiting to view it.

She'd never had the opportunity to study the amulet. Was the central stone ruby? Or the more commonly used garnet or spinel?

"I wonder if she ever got the stone tested," she mused aloud.

At Scott's questioning look, she explained that throughout most of history, all red gemstones were called rubies. Never mind that garnet, natural spinel and even natural zircon could all appear ruby-red. Then, in the late 1700s, a mineralogist started testing the red gemstones. He discovered that while ruby is made of corundum, spinel is magnesium aluminate. Garnet wasn't a single mineral, but a conglomerate of related minerals that differed by color. The most ruby-like of these was pyrope garnet.

"After that discovery, people got more exacting when describing colored gemstones," she said. "Turns out some of the famous rubies in the British Crown are actually red spinel."

"Bet that went over big."

Kim smiled at Scott's dry tone.

Finally, the last couple in front of them stepped aside and provided a clear view of the infamous amulet. Kim leaned close to the glass to study the pendant.

The central, rose-cut ruby was maybe 9 mm in diameter -- about the size of a pea -- making it two, two-and-a-half carats. Large for a ruby, but within the realm of possibility. It was surrounded by smaller rubies. These hadn't been faceted, just simply polished so that their red color glowed.

The sign beneath the case indicated Stede Bonnet wore the amulet to protect him in battle, a common practice with blood-colored stones.

Kim itched to hold the pendant, to study the ruby with a loupe. Maybe Grandpa could talk Brittany into letting him examine it.

Turning away, she spotted Grandpa, Mary and Mary's husband standing near a display of antique gemstones. Mary looked radiant in a soft blue gown, every bit the equal to her handsome, tuxedo-clad Kevin. As for Grandpa...

Crossing to him, she linked her arm through his. "I'm going to have to beat the women off of you tonight."

Grandpa chuckled, squeezed her hand, then introduced Scott to Mary and Kevin. As the two men shook hands, Kim compared them. Kevin was considerably shorter than Scott -- maybe 5'9" compared to Scott's 6'2" -- but his dark, wavy hair and slender but muscular build more fit the classic definition of "handsome." In Kim's eyes, however, Scott's professorial look was much more appealing.

Of course, she might be feeling super-critical of Kevin. When Mary had first met the man, she'd called Kim frequently to gush about something "wonderful" Kevin had done. Lately, however, whenever Mary mentioned Kevin, she'd described his role as a great father. It'd been months since she'd labeled her husband as "perfect."

Then again, Mary's focus these last few months had been the ongoing battle with Brittany.

"I've been trying to tell Mary to relax," Grandpa said. "The museum looks wonderful."

Kim studied her old friend. While her hair and makeup looked professionally done, the hand that clutched a half-filled champaign glass was white knuckled and her nails had been chewed down to skin.

She touched Mary's arm. "Brittany?"

Mary nodded and gulped her champaign.

"Don't worry; she knows better than to make a public scene."

Unfortunately. Even as a child, Brittany possessed a sly intelligence. She limited her public bullying to snide remarks and put-downs so subtle the adults were never sure if she'd been joking or serious.

"What if she fires me?"

"She can't," Grandpa said. "She may have paid for this new building, but the museum board has final say on who works here. And we're happy with what you've done with the museum."

"But Brittany's father is now on the board."

Grandpa brushed aside Mary's objection. "Stede's a businessman. He understands you don't change something that works, especially not at the whim of his daughter."

Kim bit her tongue, not wanting to add to Mary's fears. Truth was, she wouldn't be at all surprised if Stede Bonnet championed his daughter's wishes to fire Mary. He and his wife had always doted on their only child. They'd used their wealth to lavish Brittany with designer clothes, exotic trips and expensive gifts.

For Kim -- herself an only child -- the Bonnet's extravagance chafed. Her own parents couldn't afford such luxuries, not on their salaries as high school teachers. Unlike

Brittany, Kim had to earn each and every treat. She did household chores, babysat neighbor's children, even struggled with a paper route.

Her resentment had been fueled by her own cousins and aunts. Mom's three sisters had married wealthy men and, like Brittany's parents, didn't hesitate to meet their children's demands. Seemed like every Sunday, at the weekly family dinner, her cousins rushed into Grandpa's store to buy new pendants, bracelets or earrings.

Childhood jealousies tend to fade with age and Kim might have moved beyond the feelings of resentment except for one thing: To this date, her parents continually bragged about how they'd never spoiled their only child.

What's wrong with a little spoiling, providing you set limits? That's how she'd raised Rory and he'd turned out great.

Scott and Grandpa started talking local politics. Bored, Kim turned away to study the nearest display of antique jewels.

In keeping with the pirate theme, Mary had positioned an ancient-looking jewelry box on its side so that the "treasure" could spill out onto a velvet covered foreground. Gold doubloons mingled with strings of pearls, gold chains and chunky rings. Loose diamonds and colored gemstones had been strewn in between. The occasional flash from someone's camera reflected off the stones' facets.

Kim leaned closer, marveling at the amount of sparkle and shine fifteenth- and sixteenth-century lapidarists obtained with primitive cutting and polishing tools.

The collection included rubies, emeralds, sapphires, garnets, turquoise and other colored stones polished to a high sheen. Diamonds had been fashioned into squares or rectangles with stepped sides, an early version of the modern emerald cut.

Despite the beauty of the classic gems, however, it was the ancient amber that set her heart racing. Translucent honey orange, the fossilized tree resin glowed with a subtle beauty. Unlike other gemstones, amber actually felt warm. She'd discovered this when Grandpa gave her a small piece with an ancient bee trapped inside. The amber sat atop her dresser along with her other prized childhood possession -- Fluffy, the stuffed poodle.

A camera clicked, its flash catching one of the diamonds at an angle that shot piercing white at her eyes. She blinked, trying to clear the black dots from her vision. A shoulder shoved her aside.

Her vision cleared and the black-clad woman bending over the jewelry display came into view.

Dorothy Tyson.

No surprise there. The woman was so self-centered she probably hadn't noticed Kim looking at the gems. Rolling her eyes, Kim turned from the display only to find Mary's husband staring at her.

The muscles in his shoulders and neck were tight, his mouth down-turned. His eyes flicked from her to Dorothy and back. The poor man looked worried or scared or something. Maybe Mary's nerves over Brittany were contagious.

Kim aimed a reassuring smile his way and was rewarded with a flick of a smile and a nod. Then his eyes shifted to stare at someone behind her.

She turned to see Dorothy and Aunt Ruby link arms and mug at a professional looking camera.

"Say cheese doodle-doodle-doo!" the photographer said.

Cheese doodle-doodle-doo? Brooke used to say that after she got her first camera... The flash blinded her a second time as the photographer captured Aunt Ruby's smile and Dorothy Tyson's grimace.

Before her vision returned, she heard a female voice shout "Kim!" and felt arms wrap around her.

"I didn't know you'd be here tonight." Kim hugged her childhood friend.

Brooke tossed her blond hair and laughed. "Now that you're home, you'll find I'm everywhere."

Kim grinned. People had teased Brooke mercilessly when, at age eleven, she'd announced her plans to become as famous as Margaret Bourke-White. While Kim had encouraged Brooke to pursue her dream, she'd secretly worried. Photography, like the other arts, was a difficult career that depended as much on luck as on talent and effort.

"I know covering local events like this isn't the same as working in a war zone," Brooke said.

"Hey, it's a start. The important thing is you're making a living as a photographer."

Brooke beamed, then turned to Grandpa. "Hey, Mr. Hershey."

She embraced Grandpa, then Mary. Kevin, however, got only a cool nod.

Making a mental note to quiz Brooke about that later, Kim introduced Scott.

"Hmmm..." Brooke stepped back and eyed Scott from head to toe. "Combination of Indiana Jones and James Bond. Good job, Kim."

Scott, Grandpa and Mary laughed. Kim groaned. Nothing like childhood friends to find the best ways to embarrass you.

Before she could retaliate, Mary suggested everyone move to the restaurant.

"Only the head table has reserved seating," she said, "so if you all want to sit together, you'd better try to beat the crowd."

"You go ahead," Kim said. "We'll be up in a minute." She kissed Grandpa on the cheek and urged him to go with Mary. He'd been standing now for close to an hour and was starting to look tired.

As soon as everyone was out of hearing range, Kim turned to Brooke. "Okay, give. Why were you so cool toward Mary's husband?"

Brooke glanced at Scott.

"It's okay," Kim said. "Scott won't repeat what you say."

Brooke shrugged. "He reminds me a little of Leslie's husband. Good looking but easy to push around."

"Well, then he's lucky he married Mary; she doesn't push people."

The overhead lights flashed.

"Guess it's time to go to the restaurant," Kim added. "Want us to save you a seat?"

"Oh, you don't think Brittany would allow the hoi polloi to actually sit at one of those fancy tables, do you? I'm only allowed in here to take photos." Brooke rolled her eyes. "Do you know how many times the paper has sent me out to photograph Brittany since she's returned? Her parents have thrown a million parties and benefits in her honor. And she's only been back a week!"

"Why'd she come back? Last I heard she married some rich guy and moved to New York."

"Divorce." Brooke flashed an impish grin. "Guess we're not the only ones who can't stand her."

"Okay, you've got to tell me the story here," Scott said.

Before Kim could reply, the lights flashed again.

"Oops, I'd better get some photos of the displays before they chase me out." Brooke handed a business card to Kim. "Call me?" Without waiting for a reply, she turned and aimed her camera at the case of gemstones and jewels.

"Heavens, Brooke, watch what you're doing with that thing." Dorothy Tyson blinked rapidly.

"Guess you can tell these are quality jewels when they reflect the flash that well, right Mrs. Tyson?" Unrepentant, Brooke snapped another photo of the display, then crossed the room to photograph the case of pirate cutlasses, daggers and swords.

Kim turned away so Dorothy couldn't see her smile. Except for extreme moments -- like when Brittany sucker-punched Kim in the schoolyard -- Brooke's solution to confrontation had always been to kill 'em with kindness.

Taking Scott's hand, she led the way back toward the front of the museum where she'd seen an elevator. After navigating the hallway of pirate photos, however, she discovered the line for the elevator snaking all the way around the exhibits. At least Grandpa was nowhere in sight; they must have made it upstairs before the crowd formed.

"Uh, let's look for stairs."

"Are you comfortable climbing in your gown?" Scott said. "I don't mind standing in line."

"I'd rather chance the stairs than deal with the crowd. There's a room beyond the gemstones. Maybe there's another elevator or a staircase." As she turned, she heard Aunt Ruby calling her name.

"Have you seen Dorothy? She's supposed to make the welcoming speech."

"I saw her back by the jewelry display."

Aunt Ruby sighed. "That woman. Get her around gems and she forgets everything else."

Kim and Scott followed Aunt Ruby back to the gemstones. Sure enough, Dorothy stood alone, staring into the gemstone case.

As Aunt Ruby swooped down on her friend, Kim peered into the next room. At the far end, a red sign announced an emergency exit. To the left, however, a second sign indicated a flight of stairs. And, wonder of wonders, no crowds.

Should she tell Aunt Ruby? She glanced over her shoulder. Both women were staring into the display case with frowns on their faces.

She bit her lip. Had Dorothy found something to criticize? The last thing Mary needed tonight was a confrontation with a museum board member.

"Stop worrying," Scott said. "Mary did a great job with the exhibits and everyone looks happy."

"You don't know Dorothy; she always finds something to criticize."

"I don't want to talk about Dorothy." He caressed her cheek, tilting her chin up. "I'd much rather focus on this beautiful lady standing beside me."

Kim's lips parted as his mouth touched hers. She leaned into him, relishing the warmth of his body. His hands slid up her bare arms to her shoulders, leaving a trail of goosebumps. And then he gently pushed her away.

"Much as I'd love to continue this..." He brushed a lock of hair from her eyes. "We are expected upstairs."

Kim's stomach growled. They both laughed. Clasping hands, they headed for the staircase.

🐩

The stairs led to a red-carpeted lobby with high, gilded ceilings. Over the buzz of conversation, they could hear the pop of champaign bottles and the clink of glasses. The scent of Old Bay seasoning -- the spicy mix used heavily in local crab-based dishes -- made Kim's mouth water.

To their left, the elevator dinged. The doors opened to disgorge a chattering group of formally clad people. Kim and Scott followed the crowd to the right into the restaurant.

"Wow." She'd been prepared to dislike the restaurant -- she'd heard Brittany owned it -- but the wall of windows overlooking the Chesapeake Bay left her breathless.

"The newspaper said that during the day, they'd serve food buffet style," she told Scott. "And after the museum closed in the evening, they'd switch to normal restaurant seating."

Indeed, a buffet station -- now dark -- stood near the right wall. Round, linen-covered tables dotted the rest of the large room. A long head table sat in front of the windows, its seats facing the crowd. A woman dressed in jeans stood near the table-top podium, adjusting a microphone.

Kim scanned the room. Judging by the cluster of people and purses draped over chair backs, it appeared that most seats had already been claimed.

"There's your mom," Scott said, nodding toward a table near the front.

Mom had risen and was indicating a pair of chairs to her right.

"Looks like she saved seats." But as Kim approached her parents, she identified the others at the table: Aunt Emerald, Uncle Thomas, Aunt Sapphire and Uncle Don.

Did she really want to sit through an entire meal with Aunt Emerald quizzing Scott about his intentions and Aunt Sapphire babbling about the stars? On the bright side, Aunt Ginny sat beside Dad; maybe she could help diffuse the interrogation. Even so, the thought of spending the evening dodging embarrassing questions made her head ache.

"Kim, over here!"

Turning, Kim spotted Tiffany, Tiffany's husband, cousin Tony and a woman that must be Tony's date. Tony pointed to a pair of chairs beside him.

Relieved, Kim veered toward them.

"Haven't seen you in ages," she said, dropping her purse onto the chair and embracing her only male cousin. A lawyer specializing in white-collar crime, Tony spent much of his time in court. "You remember Scott."

The two men shook hands, then Tony introduced his date, a perky blond wearing a low-cut gown. As the woman gushed over Scott -- she'd apparently read the Pulitzer-prize winning story he'd written years ago for *The Washington Post* -- Kim rolled her eyes at Tony. Judging by the woman's comments, she only vaguely remembered the article and was simply trying to impress the hot-shot reporter turned professor. When was her handsome cousin going to date someone who could keep up with his high IQ?

Well, at least this woman could read.

Tiffany looked stunning in a red silk gown. Richard's red cummerbund and bow tie exactly matched the color of Tiff's gown.

"Thanks for saving seats." She hugged Tiffany. "Let me go say hi to Mom and Dad and I'll be right back."

Scott, bless him, accompanied her to the other table. After hugging her parents and saying hello to the others, Kim introduced Scott to her aunts and uncles.

"Kim said you teach at the university," Aunt Emerald said. "I didn't realize they allow journalists to teach."

Given that her aunt was too far away to kick, Kim opted for a scowl.

Scott, however, diffused the comment with a laugh. "I think the Pulitzer helped," he said. "But I also acquired a PhD in history."

"Oh, I just love history," Aunt Sapphire said. "Especially the parts about the ancient use of crystals for healing. Did you know one of the gems found in King Tut's tomb was amber?" She brandished the amber pendant she wore. "Amber connects you to your inner wisdom, you know. I'd have named my daughter after it, but Tony came first and you can't name a boy Amber. By the time Tiffany came along, Ruby had already claimed the name for *her* daughter." She glared at the head table, where Aunt Ruby, a museum board member, chatted with one of the others.

As Scott struggled to maintain a straight face, Mom whispered in Kim's ear. "Okay, I forgive you for not sitting with us. But promise me you'll bring your young man to dinner sometime soon."

Kim hugged her mom, marveling at her good fortune in having been raised by poor, but sane, parents. As a psychology professor, she knew part of the credit belonged to Grandpa. When his eldest daughter had turned ten, she'd insisted on being called Tina instead of her full name, Diamondtina. Grandma had been horrified -- after all, she'd named her four daughters after the major gemstones as a tribute to the girls' value.

Grandpa, however, had recognized his daughter's need for independence and supported her decision. As a result, Mom created a small barrier between herself and her sisters' jewel obsession. True, she still drooled over Grandpa's display cases and, judging from the diamond and ruby pendant she wore tonight, occasionally succumbed to temptation. But at least Mom understood her only child's reluctance to join the family jewelry business.

Suddenly realizing her nerves were playing havoc with her insides, Kim excused herself and went in search of the restroom. She found it in the hallway by the elevators. A few minutes later, as she was washing her hands, a voice hissed: "Are you nuts?"

Kim jumped and wheeled around. There was no one behind her.

"He was drunk on duty," a second voice said.

Frowning, Kim checked beneath the stalls. But she was quite alone. The voices seemed to come from one of the wall vents.

"Who's going to protect my pirate's ruby?" Brittany's voice had a whine to it.

"A drunk watchman would be no protection against thieves," Dorothy Tyson replied. "Besides, by the time the banquet is over, there will only be a few hours left before the day guard arrives."

Kim stood frozen, afraid of making a sound. Were they standing just outside the door or farther away? If they found her eavesdropping, they'd be furious.

"If you have the power to fire the night guard without consulting the rest of the board," Brittany said, "why can't you fire Mary?"

"No one's going to question my firing a drunk guard," Dorothy said. "As for Mary, let me worry about her." Dorothy's voice was ice. "Max Hershey might not go along, but I've got ways to convince the others. Now pull yourself together and let's get back to the banquet."

The sneering tone of Dorothy's voice as she said Grandpa's name made Kim shiver. She couldn't hear Brittany's response. The women must have moved away from the vent.

Kim tiptoed to the restroom door and opened it a crack. Seeing no one, she swung the door wide and slipped out.

Before entering the restaurant, she straightened her shoulders, lifted her chin and pasted what she hoped was a neutral expression on her face. She breathed easier when she spotted Dorothy and Brittany standing behind the head table.

Scott stood when he spotted her and pulled out her chair.

"Everything okay?" he whispered as she settled in the chair.

"Tell you later." Best to not think about the overheard conversation until she was alone and didn't have to control her expressions.

She reached for a napkin and used the process of shaking it open and laying it across her lap to study the people around her. Scott sat to her left with Tony on her right. Tony's girlfriend perched to his right, with Tiffany's husband Richard and Tiffany beside her. Uncle Walt sat next to his daughter.

The final two seats were filled by Mary's husband Kevin and Dorothy Tyson's husband Jared. With their wives occupying the head table, Uncle Walt, Kevin and Jared looked abandoned.

"Is this the table for displaced spouses?" she teased.

Uncle Walt grinned. "Everyone except for Stede's wife."

Sure enough, Brittany's mother, accompanied by that squirrelly looking guy, was now claiming the seats Mom had saved.

Who was that guy?

Even as she stared, Aunt Ginny leaned across the table to shake his hand. Good. Aunt Ginny was an expert at weaseling out people's life histories.

She returned her attention to her own table. Mary's husband appeared uncomfortable sandwiched between the two older men.

Maybe talking about himself would help.

"You did a great job with the new display cases," she said.

"Didn't know you were into construction," Uncle Walt said. "I thought Mary said your degree is in engineering."

"It is, but the job market..."

"Nothing wrong with construction." Jared Tyson slapped Kevin on his back.

Kevin winced and his attempted smile came out a grimace.

"I bet Mary was thrilled to have someone who could build exactly what she needed for the museum," Kim said. "Did you also build the ship replica?"

"I was one of the volunteers who wielded a hammer, but the ship itself was designed by some of the guys who worked on the tall ships. I can't wait to show Bobby." For the first time that evening, Kevin's smile reached his eyes.

Kim's breath caught. Wow. She kept forgetting how handsome Mary's husband was. Brittany must have been green when she met him.

She glanced at the head table. Brittany picked at her salad as she listened to the man seated beside her. Though she had a smile pasted on her face and she nodded occasionally, the furrows between her brows indicated concentration at odds with the man's broad grin. Brittany had always been expert at pretending to pay attention while lost in her own schemes.

"You're lucky Mary is so level headed," Uncle Walt said. "Ruby has been frantic ever since they broke ground on this building."

"Tonight's opening is all Mom's talked about for the last few weeks," Tiffany agreed. "She's been almost as obsessed as when she planned my coming out ball."

Uncle Walt grimaced. "No. Nothing could be that bad."

"Don't kid yourselves," Kevin said. "Mary's been a nervous wreck ever since she learned Brittany's financing this whole thing. I'm just grateful Brittany didn't actually arrive in town until a week ago."

Kim glanced at Jared, but his face showed no reaction to the criticism of his niece.

"Brittany's only been back a week?" Uncle Walt shook his head. "Man, seems like Ruby's been running around for a lot longer than that."

"Blame Dorothy for that." Jared grimaced. "Ever since the board elected her chairman, she's tried to micromanage everything. Even me!"

The arrival of their dinner interrupted the discussion. Kim inhaled the spicy Old Bay steam rising from the rockfish fillet. Taking a bite, she closed her eyes and moaned. Mild, moist and dense, the fish melted in her mouth.

"Oh, I've missed this." She reached for her iced tea.

"Thought you lived in Oregon for five years," Scott said. "Didn't they have good fish?"

"Wonderful fish, especially the steelhead, salmon and halibut." Kim pointed at her plate. "But no rockfish. And no Old Bay seasoning. No blue crabs, either."

Scott grinned. "Primitive place."

Kim wrinkled her nose at him, then took another bite of rockfish. The sautéed zucchini and herbed new potatoes were equally good. Kim sighed. Brittany was right; this chef was amazing.

Speaking of Brittany... She glanced at the head table in time to see Brittany turn from her chattering dinner partner to stare at Mary. Her eyes narrowed, her lips tilted in a subtle smirk -- and then she smiled one of her classic I-know-something-you-don't smiles.

Kim shuddered, remembering other times she'd seen that expression on Brittany. The worst had been in fourth grade when the teacher discovered nursery rhymes scrawled on the blackboard. The rhymes had been altered to make them sexually suggestive.

Jack Rogers had been reciting those rhymes from a book he'd stolen from his uncle. But no one spoke up when the teacher demanded a culprit. Who wants to be a telltale? For a moment silence reigned. And then Brittany's eyes narrowed, her lips tilted up and she'd tossed a sly smile toward Kim. She raised her hand.

Instead of telling on Jack, however, Brittany claimed to have seen Kim, Mary and Brooke writing on the board.

Now Brittany leaned into Dorothy Tyson and whispered something. Dorothy's eyes widened. Then she peered over her shoulder. Was she looking at Mary or Grandpa?

"Are you finished, miss?"

Kim glanced at the server hovering over her, then down at her empty plate. When had she finished? She leaned sideways to allow him to remove her plate, then turned down the offer of coffee from a second server. From a far corner, waiters dressed in black and white emerged carrying large silver trays. Lifting her chin, she strained to get a better look at the dessert. Chocolate? Oh, please, be something chocolate.

Someone cleared his throat and Kim glanced back to see one of the waiters holding a small plate. The rich fragrance of chocolate drifted from a mound of a cake-like substance. The scoop of ice cream beside it was rapidly melting.

"Chocolate lava cake?" Kim asked.

The waiter grinned. "Made with dark Swiss chocolate."

Kim moaned. As the waiter set the plate in front of her, Scott told him "Better give her two."

Kim elbowed Scott, but didn't resist when the waiter set an extra cake in front of her.

Before she could take her first bite, however, someone tapped a water glass and Dorothy Tyson's voice boomed through the microphone.

"While you're enjoying your desserts, I'd like to welcome you to Osprey Beach's brand new pirate museum," Dorothy said.

She waited for the polite applause to cease. "I hope you all had a chance to explore the museum?" More applause. Dorothy beamed. "As you probably know, none of this would have been possible without our wonderful benefactor, Ms. Brittany Bonnet." She gestured toward Brittany and again waited for the applause to stop. "I'm sure Brittany would like to say a few words to you, but before she does, I'd like to introduce some very special people who helped make this weekend event possible."

Kim tuned out Dorothy and focused on her dessert. The waiter was correct; the gooey part of the lava cake had the smooth, rich flavor found in chocolates produced in Switzerland.

"This is almost as good as the candy Grandpa buys in New York," she told Scott. Except nothing was as good as something from Grandpa.

"Maybe we'll have to come back here for dinner," he said. "Alone."

The spoon stopped half-way to Kim's mouth and she felt a warmth traveling up her neck and face. The tilt to Scott's smile told her he'd read her reaction correctly.

Setting her food down, she looked directly into his eyes. "Yes," she said. "I'd like that."

A heavy foot nudged hers. "Wipe that silly grin off your face or you'll scare him away," Tony whispered.

Kim rolled her eyes. "Since when did you become the relationship expert?"

"Since I started wondering why my favorite cousin didn't seem to be getting any."

Kim gasped, then smacked Tony's arm. Unabashed, he leaned across her and engaged Scott in a murmured conversation about the upcoming football season.

At the podium, Brittany replaced Dorothy and launched into a prepared spiel that sounded suspiciously like what she'd said to Scott earlier. Kim slipped her cell phone from her purse to check the time. Ten o'clock.

This was taking much too long. Grandpa should be in bed. The doctor said he needed rest.

She checked the end of the head table where Grandpa was seated between Mary and Aunt Ginny's friend Wilma. Mary's smile seemed strained. Wilma looked bored. And Grandpa... Was his face a little pale?

Loud applause signaled the end of Brittany's speech. Good. They could follow Grandpa's car, make sure he arrived home safely, then maybe sit on the living room balcony for a while.

As she was reaching for her purse, however, Brittany stepped back to the microphone. "Before you leave, I think Dorothy has some last-minute instructions for the museum board members."

Brittany slid her eyes toward Mary, the smirk on her face unmistakable. Goose bumps climbed Kim's arms. Now what?

Dorothy took Brittany's place at the microphone. "I'd like to ask the board members to remain behind for a brief meeting." She beamed at Brittany. "We have a very important proposal to consider."

"Aww, geez..." Jared Tyson pushed his chair back with a loud scrape. "Now what is that woman planning? I swear, if I don't stay on top of her every minute..." The rest of his words disappeared in the crowd as he headed for the podium, Uncle Walt and Kevin on his heels.

"I don't like the looks of this," Kim said to Scott. "You mind?" She gestured toward the head table where Grandpa and the other board members and their spouses were gathering.

They wove through the departing guests, arriving in time to hear Dorothy Tyson tell Mary "You don't need to stay."

"I don't mind," Mary said. "Kevin and I came in separate cars so he can go relieve the babysitter."

"I'm afraid this meeting is for elected board members only." Dorothy held out her hand. "If you'll give me the new key, I'll be sure to lock up."

"But... I don't understand."

"You will." Brittany lifted her nose and peered down at Mary.

"You'll need to leave too, Brittany," Dorothy said as her hand closed over the key Mary held out.

"I most certainly will not. It's my proposal!"

"Why does anyone have to stay?" Kim said. "It's late and everyone's been working on this event the entire day. You all look exhausted."

"This will only take fifteen minutes, thirty at the most," Dorothy said.

"Grandpa just got out of the hospital! Surely you can schedule a meeting for later this week." And give her time to find out what, exactly, Brittany had proposed -- and figure out a way to stop it. Kim was certain Brittany's scheme involved some way to hurt Mary.

Mary seemed to think so, too; her face had lost all color, giving her the appearance of one of those Suzy Sad Eyes dolls from the 1960s.

"We can stand here arguing for fifteen minutes or we can just hold the meeting." Dorothy turned to her husband. "Walter, would you please drive Jared home? I'll drop off Ruby after the meeting."

Uncle Walt shrugged and the two men shuffled off.

"And, Brittany, I meant it when I said you couldn't stay," Dorothy continued.

A waiter whisked past, arms loaded with dirty plates, effectively cutting off Brittany's protest.

"I think we'll hold the meeting downstairs in the museum," Dorothy said. "Come along."

She swept toward the elevator. After a few minutes, the board members fell in line behind her.

"Grandpa?" Kim grabbed his arm. "Let's go home, okay?"

He patted her hand. "I'd better see what this is all about. Don't worry. I can drive; it's not far." He gestured toward Scott. "Go and enjoy your fellow. I'll be home soon."

Kim watched him trudge to the elevator, his shoulders hunched. Her own shoulders sank as she realized her romantic evening was about to end. No way could she allow Grandpa to drive himself home. The doctor had warned him against over-exertion. Under the best of circumstances, he was uncomfortable driving at night and now he looked like he was about to wilt.

She turned to her date. "Scott, I..."

He silenced her with a finger to her lips. "It's okay." He smiled down at her. "I don't want him getting into a wreck, either. He's a good man."

So are you, she thought.

"You two go ahead; we'll bring Dad home."

At the sound of Mom's voice, Kim turned. She smiled. She'd never seen Dad in a tux or Mom in a gown. They made a handsome couple with their matching chocolate brown hair and warm eyes.

For a moment, Kim was tempted to accept Mom's offer. She seldom got the opportunity to wear a gown and didn't want the Cinderella feeling to end so soon.

But her parents lived a good forty minutes away. As high school teachers, they embodied the early-to-bed, early-to-rise mentality even on weekends. It was already way past their bedtime.

Besides, when Kim accepted her new job at the University of Maryland, she'd also accepted Grandpa's offer to stay with him until her house in Oregon sold. That he'd created a second master suite for her and fenced the backyard for Rory had made the offer irresistible.

As much as she wanted to spend more time with Scott, she was the logical person to wait for Grandpa.

Again, Scott read her mind. "Thanks for the offer, Mrs. West, but I probably should head home to see what kind of damage Al did in my absence."

Kim frowned. "You didn't give Al complete range of the house, did you?"

At only nine inches tall, the longhaired dachshund -- inherited from Scott's uncle -- had an amazing ability to climb chairs, tables and boxes in his quest for unattended food.

"Don't worry, I put all of the food away before I left," Scott said.

Kim pushed aside the vision of the black and tan dog trying to open the refrigerator by tugging on the kitchen towel most people hung on the door handle. Surely he wasn't as strong as Rory, who'd sneaked a raw steak and half a ham from Grandpa's refrigerator before she caught on and started hanging the towels elsewhere.

Yes, it was probably a good idea for Scott to return home to check on the little dog.

She said goodbye to her parents and shared a sweet, too-brief kiss with Scott.

"Be safe," she told him. Like her parents, Scott didn't live in Osprey Beach and would face a long drive home.

With a sigh, she turned and trudged down the back stairs to the museum.

She could hear voices coming from the room with the gemstone exhibit. Peeking inside, she spotted Grandpa, Dorothy, Aunt Ruby, Wilma, Stede Bonnet and the others gathered around Brittany's pirate amulet.

"What's so important that it couldn't wait for a more civilized time to meet?" Matt Garfield, manager of the new 24-hour gym, crossed his arms and glared at Dorothy.

"Brittany has made another generous offer, but we have only a few days to accept," Dorothy said.

"Typical Brittany," another man said. "Do we really want to play her game?"

Kim recognized the speaker as Mr. Jefferson, the fourth-grade teacher who'd chased her that awful day when she'd fought Brittany on the playground. His dark hair was now speckled with gray and he'd grown a short goatee, also grizzled; the combination reminded her of Morgan Freeman, one of her favorite actors.

Dorothy's eyes flashed. "When there's this much money involved, you're damn right we'll play her game."

"For heaven's sake, Dorothy," Aunt Ruby said, "just tell us what she wants so we can all go home."

Dorothy folded her arms. "She's offered to contribute $100,000 to the museum's operations endowment."

Grandpa frowned. "In exchange for what?"

Dorothy lifted her chin. "Mary's resignation."

Someone gasped, but the sound came from behind Kim. She wheeled around. Mary stared at her, her mouth opening and closing like a goldfish.

Fortunately, all of the board members started talking at once, effectively masking Mary's reaction. Gripping her friend above the elbow, Kim pulled her away from the meeting room.

"What are you doing here?"

"I knew it! I knew Brittany would find a way to get me fired."

"Shhh, keep your voice down."

Mary grabbed Kim's forearms. "I can't lose my job. I can't! Construction is bad now and the museum has been Kevin's only client in months and he can't find a job in engineering and Bobby needs braces and--"

Kim broke Mary's hold, grabbed her shoulders and shook. "Stop that. Take a deep breath; you're turning purple."

"P...purple?"

"Yeah, like the purple people eater." Kim held her breath, wondering if her reference to a childhood joke would break through Mary's panic.

For a moment, Mary gaped at her. Then, finally, she blew out a breath, shook her head and offered a wane smile. "Lame, Kim. Very lame."

"But effective." Kim stepped back and suddenly noticed Mary wore no shoes. "Why are you barefoot?"

Mary's face flushed. "Broke a heel. This day's been a disaster."

"Hey, it's not that bad. Brittany can make all the demands she wants, but the decision belongs to the museum board.

And they know you and love you and understand what a good job you've done."

"Yeah, but--" Mary gestured toward the meeting, where loud voices seemed to be speaking at once. "Doesn't sound like they all agree with you."

"You know they need to at least consider Brittany's proposal; it's a lot of money. But the board has always made rational decisions in the past."

"That was before. We've got three new members, one of which is Brittany's father."

Kim flinched, but pushed back the rising concern. Right now Mary needed reassurance, no matter how Pollyanna. There'd be plenty of time later to deal with reality.

"Stede Bonnet is a single vote," Kim said. "There are six other people on the board and you know Grandpa will support you."

Mary studied Kim's face. Then her eyes narrowed and she wheeled around, stomping toward the room where the voices had finally lowered to normal volume.

"Mary, wait!" Kim hissed.

Mary ignored her. Slipping off her heels, Kim ran after her. If Mary crashed the meeting, she'd just fuel Brittany's campaign to oust her.

But Mary stopped outside of the room, close enough to understand what people said but far enough away that a casual glance wouldn't reveal her presence.

Kim reached her in time to hear Grandpa say "We can raise money without Brittany. Once people see the museum, they'll be willing to contribute to its upkeep."

"Dad, you know how hard it is to convince people to donate to something intangible like maintenance," Aunt Ruby said. "People want to see something concrete like a building or a painting."

"Precisely," Dorothy said. "That's been an issue all along. And Brittany is offering a solution."

"At what price?" Wilma said. "Mary has single-handedly kept the museum alive when some of you weren't even involved."

"My daughter isn't downplaying Mary's prior role in the museum," Mr. Bonnet said. "But we've got to face facts here. This new museum has the potential to draw tourists from all over. Brittany says--"

"We don't need to hear about Brittany," Aunt Ruby said. "Our job is to ensure the best for this museum."

"Then we all agree," Dorothy said. "The best thing we can do for the museum is accept Brittany's offer."

Several people shouted "no" and once again the meeting deteriorated into a cacophony of voices. Kim pulled Mary away from the door.

"Looks like Dorothy and Stede are the only ones really pushing for this."

"Don't forget Brittany always gets her way." Before Kim could respond, Mary's fists clenched and her face flushed. "But not this time."

"That's the spirit. We'll find a way to stop this."

Mary's brows drew together and her eyes flashed. "I hate her. I hate her!" With a sob, she turned and ran toward the back door.

Chapter 3

Mary's angry voice echoed throughout the deserted museum. So Kim wasn't surprised when she turned back toward the meeting room to find Dorothy Tyson standing in the doorway.

"What is going on out here?" Dorothy folded her arms and tapped her foot.

"I've come to take Grandpa home."

"We haven't finished our meeting yet."

"Yes we have." Grandpa appeared behind Dorothy. "Everyone's heard Brittany's proposal. There's no way we'll reach an agreement tonight."

"You can't just stop a meeting! We have to vote."

"While you were out of the room, we voted to table the discussion." Aunt Ruby peeked around Grandpa's shoulder. "C'mon, Dorothy, I'm tired. And you look like you're ready to drop."

Kim suppressed a smile, hooked her hand around Grandpa's arm and headed for the front door. He didn't protest when she led him to the passenger side of his car, a testament to his exhaustion. They drove home in silence.

Rory greeted them at the kitchen door with furious tail wags and a high-stepping prance.

"Go on up to bed," Kim said. "I need to take Rory outside."

"Actually, I'd like to spend a few quiet minutes with you on the balcony," Grandpa said.

Kim eyed the black standard poodle, who was now running circles around them while squeaking a stuffed hedgehog.

Grandpa chuckled. "Okay, maybe not so quiet. But let's do it anyway."

"You just want to quiz me about Scott."

He dropped his chin, gazed up at her and waggled his eyebrows. Ever since she was a child, Grandpa had used that gesture whenever she'd appeared nervous. It never failed to make her giggle.

"Let me take care of Rory and change out of this gown. I'll meet you outside."

Ten minutes later, dressed in comfy shorts and t-shirt, she carried two glasses of decaf iced tea out to the living room balcony.

Grandpa had taken off his shoes, tuxedo jacket, tie and cummerbund and unbuttoned the starched shirt. He leaned back in the patio chair, feet propped on a deck railing.

Kim handed him a glass then leaned against the railing. A half-moon illuminated the black Chesapeake Bay. From somewhere nearby, a katydid chirruped. The breeze smelled of water and sand and the bittersweet joy of summer coming to an end. Rory leaned against her and she buried her free hand into his topknot.

"It's so good to be home," she said. As beautiful as Oregon had been, Kim had pined for the beach town where she'd grown up.

"It's good to have you back," Grandpa said. "So how was your date?"

Smiling, Kim turned. "Okay, you were right. He's wonderful."

Grandpa had first mentioned Scott Wilson when Kim was still living in Oregon, struggling to finish her thesis while teaching three sessions of psychology 101 at the university. Like many assistant professors, she'd had little time for a social life.

That hadn't prevented Grandpa, Aunt Ginny, Tiffany and a whole passel of other relatives from trying to fix her up with dates -- from 3,000 miles away!

When Grandpa found out she'd accepted the teaching position at the University of Maryland, his matchmaking attempts became less subtle until he'd finally extracted a promise that she'd at least meet his friend's nephew.

Ironically, Kim met Scott without Grandpa's help. After a robbery that landed Grandpa into the hospital, Scott had unknowingly entered the jewelry store looking for him. The two ended up joining forces to figure out who was trying to steal a priceless blue diamond and why that same someone wanted to kill Grandpa.

"So you had a good time?"

"Yeah, it was great." Before Grandpa could quiz her further, she changed the subject. "Can Brittany really get Mary fired?"

"Not without a fight. If Dorothy had convinced the board to actually vote tonight-- Well, I'm glad you stepped in when you did."

"You mean most of them would have voted against Mary?" Kim's mind flashed onto Mary's anguished face.

"It would have been close."

"Who would have voted against her? Besides Dorothy and Brittany's father?"

Grandpa grimaced. "Ruby."

Kim groaned and settled into a seat. She'd never understood her aunt's friendship with Dorothy Tyson. Dorothy was an even worse snob than Brittany's parents. While Aunt Ruby always fretted about what the neighbors thought, she'd never bought into the classism that drove people like the Tysons and Bonnets.

"Maybe we can change her mind," she said. "But aren't there seven board members? You only named three opposed to Mary."

"I couldn't get a read on Robert Jefferson."

"He's not easy to read." When he'd chased her that day in the playground, she'd been certain his intention was to haul her into the principal's office and demand she be expelled. Instead, she'd learned later, he'd actually defended her.

Grandpa's cell phone rang.

Frowning, he pulled it from his pocket and glanced at caller ID. "Dorothy Tyson," he groaned.

"Don't answer it."

Nodding, Grandpa silenced the phone and set it on the table. A few minutes later, the home phone rang.

"She can be persistent." Grandpa started to stand.

Kim touched his arm. "Let the answering machine deal with it."

The machine clicked on and Dorothy's voice boomed from the living room. "Max? Max, I know you're still awake. You haven't had time to fall asleep. Pick up now; this is important. Oh, here, *you* talk to him."

Aunt Ruby's voice replaced Dorothy's. "Dad? Please pick up. Otherwise none of us will sleep."

Sighing, Grandpa rose and crossed into the living room to pick up the phone.

"What's so important it can't wait until tomorrow?" Grandpa listened, grunted, listened some more. "I don't believe it." He ran a hand through his silver hair. "All right. Yes, if this will clear Mary, I'll be there in ten minutes."

"Clear Mary?" As Grandpa disconnected, Kim charged into the living room. "Clear Mary of what?"

He sighed. "Dorothy says she has proof that Mary has been stealing from the museum."

"*Mary?* The same Mary who returned pennies that fell out of people's pockets?"

"I don't believe it either, but Dorothy says she can show me proof at the museum."

"So she's demanding all the board members return?"

"Just me."

"Why just you?"

Grandpa slumped onto the couch. "She wouldn't say. Wouldn't even tell Ruby."

Kim studied the man who'd been the primary influence in her life. Normally, his flashing eyes and mischievous smile hid the fact that he was now in his early 70s. Right now he looked every bit his age.

"Couldn't you maybe just not show up?"

Grandpa snorted. "You know how Dorothy gets when she's got a bee in her bonnet. If we ignored her calls, she'd just come pound on the door and wake the neighbors."

"Okay, I'll drive. But you need to promise that tomorrow you'll do nothing but rest. Don't even go into the store or office."

Sunday was the only day Grandpa closed the store, but he liked to use the quiet time to tinker with watch and jewelry repairs.

"You always were a bossy little kid."

She crossed her arms and shot him her best the-professor-is-not-happy look. Grandpa chuckled.

"Okay, okay, I agree." He stood. "Before we meet Dorothy, I need to change out of this monkey suit."

He trudged past the interior stairs, heading for the elevator he'd installed several years ago.

Rory butted his head against her hand. Smiling, she scratched his ear.

"He'll be okay," she said.

And on Monday, if his complexion still had a gray tinge, she'd ask Aunt Ginny to help in the store. The doctor had warned of possible setbacks if Grandpa didn't rest.

She settled onto the couch to wait. Rory, sensing an opportunity, slapped a hairy paw onto her knee. Kim giggled and reached for the treat jar. Encouraged, Rory proceeded to run through his repertoire of tricks: spin, back, curtsey, jump. Finally, adrenaline spinning out of control, he scooped up his stuffed hedgehog and raced around the room.

Poor fellow had been cooped up in the house all day. She hated to leave him again for who knows how long; Dorothy tended to take forever to make a point.

She could bring him along, but didn't want to risk leaving him in the car. Even at night with the windows cracked, the car would become too hot. And if she didn't leave him in the car, Dorothy Tyson would freak...

Kim grinned.

Ten minutes later, she parked her van next to Dorothy's Mercedes. She opened her door and stretched, looking around. While a few spotlights lit the museum's exterior, most of the parking lot remained dark. The surrounding woods absorbed the moon's light. Despite the heat, Kim shivered.

"Looks like she didn't wait to go inside," Grandpa said, peering into Dorothy's empty car.

Kim shrugged. "She's never been good at waiting." Slipping the collar and leash over Rory's head, she gave him permission to jump out.

Grandpa peered down at Rory. "Sure you want to take him inside?"

"You wanna let Dorothy go at her own pace or speed things up?"

Without responding, Grandpa headed toward the museum.

Even with an enthusiastic two-year-old bouncing at the end of the leash, traversing the front stairs was much easier in tennis shoes than high heels. The front door was unlocked. Grandpa held the door open and Kim followed Rory inside.

The entryway was lit by a single bulb. Apparently, the oh-so-economical Dorothy Tyson hadn't turned on the overhead lights. The safety lights barely illuminated the area.

"Dorothy?" Grandpa peered into the shadows.

Kim stepped around the ticket counter and started toward the pirate ship replica. Rory slammed to a stop. Planting his feet, he sniffed the air. The hair on his back bristled and his throat rumbled.

Grabbing Grandpa's hand, she hissed, "Something's wrong."

"He's just never been in a museum."

She started to point at Rory's raised hackles when he suddenly charged forward, pulling the leash from her hand.

Kim ran after him. "Rory, no!"

Rory barked and seemed to increase speed. She followed him around the pirate ship, but slipped as they rounded the corner into the dark hallway of pirate photos.

Somewhere ahead, a door alarm clanged.

"Rory!"

She skidded around the last narrow turn in time to see him disappear through the far doorway into the gem exhibit.

She raced after him. Through the door, careening left, her mind barely registering something wrong with the exhibit on the right, no time, gotta catch Rory, through the entry into the final exhibit.

There, just ahead. The big poodle stood at the back door, barking and scratching. She snagged his leash, her heart racing, her mind trying to make sense of what just happened.

Someone had been in the museum, had run from Rory. Dorothy?

No. Rory had met the woman and, though he was normally a good judge of character, treated her like any other new friend: He'd leaned against her expecting an ear scratch. His hackles wouldn't have risen if Dorothy was the only one in the museum.

So who just ran through the door?

She turned to look for Grandpa. But the large room was empty. Hadn't he been right behind her?

"Grandpa?"

"In here." His voice sounded strange, like his throat muscles were too tight.

She glanced at Rory. He'd turned his attention from the door and was now sniffing the floor in front of it. But his fur was back to normal. That meant no immediate danger. Right?

"C'mon, buddy." She had to tweak his topknot to get his attention, but he finally fell into step beside her. They retraced their steps to the entrance of the gemstone exhibits. Rory braked to a halt and refused to enter the room.

Kim told him to lay down, then gave him the stay command. Turning, she entered the gem exhibit. Something crunched under foot. Glass.

Now she could see that more than half of the display cases had been broken. Glass and scattered artifacts littered the floor. The case that once held Brittany's ruby amulet was empty. Bare spots dotted the display of pirate weapons.

Grandpa knelt in front of the empty jewelry display, his back to her. She could see a woman's stocking-covered foot; her shoe lay a few inches away.

"Grandpa?"

He slowly rose, revealing the woman's face. Dorothy Tyson.

"Is she...?"

Grandpa nodded. "She's dead."

Chapter 4

They decided to wait in the van for the police to arrive. While Grandpa climbed into the front passenger seat, Kim joined Rory in the back. The warmth of his head on her lap drove away some of the night's terrors.

But nothing could erase the memory of Dorothy Tyson laying in front of the shattered, empty display cases. The poor woman may have been a bully and snob, but she didn't deserve a violent death.

"They've never killed before," Grandpa said.

"Who... who are you talking about?"

"The local jewelry thieves. Don't you remember reading about the school teacher who interrupted them?"

Her sluggish mind conjured up the newspaper story. During the last year, a dozen or so Osprey Beach homes had been burglarized. The thieves seemed to know when the houses were vacant. They'd taken small, easily pocketed items, mostly jewelry.

A few months ago, a local school teacher left work early and arrived home to discover a burglary in progress.

The thieves had tied the terrified woman to a kitchen chair with duct tape. The teacher hadn't been harmed, probably because she couldn't identify the burglars; they'd worn balaclavas and gloves.

"Dorothy must have interrupted them," Grandpa continued. "But why did they have to kill her?"

Kim squeezed his hand. "Maybe they didn't. Maybe she had a heart attack or fell and hit her head or something."

Grandpa shook his head. "When I checked for a pulse, I saw blood on her chest. I think she was stabbed."

Kim shivered. The thieves stole a fortune in diamonds, emeralds and rubies -- including Brittany's pirate amulet -- and a collection of gem-encrusted daggers.

They had a million reasons to commit murder.

Rory's ears perked. A moment later, Kim heard the sirens, too.

She reached for the door handle. After much arguing, Grandpa had agreed to stay in the car with Rory while Kim showed the police the body and answered questions.

The ambulance arrived first, followed by a black-and-white sheriff's car. Kim didn't wait to see who was in the car;

instead, she headed into the museum with the emergency crew behind her.

"Do you know how to turn on the lights?" one of the EMTs said.

"I suppose the switches are somewhere near the front doors."

While one of the rescue workers searched for light switches, Kim led the way past the ship replica. As they entered the hallway lined with pirate photos, she was grateful for the two strong-looking men walking behind her.

The lights flashed on and Kim pointed to the entrance to the gem room.

"She's laying on the right side in front of one of the cases." No way was she going back in there.

"You the one who found the body?" a woman's voice said.

Kim turned. A woman officer stared up at her with a piercing don't-mess-with-me expression.

The officer stood just barely above five feet. Her department-issued black uniform clung to narrow hips, small waist and large bust. Her blond hair had been pinned into a severe knot at the back of her head. The tag on her uniform said "Darnell."

Kim answered the woman's question with a nod.

"Wait here." Officer Darnell disappeared into the gem room. A few minutes later, she returned and gestured for Kim to follow her back outside.

Kim sank onto the top step and waited while the officer trotted down to her car and removed the radio microphone. Officer Darnell babbled a few numbers -- geez, cop speak was as impenetrable as psychology speak -- then added "Better send Lieutenant Brockley."

Brockley. He of the dark hair, flashing eyes and wicked smile. The poster child for "bad boy."

She should have expected someone would call Brockley. After all, Lieutenant Bill Brockley was the county's new hot-shot investigator. She was probably the only person in the state who wasn't impressed.

After the botched robbery that sent Grandpa to the hospital, Brockley insisted the thieves were part of the local burglary ring. He'd listened with raised eyebrows while Kim explained why she thought the robbery had been planned by a jewelry insider. Then he'd essentially patted her head and told her to mind her own business.

Brockley's mistake almost cost Kim her life.

Maybe Officer Darnell would be more open to ideas. It certainly couldn't be easy earning respect in a man's world when you were tiny and cute. Kim vowed to help this woman as much as she could.

"Okay, let's start this again." The officer now loomed over her. "I'm Officer Darnell. Wanna tell me what happened here?"

"Not sure. Dorothy insisted we meet her back here..."

"Dorothy the deceased?"

"Uh, could you please sit down? I'm getting a crick in my neck."

Instead of sitting, however, Darnell pointed toward a row of concrete planters. "Let's go over here, get out of people's way."

Kim stood and followed Officer Darnell to the planters. She leaned against one, her legs still a bit rubbery.

"Yes, the, er, woman inside is Dorothy Tyson. She's chairman of the museum's board of directors."

"So she was at the shindig tonight. Why was she still here?"

Kim opened her mouth, closed it. No way was she going to tell anyone that Dorothy had accused Mary of stealing.

She opted to reveal half of the truth. "She was on the way home when she decided she needed to show Grandpa something in the museum. She insisted we meet her here."

"And it couldn't wait till morning?"

"That's exactly what we told her." Kim attempted a casual shrug. "You have to understand Dorothy; once she got an idea in her mind, there was no dissuading her."

"So what did she want you to see?"

"Don't know. When we got here, the front door was unlocked. Rory, my dog, sensed something wrong and, well, I think he chased someone out the rear door. I heard feet running and then the door slammed."

"You see anyone?"

"No. Didn't get close enough."

Before Officer Darnell could ask another question, the county's crime scene van pulled into the lot followed by an unmarked dark car. Officer Darnell straightened as Lieutenant Brockley stepped from his car and strode over.

With only a glance at Kim, he addressed Darnell. "What have we got?"

While Darnell gave her report, Kim studied Brockley. The last time she'd seen him, he hadn't slept for 48 hours and sported a pasty complexion, beard stubble and undereye bruising. If anything, the combination had made him more attractive.

Now he was freshly shaved, his hair neatly combed, his dark shirt and pants clean. Yet she found this Brockley easier to resist. Maybe because he resembled every other bad boy who'd broken her heart? Or because she was falling for Scott?

She heard her name and tuned back in to hear Darnell say "She's the one who found the body."

Brockley finally turned his eyes on her. They seemed to soften. "I heard Mr. Hershey was released from the hospital. How is he doing?"

"Great until today." Emboldened by his sympathetic expression, she added "He's so tired right now that I'm worried about a relapse. Could we maybe wait till tomorrow to give our statements?"

"Tell you what," he said. "Let's get initial statements while everything is fresh in your mind. You can fill in the rest in the morning."

He turned to Officer Darnell. "Why don't you finish up with Ms. West while I talk with Mr. Hershey."

Without waiting for a reply, he headed toward the car.

Kim turned back to Officer Darnell to find the woman's icy eyes boring into her. Kim's breath caught as she identified the drawn brows, narrowed lips and clenched teeth as anger.

And then the muscles in Darnell's face metamorphosed back into a blank, neutral expression.

The change from professional cop to enraged woman and back happened so quickly that Kim might have imagined it. But when Darnell spoke, a slight tremble in her voice betrayed the otherwise hidden emotion.

"Tell me again why you and your grandfather came back."

Kim repeated what she'd said earlier, but her thoughts kept drifting to the unguarded expression she'd seen.

Why was Officer Darnell angry at her? Was she annoyed because Brockley had been kind?

Or did she suspect Kim had killed Dorothy?

Despite Lieutenant Brockley's assurance that he wouldn't detain them long, they didn't arrive home until just before dawn.

Kim pulled the van into the garage and turned to Grandpa. "Why don't you go inside while I take Rory into the backyard?"

Grandpa didn't protest, a sure sign of his exhaustion. She watched him trudge toward the elevator, shoulders hunched like an old man.

No. Grandpa was not an old man. He was a tired man who needed time to recover from a long, stressful day.

Opening the car door, Kim called to Rory and led him into the fenced back yard -- where he proceeded to run. And run. And run. Slamming to a halt at her feet, he gazed up with wide eyes. When she didn't respond immediately, he snagged the leash dangling from her hand and shook it.

She chuckled. "Yeah, I bet you need a w-a-l-k, but I'm not sure--" She broke off as Rory leaped into the air, then ran to the gate.

Shoot, when did her poodle learn to spell?

A wave of guilt washed over her. While she'd been helping with the children's treasure hunt and attending the banquet, Rory had been cooped up inside. He'd then endured the tension following Dorothy's death. No wonder the poor dog needed a return to normalcy.

She frowned, considering. She was too edgy to sleep. In just a few hours, they'd need to schlep to the police station to sign statements. Maybe a little exercise would help her through the next few hours.

"Okay, puppy, you win. Let me leave a note for Grandpa and we'll go to the beach."

As she wrote the note and stuffed dog treats and toys into her pockets, she weighed the pros and cons of walking or driving to Pirate's Cove. At this hour, the parking lot would be empty. Even so, the path from lot to beach was over a football field long.

The alternative was to follow the boardwalk from Grandpa's house, a much longer stroll that didn't require messing with the car.

She shrugged and clipped the leash onto Rory's collar. The whole point of this exercise was to relax. She followed the trotting poodle to the boardwalk.

Twenty minutes later they reached the beach. The eastern horizon glowed in reds, pinks and oranges. Kim trotted down the steps and onto the sand, proud that she wasn't even breathing heavily.

Like many college professors, she'd never paid much attention to her body; given a choice between exercise and reading a good book, the book won every time.

The fallacy of that thinking became clear a few weeks ago when she'd run from a pair of thugs. She'd been so winded she'd barely escaped.

After the men were arrested, she began jogging daily. The boardwalk, located right in front of Grandpa's house, provided a level surface with the added benefit of beautiful scenery. Rory loved it.

His all-time favorite activity, however, was running on the beach.

Glancing around to make sure they were alone, Kim unsnapped Rory's leash and grinned as he ran through the sand, kicking up his heels.

The beach was also a great place to train dogs.

"Rory, come!"

To her delight, the young dog whipped around and charged back to her. Laughing, she rewarded him by pulling a tug toy from her pocket and allowing him to snatch the other end.

"That's it, tug."

Rory pulled on his end. After a few seconds, Kim said "Out."

Rory stopped tugging. But the toy remained in his mouth.

"Is that an out?"

Rory dropped his end of the toy. She rewarded him with a treat, then cued "tug" and repeated the game, this time letting him win by releasing her end. He pranced away, tossing the toy into the air.

"Okay, bring it here."

Rory trotted back and exchanged the toy for a treat.

They played the game until Kim's arms started to ache. She told him to go play and tucked the toy back into a pocket.

The first glints of sunlight reached the water's edge, but the area beneath the cliffs remained in shadow. Movement above drew her eye to the tree leaning over the cliff's edge. The young osprey eyed her.

"See? Everything's back to normal," she called.

The bird shook its feathers and didn't respond.

Turning, she strolled along the water line, absently scanning for fossils and shark's teeth. While the osprey's world might be back to normal, hers had shifted once again.

As much as she adored Osprey Beach, she hated the small-town politics. Dorothy Tyson and her brother, Stede Bonnet, used their wealth and social status to practically run the town. If you wanted to sit on a local board, obtain a building permit or even secure a summer internship, you needed Dorothy's and Stede's support.

Dorothy was also the source of much of the local gossip. Everyone knew everyone else's business in Osprey Beach and it seemed like Kim couldn't sneeze without someone telling her parents. She'd once chased a ball into the street and, by the time her parents arrived home from work, they'd both heard about it and had prepared the appropriate lecture.

Mom insisted the local grapevine provided a way to protect people in the community. But even in this there was a clear hierarchy. When Kim was 16, she skipped her last class so she could ride in Tommy Giovanni's new convertible. Dorothy saw them driving through town and reported to her parents. Kim had been grounded for a week.

When Brittany was caught shoplifting, however, Stede Bonnet paid the shop owner more cash than the item was worth to keep the theft a secret. Only Brittany's bragging revealed what happened. Even then, she wasn't punished.

Kim never understood how Grandpa managed to function in such a cauldron of gossip, backstabbing and innuendo.

This was one of the reasons she'd left Osprey Beach. But she'd missed her family and the Chesapeake Bay. She knew when she decided to return, she'd have to find a way to avoid the small-town intrigue she'd hated as a child.

Dorothy's sudden death would certainly make life easier for Kim and many other town residents. As the town gossip, Dorothy had never hesitated to resort to blackmail to obtain her own way.

Blackmail.

Kim slammed to a halt. Would one of Dorothy's blackmail victims resort to murder?

What if the museum theft was intended to disguise the reason behind Dorothy's murder?

She imagined a killer following Dorothy from the banquet, perhaps planning to run her off the road when she started her trip up the steep, winding road that skirted the Bay. Instead, after dropping off Aunt Ruby, Dorothy returned to the museum.

So the killer followed her inside, maybe stabbed her with one of the ornamental daggers and cleaned out the display cases to make the police think Dorothy interrupted a burglary.

A sudden wave splashed cold water over her tennis shoes. Squealing, she retreated to dry sand.

She shook her head, embarrassed by her imagination. Real people didn't kill because an old gossip might reveal a secret. She'd been reading too many mysteries.

She turned to call to Rory and spotted him digging in the sand at the base of the cliff.

"Rory, no!" He glanced her way, his face, chest and front paws speckled beige and brown.

Groaning, Kim jogged toward him. It would take her hours to brush the fine grains from his hair. As she approached, he dropped his head into the hole he'd made.

"Rory, leave it."

Rory lifted his head and trotted to meet her. He carried something grayish brown in his mouth.

Kim pulled a dog biscuit from her pocket and exchanged it for the item he carried.

"This is your idea of buried treasure, huh?" She frowned at the thing in her hand. Strips of some kind of smelly, disgusting cloth -- leather maybe? -- clung to a piece of driftwood six inches long and maybe an inch wide. Rusted metal jutted out about two inches from the wood, a perfect place to cut a dog's lips.

She looked around, trying to figure out where to put the thing so Rory wouldn't simply retrieve it. Good heavens, there were signs of digging all along the base of the cliff. While she'd been woolgathering, her poodle had been busy. There was no place to discard his ratty treasure.

Sighing, she tucked the wood into her belly pack. Best to get rid of it at home.

"I think you've had enough fun for this morning."

Rory wagged his tail. Sand flew in all directions. Shaking her head, she clipped the leash to his collar and headed for home.

She spent thirty minutes brushing the dirt and tangles from Rory's coat, then another hour bathing and blow drying him. Given the warm day, she could have let him dry naturally. But the mindless action comforted both of them and she loved the cottony feel of his fur when she'd groomed him properly.

By the time she'd taken her own shower, Grandpa was awake, dressed and looking much more himself.

"How 'bout I buy you pancakes before we head to the station?"

She kissed his cheek. "You sure know the way to a girl's heart."

The restaurant was crowded, so they didn't arrive at the police station until 10 a.m. As they stepped from summer heat into air-conditioned building, their glasses fogged. Grandpa whipped a handkerchief from his pocket, wiped his glasses then handed the cloth to Kim.

The first thing she saw when she perched the now-clean frames on her nose was Aunt Ruby and Uncle Walt. Aunt Ruby's red eyes and sagging shoulders indicated a restless night. Uncle Walt looked befuddled.

"Oh, Dad!" Ruby threw her arms around Grandpa and started sobbing. "I can't believe she's dead! They're saying she was stabbed with a knife or sword or something.

"She wanted me to return to the museum with her and I refused. Maybe if I'd gone along she'd still be alive!"

Grandpa's arms tightened around his daughter. "And maybe you'd have been killed, too. We have no idea who did this or how many there were."

While Grandpa patted Aunt Ruby's back, Kim laid a hand on Uncle Walt's arm. "How are you doing?"

He shook his head. "I'm worried about Jared. He's feeling guilty for being angry at Dorothy last night. And with Jennifer's wedding in only a few months..."

It took a moment for Kim to place the names. Jared, Dorothy's husband, had been at last night's banquet. But who was Jennifer? She frowned until an image swam into view: Dorothy's daughter.

She'd met Jennifer while Grandpa was in the hospital. The timid young woman and her fiancé had come into the store to buy an engagement ring. Dorothy had given Jennifer a list of requirements for the diamond.

Kim had studied the list, growing angry. Not only was a diamond that met Dorothy's "must-haves" rare -- so rare that a small jeweler like Grandpa would have difficulty finding one -- but it was well beyond the range of the fiancé's budget.

Dorothy's unrealistic instructions had set her daughter up for a huge disappointment.

Biting back a snide comment, Kim had explained the ins and outs of choosing a diamond and urged Jennifer to try on several of the rings Grandpa stocked. The girl had fallen in love with a marquis-shaped diamond, an excellent choice. The slight-yellow hue lowered the diamond's value, but complimented Jennifer's complexion while the long, narrow style elongated her fingers.

Kim had delighted in selling a diamond to the couple *and* helping Jennifer stand up to her bully of a mother.

And now the mother was dead.

"Do you think Mary Klein could have done it?"

Aunt Ruby's comment cut through Kim's thoughts. She stared at her aunt, wondering if she'd heard wrong.

"Why in the world would you think that?" Grandpa said.

Aunt Ruby waved toward the rear offices. "Brittany's in there right now telling that Lieutenant Brockley that Dorothy planned to fire Mary, which gives her a motive."

"That's ridiculous!" Grandpa crossed his arms. "Mary doesn't have a mean bone in her body."

Kim pictured Mary's flushed face last night as she'd screeched "I hate her." Mary might not be mean, but like most people, she could only be pushed so far before pushing back.

But defending oneself was a world away from cold-blood murder.

A door opened and Kim turned to see Lieutenant Brockley approaching, Brittany at his side. Brittany tossed her hair and peered up at him through long, probably false, lashes.

"If I can be of any further assistance, please call me," she cooed.

Brockley's only response was a polite thank you for coming in. That didn't stop Brittany from licking her lips and offering a Marilyn Monroe smile.

She sashayed toward the door. As she drew even with Kim, Brittany tilted her chin and smirked. Kim's hands clenched, but she refrained from comment.

Instead, she turned and followed Grandpa into Brockley's office.

Brockley waited until they were seated before leaning forward and saying, "So, tell me about Mary Klein."

An hour later, Kim unlocked the kitchen door, marched inside and slammed her purse on the table. "I can't believe that idiot thinks Mary murdered Dorothy!"

"He's just exploring all possibilities."

"Only because Brittany implicated Mary."

Grandpa dropped into a chair and leaned over to greet Rory. "Thanks to you, he won't be able to go too far in that direction. We all saw Mary hand her only key to Dorothy. And, as you pointed out, anyone from the banquet could have hidden in the museum to gain access to the jewelry."

"Brockley had a lot of nerve ordering me to keep out of his investigation." She opened the refrigerator and pulled out a pitcher of iced tea. "By the way, thanks for stopping me from saying something stupid."

She'd been about to respond to Brockley's "order" when Grandpa squeezed her shoulder -- a silent warning he'd often used with his outspoken granddaughter.

"Try not to worry," he said. "It's pretty obvious Dorothy interrupted a burglary."

A pounding on the kitchen door sent Rory into a barking frenzy. Kim peered outside. Mary stared back, eyes wide, face white.

As soon as Kim swung the door open, Mary threw herself into her arms. "Kim, you've got to help me. They think I killed Dorothy."

Chapter 5

Kim patted Mary's back and repeated Grandpa's words. "The police are just exploring all possibilities." She gently extricated herself and smiled into Mary's tear-stained face. "Let's go into the living room and talk."

Mary nodded and allowed Kim to step back. Rory pushed between them. He showed Mary his stuffed hedgehog, but turned his head when she reached for it, offering his back to pet. Mary laughed and stroked his fur.

"Oh, he's darling. What's his name?"

"Rorschach. I named him after Hermann Rorschach, the Freudian psychiatrist who developed the ink-blot psychological test." Kim poured another iced tea. "I call him Rory."

"So you're black like an ink blot," Mary told Rory. To Kim, she added, "You always had clever names for your stuffed animals and things."

Kim smiled and handed the glass to Mary. "Ever see a photo of Rorschach? The man, not the test? He was kinda hunky."

Mary threw back her head and laughed.

Glad her friend had finally relaxed, Kim pointed down the hall.

"Living room's this way."

Grandpa had already retired to the living room, correctly sensing Mary's need to be alone with Kim. Now, as they entered, he embraced Mary and waved her to a seat.

"So, why do you think you're a suspect?" Kim sank into the sofa beside Mary. Rory deposited his hedgehog into Kim's lap, retrieved a rawhide and plopped down at her feet.

Mary took a long sip of tea before responding. "Early this morning, the police called and told me to bring a copy of the banquet guest list to the station."

"Did they tell you why they needed it?"

"Whoever called wouldn't answer my questions. When I got there, I was told to talk to this tiny blond cop, this Officer Darnell. She kept asking me about those stupid museum keys. How many did I make, who did I give them to, what did I do with the rest. I finally refused to tell her any more until she explained why she was asking."

Mary bit her lip and breathed deeply. "That's when she told me Dorothy was dead and someone saw me sneaking into the museum."

"*You're* the one Rory ran after?" Kim looked down at the curly haired dog happily gnawing a rawhide bone. Why would he chase Mary last night, then greet her with wagging tail today?

Mary frowned. "What are you talking about? You didn't have your dog when I saw you."

"When you-- Oh. You mean someone saw you sneak in while the board members were talking?"

"Not just someone. Brittany. I saw her and some guy skulking around the parking lot when Kevin and I were fighting." Mary's shoulders crumpled. "My life is such a mess."

Grandpa shifted in his chair, clearly uncomfortable with the turn of the conversation.

Best to get Mary back on track. "Uh, maybe you'd better back up here, start at the beginning. What did you do after Dorothy demanded your key and wouldn't let you or Brittany attend the meeting?"

Mary nodded and took a deep breath. "Kevin and I went outside. I was telling him how I just knew Brittany had found a way to fire me and, well, he got mad. He said he was sick of hearing about my childhood battles and I should stop acting like a baby, that I'm just being paranoid."

Kim winced. "Ouch."

Mary sighed. "You have to understand. Kevin's been under a lot of pressure lately. The construction industry is a mess. The contract to build museum cases was the first one he's had in months."

"Even so, it's not your fault Brittany's driving you nuts."

"No, but it's my fault we're living in Osprey Beach." Seeing the question on Kim's face, Mary continued. "I never told you that, did I? You remember how Kevin and I suddenly got married in our last semester of college?"

"Yeah. You were pregnant with Bobby."

"Well, what I didn't tell you is that when we decided to get married, we made a pact: Whoever landed the first good job offer would determine where we'd live."

Mary shrugged. "I thought for sure Kevin would find a job first. Engineering degrees are a lot more in demand than museology.

"But then the board offered me the job here. The salary wasn't much, but it was high enough to live on until Kevin found a job. We moved to Osprey Beach because it's a great place to raise kids."

She paused to sip her tea. "We figured Kevin would find an engineering job in Annapolis or Washington and Baltimore's not too far to drive, either."

"But he didn't?"

"The economy was such a mess. And then after Bobby was born, we could no longer live on my salary -- babies are so expensive! So Kevin started doing construction. That's what his dad did."

Kim reached for her own tea. "Okay, so Kevin is unhappy with his job. That's no reason to ignore your concerns."

Mary sighed and dragged fingers through her hair. "Well, he's right that I've been complaining a lot lately."

Her hands clenched. "But last night when Kevin called me paranoid, I got so mad that I said some things I probably shouldn't have. After he stormed off I thought maybe he was right -- about me being paranoid -- so I decided to eavesdrop on the board members' discussion."

"And you discovered you weren't being paranoid after all." Kim slipped her bare feet out from underneath Rory and tucked them under her. "But I still don't hear anything that indicates you killed Dorothy. If you were going to kill someone, wouldn't it have been Brittany?"

Kim's attempt at a joke fell flat.

"Thing is," Mary whispered, "I don't have an alibi."

The memory of Mary's angry eyes when she fled the museum flashed through Kim's mind. She struggled to keep her face neutral. "Didn't you go straight home after the board meeting?"

"No. I was too upset to face Kevin. I drove to the boardwalk and stared at the water until I felt better."

"And no one saw you?"

Mary shook her head, her eyes blinking back tears. Kim reached for her friend's hand. Mary's fingers closed over Kim's, pressing so hard Kim winced.

"The police told me not to leave town." Mary stared at Kim. "I'm their main suspect. Will you help me?"

Gently, Kim extricated her aching fingers from Mary's grasp. "Help you what?"

"Find the real killer, of course."

Kim's "are you nuts?" drowned out Grandpa's exclamation.

Mary crossed her ankles, folded her hands in her lap and straightened her shoulders, presenting an image of calm rationality.

"I'm perfectly serious. Think about it. With Dorothy's standing in the community, the police are going to be under pressure to quickly arrest someone. Right now I'm the most likely suspect."

Before Kim could protest, Mary began ticking off reasons on her fingers. "I had the means: Access to the museum and whatever sharp weapon killed her..."

"Anyone who attended the banquet had museum access."

Mary dismissed Kim's comment. "But I also had motive: Dorothy was trying to convince the board to fire me. And I had opportunity: During the critical time, I was walking along the boardwalk. Alone. No one saw me."

"All circumstantial," Kim said. "Besides, even if the police are leaning that way, what you need is a lawyer, not a psychology professor."

Mary shook her head. "You forget what it's like living in a small town. It's not enough for some lawyer to cast reasonable doubt about my guilt. If the police focus solely on me, they'll never catch the real killer. And everyone will wonder if I got away with murder."

"So hire a lawyer and let him hire a private detective."

"With what? Even if I took out a second mortgage to pay him, we don't have any PIs living in Osprey Beach. You know how people are here; they don't like talking to strangers. But they'd talk to you."

"I'm not an investigator!"

Mary dismissed that with a wave of her hand. "An investigator is nothing more than someone who understands people. You've got your psychology degree. You know how to read body language, make people open up."

"That's a lot different than tracking a murderer."

"Don't you remember the sleuth games we played as kids? You always won."

"Mary, amateur sleuths don't solve murders like in the books we read. This isn't a game."

"Don't you think I know that?" Mary leaped to her feet and began pacing. "You should have seen the way Officer Darnell looked at me, like I was some kind of worm or something. If I go to jail, people will ostracize Kevin and the kids. No one will hire Kevin -- who wants a worker whose wife is a jailbird? My family will starve!"

She stopped and stared down at Kim. "Look, all I'm asking is that you poke around a little bit, see if anyone saw or heard something that might help."

Before she could reply, Grandpa said "It wouldn't hurt for us to talk to people we know."

"*Us?*"

Grandpa nodded. "The thieves stole jewelry. If they try to sell any, one of my colleagues might hear about it."

"But the doctors said you need to rest."

"Talking to people isn't work." He crossed his arms. "Probably less work than waiting on customers."

"But--"

Mary played her trump card. "Do you really want Brittany to win?"

With Grandpa taking Mary's side, Kim capitulated. She agreed to interview people who attended the museum celebration -- but only if Grandpa promised to rest in between meetings.

Which was why, two hours after Mary left, Kim and Grandpa set off in her mini-van to interview Aunt Ruby, the last person to see Dorothy alive aside from the killer.

Ruby and Uncle Walt lived inland, away from the Chesapeake Bay's cold winter winds. From the front, their house resembled its neighbors: single story, white vinyl siding, maybe fifty feet wide with a front porch that wrapped around the sides.

The side porches, however, only extended the length of the formal living and dining rooms. Beyond the porches, the foundation widened and stretched deep into the private backyard.

The extra width and length allowed Aunt Ruby to appease her neighbors with a humble-looking abode while satisfying her own need for space. In addition to the two front rooms, the house included large bedrooms and private baths for their three daughters, a master suite for Ruby and Walter, gourmet kitchen and an airy family room that opened into a professionally landscaped courtyard.

As Kim pulled into the driveway, a surreal numbness washed over her. It'd been... six? seven?... years since she'd visited this house. But the outside looked the same as when she'd climbed trees to avoid playing dress up with her cousins.

"Nothing's changed," she said to Grandpa.

He snorted. "Think Ruby would allow change?"

Kim grinned. Seemed like everyone in the family possessed an enduring quirk. As a child, Kim never went anywhere without Fluffy; as an adult, Rory replaced the stuffed poodle as her constant companion. Grandpa always carried a jeweler's loupe, Aunt Sapphire always dressed in blue, Tiffany's husband never removed his tie. And Aunt Ruby refused to allow anyone to change her immediate surroundings.

Ruby's fear of change reached epic proportions when the family's television broke. They'd purchased a new one and Ruby positioned it in exactly the same location as the old.

But the old television had been a cathode ray tube. The new one was digital. The angle of Uncle Walt's recliner prevented him from viewing the screen.

Having just listened to Ruby's lecture on why the new television must reside in the same location as the old, Uncle

Walt knew better than to move the television. Instead, he slid his recliner six inches to the left. He figured Ruby would never notice such a small move.

She noticed. She moved the chair back.

Walt waited until Ruby was out of sight and repositioned his chair. But when he left the room to get a beer from the refrigerator, he returned to find his recliner in the old position.

For a week, the two silently struggled: move the chair, move it back.

Walt finally solved the problem by moving his chair and, at the same time, repositioning the television. Aunt Ruby, focused on the chair, didn't notice the change in the television. When she pushed the recliner back into its original position, he could view the screen perfectly.

And speaking of Uncle Walt...

"What the heck is he doing?" Kim pointed to the side yard.

Walt was swinging a shovel like a two-handed hammer, the flat side smacking the ground before he raised it again. Beside him a woman in a house dress and flip flops was waving her arms.

"Let's go see." Grandpa opened his door.

Kim clipped the leash onto Rory and followed Grandpa into the yard. Now she could hear the woman -- ah, yes, Mrs. Tailor from next door -- screeching "Don't kill it, don't kill it!" The shovel came down with a solid *fwap* and Walt raised it again.

"Uncle Walt, what's wrong?"

"He... *fwap*... bit... *fwap*... me..." *Fwap, fwap.*

Before she could inquire who "he" was, the front door opened and Aunt Ruby stepped out on the porch. "Walter, if you're not going to the hospital, at least come inside so I can clean your wound. The snake is long gone."

"He tried to kill it!" Mrs. Tailor turned to Aunt Ruby. "Black snakes are good for the environment."

"Well, he didn't kill it, did he? Go home, Betty, you're getting sunburned. Walter, you're turning red, too."

With a final *fwap*, Uncle Walt turned and extended his hand to Kim. "You're the doctor in the family. This doesn't look bad, does it?"

"I'm a doctor of philosophy, not medicine." When he continued to hold out his hand, she took it and examined the raw-looking fang marks. "I don't know much about snake bites, but I'd probably go to the emergency room to have this cleaned. If you don't want to do that, at least pour some peroxide on it."

"Jared was right." Walt snatched his hand away. "You women are all in cahoots."

With that, he swung his shovel over a shoulder and marched toward the backyard. Mrs. Tailor shrugged and headed for her house.

Aunt Ruby gestured for Kim and Grandpa to follow her inside.

"I swear, that man gets more stubborn every day." She led the way past the two formal rooms and into the family room where a tray with a pitcher of iced tea and three glasses had been arranged. "Let's sit in here; it's too warm for the courtyard. Kim, would you please do the honors?"

While Kim poured, Grandpa explained why they'd come.

"Dad, have you considered that Mary might have killed Dorothy?" Aunt Ruby passed out coasters. "Brittany saw her sneaking back into the museum last night."

"She was only there a few minutes," Kim said. She settled into a chair with Rory at her feet.

"She could have gone back."

Kim opened her mouth to protest that anyone could have gone back, but Grandpa silenced her with a look.

"Let's assume for the moment that Mary's innocent," he said. "Who else might want to kill Dorothy?"

"Dorothy fought with everyone -- her daughter, her neighbors, her friends, her husband. But I can't imagine anyone actually killing her."

"Do you have any idea why Dorothy insisted I meet her at the museum last night?" Grandpa said.

"Wouldn't tell me," Aunt Ruby said. "All I know is when we were driving home from the museum, we rounded a corner and some yahoo blinded us with his bright lights. Didn't bother turning them down even after he saw us.

"Normally, Dorothy would have launched into a tirade about inconsiderate drivers and the world going to hell. Instead she just sort of stared into the night. I wondered if she was still seeing that awful prism -- you know how lights reflect off your glasses and it's like looking through a kaleidoscope? All those colors sort of fracture everywhere?

"Anyway, she suddenly slammed on the brakes and pulled to the side of the road. *That's* when she announced we had to return to the museum." Ruby sighed. "I wish I'd have stopped her."

Grandpa patted Ruby's hand. "No one could stop Dorothy."

Ruby smiled sadly. "Remember the time Dorothy petitioned to prohibit dogs on the boardwalk?"

Kim gasped. "How did she justify that?"

"Oh, she gave several reasons," Ruby said. "She told the commissioners that dogs are unclean; they bark, bite, poop and shed. She even claimed that when people stopped to pet someone's dog, they blocked the boardwalk."

"She didn't like people petting dogs?"

"Oh, she didn't care about dogs one way or another. She just wanted another way to boss people." Aunt Ruby sighed. "I never understood why she acted that way."

"It probably made her feel powerful and in control," Kim said. "There've been a number of studies about bullies and why they act that way, but the reasons people become bullies are as varied as the people themselves."

"Well, I do know that she always thought she was helping," Ruby said. "She once submitted a proposal to forbid the sale of funnel cakes on the boardwalk because they make people fat."

Aunt Ruby started to share more Dorothy stories. As she listened, Kim realized that as Brittany's aunt, Dorothy had provided a sort of role model in bullying 101.

"Maybe it'd help if we talked about the banquet itself," Kim said. "If Dorothy interrupted a burglary, then chances are good the thief entered during the banquet and hid in the museum after everyone left."

Aunt Ruby frowned. "He couldn't have gotten into the museum without a written invitation. Those were only given to dignitaries and major donors."

"Even the wealthy and powerful can steal," Grandpa said. "Look at Johnny Rutherford." Seeing Kim's puzzled expression, he added "Mayor's son. Caught embezzling and sent to prison."

"Embezzling's different from smashing display cases," Aunt Ruby protested.

"More direct, that's for sure."

"What about that squirrelly guy?" Kim said. "The one hovering around Mrs. Bonnet? He stared at the displays like he owned them or something."

"You must mean Nigel Cummings," Aunt Ruby said. "He's some hot shot curator from London. Just moved to Washington, I think."

"So why was he at the banquet?"

"He was Brittany's date." Aunt Ruby's eyes hardened. "He's also looking for a job. If Brittany can fire Mary, she can propose Nigel for the position."

"Think he's desperate enough to, I dunno, steal artifacts to make Mary look incompetent?" Kim said. "And maybe Dorothy recognized him and he had no choice but to kill her."

"Brittany would have had to be in on that sort of scheme," Grandpa said. "She'd notice if her date suddenly disappeared."

Kim flopped back in her chair. Rats. Nigel would be the perfect suspect; he wasn't a resident of Osprey Beach and she wouldn't feel guilty pointing the police in his direction.

But Grandpa was right; Brittany wouldn't have left the party without him. And as sneaky as Brittany could be, stealing her own ruby talisman wouldn't be her first thought for removing Mary.

"We need to get a copy of the guest list," she said. "And gather together the people who were there but we know are innocent."

"And who might they be?" Aunt Ruby raised a single eyebrow.

Kim ticked the names off on her fingers: "Tiffany, Richard, Tony. Don't know about Tony's date, but let's exclude her. Mom, Dad, Aunt Ginny, Aunt Sapphire, Uncle Don, Aunt Emerald, Uncle Thomas. Scott." Just saying his name made her smile.

"You can add Ginny's friend Wilma to that list," Grandpa said. "She was sitting beside me at the head table and might have noticed something during dinner."

Kim nodded. "Counting us and Uncle Walt, that gives us sixteen people. Surely one of us saw something that would help."

"You're not including Mary and her husband?" Aunt Ruby said.

Kim sighed. "Mary's kind of emotional right now. Don't think she'd be much help."

"Why don't we invite everyone to a cookout tomorrow evening?" Grandpa said. "Ruby, you round up your sisters. Kim and I will call the others."

They agreed on a time for the dinner and rose to leave. As they stepped out onto the porch, Kim turned to her aunt.

"By the way, how'd Uncle Walt get bitten?"

"Tried to grab the snake by its tail."

Chapter 6

Early the next morning, Kim tiptoed into the kitchen with Rory at her heels. Today would be a long one, starting with helping in the jewelry store and ending with tonight's cookout. Right now was her only opportunity to exercise her young dog.

Opening her belly pack to toss in her keys, she discovered the piece of driftwood Rory had dug up yesterday. Rolling her eyes, she tossed the disgusting thing onto a kitchen chair. She'd deal with it later.

She clipped Rory's leash onto his collar and headed for the boardwalk.

It took a good thirty minutes to reach Pirate's Cove, mostly because tourists strolling the boardwalk kept stopping them to pet Rory. In typical poodle fashion, Rory performed his repertoire of tricks -- unasked -- before leaning into an admirer for an ear rub.

"Watching you suck up to people is not the same as exercising," she told him as they stepped onto the sand.

He simply cocked his head, waiting for her to release him from his leash.

"Spoiled, spoiled, spoiled." Kim studied the area, searching for signs of other people on the beach. While Rory was friendly, she'd learned the hard way that not everyone enjoyed greeting him.

The path from the parking lot appeared empty, as did the stretch of white sand she could see. She turned to study the shadows beneath the cliff. A clump of dirt fell from above. Shading her eyes, Kim look up. A child's face peered from behind the osprey's leaning tree.

Liz's eyes widened, her mouth formed the word "oops" and she disappeared from sight.

"Liz, what are you doing up there?"

No response.

With Rory still on leash, Kim trotted up the path that led to the parking lot, looking for a place to climb onto the cliff top.

Along the way, signs warned visitors to stay off the cliff. The sandy soil was steadily eroding. With each rain, the cliff edge grew more unstable as pieces dropped to the beach below. Trees like the leaning one Liz had hidden behind could tumble loose any time.

Finally, Kim spotted a winding path leading up. Beside it, two bicycles laid on their sides.

Calling Rory to heel, she climbed.

At the top, she paused to glance around. Ragged trees dotted the area, providing welcome relief from the steadily warming sun. But there was no sign of Liz.

"Liz, I know you're up here."

The enormous sigh came from Kim's left. Liz stepped from behind a tree, dragging Bobby with her.

Rory ran to greet the children, turning pouts into squeals of delight. Kim let them play for a moment. If she launched into a lecture about the dangers of the cliff, the kids would just shut down.

"Must be something pretty important up here for you to ignore the danger," she finally said with what she hoped was a mild tone. "Care to share?"

Bobby stared at the ground, shuffling his feet. Liz eyed Kim. A second passed. Two. Finally, Liz nodded.

"Looking for treasure."

Bobby's head whipped up to stare at Liz.

"*I* wanted to tell the truth, but nooooooooo, Bobby didn't want anyone to know where he found it."

"It's my treasure! I don't have to tell anyone."

"Why don't we move away from the cliff edge." Kim led the way to the foot of a tree a good twenty feet from the danger and settled at its base with Rory beside her.

Liz tossed her backpack to the ground before plopping in front of Rory. After a moment, Bobby joined them.

"I take it you didn't find that red gemstone in the new sand," Kim said.

Bobby sighed. "It was in the sand, right below that stupid tree."

"The one that's leaning over the beach?"

"Yeah."

"I read on the internet that pirates liked to hide their loot in tree roots," Liz said. "So we thought..." Her voice trailed off and she suddenly couldn't meet Kim's eyes.

"You do realize digging in the roots will make the tree more unstable." Both children nodded.

"But if it fell, we'd be above it not below," Bobby protested.

Kim shuddered. When she'd lived in Oregon, the newspapers routinely published stories about loggers being killed when the tree they were cutting kicked backwards as it fell, smashing the men's heads.

"You owe Mr. Hershey an apology for lying to us," she said, standing and brushing sand from her butt. "Let's go talk to him. And along the way I'll share stories about why being anywhere near that tree when it falls is not a good idea."

She hoped the logging horror stories combined with the embarrassment of admitting to a lie would discourage the children from further treasure hunting.

With the children walking beside her, pushing their bikes, Kim was able to avoid the can-I-pet-your-dog folks. They reached Grandpa's house in record time.

Assuming Grandpa would be preparing the store for opening, Kim led the way up the front stairs and peered into the window. Sure enough, Grandpa was inside arranging a display of South Sea pearls.

She used her key to unlock the front door and gestured the children to enter. Rory charged in, scooped up the hedgehog he'd left on the floor and pranced between the display cases squeaking it.

Grandpa turned and peered at the children over his glasses. "What have we here?"

"Bobby has something he wants to tell you," Kim said.

Bobby hesitated. Liz elbowed him.

"Ow. Okay, okay, I lied, okay? I didn't find the stupid ruby in new sand. I found it in old sand, at the base of the cliff."

Grandpa nodded. "I'm not surprised. That's a very old gemstone you found, young man." He turned to Kim. "You were right; it's not a modern reproduction. The facets are too worn."

"Is it real?" Bobby said.

"Not only is it a real ruby, but there's no inscription indicating it belongs to someone." Grandpa grinned. "Which makes it yours."

Bobby's smile stretched from ear to ear. For the first time, Kim could see the resemblance to Mary's husband.

"He found the stone beneath the osprey's tree," she told Grandpa. "Judging by the trunk's circumference, the tree's old. Maybe old enough to have been around in the early 1700s."

"When there were pirates?" Liz said.

Kim nodded. "And, as you discovered, pirates often hid their share of the, er, loot beneath tree roots."

Bobby's eyes widened. "You mean I found real pirate treasure?"

Even as the words "pirate treasure" left his mouth, bells jangled and the door opened. Brittany stepped inside.

"Pirate treasure?" Her eyes glistened. "What pirate treasure?"

Kim bit back a curse. If Brittany spread rumors of treasure found in Pirate's Cove, crowds armed with metal detectors would descend on Osprey Beach. They'd dig in the sand and the fragile cliffs. Not only would the ecology be threatened, but someone might get seriously injured if the activity caused a landslide.

Before she could think of a good diversion, however, Bobby blurted "I found a ruby on the beach and Mr. Hershey says it's pirate treasure!"

Brittany's eyes narrowed, her lips tightened. Uh, oh. Kim had seen that scheming expression too many times.

"Not pirate treasure." Kim attempted a casual shrug. "Just a stone styled in an old-fashioned shape."

"You found one of the museum's stolen gems?"

"No!" Kim's protest blended with Bobby's and Liz's outraged voices.

"All of the museum's stones are identified with laser inscriptions," Grandpa explained. "Bobby's ruby is clean."

"And you found it in Pirate's Cove?" Brittany speared Bobby with her baby blues. He gulped and nodded. Brittany beamed. "So why don't we display the ruby in the museum? That way everyone can see it."

Bobby finally found his voice. "But then someone will steal it!"

"Nonsense. The thief got lucky." She glared at Kim. "And the police will arrest her soon."

Kim fought the urge to fist her hands. "Brittany, I don't believe you've met Liz Powers or Bobby Klein."

"Klein? Kevin Klein's son?"

"Mary's son as well."

Brittany ignored Kim. "You know," she said to Bobby, "We could have your dad make a special display case just for your ruby."

Bobby's eyes widened.

"And," Brittany added, "we'll make a plaque with your name on it."

"Before you make plans, you'd better run that by the museum board," Grandpa said. "Even with insurance, repairing the damaged displays may wipe out our budget."

Brittany folded her arms. "I'll pay for Bobby's case."

A chill ran down Kim's back. Brittany never bestowed favors. She was up to something.

Bobby turned to Grandpa. "Do you think it'll be safe in the museum?"

"There are no guarantees in life." Grandpa's voice matched Bobby's solemn expression. Then he smiled. "But I think the odds are on your side."

Bobby grinned but managed to rearrange his face into a serious expression as he extended a hand to Brittany. "It's a deal," he said.

"Why don't we keep your ruby in Grandpa's safe until your Dad's finished with the display case?" Kim said. And give her some time to figure out Brittany's scheme.

Bobby readily agreed, then flicked a glance at Liz. Liz nodded. Both children turned wide eyes to the adults and announced their need to leave.

Kim swallowed a protest. The scary stories hadn't worked. They probably planned to return to Pirate's Cove to dig for more treasure.

But she couldn't remind them of the dangers without alerting Brittany to the location of Bobby's discovery.

She settled for a "remember what we talked about" as the kids departed.

Well, at least she could get rid of Brittany. "Grandpa and I need to finish setting up. Do you need anything?"

Brittany, however, wasn't paying attention. She stared after the children, her carefully plucked eyebrows furrowed. Her pupils suddenly dilated, the frown disappearing. Without a word, she strode through the door.

Kim crossed to the window and looked down at the boardwalk in time to see Brittany hail Bobby. The children waited while Brittany closed the distance and began talking.

Whatever she said made Liz roll her eyes and Bobby flash one of his drop-dead-gorgeous smiles.

Rory poked his head under Kim's hand.

"Yeah, I know," she told him. "Brittany's up to something."

Chapter 7

Kim didn't have time to puzzle over Brittany's latest scheme. The store opened at 10 a.m. and the clocks had already chimed 9:30. She locked the front door and hastened upstairs to retrieve the supplies she'd purchased yesterday on the way home from Aunt Ruby's.

Thirty minutes to prepare the front window. Could she finish in time?

Remembering the twinkle in Grandpa's eyes when he'd issued this challenge, she clamped her teeth together, snagged the two large bags and trotted down the stairs.

As she set her purchases near the window, she reflected that this, too, was Brittany's fault. Grandpa always designed his store window to reflect the holidays and seasons. In the summer, he usually lined the display area with a sheet of paper printed to look like sand, then arranged the jewelry on top.

But Brittany -- the woman with the money -- had asked Osprey Beach merchants to decorate their stores in pirate themes during the museum's opening week.

Easy enough if you sold beach paraphernalia; you could sell pirate t-shirts and hats, plastic daggers, jolly rogers flags.

But what the heck was a jeweler supposed to do?

A few calls to Grandpa's sources produced some cute silver charms: sailing ships, old-fashioned ship wheels, treasure chests, pieces of eight, even tiny swords. But he'd been unable to find pirate decorations that suited a jewelry store.

And so he'd issued his challenge to Kim: Design a window display that fit the pirate theme while retaining the elegance of a jewelry store.

Kim lifted a large, shallow-rimmed baking tray from a bag and laid it at one end of the window ledge. Now to see if she'd measured correctly. She pulled other jelly-roll pans from the bags and aligned them side-by-side until the entire display floor was covered. The pans lined up perfectly.

The bags rustled and she turned in time to see Rory's head disappear into a bag.

"Now what makes you think there's something in there for you?"

Rory's head popped out of the bag. A stuffed pheasant-like bird dangled from his mouth.

Kim grinned. She really shouldn't buy him a toy every time she went to a store. But Rory loved toys; each new addition to his collection sent him into prancing poodle ecstasy.

"Let's remove the tags first, okay?"

Rory pushed the toy into her hand and waited while she snipped off the tags. She tossed the pheasant high. Rory's legs left the ground. He came down with the pheasant clamped firmly between his teeth, then proceeded to high-step around the room squeaking it. Except this particular toy honked like a pheasant.

With the honking now a musical background, she removed a beige-colored sheet from a bag and draped it over the pans, tucking it into corners.

She lifted a heavy bag of white, sterilized sand and poured it into one of the sheet-covered pans. Tossing the empty bag onto the floor, she reached for another bag. By the time she'd poured the fourth -- and final -- bag, her shoulders ached.

Now came the fun part: playing in the sand. She pushed the sand around, adding some here, subtracting some there, until she'd fashioned a gently rolling beach.

Crossing to one of the tall, antique armoires she'd helped Grandpa refinish, she opened the bottom drawer and pulled out their supply of sand dollars, sea shells and locally found shark's teeth. She scattered these across the display, then returned to the drawer to extract a large, gnarled piece of driftwood.

A second drawer held an 18" long treasure chest -- the granddaddy version of the small chests they'd buried for the children.

She placed the chest on its side, lid open, in the upper right-hand corner of the window display, pressing down so that the wood was partially buried in sand. From her store bag, she removed a small, plastic shovel and buried the blade in the sand beside the chest. She arranged the driftwood on the other side of the window.

Turning, she joined Grandpa at the display cases and collected a sampling of necklaces, bracelets and earrings from the ones he was arranging.

She used most of the pieces to create a glittering waterfall of jewels that cascaded from the "pirate chest" onto the sand. She draped some of the longer necklaces over the driftwood and scattered earrings among the shells.

She stepped outside and studied the result. Attractive. Dazzling, even, with the multi-colors. But predictable.

Her eyes fell to the twelve-inch patch of sand she'd left bare. If this didn't work...

Well, she'd find out soon enough.

She trotted into Grandpa's office and kneeled in front of the safe. Grandpa stored the most expensive or unusual pieces in the safe, taking them out only to show an interested customer.

She reached inside and pulled out a tray of jewelry set with pink, blue, yellow or black diamonds. The largest piece was a round, white-gold brooch studded with faceted black diamonds.

Removing the brooch, she returned the tray of diamonds to the safe and joined Grandpa at one of the display cases. He was putting the finishing touches on a mannequin hand. He'd draped the fingers with amethyst and orange citrine rings, the wrist with bangles sparkling with purple and orange.

"Love the color combination," she said.

Grandpa grinned. "You're teaching me to be more daring."

"You haven't seen anything yet."

She removed the final item from her bags: A small jolly roger flag.

Draping the flag over a display board, she stretched it tight and tacked the overflow on the underside. The skull grinned up at her, the crossed bones beneath it stark against the black background.

"Going to be hard matching those severe colors," Grandpa observed.

"Ah, but real bones aren't pure white." And neither were pearls, opals and other gemstones customers referred to as "white."

Kim reached for a long, Biwa pearl. Rounded on its narrow end, the freshwater pearl stretched a good inch and a half before ending in a flared, jagged edge. She laid the pearl over the bottom of one of the crossed bones, positioning it so it resembled one of the ridges of ancient bones found in archeological sites.

She positioned a second Biwa above the first, extending the ridge. She filled in the rest of the bone with irregular-shaped pearls in various shades of white, creating three-dimensional light and shadows.

"I think it's going to work." Grandpa's voice was low, almost reverential.

She started on the next bone. "You don't think it's too much?"

Grandpa chuckled. "The whole idea of a skull and crossbones is too much. This actually makes it palatable."

She allowed her grin to show. "You ain't seen nothing yet."

Reaching for the black diamond brooch, she positioned it over one of the skull's eyes. The diamonds caught the light, their luminescence such a contrast with the flat fabric that the skull almost appeared to wink.

Grandpa threw back his head and laughed.

"I take it you like it?"

"It's perfect." He wiped the tears from his eyes.

He followed her to the display and watched as she gently placed the completed board in the empty spot she'd reserved it. Without a word, the two stepped outside.

Kim grinned. The pirate flag added just the right touch of humor, elevating a nice display into something special.

"Think this will bring people into the store?" she said. While Grandpa was in the hospital, jewelry sales had floundered. She hoped the museum celebrations would attract new customers.

"Wouldn't be surprised." He pointed to a spot near the treasure chest. "You forgot your sword hilt."

"What sword hilt?"

"The one you left on the kitchen chair. I assumed you wanted me to clean it. Let me get it."

Frowning, Kim followed him back inside. Sword hilt? She couldn't remember buying something like that. She'd intentionally steered away from cutlasses, swords and knives. Not after Dorothy's death.

Grandpa reached beneath one of the display cases and pulled out a stick-like piece of wood. Rory immediately dropped his pheasant and dashed to Grandpa's feet.

"You mean the driftwood Rory found?"

Grandpa shook his head. "Not driftwood. This is antler or horn. I had to throw away the leather that wrapped it and, obviously, there was little I could do with the piece of rusty blade."

She accepted the item he held out. With the crust of dirt and rotted leather removed, she could see a t-shaped piece of metal had been shoved into the bone. The jagged, rusty metal she'd noticed earlier was actually part of a broken-off blade.

"You think this came from a broken sword?"

"Or a dagger. Where'd you find it?"

"Rory dug it out of the sand in Pirate's Cove. He--" Her words were drowned out by the chiming of a dozen wall clocks. Ten o'clock. Time to open.

"I'll get the sign," she said.

She carried the sword hilt -- sword hilt! -- to the window display and pushed the rusty blade into the sand beside the treasure chest. Closing the metal barrier to the window, she locked it and crossed to the front door.

As she turned the sign from "closed" to "open," her heart beat faster. Rory had found the sword hilt beneath the osprey's tree.

Was there really pirate treasure?

Kim didn't have time to wonder about pirate treasure. Within minutes of opening, the first tourists entered the store. Instead of approaching the display cases, however, the five women surrounded Grandpa and inquired about the murder at the museum.

"I heard that pirates killed her," a middle-aged woman said.

Her white-haired companion nodded. "And cut out her heart."

"That was an Aztec practice, not pirate." Kim separated the two ghouls from Grandpa and herded them toward the special charm display. "If you're interested in pirates, you might enjoy taking home a silver sailing ship or treasure chest."

"Oh, that treasure chest is so cute!"

Kim opened the case and removed the charm. "You can put your own treasure inside and lock it." She demonstrated how to open and close the lid and how to lock it in place.

Beaming, the woman whipped out her wallet. Her blood-thirsty friend, however, opted to buy a silver cutlass.

The two women joined their companions. As the group left the store, a second wave of people entered.

And so it went throughout the day. A steady stream of tourists interspersed with locals kept both Kim and Grandpa hopping. Tourists bought sailing ships and treasure chest charms, plus the usual array of starfish, seahorse and dolphin charms. Locals wanted to discuss Dorothy Tyson's murder.

Rumors ranged from the killer whopping off her head with a cutlass to stabbing her with a sword to using her own blood to paint an X on her chest. The only consistency in the stories was the lack of surprise that someone finally murdered Dorothy.

Apparently, the woman had used her wealth to bully not only people in Osprey Beach but throughout Calvert and Anne Arundel counties. She'd bought her way onto important community committees -- symphony, planning commission, school board -- then pushed her own agendas without regard to who benefited and who was trampled in the dust.

Several people complained that Dorothy lobbied her committees to deny a building permit or a child's scholarship application because of a perceived slight.

Given the woman's history, Grandpa's customers theorized that if Dorothy's body had been found laying beside the bay or in a dumpster, the number of suspects would stretch from Annapolis to Solomon's Island.

But no one could understand why any of her victims would kill her in the museum.

"Must've interrupted our local jewelry thieves." Mrs. Johnstone, one of Kim's favorite customers, expressed the consensus. "Can't you just image Dorothy trying to lecture them about stealing people's heirlooms?"

"Heirlooms?" Kim abandoned the pretense of straightening a shelf and turned to the conversation nook where Grandpa and Mrs. Johnstone sat. For the moment, Mrs. Johnstone was the only customer in the store. "I thought the burglars stole anything that could easily be sold."

Fortunately, Mrs. Johnstone didn't mind Kim's eavesdropping. She shrugged an elegant shoulder. "Many of the burglaries went undetected for months because the thieves only took expensive pieces of jewelry that the owner didn't wear."

"Like what?"

The indignation in Grandpa's voice made Kim grin. He firmly believed jewelry should be worn, not stuffed in a safe or bank because it was too "valuable."

Mrs. Johnstone must also know about Grandpa's quirk because she leaned forward and patted his hand reassuringly. "Mostly jewelry they'd just inherited or purchased for a special occasion."

He snorted, clearly not impressed. Kim decided to change the subject.

"Have you heard anything about a crooked cop being involved?" When Lieutenant Brockley was investigating the attack on Grandpa, he'd warned her against speaking to other officers because he feared the burglars were getting information from someone at the police station.

Mrs. Johnstone nodded. "Some say a cop is feeding the thieves information about when people will be away from home. There's also speculation that someone at the insurance companies notifies the crooks whenever customers add a new piece of jewelry to their policy."

"That would require corrupting an employee at each insurance company," Kim said. "Unless the stolen items were all insured by one company?"

"I'm pretty sure there's more than one company involved." Mrs. Johnstone reached for her purse and stood. "Whatever's going on, the police better solve this soon. People were already frightened by the attack on that school teacher. Dorothy's murder might set off a panic."

The rest of the day passed quickly. Just before closing time, Aunt Ginny swirled through the front door, her arms laden with casserole dishes.

"I am here," she announced.

Kim rushed to collect the heavy bowls. "Why so early-- Ohmygosh, is this your cheddar potato casserole?" Aunt Ginny made sinfully rich, gooey scalloped potatoes.

Ginny nodded. "I thought it'd be better to heat it here instead of trying to keep it warm all the way from Annapolis."

"Let me lock up and I'll take these up to the kitchen. Rory, no jumping."

Rory cocked his head, his "who, me?" expression positively angelic.

Aunt Ginny rubbed his ear. "I'll help Max dismantle the store."

Kim locked the door, turned the sign to closed, then carried Aunt Ginny's bowls upstairs and set them on the kitchen counter. A note on the casserole instructed to bake, covered, at 350 degrees for one hour. Kim glanced at the clock. Five thirty. Ten minutes to pre-heat the oven, an hour to bake...

Grandpa had told everyone to arrive between six thirty and seven. Knowing her family, they'd all breeze in early, claiming to be enormously hungry. Kim turned on the oven.

She removed her aunt's instruction from the casserole and set it aside. Underneath she found a bowl of three-bean salad. As she carried it to the refrigerator, Rory barked then wagged his tail furiously.

She pushed the salad into the refrigerator and turned in time to see Dad standing on the outside landing.

"No jumping," she told Rory as she unlocked the door and swung it open.

"Aw, gee, I was planning on practicing for the senior Olympics," Dad teased, kissing her cheek. Like Ginny, he'd come laden with food.

In lieu of jumping, Rory retrieved his new pheasant and wove around Dad, honking it.

"Look who I found pulling into the beach parking lot," Mom said gesturing over her shoulder with her chin.

Rory gave an excited yip and leaped forward to greet the longhaired dachshund who strained at his leash.

"Gentle, Rory." Kim met Scott's eyes and smiled. "Hey."

"Hey yourself."

Scott's baritone voice sent a thrill up her spine. Conscious of Mom and Dad watching, she scooped Al the dachshund into her arms and invited Scott inside. "Why didn't you park in the driveway?"

"Thought it'd be better to save those spaces for people who prefer not to walk a long way." He held out a sealed plastic container. "Didn't know if you liked nuts, so I made a batch with and a batch without."

She set Al down and, keeping a firm hold on the notorious food thief's leash, accepted the container. Opening it, she felt her eyes widening. "You baked cookies?" The fragrance of dark chocolate wafted from the still-warm confections.

"I know you like them, so..."

Snagging a cookie, she bit into it. The flavors of real butter, chocolate and vanilla filled her taste buds. She moaned. "These taste like they were made from scratch."

"Of course they were." He offered his half smile. "They're Aunt Cary's recipe."

"But *you* made them?"

Scott turned to Dad. "You get the impression she thinks men can't bake?"

Dad laughed and held up his hands, palms facing Scott. "Don't pull me into this. I know not to tangle with Kim."

While Scott and her parents shared a laugh, Kim closed the lid on the cookie container before the temptation to snag another became too great.

"Where's your grandfather?" Mom said.

"Downstairs putting the jewelry away." Kim dusted cookie crumbs from her fingers. "I'd better go help."

"I'll join you." Mom handed Dad the stack of tablecloths she'd carried in. "Could you two gentlemen please set up the tables? Ruby should be along with the chairs soon."

The picnic table beneath the gnarled apple tree wasn't large enough to accommodate family gatherings. So, many years ago, everyone pitched in to buy folding tables and chairs. They stored the tables in Dad's garage and the chairs in Uncle Walt's.

Kim unclipped Al's leash, then sent the two dogs outside into the fenced yard. As Mom added her salads to the refrigerator, Kim popped Aunt Ginny's casserole into the oven and set the timer. She snagged another cookie before following Mom downstairs to the store.

While Mom helped Grandpa and Aunt Ginny with the interior displays, Kim grabbed a plastic box, paper and pencil and crossed to her new window display.

Companies that insure jewelry stores require the owners to lock all gems and jewelry in the safe whenever the store is closed. While the practice certainly protected the stock from casual thieves, it also forced jewelers to recreate their displays every morning.

Kim learned long ago to draw a sketch of any arrangement she'd want to reproduce the next day. With quick strokes, she noted on paper the position of each necklace, bracelet and gemstone. Once she was satisfied with her illustration, she leaned in and removed all of the jewelry, carefully laying it in the velvet-lined box.

Her fingers hovered over the sword hilt. Leave it beside the treasure chest or store it away?

She dropped her hand and she snorted. No way was the sword hilt worth stealing. Even if it was old enough to be from a real pirate's sword, it wasn't made from gold or encrusted with jewels. Its value was purely historical.

Lifting the now-filled jewelry container, she carried it to Grandpa's safe and slid it inside.

She returned to the store. Aunt Ginny and Mom were emptying the last display case while Grandpa dealt with the cash register.

"If you don't need me, I'll go help Dad and Scott."

Grandpa waved her away.

"Helping" mostly involved keeping the dogs out from underfoot. Kim tossed a ball and laughed as Al's short legs pumped furiously as he tried to keep up with Rory. By the time the rest of the family started to arrive, the two dogs seemed content to lie in the shade and watch the procession of food headed for the tables.

Using paper dishes and plastic utensils, Kim set sixteen places, eight to a side. The table now groaned with enough food to feed all of Osprey Beach. And they hadn't even added the hamburgers yet!

She joined her cousins, who were standing in the shade of the apple tree, and gazed back at the outdoor grill. Dad and Grandpa flipped burgers while the other men supervised. Tiffany's stuffed-shirt husband stood to the side, sipping iced tea. While he'd removed his sport coat, his tie still hung perfectly knotted.

"I can't believe you couldn't talk him into removing his tie for a cookout," Tony grumbled.

Tiffany shrugged. "You saw me. I did everything but promise Dick sex on the beach."

Tony snorted. "Don't bother; he'd probably keep his tie on."

Tiffany punched her brother's arm.

Kim grinned. She actually liked Dick. Unlike Tiffany's first two husbands -- both deceased -- Dick seemed to enjoy the family gatherings. The only child of a couple of shark lawyers, the poor man craved approval for something other than courtroom accomplishments. He'd accepted her family's teasing about always wearing a tie with grace.

But he still wore it like a security blanket.

"The only way to get him to remove that tie is to make the alternative more attractive," Kim said.

"So maybe I should have offered beach sex?"

Tony choked on his tea. "Whatever works," he finally said, wiping his chin. "I've got a whole dollar riding on you."

He'd started a family pool with everyone betting on who would finally convince Dick to remove his tie in public. While most people placed their bets on Tiffany, Kim risked her dollar on Grandpa.

Who, as she watched, suddenly fumbled a hamburger. The almost finished meat hung suspended, its edge caught between the grill's rails. The other men surged forward. Grandpa held out a hand to Dick, holding him back.

"Don't come any closer," Grandpa said. "A stray spark from this here fire might ignite that fragile tie."

"But I can help," Dick said.

"Not without taking off that tie you can't."

Kim held her breath. Beside her, Tony muttered "That sneaky..." She elbowed him. A second passed. Two.

Shrugging, Dick pulled off his tie, rolled it and tucked it into his pants pocket. The group broke out in cheers and clapping.

For a moment, Dick gawked at his wife's family, his wide eyes wandering from Tiffany's to Kim's to Tony's and finally to the men surrounding the barbecue grill. Then a smile lit his face and he bowed.

Grandpa clapped him on the shoulder and handed him the spatula. Conversation returned to normal.

"Okay, Tony, pay up." Kim extended her hand.

Grinning, Tony fanned the sixteen dollar bills before slapping them into Kim's outstretched palm. "Don't spend it all in one place." Turning to his sister, he added, "Next time, beach sex."

Tiffany stuck out her tongue, then turned her back on him. "So why do you think Dorothy Tyson was killed? Mom said your old friend Mary is a suspect."

"I think it's more likely that Dorothy interrupted a burglary." Kim reached out and snagged the dachshund as he attempted to leap onto the table. "After all, how would Mary or anyone know that Dorothy had gone back to the museum?"

"But how would thieves get in? Isn't there an alarm system?"

"I'm thinking the thieves were already in the museum, that they hid somewhere until everyone left."

Tiffany's eyes widened. "That would mean the thieves are people we know."

Kim shifted Al in her arms and frowned. There must have been a hundred people in the museum last night. Did Tiffany really know all of them?

"Could have been one of the workers," Tony said. "But didn't someone make sure everyone was gone before locking up?"

"I think Dorothy messed up the procedure when she fired the night watchman and demanded Mary's keys," Kim said. "You know how focused she could get. She didn't even bother locking the front door before starting the board meeting." She didn't mention that Mary had sneaked back in.

"If the front door was unlocked during that meeting, then our suspects are infinite," Tony said.

"But any old passerby wouldn't know the door was unlocked," Kim said. "Stop thinking like a lawyer and help me come up with a list of suspects before the police arrest Mary."

Tony grinned and crossed his arms. "Okay, Nancy Drew, how do you expect me to do that?"

Kim swept her arm to include the rest of her family. "That's why we're here. If we compare memories of last night, maybe we'll identify something out of place."

"Like a game of Clue!" Tiffany lowered her voice. "It was Mr. Mustard in the parlor with the candlestick." She giggled.

"Come and eat," Grandpa called as he set a tray of sizzling hamburgers on the table.

Kim snagged a chair near Aunt Ginny's potato dish and waved to Scott to sit beside her.

"Ready for a dog training lesson?" When Scott nodded, she handed him Al. "Clip his leash back on, put him under the table, tell him 'down' and 'stay', then put your foot on his leash. When he's laying quietly, tell him 'good' and slip him a treat. Rory, you need to lay down, too."

With a sigh, Rory crawled under the table and laid his head on Kim's foot. She praised his 'down' and handed him a dog treat. Everyone settled in and began passing food.

For the next thirty minutes the group chatted happily about every-day activities. Kim praised the two dogs for maintaining their down/stays, occasionally passing a dog treat to them for reward.

As the trays of food started around for people who wanted seconds, Kim asked for the group's attention.

"Mary Klein needs our help," she said. "The police think she killed Dorothy Tyson. I think Dorothy interrupted a burglary, that the thieves attended the banquet and hid in the museum so they could rob it.

"If we share what we saw that night, maybe we'll uncover a suspect or two."

"Aren't you a little old to play Sherlock?" Aunt Emerald sniffed.

Kim met her aunt's accusing eyes. "This isn't a game. Dorothy Tyson is dead and the police seriously consider Mary a suspect."

Emerald's mouth tightened into a thin line. Beneath the table, Kim's hands clenched and she willed herself to not look away. Now that she'd returned to Osprey Beach, she needed to remind Emerald that some members of this family wouldn't be bullied.

It was Uncle Tom, Emerald's husband, who broke the stalemate by laying a hand over his wife's.

"What, exactly, are you looking for?" he said.

"I'm not sure," Kim admitted. "I guess anything out of the ordinary. People acting suspicious or sneaky or nervous--"

"*Everyone* was nervous," Aunt Sapphire said. "The vibes in both the museum and restaurant were negatively charged."

Kim resisted the urge to roll her eyes at Aunt Sapphire's woo-woo. The woman meant well and maybe she'd even seen something useful.

"Can you give me an example?"

"Well..." Sapphire frowned, then began ticking off names: "The waiters and waitresses, Brittany, Mary and her husband, that man sitting next to Jessica Bonnet." She turned to Mom. "What was his name?"

"Nigel something," Mom said. "And he was probably nervous because he was trying to impress Brittany's mother."

Kim sighed. All of the people Aunt Sapphire mentioned had good reasons to be nervous at the party. Brittany wanted everything to be perfect. Mary worried about her job. The waiters and waitresses needed to please a very picky crowd.

"Tell me more about this Nigel fellow." Okay, so she was picking on him because he was an outsider and she hadn't liked the proprietary way he'd looked at the museum exhibits. "Aunt Ruby said he's a museum director?"

"An *unemployed* museum director," Aunt Ginny said. "He just moved here from England and is looking for a job. Said he met Brittany when he went to the Smithsonian to view the Hope Diamond. He's house-sitting a friend's condo in Annapolis."

Dad chuckled. "Leave it to my sister to extract someone's life history in just a few minutes."

Ginny dismissed her brother with a wave. "I'm just friendly."

Kim grinned. Friendly and nosy. But she didn't say anything; her aunt's inquisitiveness might prove helpful. "Did he say how long he'd been in town?"

"I got the impression it was just a few months." She leaned forward, making the googly eyes on her seahorse earrings roll. "Are you thinking he might be behind the local thefts?"

"I guess it depends on when these thefts began. Does anyone know?"

People shook their heads.

"Even if this Nigel is a thief, why rob houses in Osprey Beach?" Grandpa said. "Wouldn't he focus closer to home?"

Kim pitched her napkin at her grandfather. "How dare you, sir, poke holes in a perfectly good theory?"

Grandpa's grin matched her own.

"Well, maybe it was an impulse thing," Aunt Ginny said. "Maybe this Nigel couldn't resist the display of pirate jewels. Even if Dorothy had remembered to set the alarm before your meeting, the system isn't sophisticated like the Smithsonian's, is it?"

Grandpa agreed.

"There's just one problem," Mom said. "We saw Nigel leaving with Brittany."

"He could have driven her home then returned," Ginny said.

"That's what I've been trying to tell Lieutenant Brockley," Kim said. "With that front door unlocked, anyone could have sneaked back in. I think it's more likely, however, that someone never left."

"Why?" Aunt Sapphire said.

"Because they couldn't count on Dorothy forgetting to lock the door during the meeting."

"Stuffy old Mr. Massey was at the banquet." Tiffany giggled as she mentioned the librarian from high school. "Wouldn't it be neat if he was the brains behind the burglary ring?"

Tony chimed in with the name of the math teacher he'd disliked. "It's Mrs. Roberts."

Aunt Ginny tossed in names of people she disliked and with that the party dissolved into a "who can propose the most unlikely villain."

With a sigh, Kim rose to clear the table.

As Scott started to stand, she placed a hand on his shoulder. "Be better if you watch the dogs."

"Yeah," he said, "give *me* the hard job." Taking her hand, he kissed her fingers.

Goosebumps climbed her arm.

"Wanna take a walk after we clean up?" she said. "The new railway trail in Chesapeake Beach cuts back into the wetlands. I've seen bald eagles there." Plus the railway trail was the least used in the three beaches, which meant they might have a few minutes of privacy.

Scott readily agreed.

With sixteen people working together, they quickly cleared the table, tossed disposables into a plastic sack and covered leftovers.

As Kim shook out the last tablecloth, Mom snagged the opposite end and proceeded to help fold.

"Have you considered the possibility that Mary might be guilty?"

Kim's hands stilled. "No. Should I?"

"I'd hate to think so, but when we were leaving the banquet we saw Mary and her husband arguing in the parking lot."

"Yeah, she said something about that." She resumed folding.

"Did she tell you that she screamed she wouldn't allow Brittany and Dorothy to destroy their lives?"

"No, but that doesn't mean anything."

"You didn't see her face. Then she stamped her foot so hard that her heel broke. She pulled the shoe off and threw it at her husband."

Kim's stomach clenched. "Did you tell the police this?"

Mom slipped the cloth from Kim's limp hands. "Of course not. But we weren't the only ones who saw the fight.

"Honey, all I'm saying is be careful. The pressure on Mary might cause her to act out of character."

Chapter 8

Kim slept fitfully and woke with a headache. A cup of tea helped somewhat. She was fixing Rory's breakfast when the phone rang.

Aunt Ruby.

"I woke up in the middle of the night because of you and your stupid questions," Ruby said.

Kim smiled. When she'd interviewed everyone at yesterday's cookout, she hadn't expected instant answers to her questions. People often need time to dredge memories from their subconscious. The mind works on problems until it finds answers -- a process psychologists called "closure." Often those answers come late at night.

"I'm sorry you woke up," she said. She set Rory's food onto the floor. "What did you remember?"

"It may not have anything to do with Dorothy's murder, but at the party, Claude Dickinson said something odd."

It took a moment for Kim to make the connection. "Dickinson? As in Dickinson Jewelers?"

The family-owned stores in nearby Dunkirk and Prince Frederick were one of the few Grandpa trusted. Grandpa's contemporary, Claude Dickinson -- Mr. D. to his employees -- was honest as well as knowledgeable. Mr. D. employed some of the friendliest people in the county. Grandpa continually joked about stealing Mr. D.'s employees, most recently a bundle of fire named Alison.

Thinking about the Dickinsons, however, made Kim feel guilty. Dickinson Jewelers was a true family affair. Mr. D.'s son, Claude, was a master jeweler who, among other things, designed exquisite pieces for the stores. Claude's elegant wife, Kathy, oversaw the stores' marketing efforts and was always available to answer questions.

Grandpa would so love someone in his own family to work with him.

But while Kim's aunts and cousins obsessed over gems and jewelry, they showed little interest in the actual business. Only Kim asked questions about gemstone formation and history. Only Kim helped in the store.

Only Kim broke her grandfather's heart by switching her college major from geology to psychology and moving 2,000 miles away to teach at a university.

She pushed the guilt aside. She was home now and could help Grandpa whenever she wasn't teaching or grading papers. In the meantime, she needed to find other suspects for Lieutenant Brockley.

"Was Mr. D. at the banquet?" The place had been so crowded, Kim couldn't remember seeing him or his wife.

"Yes, the whole family was there."

"So what did he say that struck you as odd?"

Aunt Ruby giggled. "He called Dorothy a jinx. Jinx-It Dorothy. You should have seen Dorothy's face! I mean, Mr. D. has always teased people and you know darn well he's joking. But Dorothy turned bright red."

"Did Mr. D. say why he called Dorothy a jinx?"

"I asked him, but before he could answer, Brittany interrupted and started blathering about the museum so that was that. I did ask Dorothy later, but she refused to explain."

"No, I guess she didn't like being compared to a European woodpecker that can turn its head 180 degrees and hiss like a snake," Kim said.

"What in the world are you talking about? Mr. D. called her a jinx, not a bird."

"The origin of the word jinx is--"

"Oh, for heaven's sake, Kim. No one cares about those things. Why Dad encouraged this nonsense when you were a child, I'll never know."

Kim grinned and resisted saying "gotcha." As one of eight grandchildren, she'd competed for Grandpa's attention by, among other things, spouting off obscure facts. Like that a

Jinx torquila woodpecker could have modeled for a role in *The Exorcist* movie.

She thanked her aunt for the help and hung up the phone. Behind her, a voice said "European woodpecker, huh?"

Kim jumped, then turned and gave Grandpa a hug. "Didn't hear you come in."

"No, you were too busy terrorizing your aunt." He couldn't hide the humor in his voice. "So what did she want?"

"Sit down. I'll get your coffee." She crossed to the coffee pot that Grandpa had prepared the night before, poured a cup, added a splash of milk and carried it to the kitchen table. She handed Grandpa his coffee, fixed a cup of tea and sat beside him.

Rory pushed his head between them.

"Rory, get your chin off the table. You know better."

The big poodle rolled his eyes at her, but didn't move.

Grandpa chuckled. "Look again; his chin isn't touching the table."

She tilted her head. Grandpa was right; she could see daylight under Rory's muzzle.

Using two fingers, she gently pushed Rory's face away from the table. "I don't want you hovering over the table, either."

Rory cocked his head, giving her his best "who me?" expression. She tightened her lips, fighting the urge to laugh. She'd learned the hard way that Rory repeated any behavior that made her laugh. She did not want to encourage him to hang his chin over the table.

Rory studied her face. Then, with a doggie grin, he picked up his hedgehog and trotted away.

"Told you not to buy a dog smarter than you," Grandpa said.

"You'd think someone trained in psychology could stay one step ahead of him." She sipped her tea. "Anyway, back to Aunt Ruby. She said Mr. Dickinson teased Dorothy about being a jinx."

Grandpa frowned. "In what way?"

"Don't know, though he was obviously joking. But Dorothy's face turned red and she refused to tell Aunt Ruby what Mr. D. meant. Doesn't that sound suspicious?"

"Not necessarily. Dorothy was easily offended."

Kim stood, retrieved Grandpa's now-empty cup and crossed to the coffee pot. "I'd still like to know what he meant by jinx." She filled the cup and returned it to Grandpa.

"Want me to give him a call?"

"Thought you'd never ask."

But when Grandpa called, Mr. Dickinson wasn't available. Grandpa left a message. Frustrated, Kim and Rory followed him downstairs to prepare the store for opening.

Like the day before, a steady stream of tourists and locals kept everyone busy: Rory greeting and showing off his hedgehog, Grandpa listening to gossip about the investigation, Kim helping shoppers choose mementos of their trip to the three beaches.

With each sale, Kim grew increasingly frustrated. Why couldn't she convince people to buy something other than inexpensive pirate and beach charms?

The tourists barely glanced at the regular displays. Yet the cases were attractively arranged. Memories of her failure selling Girl Scout cookies flooded her mind, making her irritable.

Just before noon the store finally cleared. Kim rubbed her lower back. Seemed like she'd been standing for hours. How did Grandpa do this day after day?

The door opened once again and a craggy-faced woman dressed in dirty jeans and faded t-shirt stepped inside. Rory trotted over and sniffed her boots.

"Smells good, huh fella?" The woman grinned and ruffled Rory's topknot. "Best rockfish in the entire bay. Hey, Max."

"Sam!" Grandpa rushed over and shook the woman's hand. "Good to see you. I'm surprised you're out and about at this time of day."

"Just brought a group in," she said with the scratchy voice of a long-time smoker. "Next one doesn't arrive for another couple hours."

Grandpa turned to Kim. "I'd like you to meet my granddaughter, Kimberley West. Kim, this is Samantha Rockhill, the best charter fishing captain in the whole darn Chesapeake Bay."

Captain? This must be the "Captain Sam" Grandpa hired whenever he wanted to go fishing for rockfish.

Kim extended her hand and studied the woman. Mid-fifties, maybe, with pale blue eyes and dirty blond hair pulled through the hole in her baseball cap. Despite the sun's assault on her skin, the woman possessed a confident beauty often described as "handsome."

"You must get a lot of surprised reactions when the guys show up for their charter," Kim said.

Sam shrugged. "That's why my contracts make it clear there are no refunds unless *I'm* the one who cancels the trip." She grinned. "'course, after they come home with a cooler full of fish, I don't hear complaints."

Intrigued, Kim opened her mouth to quiz Sam more about her business, but the fisherwoman -- was there such a thing or was she still a fisherman? -- had turned to Grandpa and was inquiring about his health. Seemed like everyone in Osprey Beach knew about Grandpa's hospital stay.

Grandpa brushed the question aside with the flip of a hand.

"So what can I do for you?" he said.

"Thought you could tell me if this is a sapphire." Sam reached into her pocket, pulled out a red bandana and unwrapped it.

Remembering Bobby's ruby find, Kim's heart beat faster. Stepping forward, she peered over Grandpa's shoulder.

In the center of the bandana lay a cobalt blue "jewel" about the size of a pea. Whatever the original shape, the relentless scrape of sand and waves had ground it into an asymmetrical hexagon.

Deep, whitish scratches marred the surface, telling Kim the piece wasn't sapphire. Though a hard blow could break them, sapphires and rubies were one of the world's hardest minerals and highly resistant to scratches. Diamonds could scratch sapphire, but quartz -- the mineral found most often in sand -- was too soft to do the kind of damage Kim saw here.

Even so, Grandpa treated Sam's find with respect, lifting it gently by the edges and studying it with a loupe before declaring it glass.

"What made you think it was a sapphire?" He handed the glass back to Sam.

"There's a rumor going around that Bobby Klein found a ruby in Pirate's Cove, that it came from loot buried by pirates."

Kim's stomach clenched. Samantha Rockhill seemed level-headed, too sensible to believe stories of pirate treasure. If *she* believed Bonnet had buried treasure in Pirate's Cove, what was to prevent the more typical treasure hunters from flooding the beach and destroying the ecology of the fragile coastline?

"How widespread is this rumor?" Kim said.

"There were a couple other people digging in the cove." Sam pitched the glass fragment into a nearby trash can. "But I was the only one who found anything remotely resembling a jewel."

"Were they just on the beach or also digging on the cliff?"

Sam's eyes widened. "Is that where--"

"No! No, Bobby found the ruby on the beach." Kim glanced at Grandpa. He nodded, one quick dip of his chin. Reassured, Kim continued. "We don't even know if the ruby is an antique. It probably fell from some poor woman's ring."

"That was my first assumption when I heard the rumor." Sam dusted invisible sand from her hands. "I'd better get back to work. Don't worry; I'll spread the word that Bobby's ruby didn't come from a pirate cache. Not that anyone will believe me..."

Kim followed Sam to the door and watched her disappear down the boardwalk. She tossed Grandpa a rueful smile.

"Thanks for backing me up. I hated to lie, but..."

"You didn't lie," Grandpa said. "Bobby did find the ruby on the beach, right? And it could have fallen from a ring."

Before Kim could respond, the door behind her opened and a group of giggling women swept into the store. Hearing the word "wedding," Kim turned away. Let Grandpa deal with them; he was much better at feigning interest in all of the details prospective brides hurl at any poor salesperson trapped in their sights.

The phone rang, giving her the perfect excuse to not feel guilty. She lifted the receiver.

"Is this the young woman who was named after a big hole in the ground?" a man said.

Kim struggled to place the somewhat familiar voice. Not many people knew about Kim's disdain for the way her parents had spelled her name. "Uh, this is Kimberley West. May I help you?"

The man chuckled. "Last time I saw you, you had rips in your jeans, dirt on your nose and indignation all over your body."

Kim frowned, trying to put the clues together. She'd spent much of her childhood with a dirty face and frayed jeans and, if she wanted to be honest, indignant about something or other. There was the time she discovered Grandpa had embellished the story of how opals formed. And the time Brittany accused her of stealing all of the classroom's chalk. And the time she discovered she'd been named after the famous African diamond mine...

Oh.

"Mr. D.?"

Claude Dickinson laughed. "I can still picture you with your arms crossed, demanding to know why someone had named you after a big hole in the ground."

Heat rose to her cheeks as she remembered the day she'd made the connection between the unusual spelling of her name and the Kimberley diamond mine.

Until she turned eight, Kim had cherished her normal-sounding name, grateful she hadn't been burdened with a sissy name like Tiffany, Amber or Opal. Sure, it was spelled weird. But that made it special, right?

Then one day she opened a geography book and discovered an African diamond mine spelled k-i-m-b-e-r-l-E-y. Just like her own name.

Outraged, she'd rushed into the store and demanded Grandpa tell her the truth: Had she been named after a big hole in the ground?

Grandpa had tried to reassure her that she'd been named after the most precious diamond mine in history. Kim hadn't been appeased.

In hindsight, she probably shouldn't have pitched a fit in front of one of Grandpa's colleagues.

"How've you been, Mr. D.?" As he answered, she glanced over at Grandpa. The bridal party had now formed a U around Grandpa as he laid out a selection of small pendants. No way he could come to the phone.

Maybe she could convince Mr. Dickinson to talk with her.

"So Max said you're now a professor at Maryland?" Mr. Dickinson said. "What are you teaching?"

"Psychology." Before he could ask why she wasn't teaching geology or gemology or something related to Grandpa's business, she added, "Grandpa's with some customers right now, but he asked me to talk with you if you have a few minutes?"

When he agreed, she plunged in. "We're trying to help a friend piece together Dorothy Tyson's movements at the museum banquet. My Aunt Ruby said you'd had a chance to talk with Dorothy?"

"Talked with a lot of people. What are you looking for?"

"Uh..." Oh, what the heck. Mr. D. was always a straight-shooter. Just ask the question directly. "I guess I was curious why you called Dorothy a jinx. Not that I'm criticizing or anything..."

She was relieved to hear him chuckling. "Oh, she hated when I called her that. I was joking, of course."

"Of course. But what prompted the joke?"

"Well, you know how Dorothy liked to boss people." He said it as a statement, not a question. "Recently, she started dropping into the Dunkirk store just to see what other people were buying. Then she'd lecture them about buying insurance or storing jewelry in a home safe.

"I've got good salespeople and believe me, they tried to keep things professional. But it got to the point that every time Dorothy walked in, I had to distract her so she wouldn't pester my customers."

"Yeah, she could be bossy. So you called her a jinx just to get rid of her?"

"Heck, no. Woman *was* a jinx. Seemed like every time she lectured a client about protecting their jewelry, someone would break into their house and walk off with the latest purchase."

The air conditioning suddenly seemed too cold.

"Poor Stacy Harrison," Mr. D. continued, "She actually walked in on the thieves."

"Was she hurt?"

"She had a few bruises on her arm from where they manhandled her. Tied her to a chair and gagged her, then proceeded to make off with her grandmother's antique sapphire bold as you please. She said later the worst of it was listening to Dorothy saying I told you so."

"Told her what?"

"Same thing she told everyone else. Dorothy walked into the store as I was examining Stacy's inheritance and launched into her speech about storing jewelry in a home safe."

"Sounds like good advice. Did Stacy buy a safe?"

"Wasn't time. Thieves showed up the next day while Stacy was teaching."

They chatted for a few more minutes, but the friendly jeweler had nothing more to add.

Kim hung up the phone and stared into space. A few weeks ago Lieutenant Brockley told her the local burglars seemed to have inside information about who recently purchased or inherited an expensive piece of jewelry -- and didn't own a home safe to protect it.

What if the informant was someone no one would suspect, someone like the wealthy know-it-all Dorothy Tyson?

Chapter 9

"*Dorothy Tyson?* Head of a burglary ring?" Grandpa threw his head back and laughed.

Kim sighed and sank onto a stool. She'd been so excited to share her theory with Grandpa that, as soon as the wedding party departed, she'd blurted out her suspicion without first explaining what Mr. Dickinson had told her.

"Mr. D said Dorothy was always coming into the store to see what people were buying."

"Yes, that sounds like Dorothy."

"And whenever someone bought a new piece of jewelry, Dorothy lectured them about jewelry insurance and home safes." Grandpa nodded, but she could see he still wasn't convinced. "Mr. D also said that right after Dorothy gave someone that lecture, thieves broke into the person's house and stole that specific piece of jewelry."

"And that's when he started comparing Dorothy to a European woodpecker that can turn its head 180 degrees?"

Kim grinned. "Yep. Don't you find that suspicious?"

"That thieves were able to steal jewelry that wasn't protected in a safe?"

"That they knew someone just acquired expensive new jewelry and had no way to protect it."

Grandpa's eyes widened. "You think Dorothy told the thieves where to go? But why? Dorothy had no reason to steal."

"She might be one of those sensation seekers. We studied them in school." Kim shifted a display of earrings slightly to the left. "You know, people who aren't happy just jumping from planes, climbing rocks or zipping through tree tops on a line. They have to find more risky ways of doing those things. They get some kind of emotional rush from putting themselves in danger.

"My professor told us about several wealthy, highly respected people who'd been caught stealing from friends, stores and even museums. From the outside, these people were model citizens. When captured by police, however, they vibrated from an adrenaline high as if they were on drugs."

Grandpa frowned, then shook his head. "Can't see it. Dorothy was too controlling to get involved with a couple of thieves."

Kim sighed. Sometimes Grandpa's calm logic could be so frustrating.

However, just because he didn't agree with her theory didn't negate the possibility that Dorothy was involved, even if unwillingly. She needed to learn more about the woman.

And there was one person who might know something.

"You know, we really should pay a condolence call on Dorothy's husband."

Grandpa raised an eyebrow and studied her. She widened her eyes, attempting an innocent expression, telling herself to not look away. Rory saved her by choosing that moment to push between them and drop his hedgehog in her lap.

Kim tossed the toy and grinned as Rory snagged it out of the air. "Maybe I should bake a casserole or something."

"Please don't."

"Hey, I can cook. Some."

Grandpa chuckled. "How 'bout we pick something up on the way, okay? We'll go after supper?"

"Deal."

They closed the store for lunch and grabbed a quick sandwich. After reopening, a flurry of shoppers rushed in. As the day wore on, however, the number of customers diminished to a trickle. From the window, Kim could see sunbathers trying to eke out the last of summer for their tans.

"Grandpa, why don't I watch the store while you catch up on repairs?"

No sense suggesting he take a nap; he'd just accuse her of treating him like an old man. But working at his desk would at least require him to sit.

He readily agreed, leaving her with an empty store and her laptop. Time to do some research.

Settling on a stool behind the counter, she laid the computer on the display case and searched the internet for Osprey Beach burglaries.

The story about the school teacher popped up first. But the article contained little more than she already knew. A high school biology teacher interrupted a burglary when she arrived home early. The thieves tied her to a kitchen chair with duct tape.

After the thieves left, the woman hopped the chair to the kitchen phone and used her nose to dial 9-1-1. The article didn't detail the items stolen. But it gave more information about the victim: Stacy Harrison lived on Second Avenue.

The teacher lived within walking distance.

Jotting down the woman's name, Kim returned to Google, searching for details of the other local burglaries. After twenty minutes, however, she closed the computer in disgust.

Only Stacy Harrison's assault had warranted a full article. The other burglaries had been lumped under "Police Briefs," which included every single type of crime in the county. Even when she scanned for the words "burglary," she had to read through each entry to learn what was actually stolen. It would take hours to track down the movements of the jewelry thieves.

Well, there was one lead she could follow right now. Pulling out the local phone book, she searched for the school teacher. She was listed as "S. Harrison" on Second Avenue. Probably lived alone.

She glanced at the clock. Four p.m. Even if Stacy taught summer school, she should be home by now.

Stacy Harrison answered the phone after three rings. Kim introduced herself and explained that she was looking into the death of Dorothy Tyson.

"Why do you want to talk with me? I barely knew the woman."

"I think Dorothy interrupted a burglary at the museum," Kim said. "The killers might have been the same people who robbed you."

"I've already told the police everything I know."

"I'm more interested in how the thieves knew you'd inherited jewelry."

Stacy snorted. "That's easy. Dorothy Tyson's big mouth."

"There were that many people in the jewelry store when Dorothy lectured you?"

"Jewelry store? Try hairdresser."

"*Hairdresser?*"

Stacy chuckled. "Yep. Biggest gossip mill in town. Look, I'm packing for a trip to Atlantic City. I leave tonight. If you really want to talk, why don't you wait till I get back next week?"

Next week? By next week, Mary could be in jail.

"How about we talk while you pack? I'm good at folding."

As Stacy hesitated, Kim added "Please. The police think a friend of mine is involved. She's innocent. You might have information that would give them somewhere else to look."

"How can you be sure your friend is innocent?"

Not wanting to get into an argument about the difficulty of truly knowing someone, Kim opted for the simple explanation. "Dorothy was stabbed with a knife. Mary faints at the sight of blood."

"Mary? Mary Klein?" Stacy's voice softened. "So the rumors are true; the police do suspect her."

"The police are wrong. Please, I'll only take a few minutes of your time."

She heard a sigh. "Okay, if you come right now I can take a short break."

Kim hung up the phone and trotted into the office.

"Grandpa? I need to run out for a few minutes. Can you watch the store while I'm gone?"

Looking up from a watch he was repairing, he peered at her over his glasses. "Been doing it alone for years."

"Er, right. Could you also watch Rory? I'll be back sooner if I don't have to worry with him."

She kissed his cheek, told Rory to behave, snagged her purse from under the cash register and trotted out the door.

Ten minutes later, she sat in Stacy's cozy living room, accepting a glass of iced tea. The tiny cottage suited the diminutive Katherine Jenkins look-alike, her blond hair and sweet expression totally the opposite image of "high school biology teacher." Even dressed in shorts and torn t-shirt, the resemblance to the glamorous Welsh singer was uncanny.

Right now, however, Stacy oozed tension. Shoulders hunched, she perched in a floral armchair, twisting her glass in dainty hands.

"I really don't know what I can tell you to help," she said. "It was bad enough someone stole my grandmother's sapphire necklace. But to have the thieves manhandle me." She exaggerated a shiver and raised the glass to her lips, gulping as if it contained fortifying whiskey.

"I know this is hard, but the police are so focused on Mary that I'm afraid they'll arrest her if I don't find alternative suspects."

Stacy nodded and set the glass onto a coaster. "What do you want to know?"

"I guess we should start with the robbery. I heard you'd come home from work early?"

"Yeah, I was so darn sick; there was a flu going around the school. All I wanted to do was crawl into bed. I pulled into the garage, opened the kitchen door and someone grabbed me from behind." She bit her lip and looked away. "I thought... Well, let's put it this way, I was relieved that all they wanted was my jewelry."

Goosebumps formed on Kim's arms. A few weeks ago, while investigating the attack on Grandpa, she herself had fended off two thugs. But the assault happened so quickly -- one minute she was struggling, the next running for her life -- that the idea of rape never entered her mind.

Stacy breathed deeply. "He trapped both of my arms by my side and covered my mouth with his other hand."

"He?"

"Definitely. He was taller than me and wiry muscular. Said he wouldn't hurt me if I cooperated."

"Did you recognize the voice?"

"No, he spoke with a sort of whisper growl. Could have been anyone. Anyway, someone else came into the kitchen. This one was short, dressed all in black with a ski mask pulled over his head. The clothes were so baggy that he could have been a woman. He was carrying a zippered plastic bag with Grandma's necklace inside.

"The guy holding me said 'duct tape.' The second thief stuffed my necklace into one pocket while pulling a roll of silver tape from the other. I tried to kick him when he approached, but the other guy raised one hand to cut off my oxygen."

Tears formed in Stacy's eyes. "When I stopped kicking, he let me breathe while the smaller guy taped my mouth. They forced me onto a kitchen chair and tied me with duct tape. The first one, the one who'd grabbed me, had the nerve to apologize before they left."

Kim pulled a packet of tissues from her purse and passed them to Stacy. Stacy nodded her thanks, removed a tissue and blew her nose.

Stacey forced a smile. "Ever try to dial a phone with your nose? Thank goodness the emergency operator sent someone to investigate even though I couldn't talk."

Crumpling the tissue in a fisted hand, she added, "The thing is, in hindsight I don't think they wanted to hurt me. They just wanted to grab the necklace and leave. So if they were behind the museum robbery, why would they kill Dorothy? Why not just tie her up?"

"Maybe Dorothy saw their faces when she walked in. Those masks must be uncomfortable to wear."

"So why were they wearing masks when I saw them?"

Kim thought for a minute. "Maybe they heard your car pull into the garage. From inside the museum, they wouldn't have heard Dorothy return." Not ready to reveal her suspicions that Dorothy was involved in the burglaries, Kim changed the subject.

"How did the thieves learn about your jewelry? You said something about Dorothy...?"

Stacy snorted and rolled her eyes. "That woman was a menace. I assume Mr. D told you about her walking in while he was looking at Grandma's necklace? She started pontificating about the importance of home safes and, like a fool, I admitted I don't have one and don't intend to buy one. Who can afford those things on a school teacher's salary?"

"Were there people in the store who heard what Dorothy said?"

Stacy shook her head. "Store was empty. But a few hours later, I walked into the beauty shop for my monthly trim and there was Dorothy sitting under a dryer. She immediately told everyone that she'd seen my new necklace AND that I refused to buy a home safe to protect it."

Kim could imagine Dorothy's shrill, condescending voice penetrating the cacophony of hairdryers and chatter.

"As usual, the place was packed," Stacy continued. "I mean *packed*."

She seemed to expect some kind of response.

"Er, I guess people really like this place," Kim said.

Stacy beamed. "Oh, yes, we are so, so lucky to have Ryan in Osprey Beach. He trained under Fekkai, you know."

Kim had no idea what a Fekkai was, but she widened her eyes and nodded, trying to look impressed.

Stacy patted her silky hair. "Ryan Hardy's the only one who can control my curly hair."

Kim frowned. Ryan Hardy. Why was that name familiar?

Stacy misinterpreted Kim's frown. "Yeah, I know, he's expensive. But, trust me, he's worth it. You might want to give him a try; he's really wonderful with long hair."

Kim suddenly remembered where she'd heard the name. Ryan Hardy was the beautician Brittany raved about. Odd that she and Dorothy went to the same hairdresser.

Coincidence? Or something more sinister?

"You know, maybe I will call him about getting a trim." And poke around, see who goes there and what they talk about. "Do you have his number?"

"Of course." Stacy crossed to a small table holding telephone, address book, paper and pens. Instead of writing down a phone number, however, she lifted the receiver and punched a single number.

"Tonya? Yeah, it's Stacy Harrison. Fine, fine. Look, I've just met someone who'd like Ryan to work his magic. How soon could he work her in? Really?" Stacy covered the mouthpiece. "They just had a cancellation for tomorrow morning at ten. Can you make it?"

Kim swallowed, but nodded her head. Now that she'd moved back to Osprey Beach, she'd have to find a hairdresser sometime and Stacy's hair certainly was lovely.

And sitting in this particular shop wouldn't be a waste of time because she could do some sleuthing.

Stacy confirmed Kim's appointment and hung up the phone.

"Tonya is Ryan's wife." She scribbled the salon's address and phone number on a piece of paper. "She's good, but not as good as Ryan. You're lucky he was free."

Kim stood and accepted the paper Stacy extended. "Thank you for taking the time to talk with me."

Stacy led the way to the door. Before opening it, however, she paused and laid a hand on Kim's arm. "I can tell from your questions that you're hoping Dorothy had some connection to the local thieves."

Kim opened her mouth to protest, but Stacy waved for silence. "It's okay; I won't tell anyone. And, frankly, I'd rather believe Dorothy's death was connected to a falling out among thieves than think that someone at the hair salon -- one of my friends -- is involved.

"If you're looking in that direction, however, you need to know that the day Dorothy blabbed about my inheritance, Mary Klein was in the salon."

Chapter 10

Kim leaned against the boardwalk railing and gazed out at the now empty osprey nest, needing to think through her interview with Stacy Harrison before returning to the store.

She'd hoped the school teacher's information would support the wild notion that Dorothy was involved in the jewelry thefts. Instead, Stacy had expanded the suspect list to everyone in Ryan Hardy's beauty shop the day Dorothy broadcast Stacy's unprotected inheritance.

And, darn it, Mary had been there.

Seemed like every attempt to find new suspects revealed evidence against Mary. Mary, however, was not a thief. Of that, Kim had no doubt.

Could Mary kill someone? Kim's psychology courses had convinced her that, under the right circumstances, anyone was capable of murder. Mary would likely defend her family to the death.

But Dorothy hadn't been threatening Mary's family. Sure, she'd urged the board to replace Mary with someone else. But Dorothy couldn't single-handedly fire Mary; she'd need a majority vote of the board and Grandpa thought she'd never get that.

So what was Mary's motive?

According to the mysteries Kim loved, police tended to ignore motive, focusing instead on means and opportunity. But Kim was trained in psychology. Sociopaths and psychopaths were not as common as mystery books implied. Many violent crimes were committed by average people who'd somehow been pushed over the edge into aberrant behavior. Understand the psychological motive and you should be able to unmask the criminal.

If Dorothy's death wasn't simply a matter of being in the wrong place at the wrong time, then something in her past -- perhaps her history as a bully -- had given someone a motive to kill.

The Indiana Jones "Raider's March" interrupted her thoughts. Swinging her purse onto the railing, she dug into the cell phone pocket, pulled out the phone and checked caller I.D. Aunt Ginny.

"I know you're investigating Dorothy's murder," her aunt said. "I can't get away today, but I'll be there to help first thing tomorrow."

Kim opened her mouth to protest, then decided to save her breath. She'd already involved Ginny when she invited her to Grandpa's picnic. Maybe she could convince her aunt to help Grandpa in the store while Kim poked around the beauty shop.

"Great," she said into the phone. "I'll see you in the morning."

As she disconnected, she heard a familiar voice behind her.

"You take that back right now!"

Turning, she spotted Liz Powers, fisted hands on her hips, glaring at four girls dressed in bikinis. A blond, clearly the ringleader, threw her head back and laughed before launching into song.

I want to be Bobby's girl, I want to be Bobby's girl...

The other girls quickly joined in, ignoring Liz's cries to stop. They surrounded Liz and swayed their hips as they sang.

Kim's own hands fisted. Brittany had sung that exact same song when they were eleven or twelve years old. Except Brittany and her friends had substituted "Billy" for "Bobby."

Billy was the boy who'd allowed Kim to play softball with his friends. None of the other boys wanted a girl in the game. When Brittany saw Billy and Kim on the way to a game, she'd burst into song. Billy stood there, face red, totally mortified.

He never again asked Kim to play.

Brittany's taunt had cost Kim a good friend. And now these girls were threatening Liz's friendship with Mary's son.

Kim glanced around, but didn't see Bobby. Had he already run off, unable to justify friendship with a tomboy?

She needed to stop this. But how do you correct children without acting like a bully yourself?

Not sure what she was going to say, but needing to do something, she started toward the group. At the same time, Liz reached into her backpack and pulled out her mechanical snake just far enough so the girls could see its realistic head.

"Snake!" one of the girls screeched.

Liz held the snake just below the head and jiggled it so it seemed to be writhing in her backpack. Screaming, the girls turned and ran down the boardwalk toward Kim. Liz whipped out the snake and pursued them, holding Homer in front of her.

The group parted, swirled around Kim and continued running. Liz stopped a few feet beyond Kim and scowled at the girls, who were now dodging afternoon walkers.

Wheeling around, Liz crossed her arms over her chest and raised her chin.

"I suppose you're going to yell at me for scaring them," she said. The fake snake dangled from her hand, writhing.

Kim couldn't suppress a grin. "Actually, I was about to break out into applause."

The rebellion on Liz's face faded, replaced by astonishment. Then she grinned from ear to ear. "Homer's pretty neat, huh?"

"Definitely effective. You've got a good shot at winning the science fair."

Liz sighed and pushed a switch on Homer's back. The snake stopped moving. "Only if I can get him to crawl over hills. Right now Homer only works on level ground. Bobby's right; his stupid truck does climb hills better than Homer."

"You'll figure it out. Ah, is Bobby around?"

"No." Liz stuffed the snake's head back into her backpack. "He went with his dad to pick out special wood for the display case he's making for that stupid ruby he found."

Kim took a moment to sort out the "he's" in that sentence.

"Probably just as well Bobby wasn't around to hear the singing," she said.

"Oh, he's heard them." Liz smiled. "But just wait till I win the science fair. That'll show them."

"Really? They didn't seem the type to care about science." Or anything that involved brainwork.

"Tawny's dad is an engineer and he wants her to win so bad he cheats. My teacher said it's okay to ask for advice, but we have to do all of the work ourselves. Last year Tawny said the contest was fixed because her dad did a lot of the project but she only got second place." She frowned. "But now I have to figure out how to make Homer work on rocks and things."

"Well, I can't help you with the technical stuff, but maybe we can make Homer look more realistic." She gestured toward Grandpa's house. "Wanna go see if Rory's toy snake will fit Homer?"

Liz's face brightened. Without another word, they turned and strode down the boardwalk.

"I'm gonna find my own pirate treasure, you know," Liz said. "Lots and lots of rubies."

"Don't forget; we don't know for sure Bobby's ruby came from a pirate stash. But if there's something to find, my money's on you."

Liz grinned. After a few steps, she said, "You know those ruby slippers, the ones the witch gave to Dorothy?"

Guessing Liz's next words, Kim bit back a smile and nodded.

"Were they real rubies?" Liz said.

Kim had asked Grandpa the same question after they'd watched *The Wizard of Oz* together.

"No, the shoes in the movie were decorated with sequins and beads," Kim said. "But back in the late 1800s, there was a king and queen in Burma -- it's called Myanmar now -- who each owned real ruby slippers."

"Really? So why didn't Dorothy wear those slippers in the movie?"

"Trust me, I've seen photos of those shoes. The ones Judy Garland wore were much prettier."

Seeing the disbelief on Liz's face, Kim added, "The real shoes weren't totally encrusted with rubies. The king's had a few rubies scattered around and the toes curled up like a genie's. The queen's were basically flipflops with rubies set into the sides."

Liz giggled. "Guess sometimes fake is better than real, huh? Like Homer."

Kim grinned. "Yeah, I don't think a real snake could have done a better job of scaring those girls."

They arrived at Grandpa's gate.

As they climbed the front stairs to the store, she could hear Grandpa's laughter and Rory's squeaky hedgehog. She pushed the door open, the bell tinkled and Rory charged toward her, his tail wagging furiously.

"Slow down! Rory--"

The young dog planted his feet, but it was too late. His momentum carried him across the slippery tile floor and into Kim's knees.

Kim windmilled her arms, but felt her own feet sliding out from under her. Strong arms wrapped around her and, without thinking, she grabbed the nearest support, a pair of muscular shoulders.

Which is how she found herself standing nose-to-nose with Scott Wilson, breathing in his male scent, gazing into amused hazel eyes.

Conscious of Grandpa's and Liz's intense scrutiny, Kim stepped away. "Guess I'd better get new brakes for Rory."

Liz laughed and Scott grinned.

"So what brings you to Osprey Beach?"

"Figured you'd want to pay a condolence call to Dorothy's family, so I, er..."

"He brought a chicken casserole." Grandpa chuckled. "Looks like you don't need to cook after all."

Kim threw her hands into the air. "What is it with you guys? I do know how to make a few recipes."

Scott smiled. "No need to cook when you're beautiful, smart and an excellent dog trainer."

Kim crossed her arms and looked from Scott to Grandpa and back to Scott.

"That was a compliment, right?"

Scott laughed then turned to Liz. "Don't know if you remember me, but we met at the Smithsonian when you were there with your grandmother."

Liz's eyes widened. "Oh! Grandma used to work with your dad."

Actually, Liz's grandmother had worked for Scott's uncle, but given the man had been murdered, Kim decided it was best to change the subject.

"Liz and I are going to make some modifications to her science fair project. Liz, show them Homer while I go get what we need."

She trotted upstairs and into her bedroom. Pausing for a moment, she admired the bright room with its medium-blue rug, beachy furniture and sliding glass doors leading onto a balcony that looked out over the water. In anticipation of Kim moving back to Osprey Beach, Grandpa had hired contractors to transform the top floor of his house into two bedroom suites complete with large closets and private baths.

Kim had felt guilty when she'd seen the changes. She'd planned to only stay with Grandpa until her small Oregon house sold and she could move closer to the university. After all, she was much too old to be living with parents or even a beloved grandfather.

So far, however, the living arrangements had suited them. Kim was glad she was on-hand to help Grandpa after he was released from the hospital.

She crossed to the large closet and dug out Rory's toy box. She'd purchased the box to corral the squeaky toys she couldn't resist buying him.

The stuffed snake lay coiled on the bottom. She studied it for a moment, once again marveling at the pattern imprinted on the fabric. Each scale was perfectly outlined with a bit of white. Darned thing looked just like a black rat snake.

Kim wasn't afraid of snakes. She'd played with them as a child. So she hadn't hesitated to buy the toy for Rory when his adult teeth began pushing out puppy teeth. The snake's squishy fabric rubbed his itchy gums while the draping coils distracted him from the discomfort.

The four-month-old had pranced around the house, shaking the snake and displaying it to visitors. Unfortunately, one of her visitors had been a university department head who was deathly afraid of snakes. Even stuffed, fuzzy ones.

Rory had been so upset by the woman's shrieking reaction that he'd stopped playing with the toy. Eventually, Kim had dropped it into the bottom of his toy box.

She tossed the snake onto the bed, then stood on tiptoes to pull Grandma's old sewing basket from the high shelf. Carrying the basket to the bed, she sat down and opened the lid. The faint scent of violets wafted up at her, a reminder of the dear woman who'd baked bread, read bedtime stories and kissed away tears.

Right after Grandma's death, the scent of her favorite flower had made Kim cry. But it'd been ten years since she died and, while Kim still missed her, the smell of violets now made her smile.

She pulled out black thread, needle and scissors and returned the basket to its place in the closet. Gathering her items, she trotted downstairs.

Back in the store, she found Grandpa, Scott and Liz clustered around the mechanical snake. Liz held the remote and guided it toward the front door. Rory lay at Grandpa's feet, looking bored.

"Looks like Homer moves pretty well." Kim set the supplies on top of a counter.

Liz pushed a button and Homer stopped moving. "Yeah. I just wish he'd crawl over bumps." She lifted the robot. "Of course, Homer doesn't move like a real snake. A real snake uses its muscles and scales to push sideways. My teacher said that would be too hard for me to make, even with her help.

But I'll get extra points for the display I'm making that explains everything."

Kim held up Rory's toy. "Well, let's see if we can make Homer look more real."

For the next thirty minutes, Kim cut and sewed while Liz sat beside her, pointing out the location of the underbelly switch and other important electronics that shouldn't be covered with fabric. Kim attached the fabric loosely to allow room for the mechanics to zigzag. On the underside, she cut around the wheels so they could move freely. They decided to keep the rubber snake head, which looked more realistic than the fabric one.

Grandpa was just flipping over the store's closed sign when Kim tied off the last stitch.

She set Homer on the floor. For a moment, everyone gazed down at it.

"He looks real." The joy on Liz's face made the adults smile.

Kim handed the remote control to Liz. "Let's see if he still moves okay."

Liz flipped a switch and pointed the remote at Homer. The mechanical snake undulated forward. The fabric bent in all the right places, the pattern emphasizing the slithering movement. Kim applauded.

And then Rory streaked by. Snatching the snake in the middle, he tossed it into the air, caught it, then pranced around them, the toy wiggling in his mouth.

"Don't laugh," Kim said. "Please don't anyone laugh."

Too late. Everyone was laughing.

Kim exchanged Homer for a dog biscuit and held Rory's collar while Liz tested to make sure the poodle's antics hadn't damaged the mechanism. The snake was fine; Rory hadn't even left teeth marks on the fabric. Thank goodness for poodles' soft mouths.

Liz thanked Kim for Homer's new skin, petted Rory and trotted down the front stairs.

After securing the store for the night, Scott retrieved his casserole from Grandpa's refrigerator and the three of them piled into the car and headed toward Dorothy Tyson's house.

Dorothy and Jared Tyson lived on one of the fragile cliffs overlooking the Chesapeake Bay. The view from their driveway left Kim speechless. From this height, the bay stretched as far as the eye could see, its tranquil blue interrupted only by the occasional cargo ship. Someone had mounted a two-person swing near the cliff edge, a perfect place to curl up with a book.

Carrying Scott's casserole like a shield, she followed Grandpa and Scott up a flight of stairs to the front porch. A young woman answered Grandpa's knock.

"Mr. Hershey, how lovely to see you! Did you see the gorgeous ring your granddaughter found for me?" Holding up her left hand, Jennifer flashed a marquis-shaped diamond. Then her eyes landed on Kim. "Oh! You're here!"

Before Kim could react, Dorothy's daughter wrapped her in a tight embrace. "I love, love, love my ring!"

As Jennifer continued her nervous patter, Kim pushed aside a sudden burst of anger. People handled death in different ways and Jennifer might simply be in denial. She stepped back and introduced the young woman to Scott.

"I'm really sorry about your mom," Kim said.

Tears formed in Jennifer's eyes. Jennifer brushed them aside. "You probably want to see Dad." She held open the door. "He's in the game room."

Jennifer led the way down a dark hallway. Through a doorway on the right, Kim glimpsed a magnificent room with vaulted ceilings, sweeping view of the bay and the most uncomfortable looking furniture she'd ever seen: Straight backed, thinly padded and white, white, white.

Fortunately, Jennifer continued down the hall toward the distinctive mechanical buzzes, beeps and bongs of a computer game.

Kim couldn't help grinning when she saw Dorothy Tyson's husband hunched over a control lever, eyes intent on a flat-screen television, sweat pouring from his bald head.

"Ha! Got you, you sucker! Jenny look at this score."

"Er, Dad, we have company."

Jared Tyson didn't lift his head. "Another casserole lady? Tell her I went to Tahiti."

Grandpa laughed. "Already fighting off the widows?"

The sound of a man's voice jerked Jared from his game.

"Max! Good to see you!" Jared stood and extended a hand. "Jenny, why didn't you tell me it was one of *my* friends?"

"Didn't give me a chance, did ya?" But Jennifer looked more amused than insulted.

"You know my granddaughter, Kim," Grandpa said. "And this is Scott Wilson."

As the men shook hands, Grandpa gestured toward the television. "New game?"

"Nah, Allen -- Jenny's fiancé -- bought it for me last Christmas but Dorothy never allows me to play it. Says the noise bothered her."

"You know you can turn off the sound effects," Kim said.

"Yeah, and then Dorothy says the flashing lights bother her or that I'm rotting my brain. You know Dorothy; she can find fault with anything. I'd better turn this off before she..."

The muscles in his face suddenly drooped. Grandpa laid a hand on Jared's shoulder.

"I keep waiting for her to flounce through the door, you know?" Jared said.

"Yeah, I know."

The sorrow in Grandpa's voice reminded Kim of those lonely days after Grandma died. Grandma had been gone for more than ten years and Kim still missed her.

Not wanting to add to everyone's misery by crying herself, she turned to Jennifer and suggested they place Scott's casserole into the refrigerator.

Like the rest of the house, Dorothy's kitchen projected an icy detachment. The room of white-tile floor, granite counters and stainless steel appliances contained no color, plants or homey decoration.

"We must look like a pair, both denying Mom's death." Jennifer opened the refrigerator door to reveal shelves stuffed with aluminum-foil-covered dishes. "I'm throwing myself into wedding plans and Dad... Well, you can see, he's done little but play that stupid game."

Kim found space on the bottom shelf and slipped the casserole into place. "People have to find their own ways to deal with grief."

"So you don't think it's disrespectful to move my wedding from June to December?" Jennifer reached for a pitcher of iced tea. "Mom was the one who wanted the June bride thing, but Allen and I never wanted to wait that long."

Without waiting for Kim to answer, Jennifer continued talking in a high-pitched, unnatural voice. "We found a gorgeous historic place on the Eastern Shore with a winding staircase that I can glide down just like Scarlett O'Hara. I get so excited when I think about the red-and-white decorations and the fur-trimmed bridesmaids' gowns and for a few minutes it's like Mom's still around."

"Except Mom would have hated a December wedding."

Jennifer bit her lip and for a moment looked like a lost child. "It's hard, you know? Mom was, well, Mom. Dad and I loved her. But she could be so... so overpowering."

Her voice dropped to a whisper. "Part of me's relieved that she's gone. That she's not here to tell me what to do or that I'm stupid or…"

Kim pulled Jennifer into her arms. "It's okay. Sometimes we have mixed feelings when someone dies."

She felt the younger woman tremble.

Kim could well imagine the love/hate relationship Jennifer and her father must have had with Dorothy. A daughter loves her mother simply because children love their parents. And Jared wouldn't have stayed with Dorothy if he didn't love her.

Yet the two of them must have hated the way Dorothy bossed and bullied and generally ran their lives. Unresolved angers were now complicating their reaction to Dorothy's death.

For a moment, Kim considered explaining some of the psychological dynamics following a sudden death. But she didn't know Jennifer well enough to decide if such knowledge would help or hinder.

Jennifer stepped back. Even though her face was pale, her eyes were dry. "We should probably bring the guys their drink."

Kim poured the drinks. As she helped carry the glasses into the living room, she silently reminded herself that Jennifer or Jared might have had reason to kill Dorothy.

Grandpa accepted the glass Kim handed him. "Jared was telling us that when Walt drove him home from the banquet, the two of them decided to play a few games before Dorothy arrived home."

"How long did you and Uncle Walt play?" Kim handed Scott his glass and slid onto the couch beside him.

Jared tossed her a sheepish smile. "Till Ruby got home, found the house empty and called Walt's cell." Using his glass, he gestured toward the television. "It's a pretty addictive game."

Kim turned to Jennifer. "What time did you get home from the banquet?"

"I didn't go." Jennifer shrugged. "Mom bought us tickets, of course. But Allen had to work, so I stayed home."

Seeing Kim's eyes flick around the room, Jennifer hastily added "Not here. Allen and I rent an apartment."

Interesting. Uncle Walt could provide an alibi for Jared, but Jennifer had been home alone.

"I guess you heard that the police think Dorothy interrupted a burglary," she said. "But just in case they're wrong, uh, can either of you think of anyone who might have wanted to hurt her?"

Jared shook his head. "Dorothy could make people mad. But not mad enough to kill. I mean, you'd have to be crazy to get that mad, wouldn't you?"

Kim glanced at Scott, not quite sure where to go next. He dipped his chin, then leaned forward. "Sir, you said your wife angered people. Anyone in particular?"

Jared sighed and leaned back. With an apologetic glance at Grandpa, he said, "Since becoming chairman of the museum board, she's done a lot of griping about the members."

Grandpa chuckled. "Not happy that she couldn't herd us?"

As always, Grandpa's laugh was infectious. Jared smiled.

"You could say that," he said. "Anyway..." He held out his right hand and touched one finger at a time as he mentioned a name. "Matt Garfield yelled at her because she challenged his building permit to expand his new gym. Robert Jefferson tried to get her removed from the school board, said she didn't care about the children. Wilma Bradford fought Dorothy over museum exhibits--"

"That one I heard about," Grandpa said. "Wilma accused Dorothy of trying to rewrite history."

Jared nodded. "If you really want to know about Dorothy's battles, ask the poor schmuck who got paid to listen to her."

"Dorothy was seeing a psychiatrist?" Grandpa's eyes widened.

Jennifer rolled her eyes. "He's talking about her hairdresser, Ryan Hardy."

Chapter 11

The following morning, shortly before her ten a.m. hair appointment, Kim pulled into the beauty salon's parking lot. Reluctant to turn off the car, she gripped the steering wheel and fought the rising panic.

Memories of previous experiences with beauticians flooded her mind. There was the time she'd requested a one-inch trim and left the shop feeling scalped. And the disastrous highlights that turned orange. The worst, however, had been the time she'd left the salon looking like Bozo the clown.

How the heck was she going to quiz customers about Dorothy Tyson while protecting her hair from the guy with the flashing scissors?

The shop's dirty-brown exterior did nothing to allay her fears.

She should have asked Aunt Ginny to come. Ginny would have wrung every rumor from the staff and customers before the shampoo girl finished rinsing Kim's thick hair. With Aunt Ginny here, she could have paid for the shampoo and left without going near Ryan Hardy.

Maybe she should reschedule.

Coward.

Turning off the car, she stepped out into the August humidity. Her glasses fogged.

Grumbling, she tromped inside. The stench of hair bleach and nail polish remover assaulted her. To the left, chattering female voices competed with the roar of a hairdryer while, from deeper in the store, the splattering of water suddenly cut off.

As her glasses cleared, she inspected the waiting room. A circle of cobalt blue, plush chairs surrounded a clear glass coffee table covered in hair magazines. Three women perched there, two dressed in shorts and t-shirts. The third woman, however, was draped in a heavy black gown. Silver foils dotted the top of her head, the remaining hair sticking out in all directions as if she'd stuck her finger in a socket.

Even as Kim recognized the foils as part of the highlighting process, her brain silently screamed "Run."

She turned back the way she'd come.

"Kim! Is that really you?"

Busted, Kim wheeled around to find herself face-to-face with Leslie Darling, one of Brittany's best friends.

Grandpa's voice in her head whispered: *Never show a bully fear.*

Reminding herself that Leslie had run away during Kim's schoolyard battle with Brittany -- proving Grandpa's theory that most bullies were cowards -- Kim squared her shoulders and lifted her chin. She could survive this.

She forced a smile and thrust out her hand. "Leslie, nice to see you."

"I was surprised to see your name on Ryan's schedule." Leslie shook Kim's hand, then guided her toward the reception counter. "Thought you'd moved to Timbuktu or something."

Kim stiffened, wondering if she'd just been insulted. Leslie, however, was already staring down at a large appointment book. Picking up a pencil, she checked a box, then looked up. Kim studied Brittany's friend, but couldn't see any animosity in her eyes.

"You can sit over there." Leslie pointed to the blue chairs. "Ryan will be with you shortly. Would you like a drink? We have wine, soft drinks and sparkling water."

"Ah, do you have Coke?"

"Of course. Diet?"

"No, I think high test right now." Caffeine and sugar might calm her fluttery stomach.

Leslie's brows furrowed. "High test?"

"Not diet."

With a nod, Leslie disappeared through a door, returning a minute later with a bottle of Coke and a plastic glass filled with ice. Kim accepted the drink.

Instead of retiring to the waiting room, however, she decided to start her investigation.

"So do you enjoy working here?" In high school, Leslie told everyone she'd be a doctor. In twelfth grade, however, she'd dropped out to marry Chad Martin, the school's star quarterback. The only surprise was that she retained her maiden name.

Leslie beamed. "Isn't it great? Ryan trained with Fekkai, you know." She swept her hand to encompass the front area. "He promised me that after I finish cosmetology classes, he'll let me do my interning here."

Kim poured a small amount of Coke into her glass. "How soon will you finish classes?"

Leslie frowned. "Well, I haven't started yet. The best school's in Baltimore and there's never any time what with taking care of the kids and Chad..."

Kim opened her mouth to commiserate, but Leslie had already recovered. "Husbands are high maintenance... Oh!" Leslie covered her hand with her mouth, feigning surprise. "But you wouldn't know, would you? You've never married."

Kim sighed. Some things never change.

Leslie's one-upmanship tendency might prove useful, but Kim didn't have the wherewithal to cross swords right now.

She answered Leslie's smirk with a shrug and turned away. Carrying her drink to the seating area, she settled on a surprisingly comfortable chair.

"Don't mind Leslie," the woman with the hair foils said. "She may never go to cosmetology school, but she graduated at the head of the class in Bitch School."

Kim grinned. "Probably the company she keeps."

"Ah, I see you're a Brittany fan, too."

Reaching for a glass of white wine, the woman introduced herself as "Shawn" no last name. Kim supplied her first name.

"If you want to avoid Leslie, next time schedule your appointment on Friday," Shawn said. "That's her day off."

Shawn set her glass on the table and started to return her attention to the open magazine in her lap.

Wanting to keep the conversation going -- as a regular, Shawn might know something useful -- Kim said, "I'm embarrassed to admit this, but I'm a bit nervous. It's my first time here and..." She shrugged. "I haven't had the best luck with hair dressers."

Shawn set the magazine aside. "Don't worry. Ryan really did train with Fekkai, so he's great with long hair. He won't scalp you. How'd you hear about him?"

"Several people told me about Ryan, but I also understand Dorothy Tyson came here."

Shawn's face froze, her expression carefully blank.

"Were you a friend of Dorothy's?" Shawn said.

"Oh, no, I barely knew the woman. She just seemed to have opinions..."

Shawn laughed. "You can say that again. And, lucky for you, Dorothy's support of Ryan was well-founded. The poor man had to style her hair every single week. I don't know how he tolerated it."

Hmmm... If this salon was like others she'd visited, a once-a-week appointment would certainly make Dorothy privy to all of the local gossip, including who had acquired new jewelry.

Before she could quiz Shawn further, a young woman dressed in a cobalt-blue smock appeared in a doorway.

"Shawn? We're ready to wash."

With a quick goodbye, Shawn disappeared through the door. Curious, Kim followed as far as the doorframe and peeked inside. Rows of shampoo bowls lined the wall to her right. But instead of the typical reclining plastic chairs used in most salons, the white-upholstered chairs here resembled comfy loungers.

A chill ran up Kim's spine. Free wine, high-tech shampoo chairs, hot-shot stylist... How much was this bit of investigating going to cost her?

Before she could think of a casual way to question Leslie, another blue-smocked woman appeared and called her name. Introducing herself as "Anita," the new woman led the way into a different room, this one lined with mirrors. Shelves and drawers painted white flanked the edges of each individual mirror, while cobalt-blue chairs perched directly in front.

Anita led the way past a young man rolling a woman's gray hair into perm-style curlers, a middle-aged woman snipping the hair of an executive-type man and an attractive man of about Kim's age wielding a blow dryer on a teenaged girl.

Pausing at a vacant chair, Anita instructed Kim to set her purse on a shelf and don a wrap-around nylon gown. After Kim settled into the plush chair, Anita draped a cape of heavy plastic around her shoulders and secured it at the neck with Velcro.

"Ryan will be with you shortly."

Kim nodded, then swiveled her chair so she could study the other people in the room.

The hairdryer drowned all sound, but the room was small enough that once the noise stopped she'd probably hear everyone's conversation. The woman receiving the perm chatted happily to her stylist; he responded with an occasional pat to her shoulder or laugh. The businessman appeared equally chatty with the woman wielding the scissors.

Beside her, the hairdryer shut off.

As the stylist switched the dryer for a comb, his teenaged customer said, "So, Ryan, should I hook up with him or not?"

Kim bit her lip. The girl couldn't be more than fourteen or fifteen. Though her loud voice carried throughout the salon, no one reacted to her words.

For a moment, Ryan continued to fluff the girl's shiny, straight hair.

"Not." He reached for a hand mirror, passed it to the girl and spun the chair around so she could study the back of her hair. "He sounds too immature." Returning the mirror to its place, he added, "But if you decide to do it, use protection."

Beaming at him, the girl leaped from the chair. "Thanks, Ryan, you're the best." With a toss of her head, she strode toward the front room.

Ryan turned to smile at Kim and for a moment her breath caught. No wonder the stylist was so popular. The wind-blown blond hair, blue eyes and smile lines reminded her of Robert Redford.

"So, Kimberley West, what can I do for you today?"

"Just a trim." Kim held up her thumb and index finger with a small space between. "And I mean an inch or so."

Ryan's eyes flashed with amusement as he turned her chair toward the mirror and stood behind her.

"Do you always wear your hear in a ponytail?" He tugged the elastic loose and handed it to her.

"I don't like it in my face."

Nodding, he ran fingers through her hair, lifting it as if weighing it.

"Lotta hair here. Waves natural?"

Kim nodded and stared in the mirror, watching as he continued to manipulate her hair. What the heck was he doing? Should she remind him again that she just wanted a trim? Tell him she's changed her mind?

Ryan's eyes suddenly met hers in the mirror. "You've got too much hair here; there's no movement."

Kim opened her mouth to protest but he silenced her with a raised hand. "I'm not saying cut off the length. But you need some shaping and long layers to make these waves lay right." He cupped the sides of her hair so that the very front cleared her shoulders. "If I angle the sides like this, add light layers for movement, your hair should be easier to style." He grinned. "And you can still pull it into a ponytail. Deal?"

"Let him do it."

Kim turned to her left, surprised to see Shawn now sitting in the chair recently vacated by the teenager. The foils were gone; her wet hair hung limp to her jawline.

"Trust me, you'll love the way Ryan will style your hair," Shawn continued.

Feeling a bit trapped, Kim gulped and agreed. Probably best to not alienate the man who'd be wielding sharp scissors near her eyes.

Ryan patted her shoulder. "Let's get you shampooed."

Anita magically appeared at her side and beckoned Kim to follow. Within minutes, Kim reclined in a cushy chair while Anita swooshed warm water through her hair.

"Have you worked here long?"

Anita shrugged. "Coupla years. Tips are good and most people are nice."

"Bet you get some demanding ones, too."

Anita worked shampoo into Kim's hair. "Oh my, yes. Not the men so much, but some of these women can be downright nasty."

"Nasty how?"

Water sluiced through Kim's hair and she strained to hear Anita's reply.

"They'll complain that the water was too hot or too cold or that I was using the wrong shampoo or wasn't scrubbing their scalp enough or I scrubbed it too hard." Turning off the water, she reached for more shampoo. "A lot of the older ladies like to boss me as I'm working." She raised her voice into a nasal soprano. "Don't put the conditioner so close to my scalp. You didn't rinse long enough."

More water splashed as Anita continued imitating her most difficult customers. When her tone grew haughty, Kim interrupted the tirade.

"Now *that* sounds like Dorothy Tyson," Kim said.

Rory would have been impressed by Anita's answering growl. "That woman would try the patience of Ghandi."

Suspecting a direct question would stop the flow of information, Kim attempted a joke.

"I guess the police have narrowed the suspect list to the State of Maryland?"

Anita laughed. "Maybe even the entire East Coast. She even tried to boss Ryan."

Now this was interesting. "Bet he didn't appreciate that."

"Oh, Ryan is so laid back, he just laughed it off. He's probably the only stylist in the world who could deal with Dorothy without getting angry."

The water stopped. Anita wrapped a towel around Kim's hair and instructed her to return to Ryan.

Kim plopped into her chair and looked around. Beside her, Ryan wielded dryer and round brush, the brush tugging Shawn's hair straight as the dryer followed its length. She couldn't distinguish where the foils had been; the copper highlights blended completely with Shawn's light brown hair.

At the far end, the young man squirted something stinky onto his customer's perm rods. In the middle, the businessman was gone, his chair now occupied by a middle-aged woman. The female stylist brushed goopy stuff -- hair dye? -- on the woman's roots.

"So did you attend the museum banquet?" the woman shouted over the dryer noise.

"We toured the museum, but Ryan wasn't feeling well so we left before the dinner."

Ryan turned off the dryer and reached for a large-barrel curling iron. "Tonya, I told you to stay," he said. "We'd already paid for the meal."

Tonya? Kim willed her too-expressive face to remain still. She'd never have connected the frumpy woman stylist with the dashing Ryan. The deep lines around Tonya's mouth and bruising beneath her eyes belonged to a woman a good ten years older than Ryan.

"We didn't go either," Tonya's client said. "I was wondering about the quality of the food."

Kim couldn't resist. "The food was wonderful."

Six pairs of eyes turned toward her. Maybe she shouldn't have spoken, should have pretended she wasn't listening. But this might be her only opportunity to bring up Dorothy Tyson's name.

"They served rockfish," she continued, "and somehow managed to cook it perfectly for all of those people."

"Oh, that's fabulous news," Shawn said. "We need another good restaurant in the county."

The others agreed. Before anyone could change the subject, Kim plunged ahead. "It was a really nice affair. It's a shame the evening ended in murder."

Shawn gasped. Ryan dropped the comb he was using. Tonya's brush froze.

Oops. Maybe she'd pushed this too fast.

"Well, if you ask me, what's surprising is that no one killed Dorothy before." The woman getting a perm scowled.

"Now Mrs. Buchannan." The youngest stylist wagged his finger. "You know it's not right to speak ill of the dead."

If he'd been standing closer, Kim would have kicked him in frustration. She needed to hear all of the gossip about Dorothy.

Tonya resumed painting color on her client's hair. Ryan retrieved his comb and reached for a hand mirror.

"Oh, don't give me that pious crap, Jacob Paul," Mrs. Buchannan said. "She got on your nerves, too. Weren't you just complaining about the way she treated you like a kid? And Ryan, I saw you clench your teeth every time she ordered you around like a servant."

For a moment, Ryan's fingers tightened on the mirror. Shawn slipped it from his hand.

"You've got to admit," Shawn said, "Dorothy always entertained us with her gossip, ha, ha." She studied the back of her long bob. "Now how will we ever know when someone joins the new gym or inherits a fortune?"

As Shawn stood, Kim searched for a way to continue the conversation.

"Was Dorothy that much of a gossip?" She widened her eyes just in case anyone bothered to look at her.

"Oh, it was worse than that, honey." Mrs. Buchannan leaned forward. "When she wasn't mouthing off or pushing someone around, she was eavesdropping on private conversations." She shook her shoulders. "What a woman says to her hairdresser should be privileged information like with a lawyer."

"Well, most people understand that," the lady having her hair dyed said. "Dorothy just ignored all social niceties."

Mrs. Buchannan was nodding her head so emphatically Kim feared she'd flip the curlers right from her head.

"Remember when she..."

But Kim didn't get to hear the rest of Mrs. Buchannan's comment because Ryan now stood behind her, combing through her hair and commenting about its thickness.

"I see why you wear it long." He reached for a pair of scissors. "The weight helps keep it from bushing out." He snipped a strand.

"That was more than an inch!"

"Of course it is. We need to shape the front, remember?" More hair fell to the floor. "And add some layers to give it movement." He jiggled his fingers through what he'd just cut and studied the way the hair fell back into place. "Trust me, you're going to love this." He lifted another chunk of hair.

Kim closed her eyes and forced herself to unclench her fists. It'll grow back. Hair grows fast in the summer, right? Except, this was the end of summer.

Mrs. Buchannan's voice intruded. "Do you know why Mary Klein killed her?"

Opening her eyes, Kim whipped around. "Mary did not kill her!"

"Darling," Ryan said. "Unless you want a mohawk, you need to hold still when I'm cutting."

"Sorry." Kim settled back in the chair. "But Mary did not kill Dorothy Tyson."

"Of course she didn't." Ryan resumed cutting. "Mary is too sweet to kill a spider let alone a human."

Mrs. Buchannan, however, wouldn't drop the topic. "Brittany Bonnet said Mary is the main suspect."

Kim ground her teeth. "Brittany lies."

"Someone said Mary was the only person to have a key to the museum," hair-dye lady said.

"You didn't need a key to get into the museum," Kim said. "Dorothy fired the night watchman. Anyone could have hidden in the museum until after it closed. Besides, Dorothy took Mary's key."

"So if it wasn't Mary, who was it?" Mrs. Buchannan demanded.

"My vote is the jewel thieves who've been breaking into people's homes-- Ouch."

"Sorry." Ryan set down the scissors and used the comb to tug at the piece of hair he held. "Knot."

"Was it only jewels taken from the museum?" hair-dye lady said.

"No," Kim said. "The thieves also took swords and daggers and things. I think some were encrusted with gemstones."

"I can't imagine jewel thieves being interested in the museum's collection," Ryan said. "I made a point of viewing those gems before we went home. The pirate's ruby, the one in the amulet, was okay. But the rest barely sparkled."

"That's because they were cut in old-fashioned styles."

"What do you mean by old-fashioned?" Ryan said.

"Before people learned to cut facets in gems, they simply polished them, usually by rubbing two gems together," Kim said. "The Burmese began mining rubies some time around 2500 BCE, but they didn't facet them until well into the 13th Century. Even then, the cuts were pretty crude and people didn't do much faceting until the Renaissance." As she talked, she felt the tension in her shoulders ease. "The round, brilliant cut that we know today was developed in the early 20th Century."

"But faceted stones are so much prettier," Ryan. "Why did people wait so long to cut gemstones?"

"Lapidarists needed to develop tools that would allow them to make precision cuts without destroying the gem. Even diamonds will shatter if you use the wrong tools or cut at the wrong angle."

"Well, if the museum gems weren't that pretty," Mrs. Buchannan cut in, "why would anyone steal them?"

"The stones were quality diamonds, emeralds and rubies."

"But surely the gems would be too distinctive for a thief to sell them to a pawn shop or something," Ryan said. "Unless they could be re-cut?"

"Yeah, you could re-cut them," Kim said. "But then you'd have smaller gems that weren't worth as much as the original. Probably wouldn't be cost effective."

Ryan returned the scissors and comb to his table and reached for the hairdryer. "Sounds like the value was mostly historical. Or maybe the gems would appeal to a collector."

The rumble of the dryer made continued conversation impossible. Even so, elation swelled Kim's chest. Ryan was absolutely correct: No pawn shop would accept gems that clearly came from a museum.

Someone who collected pirate memorabilia or historical gems, however, might be inclined to ignore the gems' provenance.

Maybe the museum thieves had been hired by a collector. Would an honest person who collected pirate memorabilia know the names of dishonest collectors? If so, would they talk to Kim?

The hairdryer cut off just as Mrs. Buchannan said, "Mary Klein must know people who collect pirate stuff."

"Mary would know the honest ones," Kim said. "But jewel thieves might know the dishonest collectors."

"Are you a detective or something?" Ryan's eyes met hers in the mirror. "You sound like you're investigating Dorothy's murder."

"Oh, no, nothing like that. I'm just a friend of Mary's. I don't want her to be arrested for something she didn't do."

Ryan separated out a hunk of hair and wound it around a curling iron. "I wouldn't want to see Mary arrested either. But you should let the police handle this."

"The police aren't looking at anyone but Mary."

"Well, just be careful." He wound another curl. "We don't know if her murder was accidental or intentional. Either way, whoever did it is dangerous."

"I'm just going to give them some other suspects; I'm not going to confront anyone or anything." Kim turned her attention to the mirror. The stylist had cut the sides of her hair so that it angled from below her chin down to her shoulders. As she watched, Ryan returned the curling iron to its holder, then proceeded to fluff the ends of her hair. Handing her a mirror, he turned the chair so she could study the back.

"Wow." True to his word, he'd left the back long. But whenever she moved her head, her hair swayed just like in the shampoo commercials. "Is this what you mean by movement?"

For the first time, Ryan flashed a full smile. "Absolutely." He turned the chair so she could face the mirrors. "You can still pull it into a ponytail." He lifted the front back to demonstrate. "But you can also just let it swing or, if you like, pull up the sides into a clip." He showed her how to pull the sides back from her face.

"But I don't own a curling iron and I'm clumsy with a dryer."

"You don't need to use either. After you dry your hair, pour a quarter size drop of product into your palm." He demonstrated. "Rub it between your hands." He held out both hands so she could see. "And starting half way down your hair, work the product in and comb through." He wiped his hands onto a towel. "When you're done, use your hands to scrunch sections of hair. This will recreate your natural waves. Then just let it air dry."

Tentatively, Kim touched her hair, expecting it to feel crunchy or sticky. Instead, it felt silky.

"So do you love it?" Ryan said.

Kim grinned at him. "Absolutely."

Waving goodbye to the remaining women, Kim strode to the front. At the cash register, Leslie presented her with a bill. She tried not to gasp.

As she tucked her credit card back into her wallet, her cell phone rang. Caller ID said it was Mary.

Before she could say hello, Mary blurted out "Kim, I need you! Please, can you come to the house?"

"Calm down." Kim swung her heavy purse over her shoulder and headed out the door. "What's wrong?"

"The police called. They're on their way here. Kim, I think they're going to arrest me!"

Chapter 12

Kim pulled into Mary's driveway, relieved to see that she'd arrived ahead of the police. She didn't for a minute believe the police were going to arrest her -- Lieutenant Brockley had told Mary he had more questions in light of "new information" -- but she wanted to be available for her friend.

Climbing from the car, she stretched and glanced around. Though she talked to Mary frequently, she hadn't yet visited her home.

Box-shaped cottages painted pastel shades lined the narrow street. Mary's was a pale blue accented by white shutters. Like the other homes, the front porch held wicker furniture (white) and a two-person swing, also white.

The cottages may have been similar, but even without the house numbers Kim could have identified Mary's: Only Mary's yard was fronted by a white picket fence.

Kim's stomach muscles clenched as if someone had punched her.

For a moment, she was back in elementary school, sitting on a playground swing, telling "when I grow up" stories. Brooke, the dreamer, longed to make her mark as a famous photographer. Kim alternated between becoming a female Indiana Jones and studying geology so she could help Grandpa in the store.

As Kim and Brooke talked, Mary remained silent, her sneaker-clad feet pumping the swing.

"What about you, Mary?" Kim had said. "What do you want to do?"

Mary's eyes had grown dreamy. "When I grow up, I want a husband who loves me, two children -- a boy and a girl -- and a cottage with a white picket fence."

Even as a child, Kim understood the underlying message: Mary wanted stability. With an alcoholic mother and non-existent father, Mary never knew family life until Kim pulled her into her orbit.

"What if the cottage doesn't have a picket fence?" Brooke teased.

Mary's mouth had stretched into a thin line. "Then I'll put one in."

Now Kim stared at that white fence, the symbol of Mary's success, and marveled that the quiet child she'd known had not only married and borne children, but also maintained a career as museum director.

But Brittany's unfair accusations, coupled with police blindness, threatened to destroy Mary's dream.

As if on cue, a sheriff's car pulled to the curb and two doors opened. Kim turned her back and unhooked Rory from his seatbelt. On her way here, she'd stopped by Grandpa's shop to pick up the young dog, reasoning that petting him would help calm Mary. Now she was grateful for the distraction.

She clipped the leash to Rory's collar and told him it was okay to exit.

With a graceful leap, he cleared the car and landed at the feet of Lieutenant Bill Brockley.

"How's the hero dog?" Brockley kneeled and gave Rory a vigorous scratch while the traitorous poodle washed his face.

Standing, Brockley offered Kim his hand. "Didn't expect to see you here."

She shook his hand, but withdrew it quickly. The man oozed sexuality and she couldn't afford to be drawn into his dark eyes. She needed to remember he was the enemy.

Brockley's mouth quirked, but he wisely didn't comment. Instead, he nodded at the woman beside him. "I think you've met Officer Darnell."

The petite blond -- the officer who'd been the first to arrive at the museum the night of the murder -- didn't offer to shake hands. She eyed Rory, jumping back when he took a step toward her.

"Don't worry; he only attacks bad guys." Brockley's eyes twinkled.

Darnell scowled. "I'm a cat person."

Well, that explained Kim's growing dislike for Officer Darnell. What was wrong with liking both dogs and cats? The sudden urge to punch the woman had nothing to do with the way she ogled Brockley when he wasn't looking.

She turned her back on the woman and addressed Brockley.

"Does Mary need a lawyer?"

Brockley shrugged. "That's certainly her right, but we just have some questions." He waved his hand in an "after you" fashion.

Mary opened the front door before Kim could knock. Kim inhaled sharply.

In an attempt to disguise her pale face and shadowed eyes, her friend had applied thick makeup. Then she'd nervously licked off her lipstick, leaving behind the dark lip liner. Add in the streaks of mascara from crying and Mary's face now resembled a French mime.

Kim threw a protective arm around her.

"It'll be okay," she whispered.

Stepping away, she bumped into a hallway table. A metal bowl holding keys and loose change tinkled.

"Sorry." Mary gestured to the cluttered tabletop. "I know it's crowded, but it's the only way to corral all of the stuff."

"Do you want us in there?" Kim gestured to the closest room, an airy space decorated in blue and white.

When Mary nodded, Kim whispered, "Go wash your face; we'll meet you in there."

Mary moved off and Kim led the others into what appeared to be the main living room. Rory's paws skittered on the hardwood floor until they reached the hemp-colored area rug -- the kind of rug that never showed dirt.

She moved a yellow throw pillow and settled onto the overstuffed sofa. Rory plopped onto her feet. Brockley reclined on a chair across from them. Darnell remained standing.

Kim glanced around, noting Kevin's handiwork in the custom-designed recessed bookshelves and cupboards. In addition to the usual family photos and books, Mary had filled the shelves with what were clearly the children's prized possessions: framed drawings, sea shells, fossils, an osprey feather.

Darnell lifted the feather, snorted and returned it to the shelf.

Mary returned and settled beside Kim. She'd not only scrubbed her face, but had replaced her contact lenses with glasses. Now she looked totally like the frightened child who'd stood in the principal's office. Kim took her hand.

"Where are the children?"

"Bobby's off somewhere with Liz." Mary's eyes followed Officer Darnell. The pushy woman roamed the room, studying books, lifting photographs and children's treasures and replacing them incorrectly.

With each reach of Darnell's hand, Mary's neck muscles grew tighter. "I took Kimmy next door; my neighbor loves to babysit."

Kim glared at Darnell. Clearly, the woman was trying to keep Mary off balance. Maybe standard cop practice?

But there was something more in the woman's swagger, a silent assertion of the right to be here, to mess with Mary's things.

Well, two can play psychological games. Thanks to Brittany, Kim knew exactly how to deflate Darnell's confidence.

She turned to Brockley and carefully composed her words. "Please ask Officer Darnell to join us so we can get this over with."

Darnell froze. Back rigid, she twisted toward Kim, blue eyes narrowed. Kim fought the trickle of fear. She'd made an enemy. But the woman couldn't arrest her -- she and Grandpa both had alibis for the time Dorothy died -- so there was nothing to fear. Right?

Kim looked away first.

Brockley, in typical male fashion, totally missed the emotional interplay. Probably thought it was perfectly reasonable for Kim to defer to the higher-ranking officer instead of making the request directly to Officer Darnell.

He nodded to the remaining chair. "Officer Darnell."

The woman sat and transferred her scowl to Mary.

"We just want to go over the statement you gave us." Brockley's voice was gentle. "You said you were responsible for making duplicate keys for the museum."

Mary nodded. "We needed to change the locks after the workers finished. The locksmith was going to come on Monday to do that. But, without telling anyone, Dorothy insisted the locksmith make the change on Saturday. The first I heard about it was when she gave me the only key to be copied."

She flicked her eyes to Kim. "You remember her giving me the key, at the beach?"

Not sure where Brockley's questioning was heading, Kim simply nodded.

Mary turned her attention back to Brockley. "It was a last-minute thing and there was so much to do before the banquet and, well, you know it seems like it takes forever to make a single key when you're in a hurry. So rather than wait for keys to be made for everyone, I told them to just make enough for the people who needed a key immediately. I'd come back when there was more time to make the others."

Brockley leaned back, feigning nonchalance. But Kim saw the slight narrowing of his eyes. Whatever he asked next was important.

"And how many keys did you make?"

Mary ticked off names on her fingers. "One for the restaurant manager so he could close up after the banquet. One for the guard who works days and one for the night guard.

"I thought I'd made four keys -- one for Dorothy -- but I guess I forgot."

"Why do you say you forgot?" Brockley said.

Mary gestured toward the hallway table and the bowl holding keys and change, then shrugged.

"After making the keys, I tagged them all with yellow so they'd be easy to find and tossed them into the bowl. Then I got ready for the banquet. But when I collected the keys from the bowl to take with me, well, there were only four with yellow tags. The original one and the three duplicates."

"So when you left here for the banquet, you had four keys in your possession."

Kim frowned. Where the heck was he going with this?

"Well, I didn't have them very long. When I got to the museum, I gave a key to the restaurant manager and the two guards-- Hey, did you get the key back from the night guard?"

She turned to Kim. "Would you believe Dorothy fired the poor man right before the banquet because she smelled beer on his breath? That's why no one was there when Dorothy..." Mary gulped.

Kim's heartbeat quickened. She'd forgotten about the argument she'd overheard when she was standing in the museum bathroom.

"Yeah, I heard Brittany and Dorothy fighting over it." She stared at Brockley. "Shouldn't the fired guard be considered a suspect?"

Brockley frowned, irritated with her interruption. Too bad.

"Mr. Faulkner, the guard, said he gave the key to Mrs. Tyson when she fired him." He met Kim's eyes. "And before you ask, we found an extra museum key in Mrs. Tyson's possessions."

"But... I don't understand," Mary said. "If Dorothy already had a key, why did she need mine?"

"You tell me." Brockley's voice held no emotion.

"Oh, for heaven's sake." Kim crossed her arms. "Dorothy was a bully. Demanding Mary's key in front of everyone was an opportunity to exert her power and embarrass someone. She'd have done the same if she had a pocketful of keys."

Brockley raised an eyebrow. Officer Darnell, however, couldn't contain her animosity.

"Then how do you explain this?" Darnell tossed a clear bag on the coffee table.

Kim peered over her friend's shoulder as she lifted the bag. Inside was a credit-card receipt with the name of a hardware store on top. Mary's signature was at the bottom.

Mary shrugged. "Looks like a copy of my receipt for making the keys."

Officer Darnell leaned forward and tapped a pointed fingernail on the bag. "You told us you made three keys. Says here you made four."

"I *intended* to make four. I must have run out before the fourth one was ready."

"The man who made the keys says he doesn't create an invoice until after he's made all of the keys," Darnell said. "If you paid for four, then you were given four."

"That makes no sense!" Mary stood and marched to the table by the front door. "I keep all of the keys in here." She rummaged through the bowl of keys. "Saturday night, I could only find one..." She frowned and lifted a key.

Kim could see the yellow tag dangling from it. Officer Darnell shot Brockley a triumphant grin.

"That means nothing." Kim pointed at the bowl of keys. "Did you see how many keys are in there? Anyone could miss a single key when pressed for time."

"But not anyone was seen sneaking back into the museum after the victim evicted her," Darnell said.

Mary gasped. "But..."

"Don't say anything more." Kim stood. "It's time to call a lawyer. My cousin Tony probably knows someone--"

"But I don't need a lawyer!" Mary lifted her chin. "I didn't do anything wrong. Sure, I spied on the meeting--"

"Mary!"

Hearing the panic in Kim's voice, Rory leaped to his feet. Kim laid a calming hand on his head and fought to keep her voice level.

"Mary, don't say anything until we get you a lawyer."

"But I can't afford a lawyer!" Mary glared at Officer Darnell. "And I shouldn't have to hire one because I'm innocent."

Darnell shrugged. "If you're so innocent, then you won't mind us looking around."

Mary threw her arms wide. "Be my guest."

"No!" Kim rushed to her friend's side. "Don't let them do this."

"Why not? What are they going to do, arrest me because there are dust bunnies under Bobby's bed?"

Kim turned to Lieutenant Brockley. "Don't you need a warrant to search someone's house?"

Brockley stood. "Not if we have the homeowner's permission to search."

"Mary, tell them they don't have permission."

But Mary's eyes were locked on Officer Darnell's. "Do it then get out of my home."

Darnell returned Mary's glare.

"Mrs. Klein, would you care to accompany us?" Brockley's voice was mild.

Mary shook her head. The two officers clomped upstairs.

As soon as they were out of hearing range, Kim wheeled on her friend. "You know better than to give blanket permission to cops."

"That woman's a bully. She'll hound me until she gets her way." Her face softened and she touched Kim's arm. "There's nothing for them to find. Let them search and then she'll leave me alone."

"Leave you alone? You're acting like this is personal."

Mary turned away, folding her arms across her chest. "Just drop it Kim, okay?"

Kim sensed a story here, maybe even something important, but the stubborn set of Mary's shoulders indicated the topic was closed. For now.

A thumping from upstairs reminded her of the immediate danger.

"Well, if you're not going to stop this, I'm at least going to make sure they don't damage anything. Rory, you stay here with Mary."

She found Brockley and Darnell in the master bedroom. Brockley was bent over the chest of drawers, lifting stacks of clothing and gently returning it to its original place.

Darnell stood before an open closet, flipping through the hanging garments, searching pockets and moving on. As she flicked aside a cotton dress, it fell to the floor. Darnell ignored it, stuffing a hand into the pockets of the next dress.

"Hey!" Kim marched over to the closet and scooped the fallen dress from the floor. "Mary gave you permission to search, not to destroy her house." She pointed to the other blouses and skirts laying crumpled on the closet floor. "Can't you do this neatly?"

"Don't interfere with police business or I'll have to arrest you." Darnell snatched the dress from Kim and tossed it onto the floor. She reached for another dress.

"That's enough, Officer Darnell."

Brockley's voice rumbled in her ear. Startled, Kim whipped around and crashed into a warm body. Brockley gripped her arms, steadying her. Kim stepped back, trying to put distance between them. For a moment, the corners of his eyes crinkled. Then they hardened and transferred to Officer Darnell.

"Please make sure everything is returned to its original position." Though he'd used the word "please," he left no doubt the request was, in fact, a command.

Darnell's hands tightened on the dress she clutched, wrinkling it. "Yes, sir."

Brockley held the woman's eyes for a moment, then nodded. "This will go faster if we split up," he said.

"No." Kim straightened. "We stay together." She crossed her arms, trying to ignore the trembling in her knees. "Mary may not want to watch you. But I do."

She held her breath, waiting for Brockley to chastise her. His eyes widened, then he gave a brief nod.

Kim could feel Officer Darnell's glare boring into her back. The woman's Gestapo tactics were totally out of place in this quiet county. She'd be much more at home in a big city with its rampant crime. So why was she working here?

While Darnell returned Mary's clothes to their hangars, Brockley finished searching the rest of the bedroom. Kim followed the two officers into the master bath and watched while they lifted the toilet lid, opened the medicine cabinet, shuffled through linens. Darnell even emptied the plastic hamper, searched its contents, then stuffed the clothes back inside.

They tramped into the next room, a ruffly affair with pink poodles painted on the walls. Darnell wrinkled her nose and opened a dresser that had been painted pink. In this, at least, Kim agreed with her. All that pink made her want to gag.

In contrast, Bobby's room was blue. Blue walls, blue bedspread, blue rug -- what you could see of it. In typical boy fashion, he'd decorated every flat surface with clothes, computer games and empty potato chip bags.

The remaining upstairs room was a neutral colored bathroom clearly used by both children.

Darnell stuffed the children's clothes back into the hamper and sighed. "Let's try the kitchen next."

Mary had decorated the kitchen in pale yellow with green trim. Kim leaned against the doorframe and watched Officer Darnell open a green canister. Before Darnell could put her grubby fingers into the flour, Kim said "You might want to use a spoon."

When Darnell glared at her, Kim widened her eyes. "The spoon will protect your clothes."

"Use a spoon," Brockley said without lifting his head from the drawer he searched.

They searched the cabinets and drawers in silence. Brockley sighed and closed what appeared to be a catchall drawer. Crossing to the refrigerator, he opened the top freezer.

From her position by the door, Kim could see it'd been stuffed with ice cream, popsicles and a few mystery packages with handwriting on them. When she was growing up, Grandpa's freezer always contained ice cream. Chocolate for Kim, strawberry for Tiffany, vanilla for Aunt Emerald.

Of course, the flavors in Mary's freezer had fancy names: Strawberry Shortcake, Birthday Cake, Pirates' Treasure.

Translated, the names meant: strawberry with lumps of pink cake, vanilla with lumps of white cake, chocolate with lumps of chocolate cake. Brought to you by the same advertisers who called the color of a plain black t-shirt "midnight."

"Don't you just love homes with children?" Officer Darnell peered over Brockley's shoulder. "All that ice cream."

Brockley grunted and closed the door.

Darnell's eyes narrowed. Her mouth opened, closed. She shrugged and turned away.

"I'm surprised at you, Brock," she called over her shoulder. "Thought Pirate's Treasure was your favorite..."

She whipped around and stared at the freezer, eyes wide. Brockley followed her gaze.

Yanking open the freezer door, he reached for the Pirate's Treasure ice cream container. Kim reached him in one step, in time to watch him remove the lid. The corner of a plastic bag jutted from a sea of brown goo.

With two fingers, Brockley gripped the bag and tugged. At first, it resisted, the frozen confection holding tight. But the warmth of the hand holding the carton softened the outside and, finally, the bag broke free with a slurp.

As chocolate dripped from the plastic, the kitchen light reflected off its contents: Three glittering gemstones.

Chapter 13

"Grandpa!" Kim and Rory burst into her grandfather's office. No Grandpa. His voice filtered in from the store front. A female voice answered. Darn it, he wasn't alone.

While Rory trotted into the store to greet whoever was there, Kim crossed to Grandpa's work chair and leaned against it. The familiar smells of old leather, pipe tobacco and Grandpa's cologne helped slow her racing heart.

She needed to extract Grandpa from his customers without appearing manic.

Straightening her shoulders, she plastered a smile on her face and strode into the store.

Aunt Ginny and her three sidekicks -- Maureen, Wilma and Doris -- started talking at once. Grandpa, however, must have recognized Kim's strained expression. He waved the others into silence before asking "What's wrong?"

"Is anyone else here?" She trusted Aunt Ginny's friends; they'd helped investigate when Grandpa was in danger. But she didn't want anyone else to hear what happened.

"No, it's just us," Grandpa said. "Want me to lock the front door?"

"Please."

While Grandpa locked the door, Kim pulled chairs into a circle and gestured to the others to sit. She waited for everyone to settle and for Grandpa to join them before continuing.

"They hauled Mary to the police station."

Doris gasped. "Why?"

"They found a plastic bag hidden in a carton of ice cream. Inside were three gemstones."

"Did they allow you to study them?" Grandpa used his low, solemn voice.

"No. Brockley wouldn't let me touch them. Mary denies knowing about the gems, says maybe Bobbie was playing a game with rhinestones or something."

"But?"

Oh, Grandpa knew her too well. "But the stones, whatever they are, were cut in old-fashioned styles."

"Not rhinestones," Grandpa said.

Kim nodded and dug fingers into Rory's fur. "They insisted Mary ride in the police car and wouldn't let me go with her."

Grandpa laid a hand on her shoulder.

"You're a good friend."

The warmth in his voice brought tears to her eyes. She blinked, forcing the tears away. "I called Tony. He's trying to find a criminal lawyer for her."

"Well, I guess Brittany is going to get her way after all." Wilma folded her arms and scowled.

"What's Brittany got to do with it?"

Before Wilma could answer, Aunt Ginny said "Let's discuss this over lunch. I haven't eaten all day and I've been craving cream of crab soup. Tony will take care of Mary while we figure out what to do."

Kim sighed and stood. Knots filled her stomach and she knew she'd never eat. But she'd learned long ago that when her aunt was hungry, nothing would be accomplished until she'd taken a bite of food.

Judging by the way Ginny's friends leaped to their feet and began gathering their purses, they also knew her one track mind when it came to food.

"We can probably all squeeze into my car," Maureen said.

"You all go ahead," Kim said. "I need to take Rory up to the apartment." The last thing she needed was the mischievous poodle loose in a room full of glittering toys.

Grandpa gestured to the women to leave without him, saying he'd wait for Kim. As he escorted them through his office and out the back door, Kim called Rory and headed up the stairs.

After checking Rory's water bowl, she handed him a dog biscuit and promised more if he was good. Rory sighed and plopped onto the kitchen floor, his whole body broadcasting his displeasure at her leaving without him. Rolling her eyes, Kim locked the kitchen door behind her and trotted down the outside stairs.

Grandpa had already backed his Toyota Camry from the garage into the driveway. Kim climbed into the passenger seat.

"Shame on you for disappointing Ginny's friends," she teased. "They don't often get to ride with a handsome man their age."

Grandpa chuckled and patted her knee. "I'm at least ten years older, but thanks for the compliment."

He backed the car onto the gravel alley that provided the only auto access for the houses and shops built along the boardwalk.

As gravel clicked against the undercarriage, Kim winced and rubbed the raised scar on her left elbow. Both elbows and knees sported multiple reminders of childhood falls onto the alley. By the time she entered high school, Grandpa had gotten proficient at removing the small stones with tweezers.

Noticing her reaction to the gravel, Grandpa grinned. "Not planning to ride your bike, are you?" He pulled onto the paved road.

Kim gave an exaggerated shudder. "Bite your tongue."

They turned north on Route 261, the narrow street that skirted the edges of the Chesapeake Bay. The road wound past Chesapeake Beach Elementary School, up a hill and down again, library on the left, Roland's grocery store on the right. Stop for the local geese to cross the road.

"You don't seem too concerned about the gems found in Mary's freezer," Kim said.

"There were more than three loose gemstones stolen. If Mary took the jewels, where are the others?" Grandpa eased forward, using the front bumper to urge a straggling goose out of the lane. "More likely Bobby found more gems and didn't want anyone to know. You said he's still digging."

Kim groaned. "I hope he didn't really find pirate treasure. Can you imagine the mess if people thought they could get rich by digging up Pirate's Cove?"

Man-made holes in the sand and cliff would hasten erosion and destroy habitat.

"The irony," Grandpa said, "is that pirates seldom buried actual treasure chests. They usually divided money and jewels among themselves, then individual crew members hid their portion."

They passed the water park and approached the intersection with Rt. 260, the main east/west road.

Kim frowned. "Didn't someone recently find a leather pouch of gemstones at the base of a tree that had fallen over?"

Grandpa nodded. "I think it happened along the coast of one of the Carolinas."

He pulled into the left lane and hit his turn signal.

"I thought we were going to Thursday's." The seafood restaurant had two locations. The fancier one perched on the river in Galesville. The second was one block from the bay in nearby North Beach. Ginny claimed Thursday's cream of crab soup was among the best in Maryland.

"They moved." Grandpa turned onto 260 and headed away from the beach.

Kim folded her arms. "Well, that's stinky. Part of the fun of eating at Thursday's was walking on the North Beach boardwalk afterwards."

"Don't worry; the food is still good."

Another left and he pulled into an outdoor strip mall. Kim scowled at the exterior. Yeah, the place looked larger. But moving away from the beach really messed up the ambiance.

As she stepped inside, however, her mood lightened. The restaurant was not only larger, but brighter. The walls had been lined with light-colored pine. The old decorations of stuffed swordfish, painted boat oars and photos of early Calvert County could now be enjoyed without stumbling over a diner.

"Max!" A pretty brunette, maybe in her fifties, stepped from behind the hostess stand and greeted Grandpa with a hug. "I heard you were in the hospital." Stepping away, she studied Grandpa's face. "How ya feeling?"

"Good, good." He pulled Kim close. "Karen, I'd like you to meet my granddaughter Kim."

Karen stuck out her hand. "Oh, Max has told me so much about you! Did you bring Rorschach?"

Kim grinned. Anyone who remembered the name of her dog must be a good person.

"Didn't think you'd allow him in the restaurant."

"Oh." Karen waved a hand in dismissal, the motion setting her long ponytail in motion. "That's why I put tables and chairs outside."

"I'll remember that next time."

"Your friends are waiting." Karen turned and led the way. Two tables had been pushed together to accommodate the group. Menus sat in front of the two empty seats.

Kim settled between Aunt Ginny and Doris, leaving the seat across from her for Grandpa. A quick perusal of the menu reassured her nothing there had changed. Despite the August heat, she decided to order a cup of cream of crab soup and half of a club sandwich which, she knew, also included Thursday's wonderful steak fries.

After everyone placed their order, Kim turned to Wilma.

"Okay, please start over and tell us what's going on with Brittany."

Wilma frowned. "Well, you know she wants to fire Mary. Her latest scheme is to visit individual board members to tell them why that new boyfriend of hers should replace Mary."

"The board members won't replace Mary, will they?" If Mary lost her job, she'd be unable to pay for a lawyer.

"As of an hour ago, the votes were on Mary's side," Wilma said. "I haven't talked to Stede, but I assume he'll support his daughter. Bob Jefferson, of course, won't commit one way or another." She shook her head. "You'd think the man was running for office or something the way he sits on the fence."

"He sure had opinions when he was teaching." She could still hear his outraged lecture about leaving school property during the day.

"He had to become more politic when he became the principal," Grandpa said. "What about the others?"

"Dorothy's death seems to have sobered everyone," Wilma said. "I think Ruby would have supported Dorothy and Brittany, but now she isn't interested in changing things.

"Then there's Matt Garfield." Wilma looked at Kim. "He's the owner of the new gym. He told Brittany that unless our museum attracted thousands of visitors, he saw no reason to change things."

"So at the moment, the only board member supporting Brittany is her father?" Kim said.

Wilma nodded. "But if the police actually arrest Mary, the board might have no choice but to replace her, at least temporarily."

"She hasn't been arrested yet," Kim said. "And she won't be if Tony finds her a decent lawyer. But now it's more important than ever that we find alternative suspects."

The arrival of their food interrupted the discussion. Kim dug into the sweet, creamy soup. The chef had added just enough Old Bay spice to bring out the crab's flavor without overwhelming it. Kim moaned in pleasure.

For a few minutes, they ate in silence. Kim pushed her now empty bowl aside and reached for a thick fry.

"Officer Darnell is making a big deal out of the duplicate keys Mary made," Kim said. "But it's more likely Dorothy's attacker hid in the museum during the banquet.

"I've already talked to family members who attended, but no one saw anything suspicious. Maybe it's time to interview each of the banquet guests."

"Surely the police have talked with everyone on the guest list," Maureen said.

"Maybe. But I bet people would be more willing to talk with you all than with the police."

Cheshire-cat grins spread across four faces. Ah, yes, Kim had seen those expressions before, whenever Aunt Ginny and her friends were bored and looking for trouble. Still, Kim couldn't help smiling with the ladies who'd helped investigate the attack on Grandpa.

"I can get the guest list from Brittany," Wilma said. "We'll divide it up among the four of us."

"Divide it in half," Kim said. "You'll get more out of people if you visit them in person. And for safety, everyone needs to work in pairs." She grinned. "Same as last time."

"Last time?" Grandpa's eyebrows raised.

Kim bit her lip. Not wanting to upset him as he recovered from his hospital stay, she'd glossed over everyone's role in investigating the attack on him. He seemed well enough now, but she didn't want to change the subject.

Aunt Ginny came to her rescue. "We'll talk about it later." She patted Grandpa's hand, then turned back to Kim. "What else?"

"I'd like to go at this from a different angle," Kim said. "The jewels and other items stolen from the museum are distinctive. Plus Grandpa had the gems' girdles laser inscribed. Aunt Ginny, may I borrow your ring?"

Ginny had purchased the diamond she wore from Grandpa. Kim accepted the ring, held it so she could study the side of the diamond with a loupe and located the numbers and symbols that she knew Grandpa would have inscribed on the diamond's edge.

"The laser inscription helps identify individual stones without damaging the gem." She passed the ring and loupe to her left so the others could see what she was describing.

"You're saying the museum's gems are too distinctive to sell to a pawn shop." Doris peered through the loupe, nodded, and passed the ring and loupe to Wilma.

"Yeah. I'm wondering if the thieves had a buyer before they entered the museum, maybe someone who collects pirate memorabilia."

"Oh! There's someone in Annapolis." Aunt Ginny leaned forward. "He gave a talk at our condo, maybe a month ago. I can get his name from the head of the planning committee."

"See if you can schedule a meeting with him," Kim said. "He might be able to give us a list of the top collectors."

"You're not planning to interview all of them, are you?" Grandpa said. "That could be dangerous."

"No. Once I have a list of collectors, I'll turn it over to Lieutenant Brockley. He--"

The Indiana Jones march trilled from Kim's purse. "Sorry. Forgot to turn off the cell." She retrieved the phone and was about to turn it off when she noticed the caller I.D. Speak of the devil.

Taking a deep breath, she answered the phone.

Brockley identified himself. "Is your grandfather with you? I tried the store and home numbers, but there wasn't an answer."

"Yes, he's right here." Kim covered the mouth piece and told Grandpa who was calling before handing him the phone.

She dipped a fry in ketchup and, along with the others, eavesdropped.

"Yes, I can identify them," he said. He listened a few more minutes. "I'll be there."

Hanging up the phone, he passed it back to Kim.

"Lieutenant Brockley wants me to come to the station to examine the gems they found in Mary's freezer."

Chapter 14

Lieutenant Brockley's phone call should have dampened everyone's mood. Instead, it sparked a lively discussion of the best way to proceed. Kim insisted on accompanying Grandpa to the station, saying she wanted a closer look at the gems found in Mary's freezer.

Aunt Ginny and Doris offered to watch the store. That left Wilma and Maureen free to track down Brittany and obtain a copy of the banquet guest list.

Half an hour later, Kim and Grandpa entered the police station and told the desk sergeant that Lieutenant Brockley was expecting them. To Kim's annoyance, they were directed to Officer Darnell, not Brockley.

"Mary did not steal the museum's gems." Grandpa settled into one of the two chairs facing Officer Darnell's desk. "Most of the stolen gems haven't been displayed in years. If Mary was going to steal them, it would have been easier to do it while they lay in drawers rather than wait until they were on exhibit to hundreds of people."

"No one understands the criminal mind, sir." The officer's words might be neutral, but the tone was condescending.

Kim's fists clenched. Where did the county find this woman? Throughout the years, Kim had met officers from both the Sheriff's Department and the local State Police barracks. Everyone had been friendly as well as polite.

In contrast, Officer Darnell -- Officer *Paula* Darnell, according to the sign on her desk -- behaved as if she were royalty and community members were expected to kowtow.

Darnell set the plastic bag of gems in front of Grandpa. "Are these from the museum?"

"I can't tell without examining them," Grandpa said.

Darnell's eyebrows raised. "I was told you are an expert."

"He *is* an expert." Kim ground her teeth. How dare this woman question Grandpa's ability? "No one could possibly identify gems through a stupid plastic bag."

Darnell's ice blue eyes narrowed. Before she could respond, however, Grandpa asked permission to remove the stones from the bag. His gentle voice seemed to soothe the beast.

Darnell shrugged. "Go ahead; everything's been dusted for prints."

Kim resisted the urge to roll her eyes. If it didn't matter whether or not Grandpa opened the bag, why hadn't the woman said so?

Grandpa laid a velvet cloth on Darnell's desk, opened the bag and gently placed each stone on the velvet: Two red stones and one blue. Using a pair of tweezers, he lifted a red stone by the top and bottom, leaving the edges free for examination.

Kim held her breath while Grandpa examined the stone through a loupe, searching for an inscription on its girdle.

Grandpa's shoulders slumped. "This belongs to the museum." He returned the gem to the velvet.

Kim wanted to smack the triumphant expression from Officer Darnell's face. Solving the case would probably result in a promotion or raise. And yet, the animosity the woman had exhibited at Mary's house spoke to something more personal.

As Grandpa lifted the blue stone, Kim reached for the extra pair of tweezers and loupe they'd brought. With the tweezers, she lifted the already-examined stone by the edges and studied it. It was square in shape, its pavilion -- or bottom half -- containing only four facets. The top included a small, level table surrounded by triangular facets.

The color wasn't pigeon's blood, but the red was rich enough to impress any king or queen.

But was this a ruby or one of ruby's look-alikes?

Theoretically, she should be able to tell the difference by studying the way the stone reflected the light. Most gemstones -- including rubies, sapphires, tourmalines, citrines and zircons -- split the light in two when it entered the stone, a process called double refraction. Zircons, in fact, were so doubly refractive that when viewed from certain angles, the edges of their facets almost looked like railroad tracks.

While rubies shared most other gemstone's double refractive trait, ruby-like garnets and spinel did not. Light entering these stones bent, but didn't split. The only other important gemstone with this trait was diamond.

Gemologists used the way gemstones refracted light to separate, say, ruby from spinel or diamond from zircon.

Unfortunately, Kim didn't have an instrument handy to measure the red stone's refraction and she wasn't skilled enough to see railroad tracks in a stone this dark in color.

Kim returned the stone to the velvet and glanced at Grandpa. Face white, he pronounced the blue stone as museum property. Setting it down, he reached for the other red stone. She didn't need to hear his words to know it also sported the museum's identifying marks.

With a sigh, Grandpa returned the stones to the plastic bag.

"When will these be returned to the museum?" he said.

Before Darnell could reply, shouting broke the silence. Kim turned around in time to see Mary's husband storm into the room. Eyebrows furrowed, face red, fists clenched, he marched to Darnell's desk and glared down at her.

"What have you done with my wife?"

Darnell gaped up at him. Then her eyes narrowed. "Please calm down, Mr. Klein--"

Kevin slammed a fist on Darnell's desk.

"I will not calm down! You arrested my wife on trumped-up charges--"

"Mrs. Klein has not been arrested."

A pair of burly uniformed officers appeared on either side of Kevin. Darnell waved them away, saying she could handle this.

Kim wasn't so sure. Darnell stood maybe 5'2"; Kevin was a good foot taller and, due to construction work, in good shape. Plus he had righteous anger on his side.

"If you didn't arrest her, then why did you haul her in here like a common criminal?" he said.

"Mrs. Klein is helping us with our investigation--"

"The hell she is!"

"Kevin!" The new woman's voice came from behind them.

Everyone turned to see Mary race down the hall and into her husband's arms. Tony followed at a more sedate pace. Seeing Kim and Grandpa, he waved and grinned. The tension in Kim's chest loosened.

"Oh, Kevin, it was so awful." Mary buried her nose in his chest.

Kevin's arms tightened around her. "It's going to be okay, honey." Over her shoulder, he glared at Darnell. "Since no one is under arrest, I assume we can leave."

It was Tony who answered. "Absolutely. I suggest we all leave."

Darnell stood. "You're all free to go, but don't leave the county without notifying us."

Kim followed the others out of the sheriff's office and paused to inhale the fresh air. She wasn't sure if it was the station itself or the thought of being arrested that had made her claustrophobic.

Mary turned to Tony and thanked him for rescuing her.

"I'm sorry my colleague couldn't get here." Tony shook her hand. "You have Steve's card now. Call and make an appointment with him."

"But won't that be expensive? And I haven't even asked you how much I owe you."

"You don't owe me anything," Tony said. "But I strongly recommend you talk with Steve no matter the cost." He gestured toward the police building. "They're making a case against you and next time... Well, it's better to have Steve on your side."

"Don't worry; we'll find the money," Kevin said. He reached out to shake Tony's hand. "Thanks for everything."

Kevin's cell phone rang. With an apologetic glance at everyone, he opened it and scowled at caller I.D. Sighing, he pushed the button to answer.

"I'm kinda busy here," he said by way of greeting. "No, I'm not going to be able to work today; something's come up. No, I can't change it. My wife needs me... So go ahead and schedule the reporters; they don't have to go into the building. Not now, Brittany! I'll call you later."

He angrily punched the phone off. "The police have released the museum and now Brittany wants me to build new cases immediately."

Mary touched his arm. "Maybe you should go to work. We need the money."

Kevin shook his head. "The museum can wait. We're going home."

He slipped an arm around Mary, prepared to lead her away. But hearing Brittany's name reminded Kim that their investigation was stalled until Wilma obtained the banquet guest list. Maybe she could speed things along.

"Mary, when you get home, could you please email me the guest list for the museum banquet?" she said. "You do have it on computer, right?"

Mary showed no interest in why Kim might need the guest list. She simply promised to email the document.

Kim gave her friend a quick hug and watched the couple walk away.

"Got time for a cup of coffee?" Grandpa asked Tony.

"No, I'd better get back to the office. Otherwise, I will have to charge the Kleins." Tony's smile faded. "Kim, I wasn't exaggerating about the case they're building. Your friend is in big trouble."

"We're trying to identify other suspects."

"Well, you'd better work fast. I don't think you have much time before they make an arrest."

Chapter 15

The rest of the day passed quickly. As promised, Mary emailed the list of people who'd been invited to the museum banquet, but said she had no record of who actually attended. Kim sent a copy to Aunt Ginny's friends. They'd divide the list and schedule times to interview the people.

In the meantime, Aunt Ginny tracked down the collector of pirate memorabilia who'd spoken to her club. At first, Mr. Ross Peabody told Ginny he couldn't possibly meet with them. He planned to attend a dinner meeting this evening. Early tomorrow morning he was flying to Spain to negotiate the purchase of a sword used by Errol Flynn in one of his movies.

Aunt Ginny, however, sweet talked Peabody into meeting them after tonight's dinner meeting. She told him her niece was a freelance reporter doing a story about the nation's "preeminent" collectors.

Which is why, at eight forty-five that evening, Kim pulled into the well-lighted parking lot of Aunt Ginny's Annapolis condo and dialed Ginny's number.

"Be right down," Ginny said by way of hello.

Kim hung up and tapped her fingers on the steering wheel. Excitement coursed through her, along with a touch of fear. Ross Peabody was a multi-billionaire, renowned patron of the arts and local eccentric. She couldn't help comparing him to the tall, silver-haired villain from *Indiana Jones and the Last Crusade*.

She'd have to tread lightly when interviewing Peabody. As Indiana Jones discovered, just because someone was a known do-gooder did not mean he was law-abiding.

Despite her admonitions to the others, Kim would have preferred to interview the collector alone. Aunt Ginny, however, had insisted on accompanying her and Kim knew better than to argue.

The passenger door opened and Ginny climbed inside. She'd dressed for the occasion in a khaki skirt and multi-pocketed Safari jacket.

"Where's your elephant gun?" Kim said.

"Smarty. I'll have you know that this is the latest in impressing wealthy collectors."

"You're not trying to seduce him or something?"

"Of course not! But if we're going to elicit information from him, one of us needs to look like we speak his language."

"Maybe we should have borrowed a parrot." When Ginny didn't respond, Kim added, "You know. Pirates. Parrots."

Ginny rolled her eyes. "Good thing I came. Turn here."

As Aunt Ginny directed her through the shopping district, Kim glanced uneasily at the hulking shadows. Osprey Beach used few street lights, a practice that made star gazing easy but driving the curving roads treacherous. Here in Annapolis, the contrast between light and dark created gloomy pockets that oozed menace.

"So do you still think Mary is innocent even though the police found museum jewels in her freezer?"

"Absolutely," Kim said. "Someone's trying to set her up."

"How can you be so sure?"

"The jewels were hidden in chocolate ice cream. Hellooo. No parent is dumb enough to hide something in their kids' favorite flavor of ice cream."

"We need to park here." Ginny pointed to the public parking garage that bordered Annapolis Towne Centre, a collection of fancy restaurants and boutique stores.

Kim parked beneath a light and scanned the shadows. Seeing nothing, she locked the door and tucked the keys between her fingers as a makeshift weapon.

"I hear these condos start at a million dollars," Aunt Ginny said as they skirted a clothing store.

"A million bucks to live in a shopping center?" They crossed the empty street and arrived at the door of the fancy apartment building -- only to be greeted with a locked door and some kind of a keypad.

"They probably have to buzz us in," Aunt Ginny said, pushing a button.

Kim expected a voice to ask for identification. Instead, she heard a buzzer and the distinctive click of the door unlocking.

Ginny shook her head and reached for the door. "This is what happens when people get lazy. Good thing we're not jewel thieves."

They stepped into a heavily air-conditioned lobby and followed it to the elevators. Ginny pushed the button marked twelve.

"To answer your question," Aunt Ginny said, "the view from the apartments -- all those lights -- are probably pretty at night. Plus you can walk to the stores."

"But a million bucks?" Kim gave an exaggerated shudder. "For that kind of money, I'd buy something near the shore or overlooking a lake or something. This must be like living in a glass bowl."

The doors slid open and they stepped into a narrow-carpeted lobby. They followed the signs to the left, past a few discretely numbered doors, then turned a sharp corner. The hallway dead-ended into a fire door with the words "exit" printed overhead. Ross Peabody's million-dollar penthouse stood alone to their right.

As Kim prepared to knock, raised voices penetrated the door. Frowning, she leaned closer. She could distinguish two distinct voices, one clearly female. But she couldn't make out the words.

She glanced at Ginny, unsure whether to interrupt.

The door suddenly swung open. Kim jumped back as a voice demanded "What are you doing here?"

For a moment, Kim didn't recognize the petite blond glaring up at her. Dressed in an elegant beige sheath that hugged a tiny waist and curvy hips, the woman would probably be beautiful if it wasn't for the scowl on her face and the aggressive thrust of her chin... Oh.

"Officer Darnell." Kim tried what she hoped was a confident smile. "I didn't recognize you without your uniform."

Darnell crossed her arms. "I asked you a question."

Before Kim could think of a suitable lie, Aunt Ginny stepped forward and, ignoring Darnell, thrust her hand toward the man hovering just inside the apartment.

"Ross, good to see you again."

Kim studied their host, biting back a smile. Ross Peabody was as different from Indiana Jones's nemesis as one could imagine. He stood only a few inches taller than her own 5'6" and his hair and eyes were a muddy brown. He'd removed the tie and opened the collar of his obviously custom-made tuxedo, but the tailor hadn't been able to hide the man's protruding belly.

Kim glanced from Peabody to Darnell. Was the Osprey Beach police officer actually dating this dumpy looking man?

As if reading Kim's mind, Darnell's eyes narrowed and she turned toward Peabody.

"I need to meet my date," she told him. "You'll think about what we discussed." It was an order, not a question.

Ross Peabody lifted his chin. "Of course. As I'm sure you'll consider the implications."

Darnell's lips narrowed. Without another word, she turned and headed toward the elevators, hips swaying.

Before Kim could think of a tactful way to find out why Darnell was here, "call me Ross" invited them inside.

Kim gawked at the expanse of hardwood flooring that led past a formal dining room table, a fireplace and seating arrangement and a granite kitchen bar to a wall of windows and curved balcony. In lieu of interior walls, vertical support beams held up twelve-foot ceilings trimmed in extra-wide crown molding.

The walls that did exist were covered in pirate stuff: crossed swords, muskets, daggers, cutlasses, flags and even a tri-corner hat and red velvet waistcoat.

To Kim's disappointment, instead of heading toward the wall of windows and glittering view, Ross turned left and led them down a short hallway.

"Given the late hour, I hope you don't mind if we dispense with the niceties and get right down to business." He swung open a door to reveal what might have been a typical den except it held only a navy leather recliner and end table.

Display cases, illuminated by overhead spotlights, covered the walls, their contents glittering in the light.

"What you see here is the rarest of the rare." Ross turned to the wall on his right. "Here we have gold doubloons and pieces of eight from Blackbeard's own stash." He moved to the next case, a collection of scratched belt buckles, gold bracelets and carved buttons. Labels under each indicated the original pirate owner.

"How do you know for sure that the items came from specific pirates?" Kim gestured toward the buckle labeled "Blackbeard." "Archeologists still aren't certain the ship they found off the North Carolina coast really was *The Queen Anne's Revenge*."

Ross gave her a superior smile. "I have my trusted sources, of course. But explaining my confirmation process would take more time than we have." He stepped to a case of jewel-encrusted daggers. "Now here we have..."

Kim formed a smile and nodded in what she hoped were all the right places. She wasn't here to ooh and aah over some millionaire's collection. She needed names of other collectors and, if possible, an indication of whether or not Ross Peabody was the type to buy items stolen from the museum.

A flash of gold and red in the next case caught her eye. Not caring if she looked rude, Kim walked away from Ross's lecture and peered into the case. Gold pendants set with single-cut gemstones sparkled.

"You ladies always like the glitter." Peabody swept his hand at the case. "These are amulets worn by pirates to protect them in battle."

Kim frowned. She knew that Medieval warriors often wore amulets adorned with red gemstones, believing the color would help them shed their enemies' blood while protecting their own. Legend said Henry V strode into the Battle of Agincourt wearing the Black Prince's "Ruby."

But, other than Brittany's claim that her pirate ancestor had worn his ruby into battle, she'd never heard that pirates had carried on the tradition.

She slid her eyes at Ross. Unaware of her skepticism, he babbled on about tracking down the Welsh privateer Henry Morgan's ruby encrusted pendant.

"I've succeeded in acquiring the amulets of every famous pirate." He frowned. "Except one."

"Stede Bonnet."

Ross's eyes widened. "And how did you know that?"

Kim shrugged. "I went to school with Brittany Bonnet."

"Ah, yes, Brittany. I offered her good money for her family's amulet." He smirked. "I heard it was stolen, along with other museum artifacts."

At last! A reason to talk about the museum theft.

"Brittany's quite upset that her family heirloom was stolen. I can't imagine what the thieves plan to do with it. It's so distinctive that if they try to sell it, someone will recognize it came from the museum."

"My dear, there is always a market for quality antiques."

"Even if it's stolen?"

Ross shrugged. "There have always been and always will be unscrupulous collectors."

"So what would you do if someone offered to sell you Bonnet's pendant?" She gestured at the collection. "Since that's the only pendant you lack?"

"Why, I'd call the police, of course." The smile he gave her was oily. She didn't believe him. "Now, if you ladies will excuse me..."

"What's this thing?" From across the room, Aunt Ginny pointed to a case.

Kim tossed her aunt a grateful smile. Ross had been about to throw them out and, though she now doubted Ross Peabody's honesty, she still needed to gather the names of other collectors.

She joined Ginny and Ross in front of a case and peered at the oddly shaped item. It looked a bit like an oversized caliper compass; two straight legs with pointed tips angled back to meet at a hinged circle.

"That, my dear, is a brass chart divide," Ross said. "Pirates and other sailors used it to navigate the seas."

"Is it Blackbeard's?" Kim vaguely remembered a news report saying one had been recovered from the ship wreck.

"Unfortunately, no. That one has never come on the market."

"Speaking of markets, how do you find out about this stuff? I assume there are other collectors who compete for items?"

Ross shrugged. "As you can imagine, it's a small group so, yes, we know one another and, yes, we compete."

"I suppose Officer Darnell asked you for a list of your fellow collectors?"

Ross shifted his legs, one foot pointed toward the door. "I'm always happy to help the police."

"Would you be willing to share that list?"

"Whatever for?"

For a moment, Kim's mind went blank. Why would a supposed reporter need a list of collectors?

"Oh, honey, that's an excellent idea." Aunt Ginny clapped her hands together and tossed Ross a wide-eyed look. "When my niece told me about the article she's writing, I insisted she talk to you since I know you're the most important collector. But since you're going to be out of the country for a few days, a list of people she can contact if she has questions would be really helpful."

Ross nodded. "Fine. Why don't you come admire the view while I print out a copy of the list I gave to the police."

He strode to the study door and waited for them to follow before turning out the light and closing the door with a decisive click. As they walked deeper into the apartment, Aunt Ginny questioned him about living in "such a locally famous complex."

"It's so quiet here!" Ginny said.

"That's because the place is so well-built." Ross patted a wall. "Eight inches of concrete in the walls insulate against noise and temperature fluctuations. This apartment is well over 3,500 square feet but it costs less to heat and cool than my 2,000-square foot fishing cabin."

Kim resisted the urge to roll her eyes. Two thousand square feet was not her idea of a "cabin." Her entire Oregon house -- the one she now desperately needed to sell -- was only 1,200.

"And what a breath-taking view." Ginny stood before the windows. "But why no curtains? Aren't you worried about peeping Toms?"

Ross's chest swelled. "No one can see inside. All of the windows are made of one-way mirrors."

"What a clever idea," Ginny said.

"I confess it wasn't mine. The builders installed the one-way mirrors in the bedroom windows. When I discovered how much I enjoyed gazing out without anyone seeing me, I replaced the other windows. Now, if you'll wait here, I'll get you that list."

Turning, he marched through an open door to their left, crossed to a large walnut desk and opened a laptop computer. Under pretense of studying the view, Kim shifted position, trying to see the computer screen. The typeface, however, was too small to read.

Sighing, she scanned what she could see of the room. Like everywhere else in the apartment, the walls were crammed with pirate stuff. The only variation was an oil painting that had been pulled away from the wall to reveal a large safe. The door hung part-way open.

Below the safe, a narrow, brown-paper-wrapped package leaned against the wall. Maybe three feet long, the package was free of handwriting or markings. A large, greasy looking blotch marred the top third of the paper.

The sound of a printer clacking drew Kim's attention back to the desk. She swiveled to find Ross Peabody staring at her. His eyes shifted from hers to the safe, back to her.

His brown eyes grew hard and flat. The hostility took Kim's breath away. Clearly, he hadn't wanted her to see the safe. She tried to assemble her expression into one of innocence. But her body felt frozen, like a rat trapped by a king cobra.

Pounding on the front door broke the spell. Hurrying back to Aunt Ginny, Kim leaned in and whispered, "Let's get out of here. Now."

With a raised eyebrow, Ginny fell into step beside her. Kim could hear Ross's leather-soled shoes slapping the hardwood behind them.

Peabody had said the windows were one-way glass, the walls eight-inch concrete. If she waved for help, no one would see. If she screamed, no one would hear.

But help was at the front door.

She grabbed Ginny's hand and broke into a trot. They reached the door with Peabody just a few steps behind them. Grabbing the handle, she swung the door open.

"Where's that thieving..." Brittany Bonnet flew passed Kim, hands curled like claws. "Where's my ruby?" she screamed.

Ross Peabody didn't hesitate. With a casual swipe of his hand, he back-handed Brittany across the face. Brittany toppled over backwards.

Chapter 16

Kim watched in horror as Brittany hit hard, the back of her head slamming the hardwood floor with a sickening thud. Brittany groaned and stared at the ceiling, blinking back tears.

Aunt Ginny turned away and started wrestling something from the wall. Kim dropped to her knees and studied Brittany' eyes. Her pupils appeared normal.

Releasing the breath she'd been holding, she glared up at Ross. "Are you nuts?"

"I've a right to protect myself in my own home."

"By striking a woman?" Kim helped Brittany into a sitting position and ran trembling fingers across the back of her head. A small bump was forming.

"Ouch." Brittany batted Kim's hand away.

"We need to get ice on this."

"Later." Brittany tried to stand.

Kim rose and helped Brittany to her feet, wincing at the hand-shaped red mark that covered Brittany's cheek. The curvy, black and white diamond earrings dangling from Brittany's ear emphasized her inflamed cheek.

Brittany pushed Kim away, turned to Ross and crossed her arms. "I want my ruby."

"We all want something."

Despite his assured tone, he took a step away from her. The movement brought Aunt Ginny into his line of sight. His mouth dropped open.

"And what do you plan to do with that?"

Ginny looked at the sword in her hand, then back at Ross. "Prevent you from hitting another woman."

Ross sneered. "Do you know what it's like, slicing a man, feeling the soft tissue give way, smelling the hot blood as it drains from the body?"

Kim hurried to her aunt's side, wondering if she should remove the second sword from the wall behind them.

"So first you hit a woman and now you're trying to terrorize a helpless old lady," Kim snarled.

"I think it's time for all of you to leave." Ross extended a hand to Ginny. "Return my property."

Instead of giving Ross the sword, Ginny passed it to Kim. Kim stared down at it, startled by the weight. It was much heavier than the foils she'd used in her one and only fencing class.

"Huh." She peered at the hilt. "Made in Japan."

"What?" Ross snatched the sword from her hands.

While Ross was distracted, Kim grabbed Ginny and Brittany and hustled them out the door.

Rather than wait for the elevator and give Ross the opportunity to come after them, she pointed everyone at the staircase. No one spoke until they'd safely gained the floor below and tramped to the elevators.

"Did the sword really say 'made in Japan'?" Brittany said.

"Nah. I just wanted to give him something else to think about. How are you feeling?"

"Angry."

"I was asking about your head."

"It hurts." Brittany scowled. "Just one more reason to hate that man."

"What made you think he'd have your ruby?"

"He's been trying to buy it from my family for years. When Dad turned him down, Ross threatened to make trouble at their club. Instead, Dad got Ross thrown out by telling club members Ross was buying stolen items."

"Any truth to the rumor?" Kim said.

"I wouldn't be surprised. He likes to brag about special deals and I know he's got a room in that condo that he never allows anyone in."

"Speaking of getting in, how'd you get into this building without Ross knowing?"

"What's it to you?" Brittany's eyes narrowed. "In fact, what are you doing here? Don't tell me you're playing Nancy Drew again?"

Kim felt her mouth fall open.

Brittany nodded in satisfaction. "Yeah, I heard all about that blue diamond and your 'investigation.' It's all Mom and Dad talked about for days." Brittany pitched her voice high and whiney. "Kim saved her grandfather's life. Kim caught the killers. Kim got her PhD. Kim helps in the store. Kim gets straight A's. Kim saved the Hollis boy. Kim, Kim, Kim."

Kim stepped back, startled at the venom in Brittany's voice.

The Hollis boy? That was decades ago! She'd been thirteen, gangly and awkward in her new swimsuit, waiting for her turn on the high dive, when six-year-old Tommy Hollis came barreling around the corner of the swimming pool, slipped and plunged into the deep end.

Kim hadn't hesitated. She was a strong swimmer and Grandpa had instilled the need to watch out for her younger cousins whenever they were around water. She dove into the pool, snagged the boy by his arm and hauled him to the side where the lifeguard whipped him from the water. It'd all happened so fast that Tommy hadn't had time to even realize the danger.

Her main memory of the event was the awful photo that appeared in the local newspaper. Under the headline "Girl Hero," Kim and Tommy, wrapped in towels, stood side by side, beaming at the camera. It should have been a proud moment.

Brittany ruined it by pinning the photo to a school bulletin board and pointing out the wet hair that hung in Kim's eyes, her skinny legs and "that awful swimsuit" that peeked from beneath the towel.

In the midst of Brittany's current tirade, the elevator doors opened. Brittany swung her nose into the air and stepped in -- and immediately tottered on her high heels. Kim grabbed her upper arm, steadying her.

"You shouldn't drive with that head wound."

"Don't worry; I won't be driving." Brittany shook off Kim's hand and jabbed the five button.

Kim pushed the button for the lobby and joined Aunt Ginny on the far side of the elevator. The car descended in silence.

At the fifth floor, the doors opened to reveal Nigel Cummings, the man Brittany was dating.

"I was just coming to get you," Nigel said as Brittany fell into his arms. "What happened to your face?"

The elevator doors started to close. Kim slapped her palm on them, stopping the movement. Brittany's nastiness was no reason to ignore her injury.

"Nigel, she may have a concussion. You should probably keep an eye on her."

Nigel's eyes widened and he tipped his chin, a very British nod. Kim let the elevator close.

"Wasn't that the guy Brittany wants to hire to take Mary's place?" Aunt Ginny said.

"Yeah. I wonder how an unemployed museum worker can afford a place here, even if he's only renting."

Ginny shrugged. "Brittany's probably paying for it. What'd you think of Ross's reaction to Brittany's accusation?"

"Interesting that he didn't deny he had her ruby." The elevator opened and they stepped into the lobby. "Makes you wonder, doesn't it?"

"And what's the idea calling me an old lady?"

"I know you're not old or helpless. I was trying to make a point about what an ogre that man is." They crossed the street and headed for the parking garage.

"Well, just so you know I'm not some fragile flower."

Kim grinned. "That thought would never occur to me."

As they entered the garage, Ginny added, "I gotta say, his description of what happens when you stab someone was creepy. Almost like he'd done it."

Not wanting to dwell on that image, Kim changed the subject. "Did I ever tell you about the one fencing lesson I took in college?"

"No, but I'm not surprised you tried fencing. You were sure taken with those old pirate movies." She swiveled around a pillar. "So what happened?"

"Well, the first class was free and they supplied the equipment. I got really good jabbing at the wall." She smiled, remembering lunging with the foil, imagining herself as Olivia de Havilland fighting alongside Errol Flynn -- never mind that Olivia never wielded a sword in Flynn's movies. "But then we had to pair up and jab into one another. I just couldn't do it."

"Weren't you wearing padding?"

The car came into view. Kim aimed her keys at it, clicking to open the door. "Yeah, padding and helmets. But you could still feel the jabs. I had a bruise--"

The shadow moved so quickly Kim didn't have time to react. She watched in horror as an arm snaked around Aunt Ginny, pinning her arms at her side, while a hand covered her mouth. Kim stepped forward, intending to aim a kick at the attacker. Before she could make contact, a pair of strong arms wrapped her from behind. Her feet left the ground as the arm tightened and a hand closed over her mouth.

"Stop struggling," a male voice growled, "if you want the old lady to live."

Chapter 17

Kim stared at the masked assailant who held Aunt Ginny. Acknowledging her captor's words, she forced her upper body to go limp. Her heart, however, raced and her leg muscles cramped with the need to run, kick, do something!

The thug holding Ginny whispered something. Ginny stopped struggling.

Oh gawd, why did she allow Aunt Ginny to come?

As if reading her mind, Ginny's eyes met hers. No fear there; Ginny's eyes were bright and alert. Good. If they needed to coordinate an escape attempt, her aunt would be ready.

But what could she do without endangering Ginny?

"Now listen closely." The voice in her ear was deep, whispered, sinister. Spiders crawled up Kim's spine. "Stay out of other people's business." He tightened his hold, making it difficult to breathe. "Nod if you understand."

She dipped her chin.

"Remember what happened to the cat," he growled.

A hard shove sent her flying. Kim windmilled her arms, trying to maintain her balance. She watched in horror as the thug holding Ginny pushed her forward. Kim collided with her aunt, the impact stopping her forward momentum and allowing her to regain her balance.

Over Ginny's shoulder, she saw the assailant melt into the shadows. A glance behind confirmed the other thug was gone.

Kim stepped back, holding Ginny at arm's length.

"Are you okay?" they asked at the same time.

Kim ran anxious hands over Ginny. Satisfied that nothing was broken, she hustled her to the car. They dove in and she locked the doors.

Only then did her hands start shaking. Soon her entire body trembled. Aunt Ginny reached across the console and gripped a hand.

"It's okay," Ginny said. "They're gone and no one was hurt."

"I should n-never have allowed you to c-come with me."

"Allowed?"

Kim inhaled deeply. The trembling lessened. "You know what I mean. It's one thing to put myself into danger. But they could have broken your arm or a rib or, or something."

"I don't think she wanted to hurt me. She held me just tight enough so I couldn't get away."

"She?" Kim straightened.

Ginny nodded. "Definitely a woman; I could feel breasts digging into my back. The one holding you, though, looked pretty muscular."

Kim nodded, absently rubbing a throbbing forearm. A man and a woman? Could they be the jewelry thieves that plagued Calvert County? If so, what were they doing in Annapolis?

"I guess we'd better call the police." She grabbed her purse and started digging for her phone.

"Please don't." The muscles in Aunt Ginny's face drooped as she wilted into her seat. "There's nothing they can do except prevent us from sleeping. Let's just go home."

Kim studied her aunt's slumped form. "Are you sure she didn't hurt you?"

"Might be a few bruises, but I'll live. Right now I just want my bed."

Kim turned on the car and aimed it toward her aunt's condo. When they arrived, Ginny refused Kim's offer to escort her to her door.

"If you walk me to my door, I won't be able to watch you return to your car." Ginny scooped up her purse. "Stay here.

Once I'm in the locked foyer, I'll be safe. Sure you won't change your mind about using my guest room?"

"Thanks, but I'd better get back to Grandpa." Kim kissed her aunt. "I'm going to wait here with the doors locked. Call me when you're locked inside your apartment."

She watched her beloved aunt trudge into the building. Though she moved a bit slower, Ginny didn't seem to be overly sore.

A few minutes later, Kim's cell phone rang.

"I'm home," Aunt Ginny said. "Drive safely."

"I will. Love you."

Kim disconnected and pointed the car west on Route 2. Mercifully, the winding road was empty. Her mind whirred. She could still feel the thug's arm gripping her, smell the leather of the gloved hand pressed against her mouth.

The headlights of an oncoming car reflected off her glasses. She shifted her eyes away.

Okay, assume their assailants were the local jewelry thieves. Why were they skulking around outside of Ross Peabody's condo? Had they been waiting for everyone to leave so they could sneak in and sell the museum artifacts to Ross? Was that why Ross kept looking at his watch?

After watching the man swat Brittany as if she were a fly, Kim could well imagine him contracting thieves to steal the pirate's ruby.

She tapped the brakes, slowing the car to maneuver around the first of several traffic circles between here and home.

There was one problem with the scenario she'd just painted: If the thieves had been waiting to meet Ross Peabody, then what was in the brown paper wrapped parcel she'd spotted beneath Peabody's safe?

Judging by the man's bug-eyed reaction to her peering into his office, he didn't want anyone to see the package.

Her eyes drooped and she suddenly realized the adrenaline that had sustained her through the attack was now gone, leaving behind an exhausted, aching body. She cracked her windows, hoping the fresh air would help keep her awake. Maybe she should have stayed with Aunt Ginny.

At long last, the turn for Route 260 and the beaches came into view. Ten more minutes and she could crawl into bed.

Tomorrow, she'd call Lieutenant Brockley and outline her new theory. Surely he wouldn't overlook the coincidence of thieves lurking outside the home of a famous pirate memorabilia collector.

She snorted. Yeah, right. Brockley was like a pit bull; once he'd sunk his teeth into an idea, it was nearly impossible to turn his attention elsewhere. He'd probably claim her attackers weren't the jewelry thieves at all. Or that they weren't waiting to meet with Ross Peabody. Or...

Her head jerked back. Or the thugs' target was someone else.

What if the jewelry thieves hadn't been waiting for the collector? What if they'd been waiting for *her*?

"Why didn't you report the assault last night?" Lieutenant Brockley bellowed.

Kim winced and held the phone away from her ear. Maybe she should have waited until the morning caffeine took effect before calling the police station.

But Brockley needed to hear about last night's attack so he could interview Ross Peabody before the man left for Europe.

So she'd called early and started to tell him about being attacked in the Annapolis parking garage. Before she could explain the connection to the local jewelry thieves, he'd interrupted to chastise her for failing to notify the Annapolis police.

She took another gulp of her tea. "I'm reporting it now."

"I have no jurisdiction in Annapolis."

"You do if it's connected to the museum robbery."

The silence extended so long that she wondered if he'd hung up. Finally, a long sigh preceded his next words.

"Please tell me you aren't playing Nancy Drew again."

Kim tapped a finger against her tea cup. "Do you or don't you want to hear what happened?"

"Let's hear it. Start with why you visited Ross Peabody."

"How did you know?"

"Officer Darnell told me. Now let's hear your story. Start at the beginning."

For a moment, Kim wondered if she should share the suspicion that had wakened her in the middle of the night.

Problem was, she had no evidence to share, nothing but coincidence and a vague unease.

She brushed the thought aside.

Instead, she launched into a description of Peabody's pirate collection, the package she'd seen beneath his safe, the man's angry reaction when he saw her looking, Brittany's accusation and Peabody's response. She transitioned into the attack in the parking garage, Aunt Ginny's conviction one of them was female, the warning to stay away.

"Obviously, the thieves were there to meet with their buyer, Ross Peabody," she concluded. "You need to search Peabody's condo before he leaves for Europe."

"There's nothing obvious about anything you've just told me," Brockley said. "Even assuming your assailants were our jewelry thieves, there's no evidence they were planning to sell to Peabody. No judge would issue a warrant."

"Couldn't you talk to Ross, before he leaves?" Horrified at the high pitch to her voice, Kim swallowed and tried again. "At the very least, you need to remove Mary Klein from your suspect list." There, that sounded more confident.

Brockley snorted. "And what makes you think Mary wasn't one of your attackers?"

"That's ridiculous!" Rory bumped her hand with his nose.

Stroking Rory's head, she took a deep, calming breath. "Mary asked me to investigate. Why would she now warn me away?"

"Maybe she didn't think you'd discover her buyer."

Kim rolled her eyes. "Then who was the second attacker?"

"Mary's husband? A lover?"

"Now who's making up stuff?"

Brockley's voice hardened. "Not only was one of your attackers female, she clearly didn't want to harm you or your aunt. Thieves don't generally work that way."

"But these thieves do. Stacy Harrison said they were really gentle when they tied her to the chair--"

"You've talked with local victims?" Brockley's voice was low, dangerous.

Kim shuddered but pressed on. "Of course I talked with people! You're so focused on Mary that you haven't considered other possibilities."

Another few seconds of silence. Then she heard a sigh.

"Tell you what," Brockley said. "I'll call around, see what I can learn about Ross Peabody. But you need to promise to stay away from this investigation."

"If you'll actually investigate people other than Mary, I'll be happy to avoid Ross Peabody."

Brockley acknowledged her promise and hung up without a goodbye. Kim glared at the phone in her hand and stuck out her tongue.

"I hope that's not Scott you're sassing," Grandpa said from the doorway.

Kim grinned and leaped to her feet. Crossing the room, she kissed Grandpa's cheek.

"Good morning, sleepy head. Why don't you sit down while I make coffee?"

"Oh, please don't."

When she frowned, Grandpa tweaked her nose. "There are many things you're good at, Monkey, but making coffee isn't one of them." He crossed to the sink and began running water into the coffee pot. "So who were you talking with?"

"Lieutenant Brockley." Kim popped bread into the toaster. "I had a really good lead for him, but he wasn't appreciative."

"The pirate memorabilia collector?"

"Yeah." Opening the refrigerator, she removed a tub of margarine and a jar of boysenberry jam she'd helped Grandpa make last summer.

"How'd that go last night?"

Kim carried the jam and butter to the table. Keeping her back to Grandpa, she began laying out silverware.

"Fine." How best to reveal last night's assault? "Er, it's likely that Ross Peabody collects stolen artifacts."

"Good thing your aunt went with you."

"Yeah." Reaching for her now-cold tea, she swirled the liquid around her dry mouth.

"I take it something happened that I'm not going to like."

Kim sighed and turned. "How do you do that? I wasn't even facing you."

"Thirty years of practice." He winked. "Let's hear it."

So she started all over again, only this time she included the argument they'd overheard when they'd arrived at Ross Peabody's door.

"The thing is," she concluded, "even if the thieves had just arrived for a meeting with Peabody, they had no reason to suspect we'd been visiting him. Aside from Peabody himself, there were only two people who knew Aunt Ginny and I were there."

"Brittany knew," Grandpa said.

"Yeah, but she didn't have time to change into dark clothes and race outside to attack us."

She swallowed. "But there is someone who knew we were interviewing Ross Peabody and had time to change clothes and wait to ambush us in the parking lot: Officer Paula Darnell."

Chapter 18

"So you suspect Officer Darnell is involved with the local thefts?" Grandpa carried his coffee to the table.

"It's a possibility." The microwave beeped. Kim snagged a tea bag and carried mug and tea to the table. "When you were in the hospital, Brockley told me he suspected the local thieves were getting information from a police officer."

"So why didn't you share your suspicions about Officer Darnell?"

"You haven't seen the way he looks at her." Kim dunked her tea bag. "Right now she's the fair-haired child. *She's* the one who discovered Mary made four keys, not three. *She's* the one who tricked Mary into allowing them to search her house. *She's* the one who harped about Pirate's Treasure ice cream until Brockley searched..." Her hand stilled.

"Oh my gosh," she whispered.

What if Paula Darnell wasn't just working with the thieves? What if she was actively trying to frame Mary for murder -- a murder one of her partners in crime had committed?

"Darnell could have easily broken into Mary's house to hide those gems in the ice cream for Brockley to find," she said.

"But why? Why bother setting up Mary for murder? If Darnell really is involved with the thieves, she'd be safer keeping a low profile."

"The murder changed everything." Her hand shook as she set the tea bag onto a saucer and reached for the sugar bowl. "If the killer's caught, he won't hesitate to implicate his cop helper. Darnell needs to find a scapegoat."

Grandpa set down his coffee cup. "If you're right, then that woman is dangerous. Maybe it's time to step away and let the police handle this."

"If I'm right, Darnell will stack the evidence against Mary so tightly that she'll not only be arrested, but also convicted." She touched his hand. "Don't worry; I won't do anything stupid. I just need to gather enough information to convince Brockley to question Darnell's honesty. Maybe Scott can use contacts from his reporting days to find something. And I can certainly search the internet without Darnell knowing."

"And if you find something?"

"I'll tell Lieutenant Brockley."

Grandpa nodded and stood. "Just promise me you won't do anything dangerous."

Kim grinned. "That I can promise."

Calling to Rory, she trotted downstairs to help Grandpa prepare to open the store.

She carried a box to the front window and, consulting her diagram, began recreating her pirate still-life. The display had proven a great success, attracting locals as well as tourists.

Once they stepped into the store, however, visitors had been less willing to spend limited vacation money on a pretty sapphire, emerald or ruby.

Kim sighed. If only she could find a way to increase sales for Grandpa.

She draped the final necklace over the treasure chest, then lifted the sword hilt Rory had found in Pirate's Cove.

The cleaned bone felt cool. She wrapped her fingers around it, surprised to find it fit perfectly in her small hands. Had some long-ago pirate actually used this sword? If so, did that mean the ruby Bobby found really was part of buried pirate treasure?

Part of her thrilled at the idea of treasure right here in Osprey Beach. But she feared that even a rumor of pirate artifacts would attract treasure hunters. Treasure hunters had destroyed much of the coral reefs near Key West. She shuddered to think what they'd do to the local beach ecology.

Maybe she should remove the hilt from the display.

No, that would be extreme. With the jewelry sparkling in the sunlight, no one would pay much attention to the hilt. And if anyone did ask, she could claim it was nothing more than an oddly shaped piece of driftwood.

She plunged the broken blade into the sand and closed the glass panel that blocked access to the window. She locked the panel, returned the empty box to the office, then joined Grandpa at the display cases.

He'd arranged all but two boxes of necklaces, bracelets and earrings. Most of these would be displayed on traditional stands and velvet boards.

And maybe that was the reason sales remained low.

The flashy window display promised excitement within. Instead, visitors found the traditional jewelry store.

The psychology was all wrong.

Okay. Let's say the front pirate display draws in a potential customer. What would convince her to buy a ruby necklace instead of an inexpensive beach charm?

Kim scanned the jewelry. The customer would want something unique, something she couldn't find in her local store, something she'd have to buy right here, right now because she'd never find another one like it.

A filigree pendant caught her eye.

She lifted the necklace and held it to the light. Gold had been formed into a rounded diamond shape, the filigree fashioned to resemble twigs and leaves. A half-carat, brilliant-cut ruby nestled in the center. Though a modern piece, the pendant reminded Kim of Elizabethan jewelry.

Like something found in a treasure chest.

She smiled, an idea beginning to form.

She scanned the rest of the jewelry and found four more pendants that resembled antiques. Each had been set with a different colored gemstone -- purple amethyst, yellow citrine, blue topaz and rose quartz. The colors complemented the ruby without clashing. Perfect.

She reached for a velvet board and, one at a time, draped the five necklaces across it. She adjusted the tilt of the pendants, the curve of the chains, seeking that magic combination that would dazzle a prospective buyer.

The familiar motions allowed her mind to wander and she felt her breathing slow. Unfortunately, the drop in adrenalin revealed aches and pains caused by last night's assault. Was Aunt Ginny also suffering? She made a mental note to call later in the morning.

Stepping back, she studied the sweep of pendants she'd created. Yes, this definitely looked like a treasure-trove of jewels. And yet... Something was missing. Maybe earrings?

But not matching earrings. The contents of a pirate's chest would be mixed. Yet the earrings needed to complement the pendants.

She selected citrine drop earrings that mimicked the angles of the citrine pendant. Dangles set with orange garnets accented the purple necklace. She found several pairs of blue topaz and rose quartz earrings that would highlight those pendants without exactly matching.

But none of the ruby earrings worked well with the ruby necklace. The colors matched, but the settings were too fancy or too plain or too dissimilar.

She tried contrasting colors. The emerald/ruby combo was too Christmas-y. The blue sapphire/ruby combo too dull. As much as she enjoyed purple and red together, none of the amethysts were as saturated as the ruby; when placed next to the ruby, the purple turned pale.

In desperation, she reached for a pair of diamond studs, but they just overshadowed the poor ruby.

"Grandpa, do you have any more ruby earrings in the safe?"

"Might be a pair or two." Grandpa tucked a bust draped in pearls into the case. "Mostly what's in there are loose stones."

Loose stones. Yes, that might just be the answer. What would a pirate cache be without stolen gemstones?

Crossing into the office, she knelt before the safe. A cold nose snuffled her neck. Giggling, she reached back and ruffled Rory's ear.

"Enjoying your bone?"

In answer, Rory trotted to the dog bed beside Grandpa's workbench, lifted the enormous rawhide that had been laying on it and pranced around the small space, tail wagging.

"Yep, that's the bestest bone ever." The baby talk produced a higher prance.

But it was true; that bone was the best ever. It'd saved her life. She almost hated to see Rory chew it down.

Rory froze, eyes glued on something beneath Grandpa's chair. Dropping the bone in the middle of the floor, he ran to the chair, dropped his front end and scooched forward until all Kim could see was his wagging behind. A few seconds later he emerged with his new honking pheasant.

"Wow, good for you for saving the pheasant from that nasty old chair."

Rory cocked his head, the stuffed bird's feet dangling from his mouth. Kim's laughter produced a poodle snort. Sticking his nose and tail into the air, Rory headed for Grandpa -- someone who wouldn't laugh at his toy.

Still grinning, Kim reached into the safe and extracted a tray of jewelry envelopes containing a variety of red gemstones.

She closed the safe and carried the lot into the store.

Opening the first tiny envelope, she extracted the paper wrapped gems and teased open the package. Three rubies glinted at her. Their clean red color lacked the purple tones often found in stones from Burma. They'd probably been mined in Thailand or Cambodia.

Their color matched the stone in the pendant. Unfortunately, the ruby in the pendant came from Sri Lanka and possessed more sparkle than the Thai/Cambodian stones. When she combined the rubies, they all looked dull.

Sighing, she re-wrapped the rubies, tucked them back into their envelope and reached for the next.

Six brilliant-cut rubies winked up at her. The deep red color perfectly matched the pendant. But the stones were small, maybe a quarter carat each.

"Grandpa, what's with the teeny rubies?"

He peered over her shoulder and grinned. "Not rubies."

"But the color..." Kim frowned and reached for a loupe. She lifted one of the red gems and studied it under ten times magnification. The stone was flawless.

Rubies were never, ever flawless.

At least, that's what Grandpa told her when teaching her how to identify gemstones. Even the most valuable rubies, he'd said, contain stray crystals, feather-like spots or needle-like lines.

Kim, of course, had demanded to know why.

Grandpa told her it must have happened when rubies were formed. Problem was no one knew exactly how rubies were created.

The current theory pointed to plate tectonics, the ancient collisions of continents that formed mountains. The intense pressure and heat melted stone and refined the minerals, grouping similar atoms together. When the rocks cooled, the new minerals condensed. Among these was corundum, a rare mix of aluminum and oxygen.

Corundum in its pure form was colorless. Mix in a bit of titanium and iron, however, and corundum turned the rich blue shade of sapphire. Corundum plus a small amount of chromium created ruby's intense red.

Ruby's chemical makeup explained its rarity, but not its inclusions. Many other gems, including diamond, could form without flaws. During her undergraduate days, Kim spent many lunch hours proposing and debating possible reasons with other geology students.

The same ruby trait that drove Kim nuts, however, helped Grandpa and other jewelers differentiate between rubies and imitations. If a natural red gemstone lacked inclusions, it was one of the ruby look-alikes -- zircon, spinel or garnet.

The stone in her hand didn't sparkle enough to be zircon. Of the remaining two possibilities, she decided to guess the more expensive.

"Spinel?"

Grandpa grinned. "Nice try. But, no, these are garnets. Anthill garnets."

Kim frowned. Most of the garnets Grandpa stocked were pyrope garnets, the purple-red color most people associated with the gem. But he sometimes sold tsavorite garnets; she loved their emerald green color. And once she'd begged him to purchase spessartite garnet so she could drool over the bright orange color.

But she'd never heard of anthill garnets.

The glint in his eyes told her he was itching to tell a story.

Folding her arms, she leaned against the counter and grinned. "Okay, out with it. What are anthill garnets?"

"They're among the rarest gemstones," he said. "Found only in the Navajo Nation in Arizona."

Knowing she was falling into a trap, she played along. "Garnets aren't rare."

Grandpa flashed his "gotcha" smile. "Ah, but garnets mined by ants are exceedingly rare."

She blinked. From the gemstone's name, she'd expected his story would have something to do with anthills. But she was thinking more along the lines of "certain kinds of anthills indicate the presence of garnets" not "those nasty critters that ruin picnics don safety helmets and go mining."

"You wanna elaborate on that?"

Grandpa leaned against the counter, unconsciously mimicking her body language.

"When they're excavating their tunnels, the ants carry small garnets to the surface," he said. "No one knows who, exactly, first discovered the garnets mixed into the ants' hills, but I like to think it was a Navajo princess. Because of the blood-like color, legend claims the Navajos used the garnets as bullets." He shrugged. "I don't believe that; the Navajos were peaceful, so why would they spend time worrying about bullets?"

"Anyway," he continued, "today's Navajos collect the garnets from the anthills and sell them to gemologists. And that's why we have anthill garnets."

"Back up a second. Why do the ants bother carrying garnets to the surface?"

He chuckled. "This is why I never told you the story when you were a child. I knew you'd ask why."

"So?"

He shrugged. "I can't answer the question. No one knows why. Some people think that because garnets are heavier than sand, the ants use the garnets to strengthen their hills. Other people say the garnets are in the way, so the ants are just moving them. There are even people who claim the ants don't mine the garnets at all, that the garnets are appearing because of natural erosion."

Kim snorted. "If the worker ants were female instead of male, people would claim the ants like to see the garnets glinting in the sun."

She lifted one of the garnets and held it to the light. "It's amazing how much they look like rubies... Oh. My. Gosh. Grandpa!" She gripped his arm. "I just had a wonderful idea!"

"No, you cannot salt an ant farm with garnets."

"But isn't that the only scientific way to figure out why the ants remove the garnets? I'm kidding." She transferred the garnet to her palm. "Historically, both garnets and spinels have been mistaken for rubies, right? But most people don't know that.

"What would happen if we ran a contest? We could display a ruby, a red spinel and one of these garnets and ask people to guess which is the real ruby. The people who guess correctly would be entered in a drawing for a hundred-dollar gift certificate to the store. And maybe we could have a party here to announce the winner and you can tell your story about anthill garnets. What do you think?"

"Sounds like fun, but now I get to ask you a question: Why? Why run a contest right now? Wouldn't it be better to do something like that closer to the holidays?"

Kim shook her head. "People don't need a reason to come into the store during the holidays; they are looking for gifts. Holding a contest now -- one that we announce in the local newspapers -- will bring people into the store when we need the business." Especially after dismal sales when Grandpa was in the hospital, she thought. "It's a win/win for everyone."

Grandpa beamed. "Excellent idea from the young lady who couldn't sell Girl Scout cookies."

Smiling, Kim turned her attention back to the necklace display. She scattered anthill garnets around the ruby pendant. Stepping back, she studied the design.

"Does this look like a pirate's cache of gems?"

Grandpa peered over her shoulder. "Absolutely. Why don't you put it here in front?" He pointed to an empty space in the main showcase. "The display will be the first thing people see when they enter the store."

Perfect.

She spent the rest of the morning preparing to launch what she now thought of as the "find the ruby" contest. Or, more appropriate, "bring Grandpa some business" contest.

First she selected a garnet, spinel and ruby that were similar in size and color. She arranged them on a piece of velvet and labeled them A, B and C.

Next she drafted a contest entry form that included a place for name, address, phone and email and boxes to check off the letter A, B or C. At the top of the form, she instructed customers to select the letter corresponding to the real ruby.

She arranged the gemstones and entry forms beneath a sign reading "Can You Find the Real Ruby?" With a digital camera, she photographed the contest display, then took a close-up of the three red gemstones. She transferred the photos to her laptop and used them to create an advertisement to run in the local newspapers.

To her delight, the newspapers accepted electronic ad submissions. She purchased ad space for the next two weeks and emailed her newly created ad.

Her stomach growled. Time to close for lunch.

But the front door swung open and Lieutenant Brockley entered. Ignoring the wagging poodle, Brockley turned flat eyes her way.

"Ross Peabody is dead."

Chapter 19

After making the dramatic announcement, Lieutenant Brockley insisted on speaking to Kim alone. Grandpa remained in the store while she led Brockley upstairs and into the kitchen. She poured the last of the coffee into a mug. Selecting a special tea with a malt-like fragrance -- one that usually relaxed her -- she poured hot water over the leaves, then carried the drinks to the kitchen table.

Sliding into a seat across from Brockley, she wrapped her hands around her mug. Despite the warm sun beating through the window, goosebumps dotted her arms.

Ross Peabody was dead.

"How?" Her voice was scratchy, not her own. She cleared her throat and tried again. "What happened?"

"Do you own a gun?"

Kim shuddered. "Gawd, no. I hate those things--" She stiffened, suddenly realizing why Brockley had asked the question.

"Are you implying *I* shot Peabody?"

"Who said anything about him being shot?"

Kim plunked her cup onto the table. "First you say Ross Peabody is dead. Then you ask me about guns. It doesn't take a genius to assume Peabody was shot."

Brockley glared at her. She glared right back. In the distance, she could hear the grandfather clock start to bong. One, two, three, four... Rory poked his head under her hand and whimpered.

Great. Now the tension had scared her dog.

She wrapped an arm around Rory and leaned close, whispering in his ear. "It's okay, sweetie."

The young dog quickly recovered his normal aplomb. He charged down the hall and up the stairs to the bedrooms.

"That looks like a dog on a mission." Brockley grinned.

"Probably retrieving one of his toys." She fought the urge to smile back. After all, the man had practically accused her of killing the pirate memorabilia collector.

Brockley lifted his mug. "Look, I don't think you killed Peabody. But I had to ask the question because you and your aunt were the last to see him alive. Just be glad the Annapolis police are allowing me to interview you."

"First of all, Peabody's killer was the last to see him alive. And secondly, how did the Annapolis police even know we were there last night?"

"Officer Darnell told them."

Kim snorted. "Of course she did."

Brockley cocked an eyebrow, but didn't reply.

She looked away and reached for her tea. For a moment, she breathed in the fragrance. Finally, she met Brockley's mocking eyes. "So are you going to tell me what happened to Ross Peabody?"

"He was shot once through the heart."

"And his neighbors didn't hear a gun firing?"

"Walls are almost sound proof." Brockley sipped his coffee. "Killer might have used a silencer."

"But how did he get in? That place seemed pretty secure." An image flashed through her mind: Aunt Ginny pushing a button and the door buzzing open without anyone asking "who goes there?"

Even so, they'd arrived early in the evening. Surely no one would open the door for an unknown late-night visitor.

"The Annapolis police are still knocking on doors and reviewing surveillance videos, but my guess is Peabody knew his killer," Brockley said. "There was no sign of a break-in."

"The videos should tell you who did it."

Brockley shook his head. "Doubtful. The cameras are concentrated near the elevators. If the killer used the stairs near Peabody's condo, cameras wouldn't have captured him."

"But aren't there cameras at the building's front door? The stairs wouldn't help unless the killer was already inside--"

Kim broke off as she suddenly remembered someone she knew *was* in the building when Ross Peabody died: Brittany.

Brittany might know about the sound-deadening walls and the best ways to avoid the interior cameras. After the initial violent confrontation with Peabody, had Brittany felt the need to challenge him again?

She could picture Brittany again confronting Peabody. Maybe Peabody brandished one of his fancy handguns. She imagined a now furious Brittany spitting a curse, hurling herself at the man, wrestling for the gun, the sound of a shot, Brittany rushing from the room...

She shook off the image. Much as she'd like to accuse her childhood nemesis of murder, she had no evidence that Brittany returned to Peabody's apartment.

Quack, quack, quack, quack, quack, quack.

She grinned as Rory trotted into the room carrying his yellow stuffed duck.

Quack, quack, quack.

Brockley laughed and accepted the toy. "Is this one of our local ducks?"

Rory cocked his head.

"You know you're not supposed to tamper with the local wildlife," Brockley told him in a stern voice.

Rory slapped a paw onto the man's knee. Brockley tossed the toy down the hallway. The poodle raced after it.

"So," Brockley said, "you want to tell me what's on your mind?"

She grimaced. She'd forgotten Brockley and his all-seeing-cop eyes.

Rory dropped his duck into Brockley's lap, giving her a few minutes to consider her answer.

She couldn't count the number of times Brittany had falsely accused her of things she hadn't done -- things Brittany *knew* Kim hadn't done. But did that make it okay to throw suspicion on Brittany now? After all, this was murder not some childhood "she said/he said" prank. Did she really want to point the finger at Brittany?

Okay, maybe she did. She couldn't quite believe someone she'd known since childhood was capable of murder. But, oh, it was tempting to put Brittany into the hot seat for a change.

Of course, the killer might not be Brittany after all. What about that Nigel guy? He'd also know about the soundproofing, stairs and camera placement. Maybe he'd decided to avenge his lady love.

Yeah, right. That scrawny little Britt didn't seem the type. "I'm waiting."

At the harsh voice, Kim glanced up. How could the man sound so cheerful and fun when talking to Rory and, in the very next sentence, formal and stern to her?

She sighed. "Ross Peabody assaulted Brittany Bonnet last night." There, that didn't sound accusatory.

She described Brittany's arrival, the angry exchange and Brittany's attack. As she talked, Brockley wrote in his notebook.

"Peabody swatted her aside as if she was nothing more than a bug," she said. "Left a huge hand print on her face. Anyway, it looked like Brittany was spending the night with her boyfriend, Nigel something-or-other. He lives a few floors below Peabody."

Brockley jotted another note, saying he'd pass on Nigel's name.

"You also might want to ask the Annapolis police about the package Peabody was hiding in his safe. It was about the right size for the museum's swords and cutlasses. I'm sure the museum will want them back."

Brockley frowned but didn't respond. Gulping the last of his coffee, he stood. "I need to interview your aunt. She planning to visit today? It'd save me a trip to Annapolis."

Kim followed him to the kitchen door. "I'll call and ask her to come help with the store."

And warn her about Peabody's death.

Kim called Aunt Ginny to share the news of Ross Peabody's murder.

"Brockley wants to interview you, but would like to do it here," she concluded. "Do you have time to visit?"

"I'm meeting someone for lunch, but I can come your way afterward."

"Call me before you leave so I can tell Brockley when you'll be here?"

Aunt Ginny agreed and they said their goodbyes.

One more call to make. Before she could lose her nerve, she dialed the phone.

"Hey, gorgeous," Scott purred as a greeting.

His deep voice sent chills down her spine and she felt her toes curling.

"Hey, yourself." Oh, geez, was her voice breathless? She swallowed and tried again. "Uh, we've had a bit of excitement that I wanted to share."

She launched into a description of meeting Ross Peabody last night, finding Paula Darnell already there, Peabody's reaction to her seeing the open safe, Brittany's arrival, the attack in the parking lot and, finally, Peabody's death.

To Scott's credit, he only interrupted once, cursing the people who'd grabbed her in the parking lot. But when she suggested he ask his former police informants about Peabody's murder, he squawked a protest.

"This is getting too dangerous. There are two people dead and you were attacked."

"They didn't intend to hurt me."

"How do you know?"

Kim flashed back to three weeks ago, to the night when two hired thugs assaulted her. She could still see faint outlines of the resulting bruises.

"Believe me, I know the difference between a simple warning and an all-out attack," she said.

"Even so." Scott's voice was gentle. "Maybe it's time to back off, let the police handle this."

"Would you back off?"

Scott sighed. "What can I do?"

"Brockley said the police are studying the building's surveillance tapes, but they're not hopeful because the cameras only cover the lobby and the areas near the elevator. I'm thinking the killer may have already been inside."

"Brittany or her boyfriend."

"Or Paula Darnell. After she left Peabody's condo, she could have hidden in the building until everyone was gone."

To his credit, Scott didn't argue the possibility of the killer being a police woman.

"I'm going to do an internet search on Officer Darnell," she said. "Maybe you could ask around, see if there are any rumors about her. And, this may not be possible but I'd love to hear what Brittany tells the police about last night."

"I'll see what I can do on one condition: Next time you interview someone in person, invite me along. I'm not much of a fighter, but most criminals avoid attacking a woman who's accompanied by a man."

Kim smiled. "That I can promise."

They agreed to talk later.

Before returning to the store, Kim slapped together two peanut butter and jelly sandwiches. Calling to Rory, she trotted downstairs to find an empty store and a grinning Grandpa.

"Your pirate display is a huge hit." He gestured to her new jewelry arrangement. "I've already sold the amethyst pendant."

She set the sandwiches on the counter and joined him behind the showcase. Grandpa had filled the empty spot where the amethyst had lain with another old-fashioned looking pendant, this one set with a purple charoite.

Kim squealed and kissed Grandpa on the cheek. "It's working!"

"Your displays have always attracted customers," he said. "Sure you don't want to join me in the business?"

A wave of sadness swept over her. With four children and nine grandchildren, Grandpa naturally assumed a family member would eventually join his jewelry business. But while all the females enjoyed buying and wearing jewelry, only Kim expressed interest in the business. The others treated Grandpa's store as their personal jewelry box.

As much as Kim liked helping Grandpa in the shop, however, her aspirations lay elsewhere. In college, she'd studied both geology and psychology. The psychology courses offered insight into her jewel-obsessed family and she discovered she enjoyed teaching.

Reasoning that teaching was an honorable profession -- after all, she'd be helping others, right? -- she'd steeled herself for the long journey to become a tenured psychology professor. Now that she'd landed a coveted position at the University of Maryland, she couldn't imagine giving up the job to work in the store.

The fact that she dreaded the start of the school year was no reason to think she'd made the wrong career choice.

"You know I love you, don't you Grandpa?" She reached out and hugged him, then quickly changed the subject. "Wanna hear what Brockley said?"

She gestured toward the sandwiches and waited until Grandpa began chewing before summarizing her discussions with Brockley and Scott. As she talked, Grandpa's face grew increasingly somber.

"I have to agree with Scott," he said. "Peabody's murder changes everything."

"Mary didn't do it."

"Of course not." He sighed and ran fingers through his gray hair, leaving tufts sticking every which way.

"Maybe there's a safer way to help," he said. "We could hold a fundraiser, donate a portion of sales to pay for a good lawyer."

Kim winced. A fundraiser might help Mary, but it would push Grandpa's store further into the red.

"All I'm going to do right now is search the internet." She reached over and smoothed Grandpa's hair into place. "If I need to talk to anyone in person, Scott said he'd come with me."

"You should keep Rorschach with you, too."

Kim glanced down at the standard poodle laying at her feet, eyes closed, a squeaky toy clenched between his teeth. A month ago, she'd have scoffed at Grandpa's confidence in her curly companion. But that was before she saw Rory drive off Grandpa's attacker and defend her from a man with a gun.

"Deal."

The front door bell jingled and two middle-aged women entered. Rory opened an eye, assured himself that Kim was nearby and went back to sleep. Clearly, playing store dog had exhausted him.

While Grandpa assisted the women, Kim powered up her laptop and typed into the search engine "Paula Darnell Calvert County." She bit into her sandwich and scanned the results.

The top entry linked to a two-year-old article published when Darnell joined the local sheriff's department. Written in typical press-release fashion, the story quoted the sheriff and other law enforcement bigwigs professing Darnell's importance. A single paragraph near the end of the article summarized the woman's career history.

After graduating from Annapolis High School, Darnell attended the police academy. She worked for the Annapolis Police department for several years, then became head security guard at National Towers in Annapolis.

Kim frowned and finished her sandwich. What an odd career progression. Surely it would make more sense to work for a small department like Calvert, advance to the Annapolis Police and then retire to security guard. Instead, Darnell had started large, moved into security work, then joined the small local force.

Why? Had she been fired from the Annapolis police? Been forced to resign?

Returning to the search engine, Kim typed in "Paula Darnell Annapolis Police." Two links appeared.

A press release described Darnell's success in recovering a collection of Faberge eggs that had been stolen from the wife of an Annapolis politician. She scanned the article. The chief of police praised Officer Darnell's diligent efforts blah blah blah.

Kim sighed and clicked on the second link, another press release. This one announced Darnell's appointment as a security guard for National Towers in Annapolis. The building's owner, a Robert Markey, gushed about Officer Darnell's success at the Annapolis Police Department.

She jotted down Markey's name. She'd call him later.

Clicking to a new screen, she searched for information about the National Towers. The builder's site claimed the newly constructed high-rise housed "some of the city's most influential lawyers, medical specialists and businessmen." The building itself was located near Ross Peabody's condo.

Had Paula Darnell met the wealthy collector while working at National Towers?

She searched for "National Towers" and "Ross Peabody," but found no matches. A link to a police brief, however, caught her eye. The article reported a series of thefts at National Towers. Among the items stolen: An antique cutlass that once belonged to Captain Kidd.

Heart racing, she checked the date of the robbery. The cutlass had been stolen while Paula Darnell worked for National Towers as a security guard.

She frowned and leaned back in her chair. Was it a coincidence that pirate memorabilia disappeared whenever Darnell was near?

Maybe she should tell Lieutenant Brockley. No, to investigate, Brockley would need more than coincidence; he'd want real evidence.

Too bad Scott didn't still work for *The Washington Post.* He could call Darnell's old boss, say he was writing an article...

Wait a minute. Why couldn't *she* say she was writing an article? She couldn't claim to work for the *Post,* but maybe... Before she lost her nerve, she dialed the number for National Towers. Within minutes she had an appointment to interview Robert Markey for a fictitious specialty police magazine.

She glanced at the clock on her computer screen. Two p.m. Markey's secretary had scheduled a 3 p.m. meeting. Plenty of time to change clothes, brush her hair and drive to Annapolis.

She explained to Grandpa her plans, reminded him that Aunt Ginny would arrive mid-afternoon to talk with Lieutenant Brockley and hurried upstairs to toss a light-weight blazer over her t-shirt. Considering this was the second time in as many days that she'd posed as a reporter, she made a mental note to ask Scott how real ones dressed. If the women wore skirts, she'd have to devise a new cover story for these types of interviews.

"Be good for Grandpa." She ruffled Rory's ears, then hurried out to her car.

Despite construction on Rt. 2, she arrived at National Towers with five minutes to spare. She followed a couple of lawyer types into the chilly, gray lobby. Banks of elevators lined the two side walls. A brawny man dressed in a charcoal uniform and gun belt stood next to a reception desk, legs planted, arms crossed, a don't-mess-with-me expression on his face.

One of Paula's former colleagues? She made a mental note to attempt conversation after her interview with Markey.

Markey's secretary had instructed Kim to check in at the desk. Unlike the burly guard, the white-haired man perched behind the desk gave her a welcoming smile.

"What can I do for you, young lady?"

She returned the smile. "I have an appointment with Robert Markey."

The man reached for a phone. "Name?"

"Er, Kimberley West. I'm with *Police Life Today.*"

As the older man announced her presence, the guard sidled close. "Never heard of *Police Life Today.*"

"Brand new magazine for policemen and women." Thank goodness she'd come prepared for that question. "I'm doing interviews for the premier issue."

The guard's eyes narrowed, but before he could say anything a young blond appeared, introduced herself as

Lindsey and led the way toward the back of the building. To Kim's disappointment -- she'd hoped to stroll past some of the offices and view the personal items on display -- Robert Markey's domain was down a plain hallway lined with doors marked "utility" and "employees only."

Markey greeted her at his office door. Tall, silver-haired and dressed in a gray silk suit, the man oozed traveling salesman confidence.

"Paula Darnell will make a great profile subject." He waved her to a burgundy leather guest chair. "Before I hired Paula, my tenants suffered from all sorts of petty thefts."

He settled into his own leather chair and folded his hands on top of the mahogany executive desk. The desk's surface was bare of everything except a photo of a plain brunette and three boys ranging in age from maybe six to twelve.

"What sorts of things were taken?"

"Purses, cash, personal items, anything small that could be pocketed without someone noticing," Markey said. "It was damn embarrassing having all of that disappear in broad daylight."

"But I noticed security cameras in the lobby..."

"Ah, but we don't have cameras in the actual offices." Markey snorted. "Lawyers don't want cameras freaking out their customers."

"So the cameras are only in the lobby?"

"In the lobby and covering the elevators."

Interesting. The security set-up was similar to the one in Ross Peabody's condo.

"So how did Officer Darnell stop the thefts?"

"She actually patrolled the building," Markey said. "Moved around the hallways, entered offices, got to know the tenants by sight. Potential thieves never knew when Paula might stroll in. She once caught someone from the mailroom trying to remove cash from a secretary's desk."

Entering offices would also allow Darnell to scope out the personal items in the offices.

Time to push Markey a bit.

"But the thefts didn't stop, did they? I read somewhere that a pirate's cutlass was stolen?"

"Those thefts happened at night, under other guards," Markey said. "I told Paula if I could clone her, the world would be a safer place. I said--"

"Wait a minute." Kim resisted the urge to lean forward. "You said thefts plural. Were other items stolen besides the cutlass?"

Markey sighed. "Yeah. But it was all stuff the tenants have no business stashing in their offices."

"Like what?"

Markey leaned back and used his fingers to tick off items. "A Mickey Mantle baseball card, an antique sheriff's badge, a Civil War Calvary sword, a signed Walt Disney photo, a signed Pirates of the Caribbean poster. Would you believe there was even some stupid egg that was worth more than the baseball card? I mean, c'mon, we're talking Mickey Mantle here."

Kim felt her heart rate increase. "An egg? You mean, like a Faberge egg?"

Markey flipped a hand. "Yeah, yeah, that's what they called it. What's up with that?"

He continued on a rant about societal values. When he wound down, she asked several more open-ended questions. But Robert Markey had nothing else to add.

"One final question," she said. "Do you have any idea why Officer Darnell left the Annapolis police? Usually police officers don't go into security work until after they retire."

"Which is why most security guards are nothing more than beat-up cops." Markey crossed his arms and looked smug. "That's why we pay our guards a lot more than what they'd make as police officers. So we can get the best. Paula had a good thing here.

"And before you ask, I have no idea why she left me to join that rinky-dink sheriff's office."

"You didn't want her to leave?"

"Absolutely not. Tried to talk her out of it. Even offered her a raise. But she said she missed police work. Go figure."

Kim thanked Robert Markey for his time and stood. Promising to send him a preview copy of the magazine, she hurried away before he could question her further.

As she neared the information desk, the guard stepped in front of her. "Get what you needed?"

Kim shuffled sideways, bumping against the desk. The guard followed, trapping her.

Oh, goody, another bully.

Folding her arms, she lifted her chin and met his eyes. "Actually, I'll be writing an article about an amazing guard who actually patrolled the offices instead of hanging around the lobby pushing people around."

The guard's hands clenched and for a moment Kim feared she'd pushed him too far. Then the man threw back his head and laughed.

"Hey, Ralph, you hear this dame? Thinks she can tell me how to do my job."

The elderly man behind the desk stood. "Let her pass, Johnny."

Johnny the guard stepped back, raising his hands to show his palms. "Hey, we're good."

Kim hurried through the opening and headed for the door.

"Don't you want to hear the truth about Paula Darnell?"

She stopped and glared at Johnny. "What makes you think I was talking about Paula Darnell?"

Johnny shrugged. "Markey thought she walked on water. Only us peons got to see her real side."

"Oh? And what was that?"

The guard snarled. "She was a first-class bitch. Flirting with everyone, playing one guy against another, causing fights. And the only one she ever actually put out for was Markey."

She tried to hide her surprise, but apparently, wasn't successful. Johnny smirked.

"Oh, yeah, Ms. Perfect had an affair with her boss."

"C'mon, Johnny, you're not being fair." Ralph, the older man, leaned on his desk. "The girl had a rough upbringing. And it couldn't have been easy for a lower-class woman to marry into the Annapolis Darnells and Peabodys."

"Peabodys?" Kim turned to the desk man. "As in Ross Peabody?"

Ralph nodded. "Ross and Katherine and that whole bunch." Seeing her interest, he added, "Want to hear the real story of Paula Darnell?"

Chapter 20

The return trip to Osprey Beach passed in a haze as Kim tried to digest the story Ralph the desk clerk had related. If true, the events that shaped Paula Darnell explained her transformation from honest cop to sneaky thief. Whether Kim could find a clue to the killer in Ralph's story remained to be seen.

She pulled into Grandpa's driveway, easing the van next to Aunt Ginny's red convertible. Good. Maybe between the three of them, they'd find something to lead Lieutenant Brockley away from Mary.

Rory greeted her at the kitchen door, but her grandfather and aunt were nowhere to be seen. Voices drifted from the living room. Kim followed Rory down the hallway and paused at the living room door. Grandpa and Aunt Ginny perched on the sofa, staring at the television.

A map of the East Coast filled the screen. A series of colored dots trailed along the shoreline.

The perky blond weather girl pulled a long face as she pointed to the largest of the dots just southeast of Florida.

"Hurricane Dan has been upgraded to a Category 3 hurricane with 112 mile-per-hour winds," she said. "At the moment, Dan is expected to make landfall somewhere between Georgia and North Carolina. If Dan follows Isabel's path and continues to the west of the Chesapeake Bay, we could experience historically high storm surges."

Grandpa groaned.

"How high is historically high?" Kim said.

"Isabel produced eight foot surges."

Kim shivered.

Hurricanes seldom traveled as far north as Maryland. The most damaging tended to land near North Carolina's Cape Hatteras, 350 miles south of them. Such storms could produce a combination of high winds, rain and tide that carried bay water over the boardwalk and into people's homes.

Years ago, Grandpa decided to protect his business and home by hiring people to elevate the building ten feet above the boardwalk. Concrete block walls now supported the building, creating a buffer against flooding. Grandpa used the open area beneath his home as a garage; in severe storms, cars could be moved to higher ground.

She'd been living in Oregon when Hurricane Isabel hit her hometown. When she'd placed a frantic call to Grandpa, he'd downplayed the storm. Yes, the basement had flooded and he'd lost electricity. But Grandpa, his store and home had all escaped damage.

If Hurricane Dan produced higher storm surges than Isabel, however, the store itself might be in danger.

"As long as it stays south of Cape Hatteras, we should be okay," Grandpa said.

"Shh." Aunt Ginny pointed at the television.

A dark-haired anchorman beamed at the camera. "We thought we'd end this report on the lighter side. Is there buried pirate treasure in Osprey Beach?"

Kim's stomach plummeted.

But the smiling face continued. "Let's go live to Connie Burns. Connie?"

The picture switched to a wide shot of the new Pirate Museum. As the camera slowly closed in on a group of people, a woman's voice said "Less than one week ago, the joyful opening of Osprey Beach's newest attraction turned to tragedy when a burglar broke into the Pirate Museum and not only stole millions of dollars' worth of priceless items, but also murdered one of the museum's board members."

The camera zoomed in on a smiling, immaculately coiffed reporter. "But thanks to a recent discovery, the Osprey Beach Pirate Museum will reopen with even more exiting exhibits."

The camera zoomed back and there stood Brittany, dressed in designer shorts and high heeled sandals, posed like a model, nose slightly elevated, slight smile on her perfectly painted lips.

Connie the reporter said, "I have with me today Brittany Bonnet, the generous donor behind the new and improved museum." She turned toward Brittany. "I understand that a personal family heirloom was among the items stolen." The reporter tipped the microphone toward Brittany.

"That's correct," Brittany said. "The thieves stole a ruby amulet that belonged to the Gentleman Pirate, one of our ancestors."

Kim rolled her eyes and sank onto the sofa next to Grandpa.

"Throughout the years," Brittany continued, "many people tried to convince my family to sell the amulet. But naturally we'd been reluctant to part with such an important part of our heritage." She wiped an imaginary tear from her blue eyes. "I just hope the police can find whoever did this."

"Well, let's talk about something more upbeat, shall we? I understand that the museum will re-open and you have a very special exhibit planned."

"Yes, we'll be exhibiting the only pirate treasure ever discovered right here in Osprey Beach!"

Kim groaned. Brittany had just doomed Osprey Beach to an influx of treasure hunters.

She'd seen photos of other places rumored to contain pirate treasure. The soil had been pockmarked with holes as if giant prairie dogs had moved in, then abandoned the area. The so-called "Money Pitt" -- a Nova Scotia island purported to hold Captain Kidd's buried treasure -- was so riddled with man-made craters that you took your life in your hands just trying to walk across the island.

And now Brittany was telling the world that Osprey Beach contained buried treasure.

The camera now widened to reveal Mary's son Bobby. To his left, the three girls who'd tormented Liz with their singing waved and mouthed "Hi, Mom" at the camera. Liz stood on the outside of the line, frowning down at her sneakers.

"This is Bobby Klein, the young man who discovered the treasure. Bobby, tell us about your discovery." Connie held the microphone down to Bobby.

His brown eyes widened and for a moment he looked as if he might cry. Then he puffed out his chest.

"Well, I'd been studying pirate history, you know, what Blackbeard and his gang did with the loot they found."

Liz's head swiveled toward Bobby, her eyes wide. The cameraman, obviously annoyed with the other girls who'd continued to mug to the camera, zoomed in on Bobby's face.

"And from what I read," Bobby continued, "I just knew there must be treasure here somewhere. I--"

The reporter interrupted, trying to hurry him along. "So you went digging in Pirate's Cove. Please tell our viewers what you found."

"A huge red ruby!"

"And why do you think it belonged to Blackbeard?" Connie said.

"Well, Mr. Hershey said something about the way it looked--"

"Bobby's ruby," Brittany interrupted, "is similar to the one my pirate ancestor wore into battle. The two rubies might have come from the same pirate stash."

"And do you think there's more where this came from?"

"Who knows?" Brittany grinned at the camera. "You all will just have to come to the museum and find out."

Kim leaped to her feet. "I'm going to kill her."

Chapter 21

As she raced to her car, Kim dialed the cell phone number Brittany had given to the museum board members. It immediately clicked into voice mail.

She didn't bother leaving a message. Maybe it was better to not warn the creep that she was coming.

She flung open her car door. A black blur pushed her aside, scrambled past the steering wheel and into the passenger seat.

"I don't remember inviting you."

Rory stared out the windshield, ignoring her, his pink tongue hanging out in anticipation of a car ride.

Kim looked back to see Grandpa standing at the top of the outside stairs.

"You promised you wouldn't go anywhere alone," he said.

"It's too hot to leave him in the car!"

"So bring him into the museum with you." Turning, he disappeared inside.

Kim sighed. Rory continued to look away from her. He knew he was supposed to sit in the back, but there wasn't time to argue with him. Defeated, she retrieved his seatbelt and secured him in the passenger seat.

Ten minutes later, she turned into the museum parking lot. She'd expected to see a crowd of media vans, but only a single car remained. The baby blue convertible most likely belonged to Brittany.

"Figures," she muttered to Rory. "Brittany gets the hot car and I get the soccer mom van."

Brittany probably also had the hot-car lifestyle, while Kim's was definitely soccer mom. Or, rather, dog mom. Even though Rory didn't shed, he liked to paddle in whatever body of water that presented itself. Muddy poodle paws and fancy convertibles didn't mix.

Sighing, she pulled into a parking space well away from the blue car. No sense giving Brittany the opportunity to accuse her of dinging the convertible.

She clipped Rory's leash to his collar and allowed him to leap from the car. Figuring Brittany was inside, she started toward the museum.

Rory, however, had other ideas.

With a muffled woof, he tugged her in the opposite direction. Kim planted her feet; the last thing she needed was this exceptionally bright dog thinking he could drag her wherever he wanted.

Unrepentant, Rory strained at the leash, tail wildly wagging. Kim followed his line of sight and spotted a girl's bicycle leaning against the low stone wall that edged the parking lot. On the other side of the wall, a gnarled tree leaned toward the bay and a narrow strip of unstable land ended in a sheer drop to the beach below.

Kim's heart raced. Where was the bike's owner? Had someone fallen off the edge?

No longer worried about training her dog, she followed Rory to the bike and peered over the wall. No footprints showed in the dry soil. If someone had fallen, surely she'd see scuff marks on the edge of the cliff.

Rory slapped his front feet onto the wall and woofed into the air. Kim looked up and spotted the girl sitting high up in the tree.

Liz.

"Liz? Are you okay?"

"Go 'way." Liz didn't even look around. She sat with bowed head and hunched shoulders, long hair hiding her face.

Kim glanced back to the museum. She really needed to confront Brittany, put a stop to the treasure rumors she was spreading. She looked back at Liz. The girl's body language screamed dejection.

Sighing, she tied Rory's leash to the tree trunk, draped her purse cross-body and stepped onto the low wall. She snagged the lowest branch and started to climb. By the time she reached the branch Liz occupied, she was out of breath.

"Scoot over."

Liz's head whipped up. Kim allowed herself a moment to enjoy the girl's reaction to finding an adult in the tree: her mouth dropped open and her eyes widened. Then, without a word, Liz shifted to allow room on the branch.

For a few moments, they sat in silence, Kim gazing at the water, Liz shooting sideways glances at Kim.

Kim finally broke the silence. "Great view. Wish I'd have known about this tree when I was your age."

Liz dropped her eyes and shrugged. Now Kim could see the mini iPad clutched in the child's hands.

"Reading a good book?"

Liz sighed and handed the iPad to Kim. But instead of a book, the screen showed an internet search for pirate treasure.

"How'd you get internet connection out here?"

"Hooked into the museum's system."

Hmm. Surely the museum's computer system was password protected. Probably best not to ask.

Instead she scanned Liz's search results.

"Find anything interesting?"

Liz gestured toward the bay. "How am I supposed to find treasure when it's all out there?"

"You found the ruby."

"Bobby found the ruby. And he won't let anyone forget it."

Ah. That might explain Liz's mood.

"Boys can be jerks sometimes." Kim returned the iPad to Liz.

"Tell me about it." Liz stared at the water, fingers clutched around the tablet.

Kim mimicked Liz's body position and allowed a few minutes to pass. "Sometimes it helps to talk."

"You wouldn't understand."

"Why? Because I'm older than you? That just means I've wrestled with more jerky boys than you have."

That produced a small smile, which quickly faded. A breeze lifted the girl's hair, tossing a piece across her brow. Kim resisted the urge to brush it aside.

"He's not really a jerk. Not unless *Tonya's* around."

Kim tried to recall the three girls who'd stood near Bobby as the reporter interviewed him. Two blonds and a brunette. The blond nearest Bobby had leaned possessively toward him.

"Tonya the blond bimbo who couldn't stop mugging at the camera?"

Finally, Liz's smile reached her eyes and the story poured out. "I was supposed to be on TV with Bobby; he said so. But nooooo, he'd bragged to Tonya about appearing on television and she showed up and--" Liz bit her lip.

"Pushed you aside?"

Liz nodded. "And Bobby didn't stop her! He just stood there grinning at that reporter, acting like the center of the world. He promised to let me tell about how it was my idea to dig below that tree. But he just acted like I wasn't there. And then, afterwards, he went off with *her*."

Kim didn't need to ask for the identity of "her." Throughout the years, starting with Brittany, she'd struggled against her own share of sneaky blonds. Her heart ached for the little girl slumped beside her. Betrayal cut deep no matter your age.

She struggled for a response that would ease the pain. Grandpa used to say life would ultimately humble people like Brittany. Yet Brittany came roaring back to the three beaches, wealthy, beautiful and determined to position herself as an Osprey Beach hotshot. Where was the justice in that?

She wrapped an arm around Liz and whispered in her ear. "Sometimes the best revenge is to go on living your own life."

Liz returned the hug. "That's exactly what I'm gonna do." Her voice quivered and for a moment Kim feared Liz would cry. But then Liz's shoulders straightened.

"And when I discover the real pirate treasure, I'm not gonna share with Bobby." She frowned and pointed at her iPad. "But it says here that the boats sunk with the treasure still inside. So that means everything is under the bay. To find it, I'd need to--" Her eyes widened. "Can you teach me to scuba dive?"

The laugh exploded from deep within her. "I'm sorry." Happy tears streamed down her face. "I'm not laughing at you. It's just... Liz, I love your style."

To her relief, Liz smiled back.

"I don't think we need to scuba dive to look for treasure," Kim continued. "Grandpa used to tell stories about pirates. As you found out, they didn't tend to bury actual treasure chests.

"But they *did* bury small pouches of jewels and coins, basically their share of their recent plunder."

She nodded toward the museum. "I need to talk to someone, but how 'bout afterwards we go to the store and talk to Grandpa? He knows about the area's pirate history. Maybe he can give us ideas of where to dig."

"You mean you'll help?"

Kim couldn't resist tugging Liz's ponytail. "Wouldn't miss it. Would you mind keeping an eye on Rory while I go to my, er, meeting?"

Liz readily agreed. Swinging a leg over the branch, Kim started the long climb down. As she neared the bottom, the strap of her purse caught on a twig. She tugged it loose, lost her balance and snatched at the trunk. The rough bark slowed her downward slide. She landed on her feet and surveyed the damage.

The blue jeans protected her legs, but the t-shirt was torn and her hands and arms sported long, bloody scrapes.

"Interesting technique."

Kim glared up at the grinning child. "Watch it, kid. I'm still bigger than you."

Liz giggled, then sobered. "Seriously, you okay?"

Kim reassured the girl, then glanced at the museum. Still no sign of Brittany. But she didn't dare run home to change clothes; Brittany could leave any minute.

She'd just have to wash the scrapes in the museum bathroom and ignore Brittany's taunting.

She kneeled down to Rory. "You need to wait here with Liz, okay?"

He cocked his head, then licked her glasses. Kim fished glasses cleaner from her purse and scrubbed the lenses. When she could see again, she touched Rory's fur and nose. Both were cool. The shade from the tree coupled with the breeze from the bay prevented overheating.

"I'll be right back."

Straightening, she marched toward the museum. Maybe, when faced with Brittany's inevitable insults, she'd remind the woman who'd won their childhood scuffles.

Brittany had left the front door unlocked. Kim headed for the nearest bathroom to clean her scraped hands.

The anti-septic soap stung. Wetting a paper towel, she scrubbed at the dirt on her jeans and top, then ran a brush through her hair. She still looked like she'd been wrestling a black bear, but that couldn't be helped.

Stepping from the bathroom, she called Brittany's name. No answer. The maze of rooms did a good job of deadening sound. She'd probably find Brittany in back where the gemstones had been exhibited, planning her triumphant re-opening showcasing Bobby's ruby.

Adjusting her purse and lifting her chin, Kim stomped toward the rear of the museum.

Even in the daylight, the empty building spooked her. The wall exhibits -- photos of glaring pirates interspersed with cutlasses, muskets and swords -- reminded her of the last time she'd been here.

She slipped the purse from her shoulder and wrapped the straps around her fist. In a pinch, the heavy, over-sized bag served as a weapon.

As she neared the entry to the jewelry exhibit, she called Brittany's name. No response. Surely the woman could hear her. Was she just ignoring Kim? Or...

Kim slowed. "Brittany?"

Still no answer.

Maybe the woman was upstairs? Kim tightened the hold on her purse. She'd finish checking these rooms before climbing the stairs.

Stepping through the open doorway, she automatically searched the area where they'd found Dorothy's body. The blood had been removed, the floor swept clean of glass. Wood piled in the corner marked the former location of the gem exhibit. The pedestal that once held Brittany's amulet had already been restored and positioned in the center of the room.

Kim stepped around it and froze.

A woman lay sprawled in the doorway to the next exhibit. From this angle, Kim could only see shapely legs clad in shorts and high-heeled sandals.

No. No, no, no, no. Kim started to back out of the room, then forced herself to stop.

What if Brittany had simply fainted? Or tripped on those ridiculous shoes?

She forced her breath to slow and crept forward. The woman's face came into view.

A moan escaped her lips. She turned away. She made it as far as the pile of wood before losing her lunch. When her stomach was empty, she pulled a tissue from her purse and wiped her mouth.

Nothing, however, could wipe the vision of Officer Paula Darnell's bulging blue eyes or the cord tied around her neck.

But there was something else...

Turning, she forced herself to return to the body. Avoiding looking at Paula's face, she focused on the sparkling earring caught in her hair. The graceful curves of platinum gleamed with black and white diamonds.

Kim recognized that earring. Brittany had worn it the night she accused Ross Peabody of stealing her amulet.

So how did it get here? She shifted her eyes lower. Paula's ears were adorned with a pair of plain gold studs.

Had Brittany attacked Paula and lost an earring?

Brittany. The blue convertible was still parked outside.

And Liz was alone.

Whipping around, Kim raced through the museum.

Chapter 22

Kim ran from the museum, calling Liz's name. The little girl looked up from petting Rory.

"Get in the car!" Kim pointed at her van and aimed the remote to open the rear doors.

Liz bent to untie Rory's leash from the tree.

"Don't worry about Rory; I'll get him." All that mattered right now was making sure Liz was safe.

With a backward glance at Rory, Liz dashed to the van and crawled into the back seat.

Kim scanned the parking lot as she ran. Other than the empty blue convertible, she could see no other cars. Did that mean the killer was gone? Or was he watching from the nearby woods?

She reached Rory, unsnapped his collar from the leash and sent him into the car after Liz. She closed the rear doors as she rounded to the front, jumped in and pushed the automatic lock button.

Her hand trembled, making it difficult to shove the keys into the ignition. The car started immediately -- thank you Toyota -- and Kim peeled out of the parking lot.

"My bike!" Liz protested.

"We'll get it when we come back," Kim said. "Don't worry; we won't be gone long."

She pulled onto the main road. Maybe the killer hadn't seen them. She glanced at the rear-view mirror, but the typical beach traffic prevented her from identifying a car that might be pursuing them.

She bit her lip. If someone *was* following, she sure didn't want to lead him back to Grandpa's.

No, she needed to find a nearby place to pull over and call the police, a public place with lots of people. She turned into the parking lot of the new 24-hour gym. For a moment, she stared into her rear-view mirror, left foot on the brake pedal, right foot on the gas. But no other cars turned into the crowded lot.

Satisfied that they hadn't been followed, she shifted the car into park, applied the hand brake and reached for her phone.

"What's wrong?" Liz's voice trembled.

"There's been an accident at the museum."

Liz's eyes narrowed. "You're lying. An accident wouldn't make you run away. I thought you were my friend."

Kim's shoulders slumped as she mentally kicked herself. She, of all people, should recognize a child's need for honesty. From the time she'd turned six, she demanded total candor from the adults, even chastising Grandpa for making up fairy tales.

Now, in a misguided attempt to protect Liz, she'd committed the same error.

"I'm sorry; I was trying to minimize what I saw in my own mind." She inhaled deeply. "I found a dead woman in the museum."

Liz gasped and for a moment Kim feared she'd misunderstood the girl's needs.

But then Liz's face cleared and she leaned forward, eyes bright. "Was she, you know, murdered? Like in the movies?"

"I'm afraid so."

"Wow."

Suppressing a smile, Kim turned away and dialed 9-1-1.

An hour later, she wished she'd never called the police.

"I have a few more questions."

Lieutenant Brockley loomed over the open door of her van. With his broad shoulders and small waist, the man was built to loom.

Too bad she was too frustrated to appreciate the view.

She'd planned to take Liz and Rory to Grandpa's before meeting the police at the museum. But the dispatcher who'd answered her call insisted Kim return to the museum immediately.

A police woman had escorted Liz and Rory into her air-conditioned squad car. Judging by the occasional flashing lights and sirens coming from the car, Liz was enjoying herself.

Kim, on the other hand, had spent the hour standing in the heat, recounting the events that led to the discovery of Paula's body. She'd told her story once to the first officer to arrive, then again to Lieutenant Brockley, then a third time to Brockley.

By the time she'd been released to collect Rory, Liz and Liz's bike, she was dripping in sweat. All she wanted to do was return to Grandpa's and take a cool shower. Before she could escape, however, Brockley stopped her, saying he had yet more questions.

"Can't we do this another time? I've told you everything I know."

Brockley glanced into the back seat. Liz and Rory stared back, wide-eyed. His eyes moved to the scrapes on Kim's bare arms, then to Kim's face.

"Just a few more questions."

He thinks the scratches came from a fight.

As the thought formed, Kim's chest muscles contracted.

"I told you, I scratched myself climbing down from that tree." She pointed to the other side of the parking lot.

"She's right; I saw her do it," Liz said.

Brockley sighed, ran a hand across his smooth-shaven cheek, then kneeled.

"Look, I believe you had nothing to do with Paula's death. But someone murdered one of our own and I don't have the luxury of letting my feelings get in the way of the investigation."

"Even if your own officer was a crook?"

Brockley stood so quickly that he bumped his head on the door frame. He started to curse, spotted the young face watching him intently and settled for rubbing his head.

Before he could reply, a female officer approached. "We found this tangled in the victim's hair." She extended a plastic bag. "It's not Officer Darnell's."

Brockley accepted the bag. "How do you know?"

"She was wearing a pair of gold earrings."

Brockley studied the contents of the bag, then held it out to Kim. "Did you lose this when you found the victim?"

The unsaid words 'or when you killed her' hung in the air.

Kim recognized the diamond earring she'd seen tangled in Paula's hair. "Are you kidding? I can't afford anything like that even with Grandpa's discount. It looks a lot like the earrings Brittany was wearing the other night."

Frowning, Brockley passed the bag back to the officer and mumbled a series of instructions that Kim couldn't understand.

Turning back, he gestured for her to get out of the car. "Let's move this conversation into my car."

"Why?"

"So you can explain why you accused one of my officers of being a thief."

"The evidence is sitting right in front of you." Kim pointed to the blue convertible she'd assumed was Brittany's. The car, however, belonged to Paula.

No way could a security guard/police officer afford such an expensive means of transportation.

If Brockley couldn't add two plus two, nothing she said would change his mind.

"Am I under arrest?" When he didn't answer, she reached for the open door. Brockley jumped out of the way as she slammed it shut. She opened the window. "I know. Don't leave the county."

Kim balanced three glasses of iced tea and headed downstairs to Grandpa's store. As she neared the bottom of the staircase, the squeal of a child's laugh made her smile. She paused at the entrance to the shop.

Liz perched on a stool with Rory sitting beside her. They both stared at Grandpa.

He wore a battered broad-brimmed hat and was miming tugging on a rope. Kim grinned, immediately recognizing the start of Grandpa's diamond hoax story.

As she watched, Grandpa the diamond prospector finally convinced his stubborn mule to walk forward a few feet. He exaggerated wrapping the mule's harness to a hitching post and knocking on a door.

Quietly, Kim set the glasses onto coasters, then leaned against the counter as she listened to one of her favorites of Grandpa's stories.

Until just a few weeks ago, she'd always assumed the tale about two 19th Century con men and a fake Colorado diamond mine had been fictional. That the story was based on a real hoax only made it more delightful.

It was also the perfect tale to distract Liz from recent events. Though she'd tried to hide it, the girl had been terrified of returning home; her mother would still be at work and the house would be empty.

Knowing Grandpa would work his magic, Kim had brought her to the store.

Of all his stories, the diamond hoax provided Grandpa with the greatest opportunity for slapstick. Kim laughed along with Liz as Grandpa pretended to lead a group of gullible businessmen to a high desert region salted with industrial diamonds. As the story came to an end, Kim joined Liz in the applause.

Grandpa swept the hat from his head and bowed, then reached for his iced tea.

Liz turned to Kim. "I wish your Grandpa could meet my Grandma."

Kim suppressed a shudder as she imagined Liz's narrow-minded, dour grandmother dating Grandpa. True, the woman clearly loved her grandchildren. But her evasions and half-truths had hindered Kim's investigation into the attacks on Grandpa. She'd prefer to avoid the woman.

Time to change the subject.

"Would you like to talk about what happened today?"

In response, Liz winced. A wave of guilt washed over Kim. But psychological studies indicated children handled trauma better if encouraged to work through the events immediately. Suppressing the fear would only allow it to fester in the subconscious.

Plus, it would be easier for Liz to talk about it now without the police hovering. An officer would interview Liz later when her mother was present.

"Why don't we sit over there?" Grandpa gestured toward the conversation nook. "I'd like to hear what this young lady has to say."

Just the sound of Grandpa's voice eased the tension in Liz's shoulders. Kim grabbed a hard-backed chair and dragged it beside the two upholstered ones.

"Why don't you start with arriving for the television interview?" she said.

"We were supposed to meet Ms. Bonnet a half hour early so she could, you know, tell us what to say," Liz said. "But when I got there, Bobby was already talking with Ms. Bonnet and Tonya, Valerie and Ashley were pushing up against him."

"Who else was there when you got to the museum?"

"Television people." Liz's eyes widened. "There were trucks and cameras and people all talking at once."

"Anyone else hanging around besides the television people?"

Liz shook her head.

"What about the blue convertible? Did you see it arrive?"

Liz frowned. "Maybe. I just don't know. I wasn't really looking, you know?"

Kim patted her hand. "You're doing great. So then what happened?"

"Ms. Bonnet told Bobby to say that Mr. Hershey," she nodded at Grandpa, "said the ruby was definitely from a pirate treasure. I tried to tell her you didn't say that, I really did, but Ms. Bonnet wouldn't listen."

Of course Brittany wouldn't listen. She needed rumors of local treasure to bring national attention to "her" museum. The truth never stopped Brittany from getting what she wanted.

"So then the reporters started asking Ms. Bonnet about the ruby and Bobby lied about what Mr. Hershey said and Tonya wouldn't let me near Bobby and..."

Liz bit her lip, clearly fighting tears of frustration.

"While all that was going on, did you notice any new cars arriving or leaving?" Hard to imagine that someone was murdering Paula while Brittany blabbed on camera -- surely a killer wouldn't be that daring? -- but it was entirely possible that the murderer was trapped in the museum when the camera crews began arriving.

But Liz hadn't noticed any cars. Like the other children, she'd been dazzled by the cameras. She might not have been standing in her rightful place beside Bobby, but she was by golly appearing on television.

When the interview ended, however, Bobby, Tonya and the others rushed away to get pizza. No one invited Liz.

Disheartened, Liz had trudged across the parking lot, climbed the tree and stared at the bay. She'd been only vaguely aware of the slam of car doors, the rumble of engines starting, the murmur of tires on asphalt.

"You didn't watch the cars leaving?"

Liz shook her head. "But I heard your car pull in."

Kim leaned forward. "Focus on what you heard after you climbed the tree. A bunch of cars left at once, right? Did you hear a separate car, one that maybe left later than the others?"

Liz frowned as she concentrated. But again she shook her head. "I just wasn't paying attention, you know? It was quiet until you and Rory arrived and--" Liz's eyes widened. "Oh, wow, I got to sit in a police car and blow the siren! And there was the ambulance! And the body! Wait till I tell Bobby!"

Grandpa's mouth opened. Kim shook her head, signaling him for silence. Liz hadn't actually seen a body. But the girl clearly needed a way to one-up her friend.

And, who knows, maybe the exciting tale would shove Tonya the bully back into the slime where she belonged.

Liz was still bubbling with excitement as she gathered her backpack in preparation for the drive home. Kim marveled at the resilience of children. Give them a safe environment and the opportunity to work through trauma and they'd often bounce right back. If Liz had nightmares tonight, they'd most likely involve Tonya and Bobby and not the sirens and police cars.

As she drove the chattering girl home, however, Kim struggled against her own nightmare. Liz hadn't seen the killer enter or leave the museum.

But had the killer seen Liz?

Chapter 23

Early the next morning, Kim, Grandpa and Rory strolled along the boardwalk toward the Osprey Beach Cafe. Rory high-stepped ahead, the breeze ruffling his plumy tail. Though a few clouds dotted the sky, the gentle waves and warm air belied the morning weather reports: Hurricane Dan's projected path was aimed straight at Maryland.

The Category 3 hurricane had torn a path across the Bahamas, killing four, and was now splattering Florida with heavy rain and high wind. Forecasters predicted the storm would make landfall Sunday night, two days from now.

"Do we need to buy plywood today?" Kim eyed a summer cottage, its windows already covered with large sheets of plywood. Year-round residents would wait a day before protecting their homes from what would be, at minimum, high winds accompanied by blowing debris.

"Got everything we need in the basement."

Kim nodded and tucked a stray hair into her ponytail. It'd been more than a decade since she'd sat through a hurricane with Grandpa, but she could still remember the sound of waves crashing over the boardwalk, the thump of wind-blown debris, the steady drum of rain.

Rory, with his fear of thunder, was so not going to like this.

Up ahead, the outdoor tables at Osprey Beach Cafe came into view. Aunt Ginny stood and waved. Kim smiled and quickened her steps, grateful that the people she'd come to think of as "the Calvary" had all responded to her late-night plea for help.

Last night, the fear that the museum killer had seen Liz in the parking lot haunted her. Her mind had buzzed with ideas to protect the girl.

She'd considered announcing to reporters that Liz had been at the museum, but hadn't seen anything suspicious. That approach, however, could easily backfire. For one thing, the killer might not believe the story. Worse, if he *hadn't* seen Liz, the revelation might put her in more danger.

Sending Liz and her family out of town until the killer was caught also wasn't reasonable. The police seemed determined to pin Dorothy's murder on Mary, which meant the real killer wouldn't be caught any time soon.

She could envision only one realistic option to protect Liz: Identify the real killer.

She wouldn't actually confront the man -- she was more sensible than that. She'd just point the police in the right direction.

With that in mind, she'd invited Scott, Aunt Ginny and Ginny's friends to breakfast. They needed to compare notes and discuss ways to identify the killer and keep Liz safe. She'd included Mary in the invitation, reasoning her old friend might shed light on why the killer seemed intent on framing her.

To accommodate everyone, Scott and the ladies had pushed three tables together. Looked like everyone but Mary had arrived.

"You haven't been sleeping." Ginny wrapped her arms around Kim.

"Hello to you too." Kim hugged her aunt, then stepped back and smiled shyly at Scott.

Though they'd talked on the phone, she hadn't seen him since Grandpa's cookout four days ago. The man still took her breath away.

Dressed in khakis and a safari-style shirt, he needed only a hat and whip to portray Indiana Jones. His little dachshund, bouncing a greeting to Rory, spoiled the macho image a bit. But when Scott flashed that half grin, a tremble coursed through her.

"I think you look great," he said, leaning toward her.

Al chose that moment to leap onto a chair. Scott scooped up Al with one arm and, holding the small dog like a football, placed a chaste kiss on Kim's cheek.

Feeling her face flush, Kim turned away to greet Doris, Maureen and Wilma. As usual, Doris wore pink; pink flamingos danced across her flounced skirt while a floppy hat adorned with a wide pink ribbon covered her white curls. In contrast to Doris's garden-party attire, Maureen and Wilma wore practical Bermuda shorts, t-shirts and comfortable sandals.

Kim hugged each woman in turn. Despite their lady-like appearances, the women were among the strongest people she knew -- especially the lady in pink. Doris had not only survived a recent kidnapping, she'd shielded Aunt Ginny from the kidnapper's sights.

"Mary not here yet?" She accepted the chair Scott held, trying to ignore his fresh Irish Spring smell.

"We're all early." Grandpa dropped into a seat beside Aunt Ginny. "Let's wait for Mary to arrive before we order."

The waitress appeared, but everyone only ordered tea and coffee.

Kim turned to Doris, Maureen and Wilma. "I know you all have been talking with people who attended the museum banquet," she said, "but before we discuss that, I assume Aunt Ginny told you all about Paula's death?"

Everyone nodded.

"How's the child?" Doris said.

"Seemed okay when I drove her home last night. I'm afraid Liz might be in danger. If the guy who murdered Paula was still inside the museum when Brittany and the media arrived, he would have waited until everyone left before making his own exit. I don't think he'd have noticed Liz sitting in that tree, but with an empty parking lot, her bicycle was pretty hard to miss."

"Which means we'd better find the killer before he finds Liz," Aunt Ginny said.

Kim nodded. "Since Paula Darnell is the most recent victim, let me start by sharing what I learned about her. Before she came here, she worked as a security guard at National Towers. The desk clerk there seemed to know her life story."

She paused, remembering her conversation with Ralph, the white-haired man who sat behind the front desk at National Towers. As he'd talked, a succession of men and women clutching briefcases called a greeting as they hurried to the elevators. To each one, Ralph responded with a personal inquiry: *How's that new granddaughter? Did you enjoy the restaurant? Did she like the anniversary present?*

Each question elicited a smile and detailed response from the otherwise harried professional. Kim quickly realized why Paula Darnell had confided in Ralph. Not only was he a great listener, but he oozed empathy.

"Paula told Ralph she was the only child of a lower-middle-class couple," she said. "When she was five or six, her parents divorced. Her mother worked two jobs to make ends meet and, apparently, urged Paula to marry a rich man."

"Don't all mothers say that?" Doris said.

"Obviously, your mother never told you that." Scott grinned at Kim.

Grandpa laughed. "No one ever told Kim what to do."

Kim rolled her eyes and continued without comment.

"Paula attracted a lot of boys -- she was tiny, blond and flirtatious -- but the one she really wanted was Tommy Darnell. Not only was he the star football player, but he was wealthy and a member of Annapolis's most elite society. They became a couple and eventually were crowned Homecoming King and Queen.

"High school sweethearts seldom survive the separation of college, so Paula convinced Tommy they should marry immediately after graduation. Tommy's parents were furious -- this was their only child -- but they weren't able to dissuade him."

She paused to sip her tea. "Last night, I found newspaper photos of the wedding on the internet. Let me tell you, his parents did not look happy."

"Afraid Paula was a gold digger?" Maureen said.

Kim imagined the photo of Paula and Tommy sandwiched between the groom's parents. Tall and thin, the blond-haired father stood erect and unsmiling. The mother, also blond and slender, wore baby blue silk and a smile that didn't reach her eyes. Give the couple a rifle instead of a pitchfork and they could pose as the Nazi version of American Gothic.

"I'm not sure any woman would have satisfied those two," she said. "Anyway, after their honeymoon, Paula and Tommy attended college. He studied law. Paula majored in history.

"Even though Tommy's parents were wealthy, Tommy couldn't gain control of his trust fund until he turned 25. He and Paula had to live on an allowance from his parents.

"The allowance was large enough to allow Paula and Tommy to continue circulating among the Annapolis elite. But Tommy's parents resented Paula and most of their friends snubbed her."

She paused to make sure everyone was listening. "The only member of Tommy's family who actually accepted Paula was Ross Peabody."

Everyone froze.

"The same Ross Peabody we visited?" Aunt Ginny said.

Kim nodded. "Ross was Tommy's uncle."

Scott blew out his breath and slumped back. "Wow, I didn't see that coming. None of my police contacts knew about the family connection."

"After the way Paula's life fell apart, I suspect she didn't want to think about Tommy or his family." She paused, her chest tightening. Ralph had had tears in his eyes as he related this part of Paula's story.

"During Tommy's second year of law school," she said, "Paula became pregnant. Her friends -- the ones from pre-Tommy days -- threw a co-ed baby shower.

"On the drive home from the party, a drunk ran them off the road. Tommy died instantly. Paula was rushed to the trauma unit in Baltimore. She survived, but the baby didn't."

"That poor woman."

Hearing the sorrow in Grandpa's voice, Kim swallowed and reached for her tea. A few minutes later, she continued the story.

"Tommy's parents blamed Paula for their son's death. They cut off all support. With a pre-nuptial agreement and no children, Tommy's parents were able to prevent Paula from receiving any of her husband's trust fund."

"Nasty," Aunt Ginny said.

Kim nodded. "So in addition to dealing with the death of Tommy and her unborn child, Paula suddenly needed to find a way to support herself." Kim shuddered. Even though Paula had been a crook, Kim couldn't help feeling sorry for the woman.

"Paula's degree in history wasn't much help," she continued. "So she entered the police academy."

"Why police work?" Scott said.

Kim shrugged. "My guess? She was probably tired of people pushing her around. Wearing a gun and strutting around in a uniform would sound like a good way to gain control of her life.

"Anyway, she did so well at the academy that the Annapolis police department hired her."

"Annapolis?" Scott frowned. "If she worked in Annapolis, what was she doing here?"

"Stalking Brittany's pirate ruby."

That statement produced a satisfying round of gasps.

"Whoa," Grandpa said. "How does a well-respected cop become a thief?"

"She gets tired of rich people pushing her around." Kim sipped her tea before proceeding. "She told Ralph that her police work required her to kowtow to the very same people who'd snubbed her when she married Tommy.

"The breaking point came when she was assigned to investigate the theft of a collection of Faberge eggs. While trying to track down the thief, Paula spent weeks interviewing pawn-shop owners. In the process, she recovered all but one of the stolen eggs and the *Capital Gazette* wrote a story about her."

"That doesn't sound like a reason to quit," Wilma said.

"Well, the reporter didn't know the whole story," Kim said. "Apparently, the owner of the collection demanded Paula be fired because she didn't find the final egg."

"Were they really going to fire her?" Scott said.

"Of course not. Paula's job was to find the thieves, not retrieve the stolen property. But the whole thing soured Paula on police work. The newspaper story attracted the attention of Robert Markey, the manager of National Towers. When he offered to double her salary to come work for him, she accepted."

"Why in the world would he pay so much for a guard?" Aunt Ginny said.

Kim shrugged. "Said he gets the best people that way. But I think he got more than he bargained for."

She pulled out a timeline of Paula's life that she'd put together and passed it around.

"Notice that a few months after Paula started working at National Towers someone stole a Faberge egg from one of the offices."

"What makes you think Paula stole it?" Grandpa passed the timeline to Scott.

"Psychology." She planted her elbows on the table and leaned forward. "After her experience with the police, she probably resented anyone who owned the eggs. Plus her investigation would have revealed where to sell them. Must have been impossible to resist taking it."

"Wait a minute." Scott pointed to the timeline. "A year after she started working there, someone stole a cutlass?"

Kim grinned. "Not just any cutlass. That one was supposed to belong to Captain Kidd."

She waited while everyone absorbed that bit of information.

"My police sources said they always suspected Ross Peabody of buying stolen items," Scott said. "But they were never able to prove it. Did you see the Captain Kid cutlass when you visited Peabody?"

Kim and Ginny laughed. "Ross had so many swords and sharp things hanging around, we'd never have noticed it."

"Like in 'The Purloined Letter.'"

Kim grinned at Doris, tickled to find another fan of Edgar Allen Poe. "Yep. Hide the stolen item in plain sight and no one will notice."

"Didn't Markey suspect Paula was stealing?" Grandpa said.

Kim shook her head. "Paula was smart enough to steal only occasionally and only when someone else was guarding the building. She actually lowered the daytime theft rate by patrolling the offices as well as the hallways."

"Also known as casing the joint," Aunt Ginny said.

"Exactly."

"Sounds like Paula found an easy way to make money," Grandpa said. "So why would she accept a job in our small community?"

"It's all Brittany's fault." She pointed to the timeline. "Notice that a little over two years ago, *The Calvert Recorder* reported that Brittany was not only financing a new Osprey Beach Pirate Museum, but that she'd be loaning her family's ruby amulet for display.

"Ross Peabody has been trying to buy that amulet for years. The Bonnets refused to sell."

She dropped her finger to the next timeline entry. "A few months after the paper announced the construction of a new museum, Paula quit her security job and joined the Calvert County's sheriff's department.

"I think she intended all along to steal the amulet for Ross Peabody."

Grandpa whistled. "How much of this can you back up with evidence?"

"I can establish the pattern, but have no actual proof Paula stole things." She slumped back in her chair. "Might be impossible to convince Brockley that his star pupil was a thief."

"The problem is she's not just a thief." Grandpa's eyes met hers. "If her goal in joining our local force was to steal the ruby amulet, then she might be the one who killed Dorothy."

"Then who killed Paula?" Aunt Ginny said.

"Maybe she had a partner," Kim said. She swept her hand across the timeline she'd written. "Problem is, this is all theory. We don't have enough information to convince Lieutenant Brockley that Paula was involved, let alone that Mary is innocent."

Aunt Ginny leaned forward, her normally cheerful expression suddenly solemn. "Speaking of Mary, I need to share a rumor before she gets here."

Kim's stomach clenched as her mind raced with possibilities. The police were about to arrest Mary. The museum board wanted to fire Mary. Nigel was replacing Mary as director.

Fortunately, Aunt Ginny didn't keep her in suspense.

"I talked to everyone on my list of people attending the museum banquet." Ginny tapped the notebook she'd set on the table. "I'll tell you what they said in a minute. What worries me is several people claimed Mary's husband has a wandering eye."

Kim took a minute to process her aunt's genteel description into modern language. "Kevin's having an affair?"

"Just rumors. No one could give me specifics. And, believe me, I asked."

"I heard the same thing," Maureen added. "Also rumors, no specifics."

"Well, no one said anything to me." Doris folded her arms and pushed out her lower lip. "Why do you all get the good stuff?"

Wilma patted Doris's hand. "Don't worry; no one mentioned an affair to me either."

While Aunt Ginny and her friends debated the pros and cons of insider information, Kim searched her memory for hints that Kevin was cheating on Mary. Truth was, she'd been so focused on helping her friend that she hadn't paid much attention to her husband. She'd noted the loving way Kevin swung his daughter onto his shoulders, the pride in his eyes as he studied his son, the protective fury as he stormed the police station searching for Mary.

And yet... Something niggled at the back of her mind, some stray observation that warned her against dismissing the rumors outright.

"Sorry I'm late!"

Kim turned to greet Mary. At the same time that Rory leaped to his feet. Before she could stop him, he'd planted his front paws on Mary's shoulder.

"Rory, no!"

"That's okay." Mary rubbed Rory's sides. "He's not heavy."

"No, it's not okay." Kim snagged Rory's collar and with a firm "no feet up" pulled him off of her friend. "Sit."

Rory wagged his tail, but made no move to drop his butt to the decking. Kim dropped her voice lower. "Wrong. Sit."

With a sigh, Rory sat.

"Good boy." She pulled a treat from her pocket and handed it to him, ruffling his ears as he chewed. "That's a very good sit."

Rory rolled his eyes sideways, drawing attention to Al. The little dachshund had his front feet on Mary's knees, his tail wagging furiously. Mary encouraged the behavior by squealing and cooing at Al.

Kim sighed. "Yeah, I know it's not fair." Popping a dog treat into her mouth, she patted her shoulders and cued "feet up." Rory eagerly flopped his front paws onto her shoulders and gently retrieved the treat from her mouth. She petted him, murmuring "good boy," then cued him "feet off." This time, he dropped his front feet to the floor.

"Hey, why are you allowed to do that and I'm not?" Mary planted her fists on her hips and for a moment resembled the little girl who'd challenged Brittany in the playground.

Kim laughed and settled Rory under the table. "He's not allowed to put his feet on *anyone's* shoulders unless invited. If I leave him to his own devices, he might knock someone over."

For a long time, she'd despaired of ever breaking the friendly poodle from jumping on people. Part of the problem had been people like Mary who liked dogs so much that they refused to cooperate when Kim tried to correct the young dog. With all of the encouragement from people like Mary, Rory clearly hadn't understood what Kim wanted him to do. The words "no" and "off" fell on deaf ears.

Kim finally resorted to the method she'd used to stop excessive barking. First, she taught Rory to do the behavior on the cue: "woof" or, in this case, "feet up." When she didn't want the behavior, she simply added the word "no." Rory had been able to connect "no" with "woof," so "no woof" had proven effective at stopping unnecessary barking.

"No feet up" was supposed to prevent the jumping. Clearly, she needed to work with him a bit more.

"So what did I miss?" Mary plunked into the empty chair beside Aunt Ginny.

Kim felt her cheeks flush. They had no proof that Kevin was having an affair and, if he was, she sure didn't want to be the one to tell Mary.

Best to direct the conversation elsewhere.

"We're pretty sure Ross Peabody bought stolen artifacts," she said. "And there's evidence Paula Darnell was his contact."

"So the cop killed Dorothy and Peabody?" Mary said. "Then who killed the cop?"

"That's one of the problems," Kim said. "We don't know how many killers we're dealing with. One person could have

killed all three people. Or Paula could have killed Dorothy
and Peabody and someone else killed her."

"Or each murder could have been committed by a
different person." Scott grimaced.

Seeing Mary's drawn face, Kim added, "Hey, look at the
bright side. The police can't suspect you of all three deaths."

"Oh, yes they can." Mary folded her arms. "Lieutenant
Brockley showed up at my door last night wanting to know
what I'd done all day and if anyone could verify my actions."

"Did you have an alibi?"

Mary snorted. "I was home alone with Kimmie when
Darnell was murdered and asleep with Kevin when someone
shot Ross Peabody. When Kevin tried to vouch for me, the
good lieutenant practically accused Kevin of lying."

"But you had no reason to kill Darnell or Peabody." Kim
refrained from adding the question "did you?".

"You saw the way Darnell was trying to pin Dorothy's
murder on me," Mary said. "That's reason enough, at least
according to the police."

"And Ross Peabody?"

Mary closed her eyes, sighed, then opened them. "A few
months ago, he came to the museum demanding to see
Brittany's ruby amulet. I guess he figured she'd store it at the
old museum while the new one was being built.

"Of course, the amulet wasn't there, so he left in a huff.
Not long afterwards, I discovered a sapphire ring was
missing." She turned to Grandpa. "I told you; it was the one
with the table-cut sapphire that Mrs. Bonnet donated."

"Brittany's mother?" Kim said.

Mary gave a fake shudder. "Oh, yeah. You can imagine how she reacted when I told her it'd been stolen. We'd just put it on display, too."

"You mean it was stolen from a display case?" Scott frowned. "How?"

"The old glass displays are easy to open," Kim said. "All you need is a pocket knife or some other thin blade to slide between the top and sides of the glass. An accomplished thief can open the display, grab what he wants and be out of the building in less than five minutes."

To Mary, she added, "I assume you weren't watching Peabody the entire time he was in the museum?"

Mary shook her head. "We had school children visiting when he came in. And before you ask, these were kindergarteners; they couldn't reach the top of the cases let alone jimmy them open. Other than the teachers, Ross Peabody was the only adult in the museum that day -- and the teachers had their hands full with the kids.

"Anyway, after the police left, I was so incensed that I called Peabody and demanded he return the ring. He denied stealing it and, well, we ended up screaming at one another. Just my luck that Dorothy came in, heard my end of the conversation and lectured me for an eternity about not offending 'clients.' And you know Dorothy; I'm sure she told everyone about my fight with Peabody."

"But that's not a reason to kill someone--" Kim broke off as the waitress reappeared to take their orders. Though she hadn't even opened the menu, Kim knew exactly what she wanted: The cafe's signature French toast. Made from thick slices of their homemade bread, the toast was seasoned with tons of cinnamon and vanilla.

After the waitress took everyone's order and refilled coffee and tea cups, Kim asked Aunt Ginny about her interviews with the people who'd attended the banquet.

"Dorothy sure didn't have many friends." Aunt Ginny squeezed lemon into her water glass. "People had a hard time finding anything nice to say about her."

"The only positive thing I heard was that she had a nice daughter," Doris said.

"Well, speaking of the daughter..." Wilma leaned forward. "Yesterday I saw Jennifer Tyson having dinner with a bunch of girlfriends. Bridesmaids, I think; they were tipsy from drink and pretty darn loud. It's been less than a week since her mother died." Wilma shook her head. "I sure didn't see any remorse there."

"When I talked with her, Jennifer seemed pretty confused," Kim said. "She was sad that her mother was gone, but... I got the impression she was astounded by how her life was easier without Dorothy breathing down her neck."

"Did she seem the type to murder her own mother?" Maureen said.

Kim shrugged. "She doesn't have an alibi." Rory pushed into a sit and lay his head in Kim's lap. "On the night of the banquet, her fiancé had to work. So Jennifer spent the evening at home alone.

"But I'm not sure there *is* a type of person who murders. We studied a lot of cases in my abnormal psychology classes and, aside from certain psychopaths, I sure couldn't predict who would kill and who wouldn't."

She absently stroked Rory's neck. "Most of us could kill in self-defense or if we were defending a loved one."

"What about the fiancé?" Aunt Ginny had been helping in the store when Jennifer and her fiancé bought their ring. Ginny turned to the other women. "Dorothy gave her daughter a list of requirements for her diamond. Jennifer's fiancé almost fainted when Kim told them a perfect diamond would cost tens of thousands."

Kim grinned. One of her finer moments had been steering Jennifer to a more appropriate diamond, one that enhanced her warm skin tones and slender fingers. That it cost a fraction of what Dorothy demanded was a small victory.

Was it possible that the purchase of the ring marked the beginning of a rebellion -- a rebellion that ended with the murder?

She sighed. "I guess we can't rule out the daughter or her fiancé."

"Did Jennifer inherit money with her mother's death?" Maureen said. "Or did everything go to the husband?"

"And what about the husband?" Doris said. "Isn't the spouse always the most likely suspect?"

"He's certainly got motive," Wilma said. "I believe the wealth came from her side of the family."

Before the conversation could disintegrate into chaotic gossip, Kim jumped in. "All good points." She turned to Doris. "When Dorothy was killed, her husband and Uncle Walt were playing video games. So he's out."

"Unless he hired someone to kill her," Aunt Ginny said.

Kim frowned, trying to picture Dorothy's husband, daughter or future son-in-law plotting cold-blooded murder. If this were an Agatha Christie style murder, she'd seriously consider a conspiracy among the three surviving family members.

But this was real life and conspiracies were notoriously hard to hold together. The human psyche was such that, as Ben Franklin said, "Three can keep a secret, if two are dead."

Still... Dorothy's heirs were now wealthy -- without a controlling woman nagging them.

"Maybe we need to look at all of these murders from a different angle." She pulled a notebook from her purse. "Let's make a list of who benefits from each death."

Flipping to a clean page, she created three columns and, at the top of each, printed the name of one of the murder victims. Under Dorothy's name, she wrote "husband, daughter, daughter's fiancé = $$$."

"So who else benefits from Dorothy's death?"

Wilma scoffed. "Probably anyone who ever had to deal with the woman."

"Can you be more specific? We need reasons strong enough to kill."

But while Dorothy had offended, alienated and bullied dozens of people, none of the confrontations were strong enough to commit murder.

Kim tapped her pen against the tablet. "Okay, let's assume for the moment that no one specifically targeted Dorothy, that she was killed because she interrupted a burglary. Why would someone murder Ross Peabody or Paula Darnell?"

"Money's often a motive," Grandpa said. "Anyone know about Ross Peabody's heirs?"

When everyone shook their heads, Scott pulled out a notebook. "I'll check on that."

Kim wrote "heirs?" under the column for Ross Peabody. She studied what she'd written. Even though money was often the prime reason for murder, people killed for other reasons.

Like revenge?

Brittany certainly had revenge on her mind when she physically attacked Ross Peabody. When Kim had imagined Brittany returning to Ross Peabody's apartment, she'd pictured Peabody pulling one of his guns and, in the resulting struggle, the gun accidentally killing him.

But what if Brittany brought her own gun to confront Peabody? As far as Kim knew, the police hadn't found the murder weapon.

"Does anyone know if Brittany had access to a gun?"

Grandpa didn't hesitate to answer. "Stede once lectured the museum board about the importance of handguns. That probably means he's got at least one at his house."

"So even though Brittany no longer lives at home, she'd know where to find her dad's handguns." Kim's heart rate increased. Could the killer, after all, be Brittany?

"Forget it," Scott said. "Brittany has an alibi for Peabody's murder."

"But I saw her in Peabody's building!"

"Her boyfriend claimed she never left his apartment after you saw her."

Kim dropped her pen, leaned back and crossed her arms. Every time she found a way to point the police away from Mary, something got in the way.

"Maybe the boyfriend is in on it," she said. "Or Brittany drugged him so she could sneak back to Peabody's condo."

"And she just happened to have her father's pistol in her purse?" Grandpa chuckled. Kim stuck out her tongue.

"Actually, Kevin thinks Brittany is behind everything," Mary said.

Everyone turned toward Mary. She'd been so quiet during the discussion that Kim actually forgot her friend was there.

With everyone staring, Mary shrank into her chair.

"Why does Kevin suspect Brittany?" Kim used the soothing tone she reserved for small children.

Mary's brown eyes met Kim's. Mary blinked, straightened in her chair and squared her shoulders. "He said none of this -- the local thefts, the museum robbery, the various deaths -- occurred until after Brittany moved back to Osprey Beach."

"I thought she's only been living here for a week," Kim said.

"She started traveling back and forth from New York soon after donating the money," Mary said. "Kevin said she hung around the construction site, driving him and everyone else nuts. When he started building display cases, she was practically breathing down his neck. She said she wanted to make sure the displays were secure. But that also gave her a chance to study security efforts."

"But why kill Dorothy? Dorothy was her aunt and one of Brittany's biggest supporter."

"Kevin thinks Brittany intended to steal her own amulet with the idea of collecting insurance money. She had that darn thing insured for a million dollars!"

Kim felt her mouth dropping open. A million dollars? For a badly cut ruby and some bits of gold?

"So Kevin thinks, what?" Kim said. "After the banquet Brittany dumped her boyfriend and returned to the museum to steal her own amulet?" It made a certain weird sense. After all, with hundreds attending the museum opening, the number of suspects would be high.

Mary nodded. "And Dorothy walked in on her so Brittany had to kill her."

"But... Brittany could have explained why she was there." Sheesh, she never thought she'd find herself defending Brittany. "She could have said she was checking things since Dorothy had fired the night watchman."

"She couldn't explain why the cases had been broken." Mary leaned forward. "Don't you see? In order to make a claim on the insurance, Brittany had to prove it'd been stolen.

She'd have broken several cases and stolen a number of items so the insurance company wouldn't question the theft."

"Brittany was one of the few people who knew Dorothy fired the guard so the museum would be unprotected that night," Wilma said.

"But to kill her own aunt--" Kim broke off as she remembered something else.

"Brittany's earring was caught in Paula Darnell's hair."

Now everyone was staring at Kim.

"And you were going to tell us this when?" Aunt Ginny folded her arms across her chest.

"I was getting to it, honestly." In truth, Kim had so much sloshing around in her head, she had no idea when that piece of information would have floated to the top.

"Besides there's no reason for Brittany to kill Paula Darnell," she added.

"Don't forget, Paula Darnell was a police officer," Grandpa said. "If Brittany did kill Dorothy or Ross Peabody and Officer Darnell suspected it, that might be a motive for murder."

Kim shook her head. "No way. I could maybe see it if Paula Darnell was shot. But someone strangled her. Brittany would have had to sneak up behind Darnell and then overpower a trained police officer. I can't imagine she'd have the strength.

"Besides, Brittany wounds with words."

"I cleaned a lot of scratches on your arms when you were a child," Grandpa said.

Kim frowned. Grandpa was right. Though the roll-in-the-dirt-till-someone-dies fights ended with grade school, in middle and high school Brittany continued to lash out with long nails if someone challenged her authority.

"Brittany desperately needs anger management therapy," she said. "But her physical attacks were always spur-of-the-moment. Sort of like road rage. I can't imagine her actually *planning* to fight someone."

"That's because you haven't heard what Brittany did to her husband's lover," Mary said.

"I thought she was divorced."

"Oh, this was what caused the divorce." Seeing everyone staring, Mary blushed.

"Well, don't just sit there," Kim said. "Tell us."

Mary cleared her throat. "Brittany suspected her husband was cheating when he was supposed to be working overtime. One day she waited outside of his office and followed him to a sleazy motel. He met some woman and they went into a room.

"Brittany drove to a nearby Walmart, bought a baseball bat and returned to the motel. She knocked on the door and when her husband answered, slammed the bat between his legs. While he was writhing on the floor, she swung the bat at the naked mistress. The other woman managed to knock it aside and Brittany attacked with her bare hands.

"The motel manager heard the commotion and found the mistress laying outside of the motel room. She was covered in scratches and had a broken nose. The husband hobbled for a few days.

"The only reason Brittany didn't do more damage was the bat was made of plastic instead of wood."

Kim folded her arms. "Why haven't we heard about this?"

Mary snorted. "You have to ask? Brittany's parents threw money around to keep everything quiet. The only reason *I* know is I met the owner of the motel where it all happened. When he tried to call the police, the mistress stopped him, said she had a better way to handle the problem. She gave him her cell phone, asked him to take pictures. He said she sent the photos somewhere and, for someone so beat up, she looked awfully happy."

"Probably blackmailing the Bonnets," Kim said. "You'd think Brittany's parents would get tired of bailing her out."

"Their insistence on protecting her may be why she's never grown up," Grandpa said.

"I got the impression Mr. Bonnet was the one who spoiled her," Kim said. "Brittany used to brag that her father overruled her mother's disciplinary actions."

"You know, speaking of Jessica Bonnet," Aunt Ginny said, "she said something weird when she gave a talk at my garden club yesterday."

"Mrs. Bonnet does her own gardening?" Kim tried to imagine the elegant lady up to her elbows in cow manure. Couldn't do it.

"I doubt it," Aunt Ginny said. "But she sits on the Save the Chesapeake Bay committee. We invited her to talk about that."

"Oh, goodie, another wealthy do-gooder."

Ginny shrugged. "Don't be so hard on her. Remember, the money comes from *his* side of the family. She's actually pretty down-to-earth, at least compared to Stede and Brittany."

"Anyway, I asked her how Brittany's face is." Ginny turned to the others. "The other night, Ross Peabody hit Brittany pretty hard. Left finger marks on her face."

Remembering, Kim winced. "Is she bruised?"

"Jessica didn't say. She wanted to talk about her daughter's obsession with the pirate museum. And she said something really odd."

Ginny held Kim's eyes. "She said Brittany's obsession with pirates was 'all my fault.'"

Chapter 24

The waitress arrived with their breakfasts, silencing Aunt Ginny. Kim waited impatiently as everyone was served and cups were refilled. When the waitress moved away, Kim leaned toward her aunt.

"Did Mrs. Bonnet say why Brittany's pirate obsession is her fault?"

Aunt Ginny shook her head. "Someone interrupted us before she could explain, but I gotta tell you, that woman had guilt written all over her face."

Guilt? Because Brittany obsessed over her pirate ancestor? What an odd focus for parental concern.

Kim reached for her fork, barely noticing the tantalizing aroma of cinnamon and vanilla drifting from her plate. Most parents worry that they'd been too strict or too lenient, too critical or too gushing. If anything, Mrs. Bonnet should feel guilty about not stopping Brittany's childhood bullying.

Instead the woman bemoaned something so seemingly innocuous.

Or was it? Maybe Brittany's obsession wasn't harmless at all.

She needed to interview Mrs. Bonnet.

She bit into her French toast and all thoughts of the investigation vanished. She ate her food in silence, only vaguely aware of the others debating the pros and cons of the various murder suspects.

After breakfast, Mary, Wilma and Maureen said their goodbyes. Aunt Ginny, Doris and Scott, however, insisted on returning to the store to help Kim plot their next move.

They set off down the boardwalk, Grandpa and the two women dropping back to allow Kim and Scott some alone time. Scott matched his stride to Kim's while the two dogs trotted ahead. Al pumped his short little legs, trying to keep pace with Rory.

Despite the warmth of Scott's presence, Kim couldn't shake a sense of urgency. It'd been close to a week since Dorothy's murder and the police seemed no closer to finding her killer. Instead two more people had died.

Scott's hand brushed hers. Startled, she jerked away.

"Sorry." She reached for Scott's hand and held it. "Guess I'm a bit jumpy today."

Scott smiled. "A meteorologist I once interviewed said people, like animals, unconsciously sense the approach of a storm." He nodded toward Al. "He certainly gets fidgety whenever the barometric pressure drops."

"Yeah, but it's more than the coming hurricane. I feel like we're missing something important. Or maybe there's too much irrelevant information."

Kim paused to watch a juvenile osprey dive feet first into the bay. His feet grazed the top of the water, but his talons clutched only air. The bird screed, flew to one of the specially designed osprey platforms and perched, glaring down at the water.

She knew exactly how he felt.

"So, I guess interviewing Brittany's mother is a priority today?" Scott said.

"Yeah. If she'll talk to me. She must know I was never Brittany's friend."

"We'll figure out something."

He squeezed her hand and they continued walking in companionable silence.

Rory suddenly stopped -- tail up, body tense -- and yipped a greeting. Kim followed the direction of the poodle's gaze. A girl's bicycle leaned against Grandpa's gate. Liz sat on the top porch step, arms wrapped around her knees, head bent.

Kim broke into a trot. "Liz, is everything okay?"

Liz stood and charged down the steps. "You need to come, quick!" She pointed back the way they'd come. "They're digging up Pirate's Cove!"

"What? Who's..."

Liz stomped her foot. "The stupid tourists! Dozens of them. They're digging in the sand and on top of the cliff!"

"Go with Liz." Grandpa removed Rory's leash from Kim's limp hand. "I'll call the police."

Aunt Ginny scooped Al into her arms. "Go."

"Leave the bike," Scott told Liz. "We can get there quicker if we take my car."

Ten minutes later Scott claimed the last parking space at Pirate's Cove. Deciduous trees, their trunks twisted and gnarled from the cold winter winds that blew off the bay, surrounded the parking lot.

Ahead of them, the forested land sloped upward before leveling off and stretching toward the bay. All along the parking lot, signs forbid trespassing on the fragile cliff.

To the left, a winding trail leading to the beach skirted the base of the hill.

"They on the cliff or beach?" Kim asked Liz.

"Both."

Kim hesitated. Grandpa was calling the police; presumably they'd round up the people on the cliff, the ones who'd ignored the danger signs.

"Let's take the beach." She trotted down the trail.

She could hear the voices before the beach area came into view. As the trail ended, she slammed to a halt and gawked.

The pristine white sand that the town had hauled in for the Pirate Festival was now flattened and pockmarked with deep holes. Sweaty men and women dressed in t-shirts and shorts grunted and cursed as they slammed shovels into the ground. She scanned the faces and recognized a few locals scattered among people who were obviously tourists.

While the majority of treasure hunters concentrated their efforts on the actual sand, an alarming number dug at the base of the eroding cliff. Fifty feet below the osprey's overhanging tree, Mr. Crisman, the owner of the local hardware store, faced down a stranger who was trying to dig "in my spot." As they argued, a chunk of sandy clay broke free and plopped to the ground beside them. Neither man noticed.

Nearby, a middle-aged woman drove a long, narrow shovel into the cliff wall. The sight spurred Kim into action.

"Are you crazy?" Kim ran over and grabbed the woman's arm before she could punch another gash into the hillside. "You're going to pull the entire cliff onto your head."

The woman jerked her arm away and glared. "How else do you expect me to find the treasure?"

"There *is* no treasure!"

The sound of digging stopped as everyone turned to stare at Kim. Tense shoulders, narrowed eyes and firmly pressed lips warned her to tread carefully. She'd get only one chance to convince this group of the fallacy of the rumor.

She inhaled deeply, grateful to have Scott and Liz now flanking her, quiet sentries offering emotional support.

"Don't you see?" She shifted her glance, trying to meet each individual's eyes. "What you saw on television was nothing more than a publicity stunt, a way to get people to come to the new pirate museum."

The man who'd been arguing with Mr. Crisman snorted. "You're just trying to keep the treasure for yourself."

A few others muttered "yeah."

"Mr. Crisman." She waited until the store owner met her eyes. "You've lived in Osprey Beach your whole life, right?"

All eyes turned toward the man. Mr. Crisman hocked up something and spit into the sand. "I reckon."

"In all the time you've lived here, have you ever heard rumors of treasure buried in Pirate's Cove?"

"Can't say as I have."

"Then why would you -- why would any of you -- now think there's treasure here?"

"What about that boy?" the woman beside Kim said. "He found a ruby here."

Mr. Crisman nodded. "Your own grandfather said it was pirate treasure."

Kim folded her arms and lifted her chin. "Grandpa said no such thing. Brittany Bonnet made that up for the TV people."

"Stede's daughter?" Mr. Crisman scowled. "That gal's had pirates on the brain ever since she were a young 'un."

"And now she's making up stories so the new museum and her fancy new restaurant are a success." She looked around at the others. "Think about it. Brittany wants you to come here, look for treasure then go have lunch in her restaurant. You've all been duped."

Mr. Crisman threw down his shovel. "I'm outta here." Turning to the man beside him, he made an elaborate bow. "This spot is all yours."

A number of people sighed and began collecting their digging tools. The woman beside Kim, however, shrugged and again dug at the cliff.

Before Kim could say something she knew she'd regret, the police arrived.

Five men in uniform paused at the end of the path and frowned at the crowd. A short, skinny officer sporting a sparse goatee and tough attitude marched onto the sand, planted his feet and crossed his arms.

Uh, oh. She recognized this guy. He'd been one of the first responders when Grandpa was attacked, a Banty rooster puffed with importance. He'd wanted to plaster the jewelry store in crime scene tape. Rory had other ideas. The rambunctious poodle had snatched the end of the tape and raced around the cop, turning him into a human Maypole.

The man hadn't been amused.

What was his name? All she could remember was what she'd labeled him: Kid Cop.

"Listen up, people," Kid Cop said. "This beach is now closed. Gather your things and return to your cars."

Everyone groaned. Several people protested, but Kid Cop responded with what he probably considered a stern look. Kim wondered if he'd practiced it in the mirror.

The other cops stepped off the path and began herding everyone away from the beach.

Kim turned to Liz and held up a hand for a high-five. "Did good, kiddo."

With a gap-toothed grin, Liz slapped Kim's hand then turned to scowl at the ruined beach. "Well, at least I know where not to look." Liz sighed.

"Let's move along, people." Kid Cop waved his hands in a shooing motion.

"Tell you what." Kim turned and, with Scott on one side and Liz on the other, started walking back up the trail. "Why don't we go talk to Grandpa? He might have some ideas of where to look." She grinned. "Besides, I know where he hides the Swiss chocolate."

Liz agreed, then skipped ahead of them. The childhood enthusiasm lightened Kim's mood. Children and dogs, gotta love them.

"Well, I'd say you now have an excuse to talk with Brittany's mother," Scott said.

"Yeah? What?"

"Tell her about what happened here." He swept a hand back toward the beach. "And that you need her help convincing Brittany to stop spreading rumors about pirate treasure."

A slow smile spread across Kim's face. Aunt Ginny had said Mrs. Bonnet was a member of the Save the Chesapeake Bay committee. Not only would she be horrified to learn people had been digging on the fragile cliffs, she'd be embarrassed by Brittany's role. That would certainly give her incentive to rein in her daughter.

And once they'd discussed the assault on Pirate's Cove, Kim could steer the conversation to Brittany's pirate obsession.

Perfect.

She started a mental list of things to do today. While Grandpa told Liz pirate stories, she'd call Brittany's mother and set up an appointment. If Brittany was indeed behind the spate of murders, maybe she could maneuver Mrs. Bonnet into revealing useful information.

They reached the parking lot.

"Liz, wait for us." Liz paused and glanced back, her expression puzzled.

Kim laid a hand on the girl's shoulder. "Let's let the treasure hunters leave first. They don't look too happy."

In fact, most of the hunters expressed their displeasure by squealing tires as they pulled out of the lot. The woman who'd been digging in the cliff held up her middle finger as she zipped by. The police watched with bored expressions.

The last car finally pulled away. As they settled in Scott's car, Kim's cell phone rang.

"Kim? This is Marie Powers, Liz's mother?"

"Oh, yes, Mrs. Powers. How are you?" Kim glanced into the back seat to see Liz frowning.

"Well, I'm looking for Liz. Your grandfather said she was with you?"

"Yes, she's here. Would you like to speak to her?" She handed her phone to Liz.

"Hello?" The girl listened for a moment. "Well, you wouldn't *have* to call all over if you got me my own phone... But Mr. Hershey was going to tell me pirate stories! Awww, Mom... Yeah, I'll be there. 'bye." Liz handed the phone to Kim. "I have to go home."

"Want me to drop you at your house?" Scott eased the car into beach traffic. "We can bring your bike home later."

"No, I have time to ride my bike home." She flopped back and folded her arms.

Kim resisted the urge to smile. "Don't worry; Grandpa's not going anywhere. We can talk to him about pirates some other time."

"Later today?" Liz leaned forward. "I just have to watch Tina and Tommy while we shop for groceries."

"I'm not sure of my schedule for today, but let me see what I can do." Maybe she could convince Mrs. Bonnet to meet with her for lunch.

All plans vanished, however, when Scott pulled into Grandpa's drive -- right beside a police car.

Chapter 25

Imagining another robbery or worse, Kim flung herself from Scott's car. Dodging the sheriff's sedan, she raced up the short flight of stairs to the door to Grandpa's office.

"Grandpa! Aunt Ginny!" No sign of them or the police in the office, but she could hear Rory's greeting coming from the store front.

"In here," Grandpa called.

Kim trotted into the store and just managed to catch an enthusiastic Rory as he leaped up to greet her. Over his curly head, she could see Grandpa and Aunt Ginny standing behind the jewelry counter. Ginny clutched a struggling Al while Grandpa leaned over the display case. Neither looked injured.

"Are you both okay?"

Hearing the panic in her voice, Grandpa looked up and offered a reassuring smile. "We're fine, honey." He gestured to the man standing across from him. "Just helping the police."

Kim breathed deeply and at last focused on the third person in the room. Lieutenant Bill Brockley's mouth tipped up into a slow smile that accelerated her already racing heart. Then Brockley's eyes focused over her shoulder and the smile disappeared.

Scott stepped beside Kim and extended his hand. "Lieutenant Brockley, I don't know if you remember me. Scott Wilson."

As the two men shook hands, Rory spotted Liz.

"No feet up," Kim warned him.

Rory kept all four feet on the ground, but his wiggling happiness almost knocked Liz to the floor. Giggling, Liz ruffled his ears. A yip from Al drew her attention to the little dachshund. Liz's eyes widened.

"You can pet Al, too, but then you'd better head for home. Ah, you don't ride on the highway, right?"

Liz rolled her eyes. "Mom's already given me lectures about where it's safe to ride my bike."

"Okay, I trust you to be safe." Kim reached across the counter for Al, then placed him in Liz's arms.

Liz snuggled her cheek against Al's. "He's so silky." Sighing, she handed him back to Kim. "Don't forget to call me."

Kim agreed and watched as Liz trudged out the front door and down to where she'd left her bicycle. Turning, she crossed to Grandpa's side and gazed down at a long package laying on the display case. The top had been opened to reveal several swords, daggers and cutlasses.

"Are those things stolen from the museum?"

"Yes." Grandpa lifted out a cutlass and pointed to a tiny engraving on the handle. "I was just showing Lieutenant Brockley the symbol we use to mark museum property."

"So Ross Peabody *did* receive stolen goods." She couldn't keep the satisfaction from her voice.

Brockley's eyebrows raised. "What makes you think this came from Ross Peabody?"

She pointed at the splotch marring the brown paper. "The stain. I saw that package sitting in Peabody's office, beneath the safe." She shrugged. "Looked like someone spilled grease from a hamburger or something on the package."

"Actually, the lab said it was corned beef."

"Did you find the rest of the stolen items in Peabody's safe?"

Brockley studied her, stone-faced. A second passed, two. Then he sighed. "This," he said, waving a hand at the package, "didn't come from Ross Peabody."

"But I saw it in his office." Kim pointed at the stain. "Trust me, you couldn't easily duplicate that smudge."

"I believe you."

She frowned. "But if you didn't find it in Peabody's office, where--?"

"It was under Officer Darnell's bed."

"No way." Kim shook her head. "That package was still in Peabody's possession after Paula Darnell left. So she must have gone back for it. Was that before or after the murder?"

"I can't discuss an ongoing investigation."

Another thought flashed through Kim's mind. "Peabody threatened her."

"What? When? And why didn't you tell me?"

Kim ran fingers through her hair. "I didn't tell you because, well, I knew there was something wrong when she left Ross's condo, but their exchange didn't make sense. But now..." She waved her hand at the package. "Now it looks like they were threatening each other."

"Go on."

"I told you that when we got to Ross Peabody's condo, we heard him arguing with a woman." She waited for Brockley to nod. "Paula Darnell was the only woman there."

"You told me this already."

Kim's hands clenched, remembering the National Towers security guard's accusation that Paula enjoyed playing men off one another. Clearly Brockley had also fallen for the woman's ploys.

But the evidence of Paula's deception lay on the jewelry counter and Kim wasn't about to let Brockley ignore it.

"As Officer Darnell was leaving, Ross Peabody said something about the *implications* of what they'd discussed. It sounded like a veiled threat."

Brockley shrugged. "Doesn't sound threatening to me."

Kim raised her chin. "You didn't hear the tone of voice or see the way they held their bodies."

Brockley's stone face and glazed eyes told her he didn't believe anything she'd just said.

"Was any other museum property recovered?" she said.

"Just this." Brockley began re-wrapping the package.

"But... What about the stuff in Ross Peabody's safe? Didn't you find Brittany's amulet?"

Brockley sighed. "I guess you'll be reading this in the paper soon enough. The Annapolis police did find a few items in Peabody's apartment that were listed as stolen. But no amulet. Nothing from the museum."

"That," Kim pointed at the now-wrapped package, "was in Ross Peabody's apartment before Officer Darnell took it."

Brockley ignored her comment, lifted the package and turned to Grandpa. "Mr. Hershey, thank you for your help." With a nod at the rest of them, he headed for the door.

"Wait!" At Kim's call, Brockley turned. "Those items recovered in Peabody's apartment? Were any of them stolen from the National Towers? Maybe a cutlass belonging to Captain Kidd?"

For a moment, she thought he wouldn't answer. When he did, his voice was tight. "Yes."

With that, he turned and disappeared down the stairs.

"Guess he doesn't want to admit Officer Darnell was involved," Aunt Ginny said.

Kim sighed. "Probably doesn't matter. Paula's death shows there's someone else out there. That's the person we need to find."

"Well," Scott said, "Maybe Brittany's mother has some answers."

Chapter 26

To Kim's surprise, Mrs. Bonnet not only recognized Kim's name -- "your grandfather is so proud of you" -- but invited her to the Bonnet home. They agreed to meet in an hour.

Kim helped the others prepare the store for opening, then trotted upstairs to search her closet for clothes suitable for visiting the lady of the mansion.

She exchanged her shorts for a flouncy, ankle-length skirt she'd bought at a pre-Labor Day sale. With a clean, fitted t-shirt and nice sandals, she hoped to pass inspection.

"Lovely," Scott said as she joined everyone in the storefront. He stood and walked toward her. "Shall we go?"

"Uh, I enjoy your company, but Mrs. Bonnet might reveal more if it's just the two of us."

Scott grinned. "Girl talk, I get it. How 'bout I just wait for you in the car?"

Kim agreed, ruffled Rory's ears and pointed at the dachshund thief. "Would you like me to get a crate for Al?"

"I'll keep an eye on him," Aunt Ginny said.

"Okay, just be sure no one leaves food within his reach. And remember he can climb."

Al cocked his head, perked his ears and donned a "who me?" expression.

Kim laughed, kissed his muzzle and led the way outside.

Scott offered to drive, so she programmed the Bonnet's address into his GPS and settled into the passenger seat.

They turned left onto Bayside and headed south, away from the other beach towns. The two-lane road climbed, dipped and twisted. At the top of a hill, they turned left onto a road that wound back toward the bay.

As they pulled into a long, circular driveway, Kim leaned forward to study the mansion where Brittany grew up. The Tidewater-style house perched on a high cliff overlooking the bay. Two stories tall and painted pale gray, the building sported porches on both levels. A broad roof swept down and out, protecting the porches from rain and wind.

Though the location wasn't prone to flooding, Kim wondered how the house had weathered hurricane-strength winds. The roof overhangs resembled sails. She could imagine a tornado carrying the house over the rainbow.

Scott parked just beyond a serpentine path that led to the front porch. The neatly trimmed evergreens and tidy perennials that flanked the stone path should have welcomed visitors. Instead, the constrained foliage made Kim claustrophobic.

"I'll finish as quickly as possible." She unhooked her seatbelt.

"Take your time." Scott held up his cell phone. "While I wait, I'll see if I can learn anything about Ross Peabody's heirs."

Taking a deep breath, Kim opened the door and stepped into the humid air. By the time she reached the house, sweat dribbled down her neck.

The woman who opened the door bore such a close resemblance to Grace Kelly that the effect had to be intentional. Mrs. Bonnet's white blond hair was swept back in a soft, wavy bob. The beige silk shirt, silk trousers and espadrilles almost perfectly matched an outfit Kelly wore in *High Society*. Mrs. Bonnet had even dangled a patterned silk scarf from a pants pocket.

The words "ice princess" galloped through Kim's mind and she suppressed a shudder.

The interior of the house, like its mistress, was decorated in pastels -- pale blues, grays and almonds. But the family room's bay-facing wall of windows warmed the interior. A set of French doors led out onto a deck furnished with white wicker.

"Would you care for some coffee or tea?" Mrs. Bonnet said.

Kim eyed the white sofa and pale blue rug, imagining brown tea stains. "Uh, no, I'm good, thank you." She eased herself onto the white leather, grateful that she didn't have to worry about black dog hair marring the pristine couch. Thank goodness poodles don't shed.

Mrs. Bonnet perched on a white wooden chair that had been upholstered in sky blue. "I'm so glad you called. I've been debating calling you."

"Oh? Why?" Kim couldn't imagine what the elegant woman would want.

"I heard about how you helped the police find the people responsible for attacking your grandfather."

"Oh, well I didn't really--"

"Nonsense. Everyone knows the police were looking in the wrong direction. Just like they're looking at the wrong person now."

Wow, she didn't see that coming. "Yeah, I agree that Mary wouldn't murder anyone."

"Mary?" Mrs. Bonnet's eyes widened. "Who's Mary?"

"Mary Klein. The director of the museum."

"Oh, her." Mrs. Bonnet waved a hand as if shooing a fly. "Do they still think she killed Dorothy? Poor thing." She leaned forward, her blue eyes seeking and holding Kim's. "Kim, I really need your help. Will you help me?"

"Uh, I guess it depends on what, I mean, if I can..." Kim's voice trailed off as she studied the stylish woman across from her. Despite the perfectly applied makeup, a closer look revealed swollen, dark circles under the blue eyes. Not sleeping? Or actually crying?

"I need you to prove my Brittany didn't kill that police officer."

Kim blew out air and slumped back in her seat. "Uh, maybe you'd better start from the beginning."

Mrs. Bonnet nodded as if Kim was a real private investigator and had said something logical.

"The police found Brittany's earring near the dead woman." Mrs. Bonnet bit her lip.

Kim remained silent. The earring had actually been caught in Paula Darnell's hair, but Brittany's mother didn't need to hear that.

Mrs. Bonnet continued. "Brittany was here, visiting, when the police arrived. They... they made her get into the back of a police car! Like a common criminal!"

"Did they actually arrest her?"

The woman's mouth dropped open. "Of course not! Said they just wanted to talk. I told her not to say anything until Frank, our lawyer, arrived.

"Frank just reported back. He said the police asked about her father's gun collection and whether or not Brittany knew how to shoot. Then they demanded details about an argument between Brittany and that woman cop. Frank wouldn't let her answer. And then... and then they showed her this diamond earring, the one I bought for her birthday.

"Frank told her not to answer, but she insisted on telling the police that, yes, the earring belonged to her but that she'd lost it and wanted it back. That's when they told her it was found on the cop. Frank terminated the interview. But he said things don't look good."

"Does Brittany have any idea how her earring ended up, er, on Officer Darnell?"

Mrs. Bonnet nodded. "She told me it must have gotten caught when the two of them were arguing."

Kim frowned. No way was an earring going to leap from one woman's ears to another's hair no matter how violent the argument. Unless... "Did they actually come to blows?"

Brittany's mother stiffened and her nose tipped upward. "My daughter is not a brawler." She studied Kim, eyes narrowed, communicating the unsaid words "unlike some people."

Kim bit her tongue. She couldn't afford to alienate this woman. She needed information.

"How did the police learn about the argument?"

Mrs. Bonnet tossed her hair. "Obviously, someone overheard and told the police. Brittany thinks it was Leslie Darling."

Kim frowned. "Leslie? But why would she implicate Brittany? I thought they were friends."

"They were until a few days before Brittany's wedding. That woman almost ruined the wedding!"

"Uh, what happened?"

Mrs. Bonnet shrugged. "They had a falling out. Leslie was supposed to be a bridesmaid, but after the argument she refused to even come to the wedding. I don't believe they've spoken since." Her fists clenched. "Brittany thinks Leslie is intentionally trying to make her a suspect."

"But why?"

"Brittany never provided details..." Her eyes slid to the left then returned to Kim's. "Are you sure I can't get you something to drink?"

Kim hesitated. The woman clearly wanted time to collect her thoughts. Would she reveal more if Kim pressed on?

Mrs. Bonnet stood. "I'm getting some water. How 'bout I bring you some, too?" Without waiting, she strode from the room.

Kim sighed. Mrs. Bonnet was hiding something, but what?

No surprise that Brittany concealed the cause of the fight with Leslie; she'd never shared confidences. But Mrs. Bonnet must suspect the reason for the argument that had destroyed a long-term friendship.

Mrs. Bonnet returned carrying a silver tray that held two crystal glasses of ice and two bottles of sparkling water. Kim wrinkled her nose; sparkling water tasted like chemicals. Well, at least if she spilled some, water wouldn't stain all of this white.

After the tray had been arranged just so, Mrs. Bonnet sat and leveled serious eyes at Kim. "I'm willing to pay you for your help."

"Mrs. Bonnet--"

"Please, call me Jessica."

Oh, yeah, like that was going to happen. "Uh, I'm not sure what you want me to do."

"I want you to find the real killer. Or at least point the police away from Brittany."

Kim studied the woman's face. She was serious. "I'm not a detective--"

"You figured out who was trying to kill your grandfather before the police did!"

"But the police--"

"The police need to stop investigating my daughter before they find out."

"Find out what?"

Mrs. Bonnet's eyes burned into Kim's. "What I tell you must remain in this room."

"I can't hide evidence of a crime."

"This has nothing to do with the murder or anything that's happened recently. It's just..." She inhaled deeply. "Do you remember when you all were in fifth grade and the teacher assigned you to create a family tree?"

Kim nodded, wondering if Brittany's mother was going to use the playground fight to guilt trip her into helping.

"You were all so young." Mrs. Bonnet stared out the window, eyes cloudy, obviously lost in thought. "Too young."

She looked back at Kim. "When Brittany brought home the assignment, Stede and I told Brittany about our ancestors. She was so thrilled to hear about the Gentleman Pirate." She smiled. "I've never seen her so excited. She read every book she could find on him. It was the first time she'd ever shown interest in books!

"I kept thinking she'd forget about the pirate as she grew older. Instead, she became obsessed. Every Halloween she wanted to dress as a different version of a pirate. She made me take her to the theater to see every *Pirates of the Caribbean* movie. Even rented old Errol Flynn movies."

She bit her lip. "I probably should have told her when she was in high school, but by then, well, it was too late, don't you see? She'd formed her whole image of herself around that damn pirate. If I'd told her, it would have shattered her world."

"Told her what?"

Mrs. Bonnet stared at Kim, expression determined, the ice queen now in full control. "That she was adopted."

Kim's mouth dropped open. She certainly hadn't seen that coming. Brittany looked so much like her mother, no one would have guessed.

"You never told her?" Brittany was 32 years old.

"How could I? It would have destroyed her." She blew air through her lips. "Do you think I wanted my poor daughter to not be able to do her homework because no one knows where she came from? It's not as if she could track down the idiot that abandoned her."

"Abandoned?"

"Someone left her on the steps of a church. We were already looking to adopt; we couldn't have children of our own. The adoption agency knew of several suitable babies, but when I saw Brittany I just knew she was the one. She was beautiful, so perfect. Even Stede thought she looked like me."

She shrugged her elegant shoulders. "My lawyer wanted me to wait, said we were taking a chance because we had no way to check the baby's ancestors. Her mother could have been a dope fiend or something. But I couldn't let her go. And I was right, too; she was the perfect baby. She slept through the night, never cried, was never sick a day in her life. And so, so pretty."

Kim's brain twisted into spaghetti. Brittany -- Miss "My pedigree is so perfect I don't need to speak to you" -- was a foundling. And Mrs. Bonnet was afraid a police investigation would reveal the adoption.

Mary would love to hear this.

She pushed aside the thought and considered the distraught woman sitting across from her. Kim was already investigating the murders; perhaps she could ease a little of Mrs. Bonnet's stress.

"How about if we do this," she said. "I'll poke around, see if I can find evidence of what really happened. And maybe I can find something before the police dig into Brittany's background."

There. She'd agreed to help without proclaiming Brittany's innocence.

At Kim's words, Mrs. Bonnet's face brightened and she looked ten years younger. A wave of guilt swept over Kim.

Part of her -- okay, a lot of her -- hoped Brittany was guilty. But she didn't want to see this poor woman in pain.

Time to change the subject.

"In the meantime, could you please talk to Brittany about her, er, stories that pirate treasure has been found in Pirate's Cove?"

"Stories? You mean that boy didn't find a ruby?"

"Oh, he found a ruby all right. But Grandpa never said it came from pirate treasure or even that the stone was old. People lose gemstones in the sand all the time." Kim held the woman's eyes. "Thing is, by telling people there's treasure, Brittany's threatening the ecology. This morning we chased dozens of people who were digging in Pirate's Cove."

Mrs. Bonnet blanched. "They were digging up the cliff? We've got to stop them!"

"The police came and closed the beach. But if Brittany keeps telling people there's treasure..."

Mrs. Bonnet's eyes narrowed and her mouth tightened into a straight line. "I'll talk with her."

The expression on Mrs. Bonnet's face raised goosebumps on Kim's arms. Here was a woman she wouldn't want to cross.

Standing, she thanked Mrs. Bonnet for her time and again refused payment for "investigating." As she turned toward the front door, someone pounded on it with a fist.

Mrs. Bonnet frowned and strode ahead of Kim to the door. Flinging it open, she glared at Lieutenant Bill Brockley.

Before she could say anything, Brockley held out a folded sheet of paper.

"Mrs. Bonnet, I have a warrant to search your house for guns."

Instead of letting him in, Mrs. Bonnet sneered. "Guns? Of course there are guns in my home. My husband collects them. What has that got to do with the police?"

"We have reason to believe one of them was used in a crime." Brockley's face softened. "We're only interested in the hand guns."

Mrs. Bonnet wheeled around. "I'm calling my lawyer."

As she stormed past, Brockley's eyes fell on Kim.

"What are you doing here? I told you I don't need you playing Nancy Drew."

"Mrs. Bonnet and I were just discussing the best way to stop these nasty rumors about pirate treasure in Osprey Beach."

Brockley's eyes narrowed, but she didn't give him a chance to question her. With a smile and a finger wave, she slipped past him and strode toward Scott's car.

"Whew," she said, slipping into the passenger seat. "That was close."

"Trouble in River City?" One side of Scott's mouth tipped upward.

"Warrant to confiscate Mr. Bonnet's pistol collection."

Scott dipped his chin. "Good. Maybe that will take some of the attention away from Mary."

"You sound worried."

"Yeah, I am." His eyes met hers. "I found someone who could tell me about Ross Peabody's will. He's divorced, but had a son from that marriage. The son inherits everything except the pirate collection. Peabody willed the collection to the Osprey Beach museum.

"The police think that gives Mary a motive for murder."

Chapter 27

The suggestion that Mary had killed Ross Peabody so that the museum could inherit his pirate collection would have made Kim laugh if Scott's expression wasn't so serious.

"That's ridiculous!" she said. "Museum directors don't kill for collections."

Scott nodded. "I got the impression from my source that the police are grasping at straws. And speaking of police..." He gestured toward the Bonnet house where several officers were now joining Lieutenant Brockley. "Maybe we'd better make our escape while we can."

Kim reached for her seatbelt. "Could you please drive to the next street and find a place to park? One of Brittany's childhood friends lives near here. She told the police she saw

Brittany and Officer Darnell arguing just before Darnell died."

As Scott drove away from the Bonnet mansion, Kim pulled out her new smart phone and searched for Leslie's address. Sure enough, Leslie still lived two blocks from Brittany.

Kim directed Scott to a two-story, cookie-cutter McMansion painted white with green shutters. The only detail separating Leslie's home from the nearby houses was the sweeping front lawn. Someone had combed the grass into golf-course perfection.

"What makes you think she'll be home mid-day?" Scott parked across the street.

"A woman at the hair salon told me Leslie doesn't work on Fridays." She frowned. "Would you mind coming in with me? Leslie and I weren't exactly friends, but she won't be able to resist a handsome man."

"And how about you?" Scott reached out and traced a finger along Kim's jaw. "Do you find me irresistible?"

Kim laughed, then slapped his hand away. "Stop searching for compliments." She opened her door and stepped into the humid air. Her glasses fogged. Sighing, she pulled a cloth from her bag and wiped the lenses clean. Dealing with Leslie would be intimidating enough without feeling blind.

Scott took her hand and they strode to the front door.

The door opened, releasing the sound of young children playing. Kim barely noticed; she was too stunned at Leslie Darling's appearance.

When she'd seen Leslie at the beauty shop, the woman had worn a professional tunic and pants that covered her arms and legs. The tank top and shorts she wore now revealed painfully thin limbs. She was so skinny that her collar bone stuck out. She glared at Kim, almost daring her to utter the word "anorexia."

"What do you want?" Leslie said.

"Uh, could we come in for a minute? We wanted to talk to you about Brittany."

Leslie folded her arms. "I haven't talked to that bitch since I caught her in bed with Thomas."

A shriek sounded deep in the house, followed by a boy's voice. "Mom! She broke my truck!"

"Did not!" a girl yelled back.

Leslie sighed and opened the screen door. "You'd better come in before they destroy something."

They followed her across a marble foyer and into a sunny living room carpeted in a thick burgundy. Leslie gestured toward an overstuffed sofa upholstered in navy flowers.

"Grab a seat while I make sure the two monsters are all right." She turned and disappeared down the hallway.

Kim glanced around at the immaculate room. Not a speck of dust marred the glass-topped coffee table or the upright piano standing against the far wall. Beginner-level sheet music was stacked neatly on the piano bench. On the other wall, a glass-fronted bookcase -- filled with trophies, not books -- sparkled.

Kim didn't need to leave her seat to know the trophies were for dressage.

Of Brittany's many accomplices, Leslie had been the one Kim envied. Not only was she slender where Kim was plump, but Leslie had owned a gorgeous black stallion and competed in dressage. She'd often change into her immaculate, tight-fitting dressage outfit and parade around the school grounds before leaving for practice.

A shout came from the hallway, then a door slammed. Silence followed.

Leslie strode back into the room. "I'm going to be so happy when they go back to school." Reaching into her shorts pocket, she extracted a pack of Salem cigarettes and lit one.

Kim stared at the cigarettes. In high school, Leslie had lectured other students about the evils of smoking, saying no true athlete could do her best if she smoked.

Seeing Kim's expression, Leslie pulled the cigarette from her mouth. "Yeah, I know, cancer sticks." She took another puff and blew a smoke ring. "But it's the only way I know to stay thin enough to keep Thomas from straying."

So Leslie intentionally starved herself into looking like a cadaver. Did she have anorexia? Bulimia?

Kim reminded herself it wasn't her business. She had no authority here, no way to convince Leslie she was too thin. Best to focus on what she needed to know about Brittany.

But how could she drag Leslie back to the topic of Brittany? The frontal approach -- "Did your best friend really seduce your husband?" -- felt wrong. She cast about for a topic that would break the uncomfortable silence.

She needn't have worried. Leslie seemed happy for a new audience for her tale of sex and betrayal.

"You looked shocked when I said Brittany screwed Thomas," Leslie said.

"Uh, that's not exactly the behavior one expects from a best friend."

Leslie snorted. "You're so innocent. Brittany always needed to be the center of attention, especially around men. You, of all people, should know what happens when someone challenges her.

"I remember that fight in the school yard. Too bad Mr. Jefferson stopped you before you knocked some sense into Brittany. Maybe then she'd have thought twice before trying to steal other people's possessions." She pulled on her cigarette.

"But to seduce your husband?" Maybe a little girl bonding would keep Leslie talking. "That must have been horrifying. I take it this happened right before Brittany's wedding?"

Leslie nodded. "A week before. I got stuck with the maid of honor duties. She had me running all over the place doing things the wedding planner should have done. Didn't make sense until the day Brittany sent me to Annapolis to discuss last-minute details with the band she'd hired for the reception."

Lines formed around Leslie's mouth as she dragged on her cigarette. "The musicians didn't show up for the meeting, so I went home early. Found Brittany and Thomas doing the nasty on my dining room table. I pitched Brittany out the door without her clothes.

"Would you believe she still expected me to be her maid of honor? When I refused, I got calls from both her mother and her father, telling me I was ruining their daughter's wedding. Papa Bonnet even threatened to sue."

"Surely he had no cause to sue."

Leslie shrugged. "Dad says anyone can sue you for any reason. I guess Bonnet thought he could scare me." She scowled. "Her parents are almost as crazy as she is."

A slow smile spread across her face. "I must admit, though, that old saying about revenge being sweeter when it's served cold? Absolutely right on."

Kim leaned forward. "So you told the police Brittany fought with Officer Darnell?"

"Damn right." Leslie stabbed the cigarette butt into an ashtray. "Couldn't believe my luck when I walked in on that."

"What happened?"

Leslie's eyes gleamed. "A couple of days ago, I was coming out of the new gym, you know the 24-hour one? Have you been there?"

"Uh, yeah, once." And she planned to never set foot inside that place again. Scott, knowing what happened there, reached over and squeezed her hand.

Leslie didn't notice Kim's discomfort.

"There was a cop car parked in back," she said, "so, naturally, I wondered what was going on. I was surprised to see the cop was a woman." She turned to Scott. "I still expect cops to be male, you know?"

Scott nodded, but remained silent.

Leslie focused on Kim. "And then I saw who the cop was talking to -- Brittany. And she didn't look happy. She was standing there with her arms folded across her chest and that expression on her face -- you know the one -- where she's looking down her nose at you?"

She seemed to expect an answer, so Kim nodded.

"I thought maybe the cop was giving Brittany a speeding ticket or something. I decided to mosey on over, get close enough to hear what was going on."

Leslie's eyes narrowed as she grinned in satisfaction. "Wasn't police business at all, just a good old-fashioned cat fight."

"Cat fight?"

Leslie rolled her eyes. "As in girls fighting over boys. The cop said something like 'Stay away from the museum when he's there.' Brittany, naturally, claimed she's got every right to be there because she's paying for that museum. Cop didn't seem impressed." Leslie sneered. "For a moment, I thought they might come to blows. Wouldn't that have been fun?"

"So why didn't they?"

"Brittany suddenly accused the cop of helping steal that stupid ruby amulet she was always bragging about -- you know the one she brought to school and you said might be spinel and not ruby? I mean, how dumb is that, accusing a cop of stealing? I thought the cop might arrest her right then and there."

From down the hall, a loud crash reverberated.

"Mommmm!"

Sighing, Leslie stood. "I'd better get that. You know the way out." Turning, she headed down the hall.

Kim leaped to her feet. "Leslie, before you go, do you know what man Brittany and Officer Darnell were arguing about?"

Leslie peered back over her shoulder, her mouth formed in a sneer. "Of course. Kevin Klein. Dowdy Mary's hunky husband."

Chapter 28

Leslie refused to elaborate on her claim that Paula Darnell and Brittany had fought over Kevin. Frustrated, Kim turned to leave. Leslie plucked at her sleeve.

"Better keep him," Leslie gestured toward Scott, "away from Brittany. Once she sees you together, she won't stop until she steals him."

As they drove back to Grandpa's, Leslie's words swirled through Kim's mind. In high school, Brittany excelled at stealing boyfriends. Her predatory behavior had sent many a girl dashing to the restroom in tears.

She'd tried to flirt with Scott at the museum banquet. Thank goodness he'd been immune.

But what about Mary's husband? Were the rumors of Kevin's infidelity true?

She could well imagine Brittany or Paula attempting to seduce Kevin. Brittany would relish stealing Kevin from Mary. And Paula hadn't hesitated to use sex to control her boss at National Towers.

Kim flashed back to the day Lieutenant Brockley discovered gemstones in Mary's freezer. At the time, she'd resented the way Paula moved around Mary's living room, lifting photos, knickknacks and books. Now she wondered if Paula's proprietary attitude stemmed from a relationship with Kevin.

"I can see your brain burning neurons." Scott smiled over at her. "Would you like a male opinion?"

Kim grinned. "Sure, let's hear it."

Scott's smile slipped away and he stared out at traffic. "It's possible that the rumors of Kevin's affairs are just that: Rumors."

"But what about Paula and Brittany fighting over him?"

His expression grew serious. "I've seen women get into heated arguments over a man who wasn't interested in either one of them. Guy could be totally innocent, but no one believes him." He frowned. "Not even his girlfriend."

"Sounds like you've had the experience."

Scott stared out the windshield, intent on his driving. As the seconds passed, Kim feared he wouldn't answer. Had she insulted him with her question?

Maybe he didn't like her probing into his romantic history. Heaven knew, she had no desire to confess her own failed relationships. There'd been the poet who talked only of himself, the lawyer who kissed like a doorknob, the ornithologist whose idea of a date was to launch a net over a tree of sleeping wild turkeys.

Before she could apologize, however, Scott tossed her a rueful smile. "Yeah, I've had it happen to me." He shrugged. "'course, that doesn't mean Kevin is innocent. I'm just saying we shouldn't condemn the guy just because a couple of unstable women fought over him."

"Agreed." Kim reached across and squeezed his hand. "And, just so you know, I trust you."

That brought a full smile to his face. For a few minutes, they drove in companionable silence. But Kim's mind wouldn't stop probing and sorting the events of the last week. So many incidents seemed off kilter. Like that business with finding museum gemstones in the ice cream.

"You know, if Paula Darnell hadn't teased Brockley about his love for Pirate's Treasure ice cream, he wouldn't have discovered the gemstones hidden in it."

Scott's eyes slid her way. "You thinking Darnell actually planted the gemstones in Mary's house? That would require relinquishing gems she'd stolen. Expensive way to rid yourself of a rival."

"Actually, not so much. Remember, there were only three gemstones in the ice cream, all cut in old-fashioned styles that wouldn't have much market appeal. Unless Darnell planned to sell the gems to a collector of historic stones, she'd have needed to hire a lapidarist to re-cut the stones before selling them."

Scott nodded and turned into Grandpa's driveway. As Kim climbed from the car, Aunt Ginny opened the office door and Rory bounded out. He flopped his front feet onto the garden gate and bared his front teeth in a poodle smile.

She ruffled his ears and tilted her cheek for a sloppy welcome-home kiss. "Missed you too, big boy. Now please back up and let us in."

She held the gate open for Scott, then turned to greet her aunt. But instead of her usual smile, Aunt Ginny's lips were pressed into a straight line.

Kim slammed to a halt. "What's wrong?"

"Hurricane Dan picked up speed," Aunt Ginny said. "They're now predicting landfall near the Virginia/North Carolina border -- right at the mouth of the Chesapeake Bay."

Kim's stomach clenched. She couldn't remember a hurricane landing so close to home.

"How soon is it supposed to hit?" she said.

"Early Sunday morning," Aunt Ginny said, "but we'll be getting rain and high wind tomorrow."

Kim breathed deeply. Two days away. There was still time for the hurricane to change directions.

But they couldn't depend on that.

"So what's the plan?" Kim said.

"Max wants to close the store early." She turned to Scott. "Would you mind helping us mount the plywood over the windows?"

"Be happy to help," Scott said. "Where does he keep the plywood? I'll haul it upstairs while you work on the store."

Kim turned toward the garage. "Follow me and I'll show you. Grandpa said he's already cut the plywood to size and labeled each piece for the matching window. You can use the elevator to cart the wood to the different levels."

After pointing out the stack of plywood and hearing Scott's assurances that he could handle the wood alone, Kim returned to the store and helped Grandpa and Aunt Ginny secure the jewelry in the water-proof, fire-proof, everything-proof safe.

Grandpa pointed at the front window. "Better take apart your wonderful display and set the material up high, away from all windows."

Kim nodded and snagged a plastic box. "You don't think the water's going to reach this high, do you?"

Grandpa shrugged. "Not likely, but best to play it safe."

Kim crossed to the window. They'd already removed the jewelry and gems from the display, so she just needed to take care of the "pirate chest," sea shells and drift wood. As she tucked the chest into the bottom of the box, she marveled that it'd been less than a week since she'd created this display.

Brittany's new museum had certainly benefited from the uproar over the thefts. She was probably reveling in all the attention... Kim's hand hovered over a shell.

Mary said her husband blamed Brittany for all that had happened, that she'd stolen her own amulet to collect the million-dollar insurance. Kim had dismissed the idea. Unlike Ross Peabody, who drew pleasure from the simple act of owning something, Brittany reveled in flaunting her possessions.

Stealing the ruby might net Brittany a million dollars, but it would also deprive her of the ability to lord the heirloom over everyone. Once she'd collected the insurance money, she could never display the ruby. The scenario just didn't fit Brittany's psychology.

But what if Brittany never intended to collect the insurance money? What if the theft of the pirate's ruby was a publicity stunt that had turned disastrous?

Kim could well imagine Brittany arranging a theft, then milking the media frenzy to bring customers to the museum and expensive restaurant. After a few days, she could place an anonymous call to the police, telling them where to find the pirate's ruby.

Or course, Brittany would never steal the pendant herself. She'd need an alibi to satisfy the police. Maybe she sent Nigel? Or she could have paid someone. Explain to a security guard or restaurant worker that she wanted to stage a theft for publicity, claim it wasn't theft at all since Brittany owned the ruby, offer money to temporarily remove it... Even an honest person might be tempted.

Kim frowned. No, that scenario didn't work. Surely, if Dorothy walked in and caught the hired hand stealing the ruby, the person would have simply explained his or her actions.

Unless... unless Brittany hired someone unstable, someone who'd panicked when discovered and lashed out without thinking. Dorothy might have threatened jail time. Perhaps her razor tongue unleashed a killer.

She sighed. Problem was, that scenario didn't explain the other two murders. And, unlike Lieutenant Brockley, she firmly believed the three murders were connected.

She reached for the last item in the window, the sword hilt that Rory had retrieved in Pirate's Cove. The bone felt smooth and organic, so different from man-made materials.

Wouldn't it be amazing if Rory's discovery really did come from a pirate's cache?

Gently, she laid it into the box.

"We're about finished here," Grandpa said. "I'm going to help Scott hang the plywood."

Oh, no. Grandpa had no business lifting heavy plywood; he'd been released from the hospital only a few weeks ago.

"Uh, why don't I help Scott while you and Aunt Ginny bring in the patio furniture?" The light-weight patio furniture.

Grandpa's shoulders straightened and his chin lifted.

Before he could say anything, however, Aunt Ginny touched his arm. "C'mon, Max. The children want to be alone. Let's clear the balconies and then you can help me prepare dinner."

Kim flashed Ginny a grateful smile, then went in search of Scott. Ten minutes later, they stood on the front porch, a piece of plywood between them.

Grandpa had cut plywood to fit each window, then attached special fittings to the wood and the window edges. The fittings secured the plywood, protecting the windows from high wind, rain and blowing debris. All Kim and Scott needed to do was lift the heavy wood and match the attached fittings to the ones on the building.

Yeah, right.

"Are you sure you want to help lift?" Scott said. "I could do the lifting while you guide the wood onto the fittings."

"I appreciate the offer, but let's try it this way first." She hated the idea of putting all of the heavy work onto Scott.

"Okay, on the count of three. One, two, three."

Kim's muscles tensed as she used her thigh muscles to raise the bottom of the wood to the base of the display window.

"A little toward your left." Scott's voice sounded strained. "Doing good."

She heard a loud snap as Scott secured the first side.

"I've got it," Scott said, reaching past her to work the fittings. Another snap. "You can let go."

"How in the world did Grandpa do all this alone?" Kim started down the sides of the wood, securing it to the wall.

"I assume he had help." Scott completed attaching the wood to the upper level, then started on the other side while

Kim worked on the bottom. "This is definitely a two-man, er, two-person job."

They stepped back to admire their handiwork. "I think this was the hardest one," Scott said. "The wood for the patio doors is bigger, but we only have to lift them an inch or two."

"Really appreciate your help with this." Kim opened the store door, waited for Scott to enter, then closed and locked it.

Scott brushed aside her thanks, saying he was always available whenever she needed him. The suggestive look in his eyes made Kim's toes curl.

They climbed the interior stairs to the living room. Scott had already laid the two plywood panels on the balcony. Grandpa had built channels above and below the patio doors. The plywood slid into the channels much like a screen door.

They lifted the panel that covered the stationary portion of the door and slid it into its tracks. After pushing it into place, they secured the plywood to the tracks with screws.

Now came the tricky part: Protecting the other half of the patio door by working from inside the living room.

First they opened the patio door and pushed it all the way open to allow themselves room to work. Still standing on the deck, they positioned the final panel into its tracks and pushed it half-way closed.

Stepping into the living room, they turned and, on the count of "three," pressed and pulled the heavy panel toward the already secured piece. They aligned the edges of the two panels, then started screwing the second panel into place.

They finished, closed the patio door and stepped back to admire their handiwork.

"We work well together," Scott said.

"Well, just as long as you never ask me to glue anything, we'll do fine."

Scott grinned. "What, did you flunk glue class in kindergarten?"

"Hey, it wasn't my fault! One of the boys kept eating his pot of glue. So the teacher took away all of our glue and I never got a chance to practice."

Scott threw back his head and laughed. Kim swatted his behind, then ran for the stairs. Scott caught her half-way up to the next level, whipped her around and trapped her against the wall, one arm on either side of her head.

Her heart ka-thumped much too loudly and her skin tingled. She stared boldly into Scott's eyes. His mouth quirked. She licked her lips. And then his mouth met hers.

She leaned into the kiss, her arms snaking around his shoulders, pulling him closer. He deepened the kiss and her throat vibrated with a low moan.

Suddenly embarrassed, Kim gently pushed against Scott's chest and broke the kiss.

"Uh, this isn't getting our work finished."

"No, but it's more fun."

She grinned and lightly kissed his lips. "Work first."

"Slave driver."

Chuckling, Kim trotted up the stairs and crossed into her bedroom.

"Careful you don't trip on dog toys." She pointed at the stuffed ducks, hedgehogs and rabbits scattered across the floor.

"Yes, I noticed the land mines when I carried the panels in." Scott lifted a giant hedgehog and squeezed it. It emitted a loud grunt. "This fellow almost sent me flying."

"That's Papa Hedgehog." Kim pointed to a slightly smaller toy. "Mama Hedgehog. And this little guy is Baby Hedgehog."

"Your dog has an entire hedgehog family?"

Kim opened the sliding door to the balcony. "Yep. Stuffed hedgehogs seem to appeal to most dogs. Actually, we should get one for Al."

"Why? So I can trip over it in the middle of the night?"

"You're not a dog owner until you've stumbled over a toy in the dark." She pointed at the first panel. "Shall we?"

As they fell into a working rhythm, however, her light-hearted mood faded. She couldn't shake the notion that Brittany had triggered the awful events by staging a publicity stunt.

Suppose she'd hired someone to steal the pirate's ruby, that Dorothy interrupted the theft and, in a panic, the thief killed her. Would he then meekly hand over the ruby to Brittany? Or would he attempt to sell it to Ross Peabody?

If Brittany suspected her partner in crime had sold her ruby to Peabody, she'd be furious. Kim could easily imagine Brittany shooting Peabody in a fit of anger or in self-defense.

Despite all of Brittany's faults, however, Kim couldn't picture her in the role of serial killer. Her sense of self-preservation was too high.

So even if Brittany had shot Ross Peabody and some unknown accomplice had stabbed Dorothy, Brittany couldn't be blamed for Paula Darnell's murder.

Or could she?

Darnell was an experienced police officer trained in self-defense. She hadn't expected the attack from her killer.

So who would Darnell consider non-threatening? Another police officer, a senior citizen, a child, a lover... a pillar of society?

Like Brittany's parents?

Brittany's parents were crazy protective. What would Mr. or Mrs. Bonnet do if Darnell threatened their daughter?

"What do we do with the windows in back?" Scott interrupted her thoughts. "I couldn't find plywood to cover them."

Kim dragged her mind back to the work at hand. They'd finished securing the patio doors and were standing in the hallway that separated Kim's bedroom suite from Grandpa's.

"They have shutters attached to the house," she said. "We can close and secure them from inside."

She suddenly noticed the spicy scent of Old Bay that drifted up from the kitchen.

"That smells like Aunt Ginny's seafood casserole!" No wonder her mouth was watering; while her mind focused on murders, her taste buds had recognized the fragrance of shrimp, scallops and cream.

The fragrance also explained the absence of Rory and Al; the two dogs must be hovering near the kitchen.

"We'd better get ready for dinner." She pointed to the door of Grandpa's bedroom. "You can clean up in Grandpa's bathroom; it's right through there. Wait till you taste Ginny's secret recipe!"

Without waiting for a response, she hurried into her own bathroom to wash and change into clean clothes.

An hour later, she set down her fork and handed the clean plate to Rory to lick.

"Aunt Ginny, that was amazing."

Ginny grinned and offered Scott another serving.

Scott shook his head. "I'd love more, but I'd blow up. Thank you for the really fantastic meal."

Grandpa also complimented Ginny, then lifted his plate and prepared to stand.

"Grandpa, no." Kim stood and removed his plate, stacking it on top of hers. "You and Aunt Ginny stay here. I'll take care of the dishes."

"In that case," Aunt Ginny said, "I'll just head for home. I'd like to travel before it's too dark."

"Do you need help securing your place?" Scott said.

"No, the condo association hires people to do that."

Kim kissed her aunt goodbye. With Scott's help, they cleared the table and loaded the dishwasher.

Afterwards, she suggested they take the dogs for a walk.
Grandpa declined the invitation to join them, so Kim and
Scott set off with Rory and Al trotting ahead of them.

A southeast wind rippled the bay water, sending small
waves crashing against the peer. They encountered no other
walkers. The beach was empty.

"I really hate it when we have to block the windows." Kim
frowned at the row of shops and houses, all covered with
plywood or panels. "Gives the beach an inner-city aura. And
it's worse from inside; when I can't see outside, I feel
claustrophobic."

Scott reached over and took her hand. "Why don't you
and Max stay with me until the worst is over? I've got a spare
room for Max, you could take my bed and I can sleep on the
couch."

Kim frowned, considering. Scott rented a farmhouse that
perched on a hill in Davidsonville. No chance of flooding
and it was far enough inland to be protected from the worst
winds.

"Thanks for the offer; I doubt Grandpa will leave the
store, but let me ask him." She sighed. "What I'd really like
to do is take Grandpa, Aunt Ginny, Mom, Dad, you --
everyone -- and head as far inland as we can go before the
storm hits."

"We can certainly make room for everyone by throwing
sleeping bags on the floors."

Kim smiled. "Thank you for the offer, but I'm afraid my
entire family is pretty stubborn when it comes to riding out

hurricanes. Actually, I used to love the storms, the whipping wind, the crashing waves. But after almost losing Grandpa and being attacked by thugs..." She dragged fingers through her hair. "I guess I'm suddenly aware of my own mortality."

Scott squeezed her hand. "Tell you what; if Max won't leave the store, how 'bout I camp in your living room? That way if there is an emergency, you'll have an extra pair of hands."

"Now there's an offer I'll gladly accept."

They walked in silence, Kim's mind alternating between the recent murders and the approaching storm.

Chapter 29

The next morning, Kim woke to total darkness and the sound of rain. The outer edge of Hurricane Dan had arrived.

For a moment, she lay in bed, stroking Rory and listening to the drum of water striking the balcony. The shuttered windows, however, preyed on her mild claustrophobia.

Swinging her legs off the bed, she headed for the shower. If the storm took down a power line, they'd lose electricity. Without electricity, they couldn't pump water from the well.

Best to enjoy running water while she could.

Half an hour later, she donned a hooded rain jacket and accompanied Rory outside. Warm, tropical air enveloped her. The wind whipped raindrops onto her glasses.

She grinned as Rory ran for the apple tree, the only shelter from the downpour, and proceeded with his morning business. He raced up the stairs to join her on the kitchen landing, his fur beaded with water.

Inside, she towel dried Rory, then fixed his breakfast. Grandpa, bless him, had started heating a pot of water so by the time she set Rory's bowl on the floor, the water was hot enough to make a cup of tea. She carried it to the table and settled beside Grandpa.

"Good thing we covered the windows yesterday," she said, blowing on her tea. "I wouldn't want to be hanging plywood in the rain and wind."

Grandpa flashed a sly grin. "Nice to have Scott around to help."

"Graandpaa!" Okay, so she sounded like a twelve-year-old. But, really, did he have to be so smug about the success of his matchmaking?

He chuckled. "Gotcha."

Kim rolled her eyes, then nodded at the local newspapers Grandpa had spread across the table. Published only Wednesdays and Fridays, the news would now be old. "What's so interesting?"

He sobered and slid a front page toward her. "The Wednesday paper carried the story about Dorothy's murder."

She pulled the paper closer and read the headline: *Local Philanthropist Murdered During Pirate Museum Celebration.*

"Philanthropist? Dorothy?"

Grandpa shrugged. "Guess she had to do something with her wealth other than buy jewelry. I know she's donated to the museum."

"Huh." She scanned the article, but it didn't tell her any more than what she already knew. Absently, she flipped through the paper. Finding nothing of interest, she pushed it aside and reached for the Friday -- yesterday's -- edition. The front page warned of Hurricane Dan. No surprise there. She turned the pages, stopped to scan the police briefs -- no more jewelry robberies, yay! -- then continued to the community page.

She froze, her eyes widening. The page was filled with photos of the museum banquet -- all taken by Brooke Swann.

She resisted slapping her forehead. How could she have forgotten Brooke slipping through the crowd, snapping pictures of everyone and everything? Was it possible her childhood friend had inadvertently captured something that might point at the killer?

Eagerly, she studied the photos. A close-up of Brittany, flanked by her parents, was prominently displayed along with a caption describing Brittany's role in building the new museum. Another photo showed Aunt Ruby and Dorothy standing beside the jewelry display. The flash had reflected off the glass and jewelry, creating odd streaks of white across the women's clothes.

Toward the bottom of the page, a large photo showed the museum board members and special guests sitting at the head table. Mary looked panicked, Grandpa bored, Brittany smug. To the left of that photo, a small close-up showed Grandpa and Mary leaning toward each other and grinning at the photographer.

Kim leaned back, disappointed. She'd hoped to find shots of strangers, people in the crowd who maybe shouldn't have been there. Instead, the paper had printed images of the usual Osprey Beach hot shots.

At least they used the photo of Grandpa and Mary. She'd have to ask Brooke for a copy... Wait a minute. Why not ask Brooke for all of the photos? She'd been using a digital camera, so it should be easy to transfer everything to a CD-ROM or flash drive. Even better, Kim could enlarge the photos on her computer. Maybe the unused pictures would reveal a clue to who killed Dorothy.

Excited now, she reached for the phone.

"Can't this wait until next week?" Brooke said. "We're pretty busy here gearing up for the hurricane."

"If the hurricane hits tomorrow, you'll be even busier taking photos. C'mon, Brooke, you don't need to sort through the photos; just copy them onto a disk or something."

Brooke sighed. "Okay, give me half an hour. I'll leave the disk at the front desk. But I don't believe for a minute that you're simply looking for photos of your grandfather. If you find something newsworthy, you'll let me know, right?"

Kim readily agreed.

Hanging up the phone, she explained the plan to Grandpa.

He nodded. "Good, that'll get you out of here for a little while. Don't look so surprised; I know you get antsy when you can't see outside."

That comment provided the perfect opportunity to pose Scott's offer.

"Scott has a spare bedroom. He said we could ride out the storm with him."

"If they order us to evacuate, I'll gladly stay with Scott," he said. "But otherwise I'd rather stay here. I'd just worry about looters."

Looters. Kim suddenly felt cold. She'd worried about the store flooding or a tree falling on the roof or how long they'd lose electricity. But she hadn't considered the repercussions of a New Orleans type disaster.

"Did you hear what I just said?" Grandpa studied her face.

"Oh, no, I'm sorry. I was just thinking. What did you say?"

"That you should take Rory and go to Scott's. There's no reason for you to stay here; I've ridden out these storms before."

"Actually, I have a better idea," she said. "Scott offered to come here; he said the couch is comfortable. Stop shaking your head before I finish. With Scott here, we can play cards or something, keep my mind off of the boarded windows."

"Fine. I'll take the couch."

"You'll do no such thing." Kim stood and reached for her purse. "You're supposed to be recovering, remember?" She leaned over and kissed his cheek. "I'm off to the paper."

"Take Rory."

Kim opened her mouth to protest, then spotted Grandpa's pressed lips and set jaw. Best to let him win this one.

Calling to Rory, she headed out into the rain.

The newspaper where Brooke worked was located south of Osprey Beach in Prince Frederick. Normally, the drive consumed fifteen minutes. Today, however, the cloudy sky, whipping rain and intense wind reduced visibility and created a traffic snarl on Route 4.

By the time Kim collected Brooke's photos and returned to Grandpa's, more than an hour had passed and her shoulders ached from gripping the steering wheel. She found Grandpa in the kitchen pulling steaks out of the freezer.

"Thought we'd better eat what's in the freezer before the power goes out," Grandpa said. "Did you get what you needed?"

"Yep." Kim tossed the CD onto the kitchen table, hung up her wet jacket and began drying Rory. "Traffic was a mess. I guess everyone is out buying batteries and canned goods. Weather seemed worse, though, when I was driving home."

"That's because the hurricane picked up speed. Supposed to make landfall in the middle of the night instead of tomorrow morning."

Kim hung the now-wet towel on a hook. "Guess I'd better call Scott, see if he still wants to come over."

"Tell him to come for dinner."

Scott answered on the second ring. Yes, he wanted to spend the night with them, yes, he'd love to come to dinner and, of course, he'd bring Al. She suggested he plan to arrive late afternoon.

Which gave her plenty of time to sort through Brooke's photos.

"Grandpa, you want to look at banquet photos with me?"

When he agreed, Kim carried her laptop into the kitchen and angled the chairs so both of them could see the screen. Kim inserted the disk and a series of tiny photos displayed. And displayed. And displayed.

"Looks like she took hundreds of photos." Grandpa peered at the tiny pictures. "This could take all day."

Kim shrugged and clicked on the first photo. "Beats worrying about the weather."

The first fifty or so photos were the standard shake-and-grin of Calvert County's most influential people. Kim blew up each photo, hoping the camera had captured someone doing something suspicious in the background. No luck.

The next hundred were shots of the restaurant.

"These are out of order." Kim enlarged a table of diners. "She must have shuffled the photos when trying to choose what to print."

"If she photographed every table," Grandpa said, "we'll learn who actually attended the banquet."

"Let me get a list of invited guests and we can check off people in the photos."

Half an hour later, Kim stared down at the guest list. They'd managed to check off most of the names.

Grandpa pushed back his chair. "Need to move a bit. Want a glass of iced tea?"

"Yes, please." Kim clicked on the next photo. "Okay, we're back to the photos taken in the museum itself."

In addition to pictures of the crowd, Brooke had snapped shots of the exhibits. Kim grinned as she zoomed in on the pirate ship. Brooke had captured the boy-like delight of the tuxedo-clad men who'd climbed aboard. Would Scott have joined them if he hadn't been with her?

The next photo showed Kim bending over the jewelry display. The flash from the camera had bounced off the display case at an odd angle, sending white rays across her face and the bodice of her gown. No wonder she'd seen black dots.

Ah, and here was a photo of Dorothy Tyson after she'd elbowed Kim out of the way. Brooke perfectly captured Dorothy's perpetual scowl.

Next came a series of photos of Aunt Ruby and Dorothy. Kim smiled. Her aunt looked pretty darn good in these. Too bad Dorothy grimaced, closed her eyes or squinted. Brooke had been patient, however, and managed to snap one photo in which Dorothy semi-smiled; this was the one they'd used in the newspaper.

Kim copied the series into a file on her computer. Maybe later she'd crop Dorothy out and print some copies of Aunt Ruby. Uncle Walt would love them.

She clicked on the next series of photos. Apparently, after capturing a decent photo of Dorothy Tyson, Brooke had shot a number of angles of the jewelry and gem display. The flash from her camera, however, reflected off the glass case and distorted the contents.

Poor Brooke. Photographing jewelry is difficult under the best of circumstances. The lovely, rich-colored photos seen in catalogs required special lighting to make the gems sparkle. Trying to shoot through the glass case increased the complexity.

The photographer also had to account for refraction, the way gemstones bent or split light. The same characteristics that helped jewelers separate light-splitting ruby from light-bending spinel or garnet wreaked havoc on a camera lens. In unskilled hands, a camera lens could magnify the double-refractive tendencies of gemstones like zircon, making them appear out of focus.

She had to hand it to Brooke, however. Her friend had been persistent and moved around the display case, changing angles, turning off the flash, placing the camera lens tight against the glass.

Dorothy Tyson hadn't helped matters. She'd continued to peer into the display case, ignoring Brooke, intent on her own agenda. Here was Dorothy's head blocking a close-up of the largest diamond, there her hand pressing against the glass.

Apparently, Brooke had resigned herself to Dorothy's interference and stepped back to photograph the woman studying the display. One photo captured Dorothy, face whitened by light reflected by the flash, grimacing at the display.

Kim clicked through the photos. Flash, Dorothy staring down, eyes wide. Flash, Dorothy leaning closer, nose almost touching the glass. Flash, Dorothy facing forward, eyes narrowed, mouth thin and determined.

Kim's hand hovered over the mouse, her thoughts darting back to a conversation with Aunt Ruby. She'd said Dorothy seemed unhappy with the jewelry display.

Wondering what had bothered Dorothy, Kim clicked through Brooke's jewelry photos until she found one that showed the entire arrangement. She enlarged the photo and studied it. But the display was just as elegant as she remembered it.

So why had Dorothy Tyson been displeased?

She clicked back to the long-shots of Dorothy peering at the gems, pausing at the one showing Dorothy's widened eyes. Looking closer, she realized the woman's mouth hung slightly open.

Dorothy wore the classic expression of surprise.

But surprised by what?

Kim returned to the enlarged photo of the display contents and studied the individual gemstones. The flash bouncing off the stones made it difficult to determine if anything was amiss. Brooke had wasted several shots aiming straight down at the few diamonds.

Kim grinned. Brooke always loved her diamonds.

She'd done a superb job with bringing out the sparkle of the smaller diamonds. But she'd been unable to bring the largest diamond into focus. The photo taken from directly above that diamond, in fact, made its facets appear doubled.

Doubled?

Heartbeat quickening, Kim zoomed in on the diamond. There, at the bottom of the stone, she could see the culet -- the small base facet that contributed to diamond's sparkle. Except there wasn't one culet; there appeared to be two.

The picture wasn't out of focus. The gemstone was merely splitting the light in two. The "diamond" was double-refractive.

"Grandpa? Could you look at this photo, please?"

Grandpa set two glasses of iced tea on the table as he slid into the chair beside her. She pointed to the screen.

"Diamond or zircon?"

He leaned in and studied the photo. "Definitely zircon. This one of Brooke's photos?"

"Yeah." Kim zoomed out so Grandpa could see the entire gemstone display. "Did the museum have zircons in its collection?"

"No. Not unless someone recently donated one and Mary hasn't told me." His mouth narrowed. "But we have three diamonds. If this is zircon, a diamond was missing before the theft."

Chapter 30

"So someone stole the museum diamond and substituted a zircon?" Kim said.

Grandpa shook his head. "That makes no sense. Zircons aren't cheap. Plus you'd need to find one that's the same size and shape as our diamond."

"Or hire someone to cut one."

"Possible," Grandpa said. "But expensive. If you were going to enlist someone to create a diamond substitute, why not use cubic zirconia?"

"A CZ is too easy to detect." Kim leaned forward. "Think about it. Stealing from a museum is riskier than stealing from an individual. Even a small museum like ours has experts studying the exhibits. You'd spot a cubic zirconia in a heartbeat."

"But the average person can't tell the difference between a CZ and a diamond," he said. "You're describing a pretty knowledgeable thief. How many people would know that natural zircon is difficult to distinguish from diamond?"

An image formed in Kim's mind: Kim, Brooke and Mary standing in the school playground, Kim expostulating about gemstones that looked alike. She pictured Brittany and Leslie, hovering in the background, Brittany glaring as Kim segued from diamonds and zircons to the red gems: rubies, garnet and spinel.

"Brittany knows," she said. "She heard me telling Mary and Brooke about look-alike gems."

"Telling?" Grandpa tweaked her nose. "If I remember correctly, you had a tendency to lecture."

Kim ignored the tease, her mind racing. "Kevin complained about Brittany hanging around while he was trying to work. Maybe she switched the diamond with the zircon as part of her publicity campaign. You know, someone steals her ruby and then an investigation reveals a missing diamond. That would attract media attention."

"Whoa, whoa," Grandpa said. "We don't even know that someone *did* substitute the zircon for a diamond. The zircon could have been a donation that Mary hasn't mentioned."

"Then where's the diamond?"

Grandpa shrugged. "Maybe it's still in the museum safe. Mary might have displayed the wrong stone."

"So how do we find out?"

"We ask." Grandpa reached for the phone and dialed.

"Mary? It's Max Hershey. Fine, fine. How are things at your place?" Grandpa frowned. "Do you want Kim and me to help you hang plywood? Okay, if you're sure Kevin will have time.

"The reason I'm calling is we think one of the stolen gemstones was a natural zircon. I don't remember a zircon in the collection... Oh, she did, huh?"

Grandpa sighed. "Yeah, I know how Dorothy was. Have you checked the safe to make sure everything's still there? No, you stay put. Kim and I are closer. What's the combination?"

Kim handed Grandpa paper and pencil. "Okay, I'm ready." He wrote several numbers, then read them back to Mary.

"Did Dorothy keep a record of these things?" He nodded. "Okay, if the gems are there, I'm going to transfer them to my own safe. If Dorothy had the combination, she might have given it to someone else.

"Where do you keep the museum's acquisition records? Good. While we're stuck in the storm, I'll compare the records with what we find in the safe.

"Now, promise to call if Kevin doesn't get home in time to secure your windows, okay?"

Grandpa hung up the phone. "Apparently, Dorothy put several new gemstones into the museum's safe."

"But how did Dorothy get access to the safe? She's just a board member. Shouldn't Mary be the only one with the combination?"

Grandpa looked at Kim. She nodded.

"You know Dorothy," they said in unison.

"Brittany gave Dorothy a few other family heirlooms to display at the museum." Grandpa stood and stretched. "But Brittany wanted the grand opening to focus on the pirate's ruby. So Dorothy secured Brittany's other stuff in the museum safe."

Kim stood. "And Mary doesn't know if it's still there?"

"She's had other things on her mind." Grandpa handed Kim her rain jacket, then donned his own. "Kevin's at the museum boarding windows, so we can easily get in."

A clap of thunder sent Rory racing to Kim's side. Reasoning he'd be less frightened if she kept him with her, she snapped on his leash and followed Grandpa down the steps.

The rain and wind had increased substantially since Kim had driven to the newspaper. Dark clouds blocked the early-afternoon sun, creating a dusk-like gloom. What should have been a ten-minute trip took seventeen minutes as drivers slowed down to peer through rain-splashed windshields.

Despite gloomy weather, however, the temperature hovered in the 90s -- too hot to leave Rory in the back seat while they located the records and retrieved the gems from the safe. Kim pulled as close to the front steps as she could without interfering with workers frantically pounding plywood over the museum's windows.

"Please go inside while I get Rory," she told Grandpa as she stepped into the rain and opened the rear door. She unhooked Rory's seatbelt harness and clipped on his leash. Together, they ran up the steps and into the museum.

The sound of metal biting through wood greeted them. Rory slammed to a halt and barked at the goggled man working just inside the front door. The man guided a circle saw across plywood that had been balanced across two sawhorses. A second man held the board firm, catching the two pieces when the saw finished the cut.

The whine stopped. The man set aside the saw, used a grease pen to mark something on the boards, then helped his assistant carry the two pieces away from the work area and lean them against the wall. Only then did he remove his goggles, revealing Mary's husband Kevin.

"Max!" He stepped forward to shake Grandpa's hand. "What are you doing here?"

"Mary sent me to get some things from her office."

Rory barked again, startling Kevin. He nodded at Rory. "He friendly?"

Kim laid a hand on Rory's head. "Normally, yeah. The saw freaked him a bit. I'm surprised you're still boarding windows."

Kevin scowled. "Mary wasn't allowed to order the wood without Board approval and after Dorothy's death, everything was in chaos. Then the police sealed the museum so no one could get in to measure. By the time they let us in, it was too late to buy the wood from our usual sources and all the local stores were sold out. I spent all day yesterday driving to Hagerstown to buy enough plywood to finish the job."

"That why you haven't boarded your own home?" Grandpa said.

Kevin nodded. "With any luck, we'll be finished here in a couple of hours and I can go take care of my own home-- Bobby, what the heck are you doing out in this weather? Does your mother know where you are?"

Kim turned to see Bobby and Liz. Water dripped from their wet hair and jackets and climbed halfway up their jeans. Their sneakers were soaking wet.

"You said I could see my display case." Bobby's chin elevated and his eyes flashed.

Liz rolled her eyes.

"Did you ride here on your bikes?" Kim said.

"Wasn't raining this hard when we left." Liz crossed her arms but wouldn't meet Kim's eyes.

"They're here now," Grandpa said to Kevin. "Might as well show them the case."

Kevin sighed. "Okay. But you'll both need to stay here until we're finished."

"I have to get right home," Liz said.

"I'll take both of you home." Kim knew Liz's bike would fit in the rear of the van; she could lay Bobby's bike on top. "But you'll need to share the back seat with Rory."

Rory, who'd been straining at the leash to reach the children, wagged his tail furiously. Liz grinned and called Rory.

"Just a minute." Kim turned her full attention to her young dog. If she let him pull her over to the children, she'd lose months of intensive training. "Rory, sit. No, look at me. That's better. Now sit."

Reluctantly, Rory's butt dropped to the floor. Kim rewarded him with a dog biscuit, then allowed him to greet the children.

"Euwwww, you're all wet." Liz giggled.

"Why don't you take the children to see what you've built," Grandpa said to Kevin. "We'll get what we need from Mary's office and meet you back here."

Kevin glanced at his watch, sighed and wrapped an arm around his son. "I don't have much time, but let's go see."

Bobby's face brightened and the two headed deeper into the museum. Liz hesitated, eyes darting from the father/son pair to Rory to Kim and Grandpa.

"If you'd like," Kim said gently, "We could load the bikes into the car."

Liz's eyes brightened and she nodded her head.

"Grandpa, do you need help..."

"No, dear." Grandpa waved a hand toward the exit. "You go load the bikes while I get what we need."

Without waiting for an answer, he turned and trudged up the stairs.

"Let's load Rory first." Kim flipped up her hood and yanked the door open.

The wind immediately whipped the hood from her head and aimed driving rain at her glasses. Kim brushed a hank of damp hair from her mouth and hurried down the stairs. Opening the rear door, she urged Rory to hop in, then secured his seatbelt. She reached for one of the dog towels she kept in the van and wiped the worst of the water off his coat. She spread a dry towel on the seat for the children.

Turning, she found Liz standing quietly, knuckles white on the bike handles.

"Why don't you get in the car while I load the bikes?" Kim handed Liz a clean towel, then walked the bike to the rear and tucked it safely inside. Bobby's bike lay against the museum steps. She half-carried, half-pushed it to the car and loaded it, then pulled the hatch shut.

Opening the driver's door, she leaned in, pushed the key into the ignition and turned the car on.

"Heat or air conditioning?"

"Air," Liz said. "It's stuffy back here."

Kim showed Liz the backseat controls where she could adjust the temperature of the blowing air.

"Wait here while I get Grandpa and Bobby."

She started up the stairs, then slammed to a halt as a black-colored snake slithered in front of her. She watched it climb the stairs, evidently seeking higher, drier ground. As it disappeared around the side of the building, goosebumps broke out on her arms. Snakes didn't scare her, but she didn't like to stumble upon them unexpectedly.

Shaking off the feeling, she trotted up the last few steps and flung open the museum door.

Bobby and Kevin stood by the sawhorses, Bobby waving his arms and babbling about the coolness of his father's display cases.

Kevin flashed Kim a smile, giving her a glimpse of the heartthrob that had attracted Mary -- and Brittany and Paula?

"I'm glad you like it." He patted Bobby's shoulder. "Now, you better head on home so I can get some work done."

As Bobby trotted out the door, Grandpa appeared at the top of the stairs.

"Need any help?" she called to him.

"No, I'm good." Grandpa trudged down the stairs carrying a small paper bag and what was obviously an accounting ledger. "I should have brought something to protect the acquisitions log."

"I'll hold it under my rain jacket." Kim reached for the book and turned to say goodbye to Kevin.

He was staring at the ledger.

"Don't worry," she said, "I'll take good care of this."

She followed Grandpa outside. Through the rain, she spotted a small, white car driving out of the parking lot. Probably one of the workers heading home.

She aimed her own car for the exit. Her mind, however, flitted back to Mary's husband.

Why had Kevin's face drained of color when he saw Grandpa carrying the acquisitions ledger?

Chapter 31

"Just wait till the others see it," Bobby gushed from the back seat. "Did I tell you there's a metal sign right below the glass top and it says 'Ruby from pirate cache discovered by Bobby Klein and loaned to museum'?"

"Only a million times," Liz grumbled.

Kim glanced into the rear-view mirror. Liz huddled in the middle of the seat, Rory on one side, Bobby on the other. Arms crossed in front of her, shoulders hunched, Liz stared at the floor. Bobby remained oblivious.

Thank goodness they'd almost reached Bobby's home.

"Imagine," he said, "my name right there for everyone to see! It was awesome! Bobby Klein, the world's best treasure hunter."

Liz's head whipped up. Her brown eyes flashed.

"All you found was one ruby," Liz said. "You just wait. I'm going to find the entire treasure and they'll have to build a whole room for me."

Kim slowed to make the turn onto Mary's street.

"No way are you going to find the treasure." Even without looking, Kim could picture the scorn on Bobby's face. "*I'm* going to find the rest."

"Are not."

"Are too."

"Not."

Thank goodness, there was the house. Kim pulled into the driveway.

"No way will you find the treasure." Bobby opened his door. "You're just a girl."

Before anyone could respond, he ran toward the house. Kim pressed the button to close the automatic sliding door, then stepped out and trudged to the rear of the van. As she opened the tailgate, Mary appeared at her side.

"Thanks for bringing Bobby home."

Kim nodded and reached for the boy's bike. Mary grasped the rear wheel and helped Kim lift the bike from the van.

"Kevin just called," Mary shouted above the wind. "He's going to be at the museum much longer than he thought and he doesn't think he'll be able to secure our house before nightfall."

Kim reached for the handle on the tailgate. "You want me to help you hang the plywood?"

Mary shook her head. "Won't do any good. The wood to the largest window was damaged in the last storm. Kevin needs to repair it before we can use it. He wanted me to ask you if the kids and I can stay with you tonight. We've got sleeping bags."

Kim's first thought was Scott. Well, he'd just have to sleep in her room; she'd take the couch. With the children and the dogs, no one was probably going to sleep anyway.

"Fine with me; we can have a slumber party. But let's check with Grandpa."

Grandpa, of course, told Mary they were all welcome.

"Thanks. I'll just pack a few things and be over. I've got a frozen pizza we can cook."

Kim climbed back into the car. Grandpa handed her a clean handkerchief to clean her glasses. As she wiped the water from the lenses, she glanced in the rear-view mirror. Liz had been awfully quiet.

"You know," she tried, "Bobby didn't mean it when he said you're just a girl."

"Then why'd he say it?"

Kim slid her glasses onto her face. How best to answer that? She backed the car into the street and set a course for Liz's house.

"Boys, and for that matter, men have this ego thing going."

Beside her, Grandpa snorted. Kim patted his hand. "Present company excluded, of course.

"Anyway, males think they have to protect females. That can be good; boys usually have more muscles, after all. But sometimes, well, that protective instinct gets skewed and they start thinking of girls as weaker and that leads to chauvinism."

"What's chauvinism?"

"It's when guys say girls can't do something just because they're girls."

"Like Bobby."

"Yeah, like Bobby." They drove for a few minutes in silence, Kim searching her psychology training for guidance of where to go from here. Liz would never believe that Bobby didn't mean what he'd said. So maybe the best approach would be to shore up Liz's bruised ego.

"Thing is, when boys say girls can't do something, the boys are usually wrong. Girls can do math and computers and science. They can climb trees and lift weights and become astronauts, doctors and lawyers." Silence from the back seat. "Girls can do most anything boys can except pee standing up."

That produced a giggle.

"I read somewhere that after a storm is the best time to look for pirate treasure," Liz said. "The rain washes away dirt and things."

Kim nodded. "After a storm is also a good time to look for sea shells and fossils. Grandpa and I used to find the best fossils after a hurricane."

They drove in silence for a few more miles. Kim increased the speed of the windshield wipers.

"I was going to invite Bobby to look for treasure," Liz said. "Now I'm going myself."

"Don't be too hard on him," Kim said. "He said something stupid, but he's still your friend."

Liz thought about that as Kim pulled the car in front of her house. Kim put the car in park and turned toward Liz.

"He really is still your friend."

Liz thought a moment longer, then nodded. "Okay. He's still my friend." She reached for the door handle. "But I'm still going to look for treasure alone."

Kim glanced at Grandpa, who shrugged. Shaking her head, Kim stepped into the rain and lifted Liz's bike from the van.

Liz grasped the handles. "You just wait. I'll show Bobby who's the better treasure hunter."

Kim hurried back into the driver's seat. Grandpa handed her a damp towel. She dried off while they waited to make sure Liz entered the house safely.

"Did I do the right thing, saying Bobby was still her friend?"

Kim turned onto Bayside Road and headed south to Grandpa's house.

"You did fine." Grandpa patted her hand. "Kids fight all the time and still remain friends. Look at you and Tony."

Kim frowned. "Tony? I don't remember fighting with Tony."

Grandpa chuckled. "When you were twelve, you didn't like him following you around."

"Well, of course not. He was eight then, totally obnoxious and always tripping over his feet."

"That why you called him Splat?"

Kim grinned. "Nah. I called him that because you wouldn't let me call him Brat."

A car came around the bend toward them. Bright headlights bounced off her glasses, creating prisms of blinding color. She tapped the brakes and steered by memory. The road straightened and she could see again.

"Why is it that glasses always make it worse when some idiot forgets to turn off his high beams..." A thought flashed through her mind and she struggled to grasp it. Someone else had recently complained about bright lights.

"Grandpa! Remember when Aunt Ruby described Dorothy's reaction to headlights reflecting off her glasses? Instead of complaining, she pulled to the side of the road and sat there thinking. *That* was when Dorothy insisted you meet her at the museum immediately."

"So?"

"Don't you see? Remember the photos Brooke took, how Dorothy was frowning at the gemstone display? She probably saw something odd when Brooke's flash reflected off the gems. But she didn't consciously figure out what was wrong until headlights reflected off her glasses.

"She wanted you to tell her whether the clear stone in the display was a diamond or zircon."

Twenty minutes later, Kim stepped out of the shower and toweled off. Despite the warm temperature, the rain had chilled her to the bone and she'd needed the hot shower to feel human again. She opened a dresser drawer, her hand hovering over a clean pair of shorts.

Though the outside temperature remained summer-warm, the whining wind and pounding rain demanded comfort clothes.

She whipped out a clean t-shirt, a pair of soft, baggy sweatpants and its matching zippered jacket. There'd be time to put on something nicer when Rory alerted her to Scott's car pulling into the driveway.

Until Scott arrived, however, she intended to spend her time comparing Brooke's photos with the museum's acquisition records and the recently donated gems Grandpa had retrieved from the museum safe.

She found Grandpa in the kitchen, slicing the steaks he'd defrosted into long, thin pieces.

"You know, Mary and I could split one of those steaks and you and Scott could eat a whole one. Or I could eat pizza."

Grandpa shook his head. "No need. I've got some green peppers from the garden that we need to eat."

"You're making pepper steak? Oh, yum. What can I do to help?"

"Slice the peppers." Grandpa pointed at the counter beside the sink where he'd already laid out the cutting board, knife and peppers. "Once you're finished, you can start looking at the museum records. I know you're anxious to test out your theory."

But Kim had barely begun chopping when Rory barked at the kitchen door. She silently cursed the boarded windows. Who'd pulled into the driveway, Scott or Mary?

The squeal of children and patter of feet climbing the stairs provided the answer. Kim set down the knife, snagged Rory's collar and opened the door.

Bobby and his little sister hustled in, dripping water from their jackets, backpacks and plastic-covered sleeping bags. Kim hesitated, unsure whether she should hang onto Rory or help the children. Mary solved the problem by rushing in and pushing the door closed with her hip.

"Set your things on the floor and do not move until you've dried off." Mary followed her own instructions by laying down her backpack and sleeping bag plus a plastic bag of something else. She set the frozen pizza on the counter beside Kim.

Kim watched Mary corral the children, fascinated. She would never cease to be amazed by the way mothers could wipe one child's face while passing a towel to the other, hang up a jacket with one hand while shaking off a backpack with the other, remove a favorite toy from one bag while sliding cookies out of reach of children and dog.

In just a few minutes, the children's faces were dry, shoes off, jackets hung, backpacks stacked neatly by the door. Kimmy approached Rory, one thumb in her mouth, the other hand clutching a pink blanket and matching teddy bear. Rory reached for the toy.

"No, leave it."

Rory looked from the toy to Kim, sighed and hurled himself to the kitchen floor with a thump, his body oozing indignation. Oh, boy, with Rory the toy thief and Al the food thief, this promised to be a challenging night.

"Is it okay if the children watch movies?" Mary pulled a stack of DVDs from a plastic bag.

When Grandpa nodded, Mary headed down the hallway with the DVDs, the children in her wake.

"Sort of like Konrad Lorenz." At Grandpa's puzzled expression, Kim added, "You know, the fellow who discovered how ducks and geese imprint on their parents? He walked past the new hatchlings and they decided he was their mother. There's a photo of him walking with a row of the adult geese following him single file." She nodded toward the hallway. "Mary's kids follow her like geese."

Grandpa chuckled. "I know your mother would like you to get married and have children, but I'm not so sure. You'd probably train the kids with a clicker."

Kim pursed her lips and blew a raspberry at Grandpa, then returned to her chopping duties. She'd only dissected half a pepper when Mary removed the knife from her hands.

"I'll do this," Mary said. "You go do your investigating. I know that's what you love."

Kim shot Mary a grateful smile. Crossing to the kitchen table, she sat in front of her laptop and called up the photo Brooke had taken of the gem exhibit. She hit the print button, then trotted up the stairs to her bedroom and the printer.

Though she was more comfortable working in front of the computer, she'd decided it'd be easier to compare the printed log book to a printed photo. She'd match the items in the acquisition record to the gems in the photo; when she found a match, she'd draw an X over the gem.

For this, she just needed an image on plain paper. She snagged the finished print and returned to the kitchen.

Mary was placing the pizza into the oven.

"I thought we'd feed the kids first," Mary said. "Then the adults will have peace while we eat. I'm looking forward to getting to know your boyfriend."

Kim shot a look at Grandpa. He winked and turned back to the meat he was sautéing.

Sighing, Kim settled at the table, closed her laptop and replaced it with the museum's record book. She turned to the first page and frowned at the date of the first entry: 1901.

"Don't worry; we haven't had that many jewelry donations." Mary leaned over Kim's shoulder and pointed at the fourth column. "If you follow this column, it'll tell you what item was donated."

Kim thanked Mary, then crossed to the silverware drawer, removed a table knife and carried it back to the ledger. Using the knife as a line-by-line guide, she began scanning.

She found the first entry four pages in. In 1927, one of Brittany's ancestors had donated a brooch containing a step-cut emerald surrounded by rose-cut diamonds.

Pulling the image of the pirate display closer, Kim located the brooch and marked an X over it.

Back to the ledger.

The smell of tomato sauce and cheese joined the fragrance of browning meat and onions. Kim's mouth watered. Maybe she'd steal a slice of pizza while she waited for dinner.

Ah, there, in 1947, another brooch contribution, this one set with a sapphire. Kim didn't recognize the donor's name. She found the brooch in the photo, crossed it out and returned to the page.

In the mid-1950s, the museum received a flurry of gifts of loose gemstones. Perhaps the director had campaigned for them? Again, Kim didn't recognize the names of the contributors.

She pulled the photo close and checked off the 1-carat diamond, the blue star sapphire, the half-carat ruby, the cushion-cut amethyst, citrine and garnet.

Back to the ledger. As the tedium built, she fell into a rhythm: Slide the knife, scan the column, slide the knife, repeat. She heard the scrape of chairs as the children joined her and Mary's whispered admonishment to be quiet, smelled the nearby pizza, tasted the basil in the slice Mary set beside her. But her eyes never left the journal.

Most of the jewelry donations consisted of Victorian necklaces, bracelets and hat pins -- all created long after the heyday of traditional pirating. Mary had clustered these donations together beneath a sign saying "Pirates would have loved these." Kim smiled. Good way to satisfy patrons while remaining true to history.

Another entry for a loose diamond, this one only half a carat. That accounted for all but one of the diamonds in the photograph.

By the year 1990, Kim had marked off all items in the photo except the three-carat, rose-cut diamond. Finally, in 2004, she located the entry. The diamond had been a gift of Brittany's mother.

Kim snorted. Must be nice to have so much money you could give away diamonds. Maybe Mrs. Bonnet didn't understand the stone's value? The old-fashioned method of faceting the stone didn't produce the sparkle of modern brilliant cuts.

But three carats was a healthy size for a diamond. If Mrs. Bonnet couldn't admire the stone for its history, she could have had it re-cut.

Lifting the pen, she hovered over the photo. The diamond-like stone was the last item to check off. Problem was, the "diamond" reflected light like a zircon.

So was the stone on display zircon or diamond?

She circled the stone, wrote a question mark above it and reached for the jewelry Grandpa had removed from the museum safe.

Laying a piece of velvet on the table, she gently removed each item one at a time and positioned it on the cloth. The collection Brittany had given the museum to display included a half-carat emerald pendant, a pink sapphire ring, gold earrings set with jet, a natural freshwater pearl mounted on a hat pin and a bracelet set with different colors of sapphire.

Though none of the cut stones sparkled like modern ones, their very simplicity appealed to Kim. The freshwater pearl was enormous, well over an inch long. Kim rubbed her finger along the irregularly shaped pearl, enjoying the silky smoothness and wondering which river mollusk had produced this lovely fluke of nature.

She reached for the acquisition ledger. Leaving the table knife to mark her place, she flipped to the final page where Dorothy had recorded the items she was storing for Brittany in the museum safe. The list matched the five pieces of jewelry recovered from the safe.

But there was no mention of a natural zircon.

Maybe someone else had donated it?

Kim flipped back to her place-marker and continued scanning the columns of donations. But she reached the end of the ledger without finding a zircon.

Closing the ledger, she pulled the photo close and stared down at the clear stone she'd circled. Maybe this wasn't a zircon. After all, she had a record of a diamond donation, not a zircon. And yet, this stone looked double refractive, a trait of zircon but not diamond.

"Grandpa? Could you look at this photo again?"

As Grandpa leaned over her, she pointed at the diamond/zircon. "This doubling we're seeing. Could that be coming from the display case or something else?"

Grandpa studied the photo, then shook his head. "I don't see glare anywhere in the photo. Let's look at the other photos."

Grandpa pulled out a chair. Kim retrieved her laptop and enlarged all of the photos Brooke had taken of the gems.

"Here." She turned the screen toward Grandpa. "Click on this arrow when you want to move to the next photo."

While Grandpa examined the photos, Kim rose and stretched. Her back and shoulders ached from the tension. She carried her glass to the refrigerator, poured more tea, then filled Grandpa's and Mary's glasses.

"What are you looking at?" Mary crossed to stand behind Grandpa. "Oh. Are those the photos Brooke took?"

"Yeah." Kim studied Mary's face, searching for an eye flick, a tensing mouth, a sign that Mary knew the stone was not a diamond. "Brooke did a good job, didn't she?"

Mary simply nodded, her eyes intent on the images. "Wait a minute. Could you go back a photo?" She pointed at the diamond/zircon. "Is that a reflection or something? It looks odd."

Grandpa sighed and leaned back. Removing his glasses, he rubbed his eyes.

"I'm afraid the stone in the photo is a zircon." He slipped his glasses back on.

"Zircon? We don't have any zircons." She turned to Kim. "Unless there was one in the safe?"

Kim shook her head. "No zircon."

Mary frowned. "So where's our diamond?" She pointed at the photo. "That's exactly where I placed the diamond when I arranged the exhibit."

"It would appear that someone switched the diamond with a zircon," Grandpa said.

Mary's eyes widened. "But, but these photos were taken before the robbery, weren't they? That means..." Her mouth fell open. "You don't think that I switched them?"

As Grandpa reassured Mary, Kim continued to study her. The facial expressions were consistent with innocence. The tension in her shoulders, however, could be caused by either surprise or guilt.

Fortunately, Mary didn't notice Kim's silence.

"We need to figure out who had access to the gems," Kim said, "and also knew that a zircon could be substituted for a diamond."

Mary collapsed into a chair. "For access, it depends on when the substitution was made. Certainly Brittany's been running around the museum a lot. Dorothy, too. And I told you Ross Peabody was alone in the old museum, when the sapphire ring disappeared."

"If he was willing to walk off with the sapphire," Kim said, "there was no reason to go through the contortions of substituting a diamond with a zircon. He'd have just stolen the diamond.

"And I think we can eliminate Dorothy as a suspect, too. We're thinking she may have asked Grandpa to return to the museum to verify her suspicion that the stones had been switched."

Mary dragged fingers through her hair. "The announcement of the new museum brought a lot of new people to the old museum. I suppose someone could have jimmied a display case open."

"So maybe we should come at this from another direction." Kim met Mary's eyes. "Who would know they could substitute a zircon for a diamond?"

"Well, I knew." Mary's eyes didn't waver. "Don't you remember, Kim? You used to tell us stories about look-alike gems. My favorite, of course, was about rubies and spinels, how the famous Black Prince's Ruby is actually spinel." She frowned. "That means Brooke knows, if she remembers. But Brooke would never steal."

"Brittany was always hovering in the background." At this point, Kim believed in her friend's innocence. "Leslie Darling was also there. Did Leslie frequent the museum?"

Mary snorted. "Are you kidding? Do something that requires thinking?"

"So that leaves Brittany. I've been trying to remember if I've told stories about look-alike gems to anyone else. Have you told anyone?"

"Only Kevin. He likes to hear stories about my childhood. I can't tell them as well as you..." Her eyes widened. "You don't think... He wouldn't..."

Groaning, she covered her face. "Oh, gawd, I'm such a fool."

Kim and Grandpa exchanged looks. Kim reached over and touched Mary's arm.

"Why do you say that?"

"He knows! Kevin knows about look-alike gems because I told him."

"That's no reason to belittle yourself."

Mary dropped her hands to reveal a tear-stained face. "Don't you get it yet? Kevin fits all of your criteria. He knew that zircons could pass for diamonds and he had easy access to the museum."

"Well, yeah, he was one of the workers, but you said the gemstones were locked in the safe."

Mary shook her head. "I'm talking about before he worked on the new museum. A year or so ago, Kevin's car broke down and, well, we didn't have the money to get it fixed. With the recession and all, there wasn't much demand for construction work.

"So Kevin began driving me to and from work so he'd have the car to use for his job hunting. I sometimes left him alone in the museum or office while I finished working on something. That gave him access."

"Even so, why would he take a single diamond? Why not substitute spinel for ruby..." Kim's voice trailed off and she looked helplessly at Grandpa.

He shook his head. "The stones I examined at the station were rubies." He grinned at her. "I checked for double refraction. There was none."

Mary shook her head, dismissing Grandpa's reassurance. "You don't understand. During this time, we were so broke that we seriously discussed taking my wedding ring to the pawn shop to get enough money for food until pay day. We figured we'd retrieve the ring after I was paid."

"Why didn't you say something?" Grandpa said. "The museum could have provided an advance on your salary."

"I was too ashamed." She breathed deeply. "I was prepared to pawn my ring when Kevin came home all excited, said he'd picked up a small job and that we should be okay."

Mary bit her lip and more tears fell. "What if he hadn't gotten a job after all? What if he hired someone to style a zircon that could be switched with the diamond?"

"But how would Kevin find a lapidarist who'd duplicate the museum gem?" Kim said. "Any honest gem cutter who suspected Kevin's motives would refuse."

"He wouldn't need to duplicate our gem." Grandpa's voice was grim. "He could just ask for a specific size of zircon styled in a rose cut."

Mary grabbed Kim's hands. "Kevin's not a thief, honestly! If he switched the diamond with a zircon, it was just temporary. He'd have pawned the diamond instead of my ring, then retrieved the diamond when we had enough money. The money from building the museum's display cases would make that possible.

"I bet he was planning to return the diamond this week; that's when we get paid."

Kim tried to reassure her friend while her mind raced in another direction. She'd speculated that Brittany had convinced a worker to steal the pirate's ruby as a publicity stunt. What if Brittany's partner was Kevin?

She could imagine Brittany sweet-talking Kevin into sneaking into the museum after the banquet. Or maybe Brittany even promised to pay him.

It would have been so simple except for one thing: Dorothy walked in while he was removing the ruby.

Kevin, of course, would insist that Dorothy's niece had hired him to steal the amulet as a publicity stunt. Would Dorothy believe him? For that matter, would Brittany admit her role?

Or would Kevin have faced a hysterical, accusing woman who insisted on having him arrested?

The phone rang, interrupting Kim's horrible train of thought. She answered.

"Kim? This is Marie Powers. Is Liz with you?"

"Uh, no, was she coming here for something?"

"She was supposed to be reading in her room. I would have seen her go out the front door, so she must have climbed out her window. Her bike's gone." The woman's voice verged on panic. "I thought maybe she'd gone out with Bobby Klein, but no one answers at his house."

Kim closed her eyes as she recalled Liz's last words: *I'll show Bobby who's the better treasure hunter.*

"Uh, I think I know where Liz might be." She pitched her voice low, trying to sound calm. Inside, however, a pack of poodles was doing zoomies around her stomach. "Don't worry; I'll try to find her."

She hung up the phone and stared at Grandpa and Mary. "Liz is missing."

Chapter 32

Kim peered through the windshield, searching for the edge of the winding road. She tried to push aside the thought of Liz riding her bicycle through this driving wind and rain. Even though it was only 5 p.m., her headlights barely penetrated the gloom. Beside her, Mary gripped the passenger door handle with white knuckles.

"I can't believe Liz was angry enough to wander out in this," Mary said. "I didn't know she was so competitive with Bobby."

Kim ground her teeth. She'd wanted to search for Liz alone, to save the poor child the embarrassment of adults making a fuss. But when she'd attempted to sneak out the kitchen door, Grandpa tried to follow. After some arguing, he agreed to stay home, but only if Mary and Rory accompanied her. Mary supported the idea.

Before they left, however, Mary insisted on telling her children where she was going and admonishing them to behave for Mr. Hershey.

Now Bobby knew that Liz had gone to Pirate's Cove to look for treasure without him. Mary's idea of honesty may have destroyed the two children's friendship.

A loud crack sounded, followed by the smack of a tree branch hitting the road behind them. From the backseat, Rory whined.

"Maybe we should call Marie, see if Liz has come home." Mary's voice had lost its confidence.

"She said she'd call as soon as she saw Liz."

They drove in silence for a few minutes, the raging storm matching the tension in the car. Leaves and small branches skittered off the windshield.

How long had Liz been missing? Was she huddled beneath a tree waiting for a break in the storm? Or pinned beneath a branch?

"I know, you know." Mary's voice cut into her thoughts.

"Know what?"

"About Kevin's affairs."

Kim's hands tightened on the steering wheel. "Maybe this isn't the best time--"

"I should have told you sooner--"

"It's none of my business."

But Mary acted like she didn't hear. "He's not evil, you know? He's just weak."

"I don't understand," Kim said. "Why do you stay with him?" No way would Kim tolerate a cheating man.

"He may be a lousy husband but he's a great father."

There wasn't much Kim could say to that. Fortunately, she could see the sign for Pirate's Cove up ahead.

Kim slowed for the left turn. As she started up the steep hill, the headlights illuminated the trunk of a large tree that had fallen across the drive.

She slammed on the brakes. A clunking sound indicated the anti-lock brakes had engaged. The pedal vibrated under her foot. She watched in horror as the tree loomed larger. They stopped just inches from the trunk.

For a moment, she clung to the steering wheel, the beating of her heart loud in her ears. An outraged yip from Rory pulled her out of her daze.

"Everyone okay?"

"I'm fine. Your dog looks pissed."

Kim unhooked her seatbelt and turned to Rory. His front feet had slid to the floor, his butt still perched on the seat. She could swear his expression was critical.

She leaned back and stroked his ear. He leaned into her hand. Her heart rate slowed.

Sitting up, she reached for the door handle. "Why don't you wait here while I look for Liz? No sense both of us getting wet."

A hand on her arm stopped her. "You know, you don't have to take care of me anymore." Mary's voice was gentle. "I asked for your help with the police and I'm grateful for all of your hard work. But I really can stand on my own two feet."

Headlights driving north on Bayside illuminated Mary's face -- the face of a woman, a woman who'd raised two children, managed a successful museum, survived police accusation of murder.

Maybe it was time for Kim to stop trying to protect her childhood friend.

"Okay, let's do this."

Kim slid her purse under the front seat, tugged on one of Grandpa's baseball hats and flipped the hood of her jacket over the hat. With any luck, the cap's brim would help keep rain off of her glasses. She slipped a flashlight into her pocket then climbed out.

Opening the rear door, she clipped a leash on Rory's seatbelt and detached the harness from the car. The young poodle leaped to the ground and began sniffing.

Kim locked the car, tucked the keys into a pocket and joined Mary in front of the van. With Rory in the lead, they trudged around the fallen tree and headed for the parking lot.

The lot came into view and Kim's breath caught. Liz's bicycle lay beneath a tree. She ran to the bike, but there was no sign of Liz. Scanning the ground, she spotted a single, child-sized sneaker print. It was pointed toward the cliff.

"That looks like Kevin's pickup."

Kim turned in the direction Mary indicated. At the far end of the lot, hidden from the road by dense trees, a battered red truck was parked next to a small white car.

The white car looked familiar. Was it the same one she'd seen exiting the museum earlier?

Mary cupped her hands to form a megaphone around her lips.

"Mary, wait."

Mary dropped her hands and shot Kim a questioning look.

Kim pointed to the car parked beside the pickup. "Do you recognize that car?"

Mary shook her head.

"Then let's not announce our presence until we figure out who's crazy enough to tromp around the cliff in a storm."

Driving to this remote area in the midst of the storm indicated a desperation that made people dangerous.

Kim turned back to the area where she'd found Liz's footprint. The overhanging, leaf-covered branches effectively blocked what daylight penetrated the thick clouds. She pulled the flashlight from her pocket.

"Since I have the light, I'll lead the way." Cautioning Rory to "no woof," she stepped over the bike and followed Liz's tracks into the woods.

The clack of overhead branches rubbing together combined with the slapping of rain against leaves masked any noise they made. Even so, Kim trod cautiously, keeping the light pointed directly in front of their feet. She didn't want to warn whoever was out here of their presence.

The roar of waves splashing the shore indicated they were nearing the edge of the cliff. If they didn't find Liz soon, they'd have to retrace their steps in a zigzag pattern, maybe even risk calling the girl's name.

A rumble in Rory's throat brought her to an abrupt halt. She clicked off the flashlight and gave Rory a whispered "quiet, no woof."

Standing in the semi-dark, she peered through the rain, searching for whatever had alerted Rory.

Something flashed silver, followed by a thunk. Another flash and she could finally see Mary's husband standing beneath a tree. He drove a shovel into the ground.

For a moment, Kim couldn't breathe. No. No, no, no, no, no. Please don't let him be digging a child-sized grave.

"Mmmf." Rory wagged his tail.

She followed the direction of his eyes. Liz squatted behind a tree, maybe thirty feet away, almost at the edge of the cliff. Her backpack lay forgotten on the ground beside her as she focused on Kevin, eyes wide.

Kim inhaled deeply, then jumped when Mary's hand landed on her arm.

Mary pointed to the right. Kim squinted. A shadow detached itself from a tree trunk. Brittany.

Kim's mind raced. Brittany must own the white car. Had she followed Kevin here? If so, why?

Brittany leaned around the tree, peering intently at Kevin.

The sound of metal striking something other than dirt drew Kim's attention back to Kevin. He dropped the shovel, kneeled and began scraping at the soil with his bare hands. A few minutes later, he pulled a box from the hole.

Kim's hand tightened on Rory's leash. Had Kevin actually found pirate treasure?

He brushed dirt from the box, revealing a plastic lid. She recognized the large snaps that held the box closed. She'd seen boaters using waterproof boxes that looked a lot like this one.

He unlatched the sides and raised the lid. The lid blocked the contents from her view. She shuffled a few steps to her left.

Kevin frowned and dug through the box with his fingers.

A few more steps and now she could see the box interior. The plastic box might not have belonged to a pirate, but it was filled with treasure.

Even in the gloom, she could distinguish necklaces, bracelets and rings. She'd be willing to bet she'd find a few loose gemstones in the bottom of the box. Maybe even the museum's missing diamond.

Kevin lifted a pendant from the box and smiled. She recognized the pirate's ruby amulet.

"So you're the one who stole my ruby." Brittany stepped out from behind the tree. She gripped a gun in her right hand, its muzzle aimed at Kevin's chest.

Startled, Kevin fell backward. The amulet fell from his hands into the mud.

Kevin scrambled to his feet.

"Whoa, whoa, I didn't steal this stuff. Paula did."

He flashed what he probably hoped was an alluring smile. It looked sickly.

"I just figured out where she stashed it," he said.

"Is that why you killed her?"

Mary's sharp intake of breath sounded loud in Kim's ear. She laid a warning hand on her friend's arm.

"I didn't kill her."

"Don't you lie to me!" The hand holding the gun trembled. "The police found my earring on Paula. The last time I wore those earrings was in the backseat of your pickup."

Mary moaned. The storm covered the sound.

Brittany glared at Kevin. "You deliberately set me up as a murderer!"

The madness in Brittany's voice pushed Kevin back a step -- back toward Liz's hiding place.

Kim shifted her attention to Liz. The child was frozen in place, eyes focused on the gun. If she moved at all, Brittany would see her.

"Brittany, sweetie," Kevin cooed. "Why would I do that?"

Kim sorted through her options. She could remain quiet and hope Kevin could talk sense into Brittany.

Yeah, right. She couldn't see Brittany's eyes, but she remembered the child Brittany's crazed expression right before she'd tackled Mary in the school yard. No way would Kevin convince Brittany to put down the gun.

Okay, option number two: Back off and call the police.

No, that wouldn't work. Unless a squad car was nearby, the officers would never arrive in time to prevent someone getting shot. And what if Brittany saw Liz?

Which left the third and final option: Fight Brittany.

Maybe she could toss a rock to draw Brittany's attention away from Liz. That might give her enough time to tackle the woman.

First, though, she'd need to get closer to the crazy woman with the gun.

She touched Mary's shoulder and stared into her frightened eyes. Kim pointed to herself, then at Liz and moved her index and middle finger in a walking motion.

When Mary nodded understanding, Kim pointed at her friend and held up a palm, the dog trainer's signal for stay. Mary agreed.

Kim whispered "quiet, good quiet" to Rory, slipped her hand around his harness and unclipped his leash. When the time came to launch herself at Brittany, she'd need both hands free. Rory would probably run with her and she didn't want his leash tangling in the brush and strangling him.

She shuffled her feet sideways, keeping her eyes on Kevin and Brittany. The couple continued to quarrel.

"I suppose I should thank you for killing Ross Peabody," Brittany said.

"That wasn't me. That was Paula." He extended his hands, palms facing Brittany. "She'd been stealing stuff and selling it to Peabody."

He took a step toward Brittany. Brittany didn't seem to notice.

"When Peabody found out you'd be exhibiting the pirate's ruby," Kevin said, "he hired Paula to steal it. But Paula got greedy, demanded more money. Peabody threatened her. So she killed him."

Kim inched sideways. So far, Kevin's story sounded true. Brittany must agree because she allowed him to take another step towards her.

"What about Dorothy?" Brittany's voice caught. "Why did she have to kill Dorothy?"

Kevin's eyes slid left. Kim froze. Had he seen her?

"Dorothy walked in while Paula was stealing the ruby." He snorted. "Stupid woman thought she could intimidate Paula into turning herself in."

Now he was lying. On the night of Dorothy's murder, Paula Darnell had been working. No way would the woman risk someone seeing her police car parked outside of the museum during the time when the pirate's ruby was stolen.

No, Paula had had a partner. And he was standing right here.

Kim continued her sideways shuffle. Liz's eyes suddenly darted her way. Kim held a finger to her lips. Liz nodded, her shoulders visibly relaxing.

Brittany sneered. "And I suppose you're totally innocent in all this."

"Hey, I'm no angel; you know that. But all I did was borrow the extra museum key Mary had made and gave it to Paula. She did the rest."

"And then you killed her."

"I had no choice!" Kevin scraped fingers through his wet hair. "First she tried to pin the murders on Mary."

Kim flicked her eyes toward Mary. But her rain-drenched glasses obscured her friend's expression.

"And when I protested," Kevin said, "she threatened to lay it all on me."

"So you killed her and implicated me."

Brittany gripped the gun with two hands and aimed it at Kevin's heart.

"No!" Mary ran into the clearing.

At the same time, Kevin threw himself at Brittany. His hands snagged the arm holding the gun and pushed up. The gun fired into the air.

Rory barked and lunged.

Even as Kim dug in her heels, using two hands to hold Rory, Kevin wrenched the gun from Brittany's hand.

He spun Brittany around and used his free hand to pin her arms against her sides. He pressed the muzzle against her cheek.

"Stay back." Kevin's wild eyes darted from Mary to Kim and back. "Don't move or I'll kill her."

Brittany whimpered and her knees buckled. But Kevin held on.

"Stand up, you bitch."

Brittany's legs straightened.

"Kevin, don't." Mary's eyes sought Kevin's. "She's not worth it."

Kevin snorted. "Damn right she's not." He shot a look at Kim. "Hang on to that dog or I'll shoot it."

"I've got him." Rory growled, his entire body tense.

Kevin backed away from Rory.

Kim peered into the gloom. If Kevin continued in his current direction, he'd crash into the leaning tree, the one the osprey had perched in.

The one right on the edge of the cliff.

Clearly disoriented, Kevin continued his backward movement. Mary followed.

"Please, Kevin," Mary said. "Let her go. We can work this out."

"How? Have the kids grow up with their father in jail?"

Kim considered her options. Kevin had a gun and a hostage. Two hostages if you counted Mary.

She had a dog she wasn't willing to sacrifice, a small flashlight that didn't weigh enough to use as a missile, a friend who might or might not convince her husband to release Brittany and a child to protect.

She looked toward Liz and her chest muscles tightened. Liz had unzipped her backpack and was slowly pulling out her mechanical snake.

As Kim realized the girl's intention, her legs began shaking. Yes, Kevin was snake phobic. And perhaps the sight of the snake might distract him long enough for Mary to pull Brittany from his grasp.

But it was equally likely Kevin would try to shoot the snake. Unless he was a brilliant marksman, the bullet could go wild and hit Liz.

Kim removed one hand from Rory's harness and wiggled her fingers, trying to signal Liz without drawing Kevin's attention. But Liz was focused on something else in her bag and didn't look up.

She glanced back at Kevin. He was staring at his wife.

She slid her left foot sideways.

Kevin's head whipped around. "I told you not to move."

The gun dug into Brittany's cheek. Brittany whimpered.

Kim held Kevin's eyes, willing him to focus on her and not notice the child placing a mechanical snake on the ground.

"What about the museum's diamond?" she said. "Did you exchange it for a zircon?"

"I was going to put the diamond back!" Kevin looked at his wife, took another step backward. "You remember, honey, how strapped we were? We might have lost the house!"

Liz aimed the remote control at the snake. It crawled forward a few inches, then stopped and writhed in place.

"I told you the house doesn't matter," Mary said.

"But it does; you love that house." His eyes turned pleading. "I just borrowed the diamond until we were back on our feet." His hand tightened on the gun. "I was going to buy it back this week."

Liz leaned out from her hiding place and nudged the rear of the snake. It crawled a few more inches.

"So what are you doing with the stolen museum jewels?" Mary's voice was small and sad.

The snake stopped its forward momentum. Kim tried to catch Liz's attention, to warn her to not move from cover.

"They're not mine; they're Paula's." Kevin dug the gun deeper into Brittany's cheek.

Liz inched toward the snake.

Kim needed to distract Kevin, keep him from spotting Liz.

"I never meant to hurt you," Kevin said. "No, Mary, don't come any closer." He stepped backward, his boot bumping against the tree's roots. He teetered, but remained upright. The gun never left Brittany's face.

Liz slid a hand toward Homer. But the snake was still too far away.

Okay, the mechanical snake wasn't going to help. But maybe...

"Kevin," Kim said. "There's a snake crawling down the tree behind you."

Kevin snorted. "Yeah, right, and probably a whole Calvary, too."

Rory suddenly broke free and raced toward the toy snake.

Snatching it in the middle, he gave it a shake, then flipped it into the air.

It landed at Brittany's feet and continued to writhe.

Kevin gaped at the mechanical snake, gave a strangled gasp and, with Brittany tight against him, leaped backwards.

The cliff gave way.

For a moment, the world moved in slow motion. The osprey's tree tilted toward the bay as more of its roots were exposed. The gun went flying. Kevin's flailing arms snagged at roots. Brittany managed to grasp a root one-handed.

Both bodies dangled in space.

"Kevin!" Mary ran to her husband and threw herself to the ground, her hands wrapping around one of Kevin's wrists.

Kim reached Brittany in a few strides, dropped to her stomach and grabbed Brittany's dangling wrist.

"Stop flailing your legs!" Kim said. "I can't hold you if you're struggling."

"I'm gonna die, I'm gonna die!" Brittany wailed.

The earth under Kim moved as tree roots slipped in the wet soil. Brittany froze, her eyes wide in horror. But she stopped moving.

"Kevin!" Kim waited until he looked at her. "Can you find a purchase for your feet?"

If they were going to get out of this alive, they needed to combine forces.

Kevin stretched a leg toward the face of the cliff. The movement caused the tree to shift. Dirt rained down and exposed more roots. Kim felt her body slide forward an inch. Rory grabbed the hem of her jacket and pulled, his feet scrabbling in the mud.

Rory's efforts sparked another idea.

"Brittany. On the count of three Rory and I are going to pull. I need you to use your other hand, the one that's holding the tree, and pull like you're doing a chin-up."

"I can't! I could never do chin-ups. My arms aren't that strong."

"You've got to try. On three, okay? One, two, three." Kim leaned away from the cliff, trying to bend her elbows enough to drag Brittany's hand on top of the cliff. She could see the muscles bulging in Brittany's arms. Then the hand that grasped the tree slipped off. Brittany screamed.

As Kim suddenly held Brittany's full weight, her own body began to slide toward the edge. Liz jumped onto her thighs, her small hands grasping at Kim's jacket. The child's weight stopped the forward momentum. But for how long?

"Don't let me die, oh please don't let me die," Brittany screamed.

The osprey tree shifted as more roots pulled free.

If the tree fell, it would take the part of the cliff they lay on with it.

"Please don't let me die." Brittany's words were muffled with sobs.

No way could she pull Brittany to safety without help. She studied Kevin. Though his arm muscles bulged, he seemed to have a firm grip on the tree roots.

"Kevin? Can you hang on while we pull up Brittany? Then we'll have three people to pull you up."

Kevin's eyebrows raised. "You would save a murderer?"

"I'm not letting anyone die!"

He stared at her a moment, then nodded. The tree shifted. Kevin gazed up at Mary.

"Go help Kim. I can hang on."

Mary bit back a sob, but held tight to his wrist.

"It's okay, sweetie," Kevin said. "Go help Kim."

"Do... do you still love me?"

"Always."

Mary nodded and reluctantly released him. She started to slide toward Kim.

"Mary? Tell Bobby and Kimmie I love them." Then Kevin deliberately let go of the tree.

"Kevin!" Mary lunged for her husband, but she wasn't quick enough.

Kim closed her eyes, but she couldn't block out the horrible thud of a falling body hitting the ground or Mary's anguished keening. Her stomach clenched as sorrow washed over her.

Dirt shifted beneath her. Her eyes popped open and she desperately dug her toes into the earth. Brittany screeched.

Mary lay nearby, silent now, her glazed eyes focused on her husband's broken body.

"Mary, help me! We've got to get away before the tree pulls loose."

But Mary's mind had shut down.

"I'll help you," Liz said.

Kim considered the idea. With Rory tugging on one side and Liz on the other, could she pull Brittany to safety? How much help could she expect from a 70-pound child and a 55-pound poodle?

She'd soon find out.

"Okay, but promise me that if this doesn't work, you'll grab Rory and get away from the edge."

Liz's eyes widened.

"Please, Liz, we can't try this unless you promise."

Liz inhaled deeply, then nodded.

"Ready? On three. One, two, three. Rory, tug!"

She felt both sides of her rain jacket jerk backward. The momentum pulled her onto her knees. Using her thigh muscles as well as her aching arms, she hauled Brittany part way onto the cliff edge. Brittany's free hand automatically clutched at the crumbling dirt. But her butt and legs still dangled into space.

Brittany screamed as she started sliding back toward the edge.

Mary pounced on Brittany's free hand, stopping the slide.

"Once more," Kim shouted. "Tug!"

Poodle and child pulled. Kim and Mary leaned back.

And then, finally, Brittany lay completely on the cliff.

Kim released Brittany's arm, flopped onto her back and stared at the sky through rain-drenched glasses. The clouds were thicker now, the wind stronger.

Rory licked her face. Kim curled fingers in his now wet fur and sat up. Liz threw her arms around her. Kim held the child's trembling body, murmuring what she hoped were comforting words.

Mary sat beside them, staring at the cliff edge, tears streaming down her cheeks. Brittany lay in the mud, sobbing. As Kim watched, Brittany raised her head and began crawling deeper into the forest.

From somewhere nearby, a tree branch thumped to the ground. Rory whimpered.

Kim kissed the top of Liz's head. "We need to get out of here."

Liz nodded, wiped the tears from her eyes, and stood. Kim pushed to her feet, reached for Mary and gently tugged her upright. For a moment, she held her friend.

"I am so, so sorry," she whispered.

"What do I tell the children?"

"Tell them their father died in an accident and that he loved them." Kim gave Mary a minute to absorb her words, then stepped back. "We need to take Liz away from here."

As she'd hoped, the comment ignited Mary's maternal instinct.

Mary's shoulders straightened and she gave a brisk nod. "I need to find the chest with the museum's property."

Kim resisted the urge to roll her eyes. Who cared about jewels in the middle of a hurricane?

"Mary, the chest will be safe until the police recover it. We need to leave *now.*"

Mary's eyes suddenly widened. She pointed at something over Kim's shoulder.

Kim whirled around in time to see the tree they'd clung to dip toward the bay, its enormous roots kicking skyward before disappearing from sight. Lightening flashed, illuminating movement to her right. She peered into the gloom.

Brittany kneeled in the mud, sweeping her hands back and forth in front of her. She seemed to be muttering to herself.

"Brittany?"

No answer. Brittany crawled forward, then performed another hand sweep.

Turning back to Mary, Kim pressed the car keys into her hands. "Please take Liz and Rory to the car while I get Brittany."

Rory, however, refused to leave her side. Placing a comforting hand on his head, she stumbled toward Brittany.

Brittany peered up at her. "My ruby! Help me find my ruby!"

"Oh, for heaven's sake." Kim reached for Brittany's arm. Brittany snatched it away.

"No! I need my ruby."

Grinding her teeth, Kim considered leaving Brittany to her madness. A crack of thunder, however, reminded her of the very real danger.

She dropped to her knees and swept her hands through the wet dirt and leaves. Rain dripped down her now exposed neck and beneath her jacket. Finding nothing, she crawled forward and felt around her. Nothing. Again she crawled forward. Her thumb brushed against something that didn't belong here. She reversed her movement. Her fingers closed over the amulet.

Leaning back on her heels, she extended the ruby pendant to Brittany. Brittany snatched it and clutched it to her breast.

Kim pushed to her feet and stared down at her childhood nemesis.

Brittany had based her entire existence on the fantasy that she was descended from pirates. That obsession had triggered the chain of events that led to four deaths.

Tears streamed down Brittany's mud-smeared face. Her blond hair hung in wet strings. She tried to stand, slipped and dropped back to her knees. She sobbed and raised blue eyes to Kim's.

Thirty years of anger, fear and loathing dissolved into a disquieting wave of pity.

Kim held out a hand. "It's all over, Brittany," she said. "Let's go home."

Chapter 33

Three Days Later

"So Lieutenant Brockley believed you when you told him Kevin's death was an accident?" Grandpa stepped off of the boardwalk and onto the sand beside her.

"Mary and I are the only ones who saw him let go of the tree." Kim bent to release Rory from his leash. "And, truthfully, visibility was so bad, I couldn't swear he didn't actually slip. It's better if the kids don't think their father committed suicide."

Grandpa nodded. "Bad enough they have to know he murdered Officer Darnell."

Four people had heard Kevin's version of the events. Kim still believed that Kevin, not Paula Darnell, had killed Dorothy when she discovered him stealing the pirate's ruby. With Kevin, Paula Darnell and Ross Peabody dead, however, the police had little choice than to accept Kevin's confession.

Rory, free from his leash, launched into the air and raced across Pirate's Cove, wet sand kicking up behind him. Kim smiled, itching to join him. But aching muscles discouraged strenuous activity.

The warm sun, however, felt delicious on her skin. Hurricane Dan had trapped them inside for three days without electricity.

But it could have been a lot worse. At the last minute, the hurricane had shifted direction and landed south of North Carolina's Cape Hatteras, sparing the Maryland beach towns from the worst storm damage.

Even so, a combination of heavy rain, high wind and tide had sent bay water over the boardwalk and into people's basements.

Once the strong winds passed, the water slowly receded. And, wonder of wonders, this morning as they left Grandpa's house for their walk, the electricity flickered on.

She turned to inspect Pirate's Cove. Most of the expensive sand imported for the museum celebration had washed away. The shoreline, however, had grown wider, a result of the cliff receding. The leaning tree -- the one they'd clung to -- now lay sprawled across the beach.

She shuddered, remembering how close they'd all come to falling.

She'd praised Liz's quick-witted assistance to anyone who'd listen and convinced Brooke to photograph the hero child for the newspaper. Bobby had been suitably impressed and, according to Mary, the two children had reached an uneasy truce.

Turning away from the tree, Kim strolled beside Grandpa while Rory ran circles around them. She scanned the clear sky for signs of the osprey, but saw only seagulls. The magnificent birds had probably used the impending hurricane as impetus for starting their long migration south.

"Something I don't understand," Grandpa said. "Why did Kevin and Paula attack you and Ginny in the Annapolis parking lot?"

"I don't think it was them. I got a good look at the woman who held Aunt Ginny. The woman wasn't muscular enough to be Officer Darnell. I think the people in the parking lot were the jewelry thieves, the ones who tied up the school teacher."

The police had recovered the jewel-filled box Kevin had dug up. Inside they'd found all of the museum's missing jewels. But the box contained none of the items stolen from local homes.

"So the jewelry thieves are still around here." Grandpa's voice was grim.

Kim slipped her arm through his. "Don't worry; they haven't hurt anyone. In hindsight, I think they wanted to warn me to not investigate the local thefts. And, believe me, I have no intention of doing that."

Rory trotted over and dropped a piece of driftwood at her feet. Kim tossed it and smiled as the happy poodle bounded after it.

The driftwood reminded her of the sword hilt Rory had dug up.

"Do you think there really is pirate treasure somewhere around here?" The recovered box had also contained no pirate treasure.

"Anything's possible." The twinkle in Grandpa's eyes told her he'd recovered his good humor. "And speaking of possibilities, I noticed that you had a perfect opportunity to tell Brittany she was adopted, but didn't take it."

"Yeah, well..." Kim shrugged.

When she'd gone to the police station to sign her statement, Grandpa had insisted on accompanying her. Which is why he'd witnessed Brittany demanding the police immediately relinquish the jewels Kevin had stolen.

Kim supported Brittany's request. The thief was dead, so the police had no need to confiscate the jewels as evidence.

But when Brittany launched into a lecture about her illustrious pirate ancestor, Kim had turned away.

"So why didn't you tell her?" Grandpa said. "She was being her usual obnoxious self and gave you the perfect opportunity to say something."

Kim sighed. Grandpa, she knew, wouldn't rest until she admitted her childhood error.

"A wise man once suggested that I think twice before using truth as a weapon," she said. "And, well, I guess I felt sorry for her."

Grandpa kissed her cheek. "My little girl is growing up."

Kim giggled and stuck out her tongue. Calling to Rory, she turned and raced along the beach.

Thank you for reading *The Pirate's Ruby*. If you enjoyed it, please tell a friend. Or tell many friends by writing a review on your favorite site. Sometimes it's hard to find a new author, so we must rely on each other for recommendations.

This book was such fun to write in part because it gave me a chance to not only explore the fascinating history and legends surrounding rubies, but also those involving pirates. Apparently, Blackbeard himself used the inlets of the Chesapeake Bay to escape capture. So maybe there is buried treasure to be found. To read more about the stories behind the story, please visit my web site.

I've never been the greatest speller, so all of my books are extensively reviewed by professional editors and proofreaders. If, however, you do find an error, please email me at Lynn@LynnFranklin.com so I can fix it.

Actually, you can email me even if you don't find problems. I love to hear from my readers. You are the reason that I write.

www.LynnFranklin.com

A Rare Blue Diamond
An Unsuspecting Jeweler

When a killer stalks a
a small beach town,
no one is safe

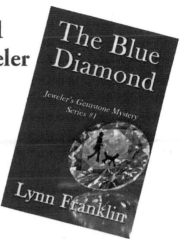

The Blue
Diamond

Jeweler's Gemstone Mystery
Series #1

Lynn Franklin

The Carolina
Emerald

Jeweler's Gemstone Mystery
Series #3

Lynn Franklin

A 60-year-old mystery
A one-of-a-kind emerald

In a small town steeped in
secrets, a romantic weekend
turns deadly.

Fact or Fiction?

Part of the joy of writing -- and I hope reading -- the Jeweler's Gemstone Mystery Series is discovering the wonderful gemstone history and lore.

The story of anthill garnets is among my favorites. The little critters really do haul garnets from the earth and deposit them outside of their hills. No one seems to know why the ants do this and the fact that no scientist has researched this question says as much about the two-legged animal as the six-legged. I'm grateful, however, to the Navajo Nation for making these gorgeous gemstones available to the rest of us.

Burmese rubies, the ones famous for their pigeon's blood red color, were first mined around 2,500 B.C.E. Throughout much of history, the largest, most beautiful rubies were reserved for Burma's kings.

The late 19th Century Burmese King Thibaw did, indeed, wear slippers encrusted with real rubies. He'd ordered his craftsmen to stick rubies onto his various crowns, robes and ceremonial daggers, so why not shoes? And, generous man that he was, he ordered a lesser ruby pair made for his queen.

The shoes are on display in Burma (or, depending on your politics, Myanmar) and photos are hard to come by. But the slippers are as Kim described: curled-toed genie shoes and flip-flops.

If you're a fan of L. Frank Baum's *Wizard of Oz* books, you'll know that in his version Dorothy's slippers are made of silver. When MGM made the movie version, the producers wanted to show off their latest technology: Technicolor. Silver slippers might look wonderful in black-and-white, but for this movie, Dorothy's shoes needed more pizzazz. Thus the famous ruby slippers were born.

Warriors in the Middle Ages did, indeed, wear blood-colored gems into battle believing the gems would shield them from harm. In fact, Henry V wore the Black Prince's Ruby as protection during the Battle of Agincourt. It was James II, however, who added the Black Prince's Ruby to England's Imperial State Crown.

As Kim points out, however, the Black Prince's Ruby was misnamed. Up until the late 1700s, all red-colored gemstones were called "ruby." But once scientists developed ways to analyze the mineral content of gemstones, they made a few startling discoveries. They identified four distinct forms of red gemstones: garnet, spinel, zircon and what we now know as ruby.

Even more surprising, rubies consisted of corundum, the same mineral as sapphire. Turns out that trace minerals create the very different colors.

Perhaps the most serious discovery was that the famous Black Prince's Ruby was not a ruby at all, but a fine example of natural red spinel. I was unable to locate an official statement from British royalty about the discovery, though I suspect, as Scott said, they weren't pleased.

I was also unable to learn if pirates regarded red gems as protective amulets, though I imagine the practice of wearing rubies into battle continued through the so-called Golden Age of Piracy.

And speaking of pirates, Stede Bonnet, the Gentleman Pirate, was a real character. A plantation owner bored with his life, Bonnet purchased a sailing ship, hired a crew and abandoned his wife and children in pursuit of adventure on the high seas. All this, it seemed, made him a laughing stock among the pirates.

Build a ship? No, no, a true pirate *steals* a ship. Pay the crew a salary? Ha! The crew's "salary" comes from dividing the treasure stolen from conquered ships.

No one knows what the other pirates thought of Bonnet abandoning both his family and his leisurely way of living. But Blackbeard considered Bonnet a greenhorn and convinced him to travel on the Queen Anne's Revenge while experienced sailors piloted Bonnet's ship.

Eventually, Bonnet insisted on returning to his own ship, which is probably why, only a year into the Gentleman Pirate's "adventure," he was captured and hanged.

No one seems to know what happened to the family Bonnet deserted. Brittany and her parents are fictional characters.

The descriptions of the places where Kim saw her first pigeon's blood ruby stem from my own childhood travels with my jeweler grandfather. Unlike Kim's grandfather, mine confined his trips to the stores in downtown Pittsburgh. I can still close my eyes and picture store walls covered with glittering jewelry and the gnarled old crone who allowed me to ogle the pigeon's blood ruby.

As for the other lookalike gems in the book, diamonds and natural zircons really do reflect light differently. If you search the internet for "zircon double refraction photo," you'll find photos of the railroad tracks optical illusion described here.

I don't know whether or not Dorothy Tyson could have spotted the illusion when the light from Brooke's camera flash illuminated the gemstone display case. Let's just call this a fictional liberty.

Also fiction is Osprey Beach, though Chesapeake and North Beaches really do exist on Maryland's Western shore. I created Osprey Beach because I didn't want to murder people in the real beaches; they are just too darn nice.

Among the most charming people in Calvert County, Maryland, are the very real Dickinson jewelry family and their employees. Like Kim's grandfather, I trust Dickinson Jewelers for their honesty.

Thursdays is a real restaurant located in both North Beach and Edgewater, Maryland. Karen, the hostess/manager, works only in the North Beach restaurant. Both locations, however, serve what Ginny Reinhart, the model for Aunt Ginny, swears is the best cream of crab soup.

If you ever find yourself in North Beach and spot a standard poodle and longhaired dachshund strolling the boardwalk, please stop to say hello. I love meeting my readers.

The Pirate's Ruby Discussion Questions

1. When they were children, Kim and Mary formed a special bond that lasted into adulthood. Do you have childhood friendships that continue as an adult? What makes these friendships so special?

2. The media are full of stories about childhood bullying. Most of these stories focus on boys. Yet, as Kim and Mary found, girl bullies can be every bit as destructive. Discuss the difference between boy and girl bullies. How would you advise your own children to deal with bullies?

3 Kim wonders why pirates like Stede Bonnet captured public imagination when they were essentially bullies, thieves and murderers. Why do you think people are attracted to the notion of pirates?

4. Brittany treasured the pirate's ruby amulet in part because it had been passed from generation to generation. Discuss the role of family heirlooms – jewelry and otherwise – in your family.

5. Psychologists have determined that people are better able to process information if it is told in story form. Throughout the book, the author weaves stories about gemstone history, legend and lore. What were your favorite gemstone stories from the book? Which stories surprised you?

6. At the end of the book, Kim has the opportunity to seek revenge on the bully from her childhood. Yet she chooses to not reveal Brittany's real heritage. Do you agree or disagree with Kim's decision?

Please Join Us!

Join *The Diamond Digest* to receive exclusive
contests, tips, insider information and
advanced notice of upcoming books.
It's Free and it's Fun!

Join at www.LynnFranklin.com

Acknowledgments

A writer's life can be a lonely one, which is why support from readers, friends and family is invaluable.

First of all, a big thank you to my first readers: Adina Gewirtz, Charlene Dunlap, Michelle (Mieke) Rockhill, Joan Rose, Virginia Rinehart and Jon Franklin. These folks read a draft of *The Pirate's Ruby*, searching for inconsistencies, jarring transitions and the like.

A conversation with Adina Gewirtz, author of *Zebra Forest*, sparked ideas for deepening the psychology of some of the new characters. If you enjoy well-written books, you should pick up a copy of *Zebra Forest*; it's marketed as a children's book, but, like all good literature, it appeals to adults as well.

Joan Rose talked me through those frightening moments when it appeared I'd maneuvered my characters into a permanent corner. She is also the best line editor I've ever worked with.

I'd like to thank the folks at Dickinson Jewelers for not only allowing me to portray them in this book, but also for throwing an amazing cocktail party for the first book in the series, *The Blue Diamond*. The party even included a display of colored diamonds! Special thanks to Alison Setzer, who makes a cameo appearance in this book, for organizing the fun, classy event. Alison bakes the best cupcakes.

Congratulations to the winners of the name-a-character contest: Brooke Steuart Swann and Dan Rose. And a special thank you to Dan for good naturedly allowing me to name the hurricane after him.

It's always been difficult for readers to discover books that will appeal to them. But now, with newspapers eliminating book reviews, it's even harder. So readers must rely on online reviews and personal recommendations.

Catie Abzug, Anne Lewis, Cindy Shiner, Anne Saker, Shauna Roberts, Elaine Riley and Nickie Seaborn Jenkins helped spread the word about the Jeweler's Gemstone Mystery Series. Their thoughtful recommendations helped other readers discover the series.

I'd also like to thank the folks on DogRead for inviting me to talk with their wonderful subscribers. The Poodle Support Group, a group of respected breeders, trainers and poodle enthusiasts, warmed my heart with their enthusiastic response to the series.

My family continues to be amazing at holding my hand whenever my confidence sags. So I'd like to thank Mom (Dolly Scheidhauer), my brother Phil Scheidhauer and my husband Jon Franklin. You are the best family ever.

Finally, thank you to all my readers who contacted me and/or reviewed *The Blue Diamond*, the first book in the series, and for your enthusiastic -- and patient -- requests for the second book. I hope you enjoyed *The Pirate's Ruby*.